used to be

Also by

EILEEN COOK

What Would Emma Do?

Unraveling Isobel

The Almost Truth

used to be

Includes The Education of Hailey Kendrick and Getting Revenge on Lauren Wood

EILEEN COOK

SIMON PULSE

NEW YORK   LONDON   TORONTO   SYDNEY   NEW DELHI

SIMON PULSE
An imprint of Simon & Schuster Children's Publishing Division
1230 Avenue of the Americas, New York, NY 10020
This Simon Pulse edition July 2012
The Education of Hailey Kendrick copyright © 2011 by Eileen Cook
Getting Revenge on Lauren Wood copyright © 2010 by Eileen Cook
All rights reserved, including the right of reproduction
in whole or in part in any form.
SIMON PULSE and colophon are registered trademarks
of Simon & Schuster, Inc.
For information about special discounts for bulk purchases,
please contact Simon & Schuster Special Sales at 1-866-506-1949
or business@simonandschuster.com.
The Simon & Schuster Speakers Bureau can bring authors to your live event.
For more information or to book an event contact the Simon & Schuster Speakers
Bureau at 1-866-248-3049 or visit our website at www.simonspeakers.com.
Designed by Angela Goddard
The text of this book was set in Adobe Garamond.
Manufactured in the United States of America
2 4 6 8 10 9 7 5 3
The Library of Congress has cataloged the hardcover editions as follows:
The Education of Hailey Kendrick LCCN 2010025608
Getting Revenge on Lauren Wood LCCN 2009938355
ISBN 978-1-4424-7514-4 (paperback)
ISBN 978-1-4424-7167-2 (eBook)
These books were originally published individually by Simon Pulse.

table of contents

the education of hailey kendrick

To Mom and Dad,
who taught me
to love books

chapter one

There was a matter of life and death to deal with, and instead we were wasting our time discussing Mandy Gallaway's crotch. I kept a neutral smile plastered on my face, but my foot bobbed up and down impatiently. More people have seen Mandy Gallaway's naked crotch than saw last year's Super Bowl. The girl's incapable of getting out of a car without flashing the sixty zillion paparazzi that follow her around. The concept of knees together and underwear on isn't that complicated, which leaves me to believe she likes the sensation of flashbulbs lighting up where the sun isn't supposed to shine.

Given that her crotch had been photographed more than most supermodels, I failed to see why one online leaked picture of her standing in her gym shorts and a sports bra was causing this much drama. The situation certainly didn't call for the public flogging and stoning the student body was advocating. All the crowd was missing were some pitchforks and torches, and we could have stormed the town. On the upside, at least people had shown up for our student government meeting, for a change.

The Evesham student body usually had more important things to care about, like planning their next vacation to a private island near the Bahamas, or deciding between another Coach or Louis Vuitton bag. Most of the time the only people who came to our meetings were those of us on the board.

It wasn't clear what had really happened, but the theory was that a female security guard had snapped the photo of the half-dressed Mandy in the locker room and had sold it to the tabloids. A few people had seen a guard doing her rounds of the gym, and she'd had her cell phone out. Given who attends Evesham, paparazzi is a common problem, but before this incident they'd tended to hang outside the school gates. No one had ever had a picture leaked from inside. This was officially big news on campus.

"We should send her to prison for violating Mandy's privacy," Garrett said. His dad is a U.S. Senator; you would think he would have a better idea of how the system works.

"We're a student government association," I pointed out. "We don't actually have the power to sentence anyone to jail time." I straightened the nameplate on the desk in front of me: HAILEY KENDRICK—VICE PRESIDENT. I managed to avoid pointing out that we barely had the authority to hold a bake sale.

"Whatever. I want her fired," Mandy said. "Like, today." She crossed her arms and stuck her chin up into the air.

"We can't have her fired, either. The school employees all belong to a union. The whole thing is outside of the student government domain. It's up to the administration." I considered pulling the copy of the employee union agreement out of my file, but I was pretty sure no one was interested in the details of due process. It wasn't exactly a big pro-union crowd. I didn't know why we bothered to have this issue on the agenda at all, except for the fact that everyone wanted to talk about it.

"Really?" Mandy raised one perfectly plucked eyebrow. "If the administration isn't interested in what students think, maybe I should have my parents give them a call."

Mandy's parents had more money than most countries. I was pretty sure they could buy up some small ones—Luxembourg or the Philippines, for example—without even breaking the monthly budget. Her great-grandparents had owned several oil and gas companies and hung out with people like the Vanderbilts. If her parents called the school administration and said jump, people there would start leaping around before even bothering to ask how high.

I looked at the clock. We were going to run out of time. In addition to tackling the safety issue I had hoped to discuss, the council meeting was supposed to be focused on choosing between the two possible themes for our spring formal dance. Any talk of Southern Nights or Old Hollywood had gone out the door when the news about the picture had spread across campus. It was standing room only in the classroom we used for our meetings. No one wanted to miss any hot dirt.

"It totally grosses me out that that dyke took my picture." Mandy made a face like she had just bitten into month-old cottage cheese.

"Careful," Joel said. As the president of the student council, he was always sure to enforce the "respect and dignity" clause in the student handbook. "Her sexual orientation isn't an issue here."

"God, it's not a gay thing. I have tons of family friends who are gay," Mandy said. "'Dyke' is just a description."

It was classic Mandy to make a distinction between okay gay people (those who design houses or clothing, work in Hollywood, or write for the *New Yorker*) and not okay gay people (women who wear flannel shirts from Walmart.) The real issue wasn't the fact that the security guard might be gay, it was that she had a cheap haircut and unshaven legs, and had made a few thousand dollars selling an unflattering photo of Mandy. Even the haircut, flannel, and legs might have been forgiven if the photo hadn't made Mandy's thighs look a bit chunky.

Joel clapped his hands together to get everyone's attention. "Hailey is right. This issue doesn't fall under student government business." The crowd in the room started to grumble and protest, and Joel held up one hand. "That doesn't mean we can't make it our business."

A cheer went up from the group. Joel was a natural politician. I was certain he would be president of the United States someday. He had written to every living former president and asked them for advice on leadership. He kept the letters he got back in a binder in his room. President Clinton had sent him at least four. Not many people can list a president of the United States as a pen pal.

Joel stood so the people at the back could see him. "Privacy and the ability of everyone to feel safe here at Evesham is critical, and is a value this government is willing to fight to uphold. This isn't just a boarding school; it's our home away from home. We go to school here. We live here. We need to feel safe here. I motion that the council write a formal letter to the school administration indicating our concerns and demanding that action be taken. All in favor?"

There was a chorus of cheers and whoops from the crowd. Joel looked at me, and I could see the corner of his mouth twitching as he fought off a smile. He knew we could write all the letters we wanted and the school administration would still do whatever they wanted. However, he'd convinced everyone that he was practically Superman standing up for truth, justice, and the American way. Saving the rich and privileged from unflattering photos. I rolled my eyes at him and pressed my mouth together to avoid smiling. If I gave him any encouragement, there was no telling what he would come up with next.

"We have to have someone second the motion and put it to a vote," I said.

"Why? Is there some rule?" Garret said. I wanted to smack the smirk right off his face. As a matter of fact, there was a rule. If he wanted the Save the Crotch letter, then there was going to be an official vote. I stared at him with a smile on my face and said nothing.

"I'll second the motion," a sophomore girl sitting on the floor said. Joel gave her one of his thousand-watt smiles. Her face flushed bright red, and she let out a high-pitched giggle.

"Great. Now we just need to get a count of all those in favor," Joel said, and called for a show of hands.

I heard a sound behind me, and I turned to see my boy-friend, Tristan, leaning in the doorway. I held up a finger to let him know it would only be a couple of minutes more. Not surprisingly, no one was opposed to the Save the Crotch letter, and it passed.

"We still need to decide on the theme for the dance," I said before Joel had a chance to dismiss the meeting.

"What theme do you want?" Tristan called from the door-way.

"I don't want to influence the vote," I said.

"I'm thinking you'd go for the Hollywood glamour option," Tristan said, cocking his head to the side as if he were picking up my brain waves.

"So, are you guessing or making a motion?" Joel asked.

Tristan flipped Joel off, and they both laughed. They'd been roommates since freshman year. As upperclassmen they'd qualified to each get their own room, but they still preferred to share. Tristan found it difficult to trust many people, and he always swore that Joel was more than his friend, that they were brothers. You could tell by looking at them they might be brothers of choice, but they weren't remotely related. Joel was tall and lanky. He always had to be in motion. I didn't have a single photo of Joel where his image wasn't partially blurred. Tristan was the opposite. He seemed unmovable. He was tall too, but broad. One of the first things that had attracted me to him was how solid he appeared. Tristan looked like he could stand straight during a hurricane.

"It's a motion, Mr. President," Tristan said with a slight bow.

"Anyone care to second?" Joel called out, and the room filled with hands raised to support Tristan. Joel was the politician, but Tristan was the charmer. It was almost unfair to have that much male charisma in one dorm room. "Great. Now a quick vote. All in favor?" The sea of hands raised again. "Anyone opposed?" He looked around the room, but no one was interested in going against Tristan. Joel looked over at me. "Looks like we have a dance theme. With our business finished, I call this meeting officially to an end."

Tristan stood next to me while everyone else streamed out of the room. Mandy paused long enough to lean into Joel, pressing her breasts against his chest (there was a running bet that they were fake, which is likely, because no one has breasts that size and that perky, unless they're filled with a space-age material) and thanking him for standing up for her. Her voice was slightly breathless, as if she were nearly overcome with gratitude. She was acting like he had carried her down twenty-two flights of stairs in a burning building. Both Joel and Tristan turned to watch her stroll out, her hips going back and forth like she was walking across the deck of a listing ship.

"Careful. Your eyes might fall out," I said.

Tristan looked away, then pulled me close to nuzzle my ear. "The girl can't hold a candle to you. She's all flash and glitter. It would be like dating a disco ball." He looked up at Joel. "You should ask her to the dance. She looks pretty grateful."

"Oh, so *I* can have the disco ball. Thanks, man. Your kindness knows no bounds."

"You need something a little flashy to keep your attention. You get distracted pretty easy. It's a good thing we're seniors, because you're running out of girls to date."

Joel punched Tristan in the arm, and they jostled around laughing.

"You can do better than Mandy," I said to Joel while I stuffed papers into my bag.

"I keep trying to convince you to run away with me, but you won't leave this ape," Joel said, ducking a headlock from Tristan. Joel darted across the room, hooting like a monkey. Very fourth grade.

"I'm glad we got the dance settled. I was afraid we weren't going to get to it, " I said.

"We can put the idea of securing the vending machines on next month's agenda," Joel said, raising his hand like he was taking a vow.

Tristan raised an eyebrow at Joel. "Vending machine safety?"

I rolled my eyes at both of them. I was used to being teased about my safety obsession. People could laugh all they wanted. The one thing I knew for sure was that the world was a dangerous and unpredictable place. Smart people do everything they can to eliminate risk. Did you know that more people are killed every year in falling vending machine accidents than in shark attacks? Our school had an entire wall of unsecured vending machines in the lobby of the gym. If someone were crushed to death trying to get a frosty can of Diet Coke, it wouldn't be my fault. I'd tried to raise the issue.

"Today's agenda sort of got hijacked. Nothing riles people up like a good scandal and a sense of righteous justice," Joel said.

"Do you think they'll fire the security guard?" I asked.

"They shouldn't. There isn't any real proof, and if she doesn't have any other disciplinary notes in her employment file, I'm willing to bet the union rules say they can't."

"They should." Tristan's voice turned serious. I wasn't surprised. Having parents with four Oscars between them meant you could have Steven Spielberg as your godfather, but never a moment of privacy. His ninth birthday had been ruined when a photographer had fallen out of a tree onto the pool deck while trying to get a picture of his parents. "You aren't taking her side, are you?" Tristan asked Joel.

"I'm not taking anyone's side. Just saying she doesn't deserve to be burned at the stake until we know what really happened."

He looked over at Tristan. "You don't have to worry, dude. No one wants a picture of your ugly half-dressed ass."

"Except you," Tristan shot back. "I've seen how you look at me."

I rolled my eyes. "I'll let you guys have some special alone time. I'm supposed to meet up with Kelsie to work on our history project."

"Hang out with us. We're going to the café to get some ice cream. What sounds like more fun, ice cream or the Revolutionary War?" Tristan held on to my hand. He rubbed his thumb against the inside of my palm, a move that always gave me shivers. "Even George Washington would pick mint chocolate chip, and he had freedom on the line."

"George didn't have to worry about college applications," I pointed out, pulling my hand away before how he made me feel distracted me from homework. I was dedicated to getting good grades, but time with Tristan was never a bad thing. I kissed his cheek.

"Fine. Abandon us," Joel said, grabbing his stuff from the table. "I'm used to you snubbing me, but I'm not sure how he's going to handle it."

"I'm sure he can soldier on without me for a few hours."

"Despite the fact that you're breaking my heart, I still have amazing news for you," Tristan said.

"What?"

"I don't know if I'm going to tell you," he said, turning away.

"I may be too devastated to talk now."

I smacked him across the shoulder. "Tell me."

"It's going to cost you a kiss," Tristan said.

I quickly kissed him.

"It's a way better secret than that," he said, leaning back against the table and crossing his arms.

I leaned in and he pulled me closer. He wound his hands into my hair and kissed me deeply, causing my heart to speed up.

"Still standing here," Joel said, interrupting us. "In fact, I'm feeling a little pervy just watching."

Tristan laughed. "Watch and learn, Grasshopper." He turned to me. "I called my mom and told her the theme to the dance is going to be Old Hollywood. She says if you want, you can borrow one of her vintage dresses. She has a gown that used to belong to Bette Davis back in the forties. My mom wore it to some awards show."

"Seriously?" I squeaked, bouncing up on my tiptoes. I hadn't even seen the dress, but I knew I wanted it. "I could kiss your mom."

"You can kiss me and I'll pass it along," Tristan promised. I planted a big smack on his lips.

"How did you know people would vote for Old Hollywood as the theme?" I asked.

"He also had his mom pick up Vivien Leigh's costume from *Gone with the Wind* in case everyone went with the Southern idea instead," Joel said. "It comes complete with a small black girl who follows you around to wave you with a fan."

Tristan gave Joel another shove, before smiling at me. "I knew you wanted Old Hollywood, which meant that's what I wanted."

"Ah, popularity. What you two want, the whole world wants. But what about me? I'm left still wanting ice cream," Joel said.

We headed out together. The guys offered to walk me back to my dorm in case any rogue security guards tried to get a photo of me, but I declined. I couldn't wait to tell my best friend, Kelsie, about the Bette Davis dress. She was going to freak out. She wants to be an actress and loves anything vintage Hollywood.

Joel was right, popularity has its advantages.

chapter two

"I can*not* believe you get to wear a dress that was worn by Bette Davis. Do you have any idea how cool that is?" Kelsie flopped back onto her bed as if she were overcome by the enormity of it all.

"I know who she is, but I don't know if I ever saw any of her movies," I admitted. I was sitting on the floor with my laptop, trying to get our presentation to work.

"I can't believe you! Bette is like an icon. She was in *Dangerous* and *All About Eve*. Tons of stuff. She won two Oscars. The dress is totally wasted on you."

"Do you have any chocolate?" I asked as I typed.

"Nope."

I looked up in surprise. Kelsie always has chocolate in her room. Her dad is the CEO of a major candy corporation and has his assistant send her huge boxes full of stuff every month. "Your dad just sent some a few weeks ago. How can it all be gone?"

"I stuck it in the common room. I decided I didn't need the temptation." Kelsie sat up and smoothed her hands down her sides.

"You aren't going through a phase where you think you're fat, are you?"

"I don't think I'm fat. I know I'm fat." Kelsie squeezed a tiny quarter inch of flesh around her middle. "Even my face is fat."

"You're not fat. You look great. You just have a round face."

"Great, I have a circle for a head. Who doesn't love a girl who looks like a cartoon character?"

"I have a weird gap between my teeth," I pointed out with a smile, so she could see it. "Everyone has something about themselves they don't like. Your face is cute."

"I'm not going for cute. Besides, a tooth gap is sexy."

"You wouldn't think it was sexy if you knew how easy it is to get food wedged in there," I pointed out.

"See, it's even a food storage device, handy and sexy at the same time. This is why I'm doomed to be alone forever."

"Is this about the dance?" I closed the laptop, sensing a serious conversation was coming, one for which PowerPoint was not going to be needed. I had a feeling the birth of our nation wasn't what was on her mind. Our history project was going to have to wait.

"No one's asked me yet."

"You should ask Joel. Seriously, it would be like a favor. I think Mandy has designs on him."

"Joel is always my backup date. We go to everything together. I want a real date. I want romance, passion. You wouldn't understand; you've got Tristan."

"You say that like he's the best thing since sliced bread," I said with a laugh.

Kelsie turned so she was facing me. "You do realize how amazing he is, right? He's hot, he's crazy for you, his parents are famous. He *is* the best thing since sliced bread. I bet when sliced bread talks about something cool, it uses him as the example."

I paused. I knew Tristan was a great guy. I just wished everyone didn't think he was so wonderful all the time. People at school act like he's perfect. Sure he's good-looking, funny, sweet, his parents are famous, and he has money, but he always does this annoying thing where he cracks his knuckles. Not only does it sound gross, but it could also cause arthritis. And he's nice, but almost *too* nice sometimes. I couldn't discuss anything with him, because he would just agree with me and tell me to do whatever I wanted. When we went out to eat, he left it up to me, saying he didn't care if we went for sushi or pizza. At the movie theater I always chose what we saw. He didn't get riled up about politics, or movies, or sports. He was so calm about everything that he made Gandhi look like he'd had an anger management problem. It wasn't that I wanted him to lose it and start screaming, but it would have been nice if once in a while he had an opinion. If I wanted a heavy discussion, I had it with Joel, who could be counted on to have an opinion about everything. However, it's hard to explain that your boyfriend can be too agreeable. No one feels sorry for you.

"You're right. Tristan is definitely bread-worthy, and I have every confidence that you will find your own bread man who will love you exactly as you are," I assured Kelsie.

Kelsie smiled at me. "There are KitKats in my bottom desk drawer."

I gave a whoop and crawled forward so I could reach her desk. Buried under a stack of folders was a package of candy bars. I tossed one to her before opening my own. "I thought you said you gave your stash away," I said.

"I did. This is different. It's an emergency fund," Kelsie explained, biting into her candy bar.

"This counts as an emergency? You've got a pretty low threshold."

"I'm an Evesham girl. Anytime I want something, it counts as an emergency," Kelsie said with a smirk. "For someone who is so keen on emergency planning, I would think you would know this."

"Well, with the crisis averted, are you ready to get back to the presentation?"

Kelsie threw herself back down onto the bed. "I hate this project. Why are they trying to ruin our senior year? We're under a lot of stress, and stuff like this could drive us over the edge. They're crushing our college dreams. I think senior year should be pass/fail."

"You're not going to college," I pointed out. "You're doing an acting class through the art center next year. How stressed can you be?"

"That's not the point. I could be going to college, and maybe I would have, if the whole thing wasn't so stressful. Not everyone is like you, Miss Ivy League."

"I'm not in yet."

Kelsie waved away my stress about getting into Yale (top choice) and Harvard (close second) with a flip of her hand. "You'll get in. You're the kind of student that admissions counselors have wet dreams over. You're spending your summer curing lepers, for crying out loud."

"They're not lepers. I keep telling you it's a study for people with hepatitis. The pharmaceutical company my dad works for is doing a summer training program for doctors."

"Whatever. If you ask me, the question is, why do you want to go to college at all? It sounds like four more years of the same thing as here—boring classes, homework, and lots of brick buildings."

"My mom went to Yale, and I've always wanted to go there."

"If I were you, I would swing by the college bookstore, pick up a sweatshirt, and then join Tristan."

Tristan wasn't planning to go to college yet either. He said he was taking a gap year to think about what he wanted to do next, but I wasn't sure if he would ever go. He seemed perfectly content to drift. His plan for the summer and next year was to travel to the different homes his parents had around the world. It wasn't like Tristan was ever going to have to worry about getting a job, so he didn't need a degree, and learning for learning's sake wasn't really his thing.

"Summer with Tristan would be good, but you have to admit my end-of-summer party will be amazing." My dad had arranged for me to be able to invite all my friends to stay in a five-star resort as one last blowout for our group. Everyone would be heading in different directions in the fall, so knowing we would have one last chance to be together was huge.

"Are you kidding me? Your summer party is already the event of the year, and it's still months away. All I'm saying is, spending the summer with Tristan in Paris wouldn't be a bad thing. In August you could swing by your dad's leper colony, put in an appearance, and then have the party."

"You know I can't do that. Part of the reason my dad arranged the party was because I'm doing an unpaid internship. It's his way of paying me back."

"I know you're looking forward to this summer with your dad, and I'm sure working for free is very rewarding in its own special way. I also get that you don't get to spend a lot of time with him, but passing up Paris? With Tristan? Croissants, fancy cheese that stinks, French wine . . ."

"I haven't spent a whole summer with my dad in forever. There is no amount of stinky cheese and wine that would make me give it up."

"And no amount of Tristan?"

"Not even Tristan." I smiled and opened my laptop. "Now back to our project. I've got a great idea for our presentation that pulls together everything. We'll take the time line you did that shows the major battles and generals and combine it with the pictures I downloaded. It will totally support the position paper I drafted."

Kelsie's eyes slid away, and she suddenly became fascinated by a microscopic chip in the polish on her thumbnail.

"Kels?" My stomach started to sink, and I felt the KitKat boiling in a rush of acid.

"I need to talk to you about the time line."

"You didn't do it?" I had deliberately given Kelsie the job of doing the time line because it was the easiest part of the project. It was time consuming, but not hard. I'd done all the research and written the paper, not to mention the bulk of the presentation.

"I started it." Kelsie pulled out a notebook. She had a line drawn on the page. Down the side it read: *War starts, Washington crosses the Delaware in the snow, War ends, Create Declaration of Independence.* I closed my eyes.

"I know I'm missing a bunch of stuff, but I can finish it now while you work on the presentation," Kelsie said.

"The Declaration of Independence happened at the beginning of the revolution," I pointed out, proving so far that 25 percent of what she had down on the page was wrong.

"Really?" Kelsie looked down, surprised, at her history

textbook. The binding didn't looked like it had been cracked yet. "Don't be pissed," she said.

"The project is fifty percent of our grade. Our presentation is *tomorrow*. Why didn't you tell me that you didn't think you would get your part done?" I wanted to kick myself. I loved Kelsie, but I knew what she was like. I should have made her show me her progress at least a week ago.

"Because I totally planned to finish it. Look, I'll talk to Ms. Brown and tell her the time line part was mine and not to have it reflect on your grade." Kelsie raised her right hand as if she were about to swear an oath.

I sighed. Kelsie knew I wouldn't let her take the fall. Besides, knowing Ms. Brown, all that would happen if Kelsie confessed is that we would get a lecture on the importance of teamwork and how learning to work together was part of the assignment. I felt like screaming, but yelling at Kelsie would be like kicking a puppy. I forced myself to take a deep breath.

"Okay. Make some coffee and do as much of the time line as you can while I work on the presentation. Then I'll take everything back to my room and polish it up." We both knew when I said "polish," what I really meant was that I would stay up until the wee hours getting it done.

Kelsie clapped her hands together and jumped off her bed. "Deal. I'll fire up the cappuccino machine in the lounge and make you a killer latte." She stopped in her doorway. "I'll make this up to you," she promised.

"Don't worry about it." I knew Kelsie. She wasn't the kind to clog up her brain with a lot of worry and stress anyway, so it was better to be nice about it. She believed stress led to breakouts, and she wasn't going to risk a zit for a war that happened hundreds of years ago. Freaking out was more my domain. I grabbed an extra KitKat. I was going to need the sugar rush to get through the night.

chapter three

I wasn't always someone who worried about everything. As a kid I assumed things would generally work out okay. My mom took care of everything. She could banish the monsters under my bed, and if I fell off my bike, she would blow on my skinned knees, which magically made them hurt less. At that age I was unaware of the dangers of septicemia (blood poisoning) and was content with a Band-Aid. Now I buy Neosporin in bulk.

While my mom was great, I thought my dad was a hero. I used to be a total daddy's girl. When I was growing up, he would take me out on Saturday afternoons so my mom could have some time to herself. He would pick me up at my bedroom door with flowers. He would always plan something for us to do, but not little-kid stuff. He would take me to fancy restaurants, the planetarium, or to the art museum. We even went to the opera a couple of times. He asked me my opinion and really listened to what I had to say.

My dad used to say that he wanted to spend all the time he could with me, because once I became a teenager, I wouldn't want to hang out with him anymore. That's not how it worked out in the end. My mom died when I was twelve. She was supposed to pick me up from school, but she didn't show up. I wasn't worried. My mom was the übermom. She made her own bread, sewed princess costumes for me to play dress-up in, and was never, ever late. A teacher found me sitting on the steps of the school hours later and called my dad when she couldn't reach my mom. The teacher wanted to know why I'd waited so long without talking to anyone. I didn't know how to explain that it didn't occur to me that anything might be really wrong. That was the last time I can remember ever feeling completely safe.

A drunk driver hit my mom. She had bought fancy decorated cupcakes for my gymnastics club meeting and was running across the street to her car. He was rushing home after spending the afternoon in the bar. She was in the crosswalk and it was a bright sunny day. There was no reason for him to have hit her, no reason for her not to have dodged out of his way. The police officer told my dad it was just a case of bad luck. She was in the wrong place at the wrong time. There were a zillion variables that might have changed things. If she hadn't stopped at the bakery, if the baker hadn't been so busy and forced her to wait, if she had stopped before crossing the street instead of assuming anyone coming would stop, if he had taken a cab instead of driving drunk, or had gone an alternate way. I used to lie in bed at night and think of all the ways it could have gone differently. Unfortunately, real life isn't a choose-your-own-adventure book where you can go back and start over if you don't like how things turned out. I overheard my grandma telling our neighbor that the man hit my mom with such speed that it knocked her right out of her shoes. They figured she was dead before she hit the pavement. There was pink frosting and sprinkles in her hair.

My grandparents moved in for a few weeks right after Mom died, to take care of things and help arrange the funeral. The first couple of days, my dad didn't even come out of his room. I would walk slowly past his bedroom, and he would be lying there staring up as if he could see straight through the ceiling into the sky and all the way to heaven, where my mom would be looking back. There were whispered conversations where my grandfather would tell him to "pull yourself together." My dad eventually came out of his bedroom, but he wasn't the same. He went back to work, and my grandma hired a nanny, even though I kept insisting I was old enough to take care of myself after school.

The day my grandparents left, my grandma took me out for lunch so we could have some "girl time." She told me that my dad was going to be okay, but that he needed my help. It was important that I be very good and not cause him any extra difficulty. I took what she said to heart and set out to be the best kid in the entire country. I made my bed every morning and went to bed promptly at nine thirty without having to be told. I washed my dishes out in the sink and put them in the dishwasher as soon as I finished eating. I flossed every day; I could have been the poster child for the American Dental Association, my teeth were so clean. If my mom had come back to life, she wouldn't have recognized me.

It was around that time that I started collecting information and statistics on risk factors, and avoided anything that I deemed too dangerous. It was like what happened with my mom opened my eyes to just how easy it was for something bad to happen. I wanted to create a safety net out of rules and systems. If I did everything right, then I could keep anything horrible from ever happening again.

The spring after she died I was mastering how to cook. Ms. Lindsey, the nanny, was teaching me the basics. After school she and I would make something together, and then all I had to do was heat it up for dinner.

I remember very clearly when the next ball dropped. I was sure my dad would say something about that night's dinner choice. I'd made a homemade green chicken curry. Thai food had always been his favorite. I placed the dish down in front of him and managed to hold in my desire to say *Ta-da!*

"I've got some good news," he said, shoveling a bite into his mouth.

I plunked down in my chair and inhaled the smell of the curry. I was hoping my dad was going to say something about summer vacation plans, since everyone I knew had exciting things lined up already.

"I've been checking around, and your grandma put in some calls to work her magic," he said, drawing out the suspense.

Maybe we would all rent a beach house on the Outer Banks together like we had years before. We could meet the boats when they came in and buy shrimp by the bucket. I could show my grandparents how I had learned to cook, and my dad could sit on the beach all day reading mystery novels. My dad would call me his Spanish peanut because my skin would turn a reddish brown from all the sun. I would sleep so well because of the sound of the waves outside that I wouldn't even notice all the sand in my bed or that my mom wasn't with us. I knew if we could only keep busy, then there wouldn't be time to let how different things were sink in. A new location meant Dad and I might not keep bumping into things that reminded us of her. I was so busy imagining the taste of salt water and burnt marsh-mallows that it took my brain a second to understand what my dad actually said.

"Boarding school?" I repeated, my fork falling onto the plate.

"Evesham Academy. It's one of the most elite schools in the country."

"I've never heard of it."

He laughed. "It's in Vermont."

"We're moving to Vermont?" My brain was still scrambling to catch up. I'd left it down on the beach in North Carolina, and I couldn't make sense of anything.

"It's a boarding school. I think I'm a bit too old to fit in." He gave a forced chuckle. "It will be a great experience for you and set you up to go to any college in the country."

"I don't want to live in Vermont."

"You've never been to Vermont," my dad pointed out. Like a person has to go somewhere to know if they would like it or not. If he told me that we were moving to hell, would I have to stop by and take a tour before I decided if it was too hot for my taste? Parent logic doesn't always make sense.

"But I like living here."

My dad took my hand and held it. "The house is too much for me on my own."

I didn't point out that he wasn't on his own. We were together. "Is it the yard work? We could get a gardener." We already had a housekeeper who came every other day and did all the cleaning and grocery shopping. I didn't like the idea of my dad doing all the mowing anyway, especially since I was coming to realize how many mower accidents occurred in a year.

"It's not the yard, Hailey. It's . . ." His voice trailed off, and I knew he was thinking about my mom. My throat pulled tight, making it hard to swallow. "I'm going to put the house on the market and find something in the city closer to work."

"I wouldn't mind living in the city," I said quickly. "It would be really cool. We could get a place in one of those high-rise buildings that have a view of Lake Michigan. One with giant floor-to-ceiling windows."

"The schools in the city aren't good, and you wouldn't want

to be cooped up in an apartment all the time while I'm at work. Evesham has a great reputation. This way, there will be tons of people your own age, lots of fresh air. They have all kinds of stuff to do, like archery and horseback riding."

Archery? Did he think I wanted to be Robin Hood? Sharp pointy sticks hurled at a high rate of speed, and no full body armor? I didn't think so. I opened my mouth to tell him no way, I wasn't going to go and he couldn't make me. I looked into his eyes. My dad was staring at me, and I could see the tension in his jaw despite his plastered-on smile. He kept swallowing. He looked like he was one step away from putting his head down on the table and crying. The kind of crying where you can't stop once you start.

"The school sounds great, Dad," I managed to choke out. I told myself maybe it would be just a year. Time for him to feel better. Then I would move home and we could go back to the way things were.

His face relaxed slightly, and I could see him take a deep breath. "Wait until you see the pictures of the place. It looks like a mini-Harvard, all those great stone buildings with lots of ivy. Some of the dorms even have fireplaces."

"Neat." I pushed my rice around on the plate. I wasn't remotely hungry anymore.

"And I checked out the science program in particular. State-of-the-art labs, and the teachers can help you organize an independent study on pretty much anything. They've also got some arrangement with the local college to use their materials if needed."

"Wow." My voice sounded flat to me, but my dad didn't seem to notice. He'd gone back to eating his dinner with gusto. "I'd come home in the summer, though, right?" I asked. "We'll spend our summers and vacations together?"

My dad smiled. "Of course we will." He took another big bite of the curry. "Wherever you ordered this from is amazing. Best curry I've had in years. Be sure to stick their menu on the fridge."

I started to tell him I'd made the curry myself, but then it didn't seem to matter. It didn't matter any more than his promise that we'd spend holidays together.

chapter four

Despite what my dad had promised about spending summers together, there was always a reason it made more sense for me to go to my grandparents' house—some project he had to work on, or construction in his new condo building.

This year was going to be different. When he asked me what I wanted as a graduation gift, I told him I wanted to have the whole summer together before I went to college. He seemed surprised, but he agreed. He even arranged the job for me with his company so I'd have something on my résumé besides working at the Gap. It was also his idea to throw the end-of-summer party. It was going to be the perfect summer. We'd have lots of stuff to talk about from working together, and after a few weeks it would start to seem easier. When I was a kid, I never ran out of things to say to him, and I was sure if we could just spend more than a day or two together, it would go back to that easy comfort. I could picture us sitting on the balcony of the resort, our feet up on the railing, talking about college and what I might end up doing, maybe even talking about my mom. I could picture him sitting at the pool with all of my friends, getting to know them. I'd been dating Tristan for almost four years, and my dad had only met him twice. Most of the time he called him Taylor by accident.

I unlocked the door to my dorm room and plopped everything down onto my bed. My room was in Elsie Hall, built in the 1920s. There was wood paneling on one wall, and the floors were a gray slate. It had one of the fireplaces my dad had seen in the brochure, although there was a strict no-fire rule. I'd put a collection of candles in the hearth. We were allowed to paint our rooms, and I'd painted the other three walls a thick cream color that reminded me of French vanilla ice cream.

Kelsie had gotten practically nothing done on the time line, and what she did have completed, I wasn't sure I could trust. Knowing Kelsie, she would have General Electric listed as one of the leaders, along with Captain Kangaroo. She was a great friend and would lend you her last cashmere sweater, but academics weren't her thing. I was mad at her for not coming through, and even more mad that I felt I couldn't tell her I was upset, because of how she would react. She would make it into a huge drama and fall over herself to apologize. It would take me longer to sort it out than it would to do the project myself. If we stood any chance of acing American History, it was going to be up to me. It was going to be an all-nighter if I was going to get it done. I pulled off my shirt and yanked on my mom's old Yale sweatshirt. I thought that I might as well be comfortable.

I wandered down to our common room to get a bottle of water. I couldn't do anything about missing sleep, but at least I could stay hydrated. Dehydration can lead to kidney failure. Also, it's bad for your skin. Besides, if I had any more coffee, I was going to get the shakes. There was a group of freshmen piled all over the lounge. They had a movie on the TV and were doing facials and painting one another's nails. Their giggling stopped when I walked into the room.

"Hey, Hailey, you want to watch a movie with us?"

I looked over. It was some slasher flick. I never saw the point in horror movies. Real life is bad enough without having someone chopping you up in your dreams as a form of entertainment. "Sorry, guys. I've got homework."

"Is it true you went to the Oscars last year with Tristan's parents?" a bucktoothed girl asked me, her mouth hanging open.

"No. They limit how many people can get into those award shows. Tristan and I just went with them to some of the after parties."

"Oh my god, that is still so cool. Did you meet anyone famous?" The group of freshman girls was now in a circle around me. I felt like someone who had introduced fire to a group of cavemen.

I pulled a bottle of water out of the fridge and wiped it clean with a paper towel. You don't even want to know what kind of germs are on those things. You might as well clamp your mouth down on a toilet. "Sure. We ate dinner with Johnny Depp. It was cool, but once you meet a few of them, you realize famous people aren't really any different from anyone else." This was true. Tristan's parents once invited me to a dinner party they had, and the guy next to me had been in a zillion box office hits, but apparently didn't know basic oral hygiene, because his breath smelled like a sewer grate. "Have fun with your movie." I raised my water bottle as a good-bye gesture.

"You can't go. Stay and tell us more about who you've met, and I'll do your nails," one girl said.

"No can do. History project due tomorrow." I turned to leave, but the girl grabbed my arm to try to convince me. She must have forgotten that she was still holding a bottle of nail polish, because a spray of bright red polish glopped onto my sleeve. We both looked down at the paint.

"Oh my god. I am so sorry." She wiped at the polish, smearing it over a larger area.

I yanked my arm back. This was my mom's sweatshirt. The one she wore when she went to Yale. It was one of the only things of hers that I had with me at school. Tears rushed into my eyes. It was ruined.

"I'm such a spaz. I'll buy you a new shirt." The freshman girl looked like she was ready to start crying too. The other girls had taken a slight step away from her in order to distance themselves from her certain social suicide. I swallowed the tight knot in my throat. She hadn't meant to do anything. It was my own fault. I shouldn't have worn the shirt if I didn't want anything to ever happen to it.

"It's okay," I managed to whisper. I waved her hands away before she could smear the polish further. "I really have to get going." I hustled back down the hall to my room.

I shut my door behind me and slid down to the floor. I couldn't believe that had happened. I pulled off the sweatshirt and looked at the stain. I buried my face into the shirt. I bet my mom would have known how to get nail polish out in the wash. Today was turning into a crappy day. I would have gladly traded the Bette Davis dress to have my mom's faded sweatshirt back without a big blob of Candy Apple Red Kiss on it.

I looked over at the clock. It was getting late. I knew I could either lie on the floor and feel sorry for myself or I could get working on the stupid time line so I could get at least a few hours of sleep. I fired up my computer, and there was the *ping* indicating new mail. It was from my dad. I clicked on it with a smile; his e-mails always put me in a good mood. But as soon as I read the first few lines, my stomach clenched tight.

Hailey—

I hope your classes are going well. I have some bad news; there's been a change of plans. I've been asked to teach a lecture series in London. The company is going to sponsor the program, and it's an excellent public relations move. It will likely result in an increase in funding for several projects. This means someone else will be heading up the training project in Tahoe this summer.

I hate to cancel our plans, but I know you'll understand. I've talked to your grandparents, and they would love to have you again. I called in a favor and was able to get you a job in the Munson Hospital Lab up there. Heck, you'll get to spend your whole summer at the beach. You won't even notice I'm not there. My lectures will wrap up in August, and we can spend some time together then, and we'll pick you out whatever you like for a graduation present. About the party you planned, your grandparents can't have all your friends at the house, but you could invite a few of them. I bet they'll love the beach too! Besides, sometimes a small group can be more fun than having everyone.

Love,
Dad

I stared at the computer screen. I hoped that if I stared long enough, the words would rearrange themselves into a different message. This couldn't be happening. He was canceling. I'd done everything I could do to be the perfect daughter, and it still didn't matter. I felt like I was going to throw up, that sour slick of spit sticking in the back of my throat. I picked my iPod up off the bed and hurled it across the room. It left a scar on the wood and made a clunk when it hit the floor. That made me feel a little bit better. I looked around for something else to destroy. I grabbed my pillow and yanked open the drawer in my desk, pulling it almost completely out. I took the scissors and stabbed them into the center of the pillow. That's what I thought of his fancy lecture series and his acting like changing my party plans was no big deal. I stabbed the pillow again. A poof of tiny white down feathers flew out, and as I pulled out the scissors, more began floating up into the air. I felt my breath coming faster.

I stood up and kicked my mom's sweatshirt out of my way so I didn't have to look at the ruined sleeve. I took my bag and turned it upside down, dumping everything onto the floor. I shoved my history book out of my way, snatched my cell phone from the pile, and immediately called Tristan. His cell didn't pick up. He never charged the damn thing. What was the point of having a cell phone if you didn't have it on when people needed to reach you? I was so frustrated, I wanted to scream. I scrolled through my list and stabbed a button. Joel picked up on the first ring.

"Is Tristan there?"

"Hi, this is Joel. Nice talking to you. Usually when people call my phone, they're calling to talk to me."

"I need to talk to Tristan." My voice snagged on the words. Suddenly the anger was sharing space with tears. I was even madder that I felt like crying.

"Hey, are you okay?" Joel's voice turned soft. "Tristan's not here."

"Where is he?" My voice came out small. "Can you get him? I really need him."

"He's in a study group down in our lounge. He's not supposed to be back until late. Do you want me to get him?"

The tears started to pour out of my eyes, laser hot as they slid down my face.

"Hailey? You still there? What's wrong?"

"I . . ." My voice trailed off. I didn't know how to explain it. How it hurt that my dad didn't want me around, and how it was even more upsetting that I'd let myself be so excited about the summer, when I should have known better. "You tell him I called?" I squeaked out.

"Yeah. I'll tell him to call you the second he walks in. Listen, you can talk to me about whatever . . ."

I clicked off the phone without even saying good-bye. My feet tapped on the floor. I couldn't just sit there. I felt like I was going to fly apart into a thousand pieces. I yanked my door open and stepped out into the hallway right into the path of our dorm matron, Ms. Estes.

"Ms. Kendrick," she said in her clipped voice.

"I have to go out for a bit."

"I'm afraid it's after eleven." She pointed to her naked wrist as if she were wearing a watch. Evesham required all students to be in their dorms from eleven p.m. to six a.m. on weeknights. No exceptions.

"I—I need to get some air." I could feel myself shaking. She stood there, unmoving. Ms. Estes had never met a rule she didn't like to enforce. I wanted to push her out of my way, but instead I stepped back into my room and slammed my door closed.

"Two demerit points, Ms. Kendrick." I heard her say through the door. Without even seeing her, I knew she was writing it down in the small Snoopy notebook she carried in her pocket, just for these occasions. I kicked the door when I was sure she was far enough down the hall not to hear. My toe gave a loud crack. I bit down to avoid yelling out. I hopped around on one foot. It felt like I had broken my big toe.

I hobbled back and forth in front of my bed, trying to shake off the pain. My phone rang, and I lunged over to grab it. *Thank God, Tristan.* I looked at the display. It wasn't Tristan; it was Joel. I threw it back down onto the bed without picking up the call. It felt like I couldn't get a deep breath. I yanked open the window and took deep greedy gulps of air. I don't remember making the decision. There wasn't a go-or-don't-go pause. It's hard to know what would have happened if I had stopped to think, but I didn't. One second I was in the room, and the next I was climbing down the ivy outside the window, jumping the last few feet down to the ground. I stood outside for a beat, looking back at the warm yellow light of my room, and then I took off.

chapter five

The problem with running away at Evesham was that there really wasn't anywhere to go. It wasn't because the campus has a giant wall around it, though it does, but because the school is several miles outside of town. Wandering around in the woods on a dark and drizzling night didn't feel like getting away with anything. It just felt wet and cold.

I paused by the front gate, next to a giant statue of the school mascot, a knight in armor holding a sword pointing toward the sky. Everyone on campus called him the Tin Man. Evesham was named after a famous battle in England in the thirteenth century. The Evesham motto—"Loyalty, Duty, and Honor"—was inscribed in brass letters around the statue's base.

That was a laugh. Loyalty and duty. Look how far that had gotten me. I was always was the one who smoothed things over, who gave in to make things work. The school could act like loyalty and duty were virtues, but my experience had taught me that all it made you was a doormat. I bent over and picked up a clot of wet mud. I stared at the statue, almost expecting the knight to beg me to reconsider, but he just stood there with his smug unreadable expression. I pulled back and let the mud fly. It smacked him in the head with a surprisingly loud *splat*.

"Screw loyalty," I said, hurling another ball of mud. "And duty, too." I was bending over, scooping handfuls of mud, and throwing them as fast as I could at the statue. I was a lousy athlete most of the time, but rage was doing a great job of improving my aim. The mud was sliding down the side of the statue, and occasionally a *ping* would ring out as a rock hit the metal.

"Whoa. What did he do to you?" a voice said behind me.

I whirled around, ready to bolt. I could make out a figure in the dark but couldn't see his face clearly. He took a step forward. It was Joel.

I dropped the clot of mud in my hand. My jeans were coated in grime, and I could tell it was in my hair, too. I looked over my shoulder at the statue in case he had anything to add that might help me explain.

"I came to make sure you were okay," Joel said, his voice calm and slow as if he were speaking to someone who might snap at any moment, which, given the circumstances, was probably a good strategy. "I tried calling you back a few times, but you didn't pick up."

"I'm not okay," I said, my voice small.

He didn't say anything else. Joel crossed the few feet that separated us and pulled me into a hug, despite the fact that I was soaking wet and dirty. "It's all right. You're going to be okay, though, I promise."

I leaned into the hug, and he squeezed me tight before pulling away and plunking me down on the closest bench. I started bawling like a two-year-old and then spilled the whole story about my relationship with my dad and everything else that had happened. "I know it's no big deal. In the big scheme of things, we're talking summer plans, not starving children or a collapsing world economy or anything." I shrugged, hoping to give the impression that I was working myself closer to sanity and off the emotional edge.

"It seems like a big deal to me. He gave you his word. He made a promise."

"But this conference is a big deal. He'll have a chance to pull in all sorts of funding."

"But he had you make all these plans and invite all these people over for a summer blowout, only to leave you in a lurch. Besides, this is still his last chance to have time with you before you go off to college."

"Yeah, but I'm not going to school in Borneo or anything. I could still come home during the summers." I wiped my nose with my sleeve.

"Are you trying to convince me or yourself?" Joel asked. I jumped a bit at the unexpected question. He laughed at my expression. "You're busted, Kendrick. You're ticked. It's fine to be pissed at your dad. Anger isn't a bad thing."

"I'm not mad. I'm disappointed," I clarified.

Joel laughed harder. "Disappointed, huh? Do you always hurl things at statues when you're disappointed?"

I looked at my hands. They were covered in mud, and I had broken two fingernails. Busted. I was mad. In fact, it was possible I had left mad behind, whipped through angry, and was plunk in the middle of really pissed off. I had been *disappointed* that my dad seemed fine with me living far away at boarding school. I felt *let down* that when I got straight A's, won state championships in debate, and made student government, all he did was pat me absently on the head like a good puppy who had managed to bring back a stick without peeing on the rug. I was *bummed* that my dad was so disinterested in my life that he could barely remember the names of my friends when he did see me, but this was a whole new level of ticked off. I felt my eyes fill up with tears again.

"He's my dad, and he acts like he wants to forget I even exist."

"No one could forget you." Joel tipped my chin up so we were looking eye to eye. "You're the kind of person that makes an impression."

"What kind of impression? Sometimes I feel like I'm not even being me. That everything is this big show. The amazing Hailey Kendrick. The worst part is, I'm trying to impress someone who isn't even paying attention, and I don't even know who I really am. I wander around here like I'm starring in a reality show, always being nice and making sure my hair is perfect. I'm the Polly Perfect Popular girl."

"I can understand that." He caught my raised eyebrow. "You think that this is all there is to me? Good guy Joel? He's such a great sport, smart. Heck, he even dresses well. You can hardly tell he's the scholarship kid."

My face flushed red. Evesham is ridiculously expensive, and the school board funds a few scholarships for kids who come from underprivileged families. Most of the scholarship kids end up dropping out; they don't fit in. It isn't that people try to be snobby, at least most people. It's just hard to know what to talk about with them. You can't really bring up your holiday plans to the south of France when you know that their parents might be on welfare. It doesn't seem right. All the Evesham students might wear the same uniforms, but the scholarship kids never have designer handbags and shoes that were custom made in Italy. The kids who don't drop out tend to be loners. They don't even seem to want to hang out with each other. It's as if they don't want to create too large a target.

It was easy to forget Joel was there on scholarship. He wasn't anything like the others. He was always in the middle of everything, laughing and cracking jokes. He never seemed bitter, or like he resented what everyone else had.

"I never think of you as the scholarship kid," I said.

"My problem is that I can't get you to think of me at all," Joel said with an exaggerated wink, and he dodged when I tried to shove him in the side with my elbow. "Look, I know I'm lucky to be here at all. If you saw the public school where I grew up, you would think you were in Beirut. They have metal detectors at the door, the ceiling is always leaking—probably asbestos—and most of the teachers are only there because they couldn't get a job at any decent school. Going here is a huge opportunity, and I get that. It's going to mean getting into a good college and doing something with my life. People can say all they want that this is the land of opportunity, but the truth is, if you don't get a decent education, you're screwed."

"Is this going to be one of your policy points when you're president?"

"Better believe it. I'm going to make so many changes that they're going to have to find space on Mount Rushmore to carve my face in next to Lincoln and Washington."

"Guess your ego isn't on scholarship, huh?"

"I figure if I act like I'm so great, the rest of you will just assume it's the truth."

"It seems to be working pretty well so far."

"Yeah, but people around here are pretty easy to fool. Sheep, most of them. Present company excluded, of course."

"Of course."

"I don't mind appreciating how lucky I am to be here," he said, "but I do hate having to be so damn grateful all the time.

It's like anything I do has to come with a caveat, that I never would have been able to do it without the kind contributions of the alumni foundation. I can't even own my own success, you know? It's like I have to share it with everyone."

I thought about the alumni banquet Evesham holds every year at homecoming. There's always a big call for donations, and last year, Joel was one of the people who had to get up and talk about how much he'd benefited from his Evesham experience. It had never occurred to me how that might have made him feel.

I touched his shoulder. "I think you're pretty amazing, with or without the scholarship," I said. "In fact, I'm counting on you being elected president someday so I can get invited to all those swanky White House parties."

"Actually, I was thinking of making you my vice president. Lots of perks. You get your own office in the White House and everything. A jet, too. Not Air Force One, but still better than flying coach."

"The vice presidency isn't really my thing. I don't mind it on student council, but I can't see me doing it long term. I might take an ambassadorship, though. Someplace good, like France or England. I don't want to be stuck in some third world country and end up with malaria."

"I would feel terrible if you caught some intestinal para-site on our nation's behalf. I think we should plan to go with London, since you don't speak French."

"Thanks. Not just for the future ambassadorship, but for

sneaking out to find me. I feel better," I said, tucking a clump of my muddy hair behind one ear. I was still mad at my dad, but I didn't feel like I was going to fly into a thousand pieces anymore.

"This is all it takes to make you feel better?" Joel shook his head sadly, as if he couldn't believe me. "I think you should raise the bar."

"I don't know. Don't forget, I've pretty well beat up our buddy here." I pointed to the statue of the knight. "I would say I've struck a blow against duty and feeling fake."

Joel's smile turned up on one side, just the tiniest bit evil. "What do you say we strike a real blow?"

chapter six

"See if you can wrap my sweatshirt around his head. Then push from up there while I pull," Joel called up to me. He was coated in mud now too. "Try to get as much leverage as you can."

We were trying to remove the mascot's head, but it was clear that this was one knight who didn't intend to be decapitated. I didn't have any artistic talent, so until that moment I'd had no appreciation for how much effort must go into making a statue. However they'd attached the head, it had clearly been done with more than a mere dollop of Elmer's glue. Whoever made these things made them to last. Our plan was to take his head off and mount it on the front gate of Evesham, but I was getting close to giving up.

I was straddling the knight's upraised arm a good six feet off the ground. I scooched forward so that I could take the sweatshirt from Joel without falling off. I wrapped it around the back of the knight's head. Joel grabbed a hold of the arms of the shirt and pulled down while I tried to push. It didn't feel as if the head was even budging. I didn't think this plan would work. Given that our earlier attempt, whacking his head with a large stick, hadn't seemed to do the trick, I didn't think we had the brute strength to just rip it off. The only impact we seemed to have made all night was a slight dent in his chin, but that might have been there before we'd started.

I leaned back against the upraised part of the knight's arm and tried to kick at his head. There was a loud *crack*, and the arm I was sitting on snapped off. It felt like I hung in the air for a split second, like the coyote in the Road Runner cartoons when he would run off a cliff. I let out a squeak, and then I fell.

Before I could hit the ground, Joel was under me, catching me with a loud "Oomph." He staggered under my sudden weight, but hung on, holding me as if he were the groom and we were headed over the threshold. We both looked up at the statue. He still had his head, but his arm had sheared right off. It was lying on the ground, the tip of the sword snapped clean off. Our eyes met, and we both started laughing.

I slipped down so that I was standing, but Joel still had his arms around me, holding me up. I was laughing so hard that my eyes were watering.

"I can't believe we did that," I said, slightly out of breath.

"I can't believe I'm going to do this."

I was about to ask what he meant, when he kissed me. He

pulled me even closer, and I could feel the heat of him through our wet clothes. It was like he was on fire. His hands were on either side of my face. I wasn't aware of the knight, the rain, or the mud anymore. Joel was consuming every sense I had. His heat, the smell of his skin, the taste of his mouth, and the look in his eyes. It was as if the entire universe had shrunk down to the space that contained us. We were a black hole pulling everything in. I wound my hands in his hair and pulled him even closer, our bodies locking together like perfectly fitting puzzle pieces, LEGO bricks clicking together to build something bigger and better. I felt the rain hit my skin and then sizzle off.

"Hey!" A voice yelled out. My brain snapped into place. I was kissing Joel. What was I thinking? I yanked back, breaking contact with his lips. I started to spin around, and a flashlight clicked on, blinding me. I threw my arm up in front of my face to shield my eyes.

"What the heck are you kids doing?"

I felt so guilty that it took me a second to realize that the voice in the darkness was talking about the statue and not the fact that I was kissing my boyfriend's best friend. I tried to see who was past the light. It had to be one of the Evesham security guards. I wasn't sure how I was going to explain what had happened. No one would believe that the arm had just fallen off while we happened to be there making out.

Joel grabbed me by the wrist. "Run." He took off, lightning fast, dragging me behind. It took me a few steps to get my feet moving in the right direction. Every time I nearly fell, Joel heaved me up by my arm and kept me running. It felt like my arm was going to tear out of the socket. He wove through the trees, staying away from any of the trails, to make it harder for the guard to follow. I could hear the branches snapping as we crashed through the woods. Behind us the guard stuck close at first, the beam of his flashlight bouncing as he ran. We were running faster, though, and I thought that Joel should have gone out for track. It was all I could do to keep up with him. After a few minutes the guard fell behind. Joel kept running long after I would have stopped. A thin branch smacked my face, stinging my cheek. I sucked in my breath. That hurt. My free hand reached up, and I felt blood.

Joel stopped quickly, and I ran into his back. We were both breathing fast. I bent over so I could suck a few deep breathes into my lungs. I rubbed my wrist where Joel had been holding me.

"I think we lost him," Joel panted.

"I can't believe we ran away."

"I don't think he'll be able to identify us. It's dark, and with all the mud, how much could he see? I don't think he could have gotten a really good look."

"We should get back, before anyone does a room check." I couldn't look directly into his eyes. Before he could reply, I started walking back toward the main part of campus. Joel walked behind me. He was so quiet that I had to fight the urge to turn around and make sure he was really there. That it, he, wasn't a dream. The whole situation seemed surreal—the statue, the kiss, getting caught. It was as if I had crawled through a portal and ended up in an alternate universe. I wouldn't have been surprised if a unicorn had wandered past to give us a ride.

When we got back to the dorms, we stood under my window. "If I boost you up onto my shoulders, do you think you can pull yourself in?" Joel asked, looking up to survey the height. "Otherwise we could try tapping on one of the lower windows and seeing if someone will let you in," he suggested. Both of us knew that option meant involving someone else in what had happened. I quickly decided that the last thing we needed was a witness.

"I think I can do it. Don't drop me, though, okay?"

"Look, about what happened . . . ," Joel began.

"It's no big deal. If the security guard identifies us, I'll talk to my dad. He can buy a new knight for this place."

"I didn't mean the statue." Joel looked serious; his face was set into hard lines. He wiped a smear of mud off my cheek and saw the cut. His eyebrows drew together in concern. "You're hurt."

"It's nothing. Just a scratch. Don't worry about it—or, you know, what happened. It didn't mean anything. Must have been all the endorphins from tearing the arm off that guy. Thrill of the hunt. You hear about that kind of thing happening all the time in battle." I looked away quickly, and hoped he couldn't tell that I was blushing.

"Yeah." Joel's voice was flat. "It was just an accident. I would never do anything to hurt Tristan. He's my best friend."

"I know. I don't want to hurt him either. Don't worry. I won't say anything. We can pretend the whole thing never happened."

"Is it really that easy? Just forget it and erase everything?"

"Exactly. Poof. Look at that—I've already forgotten." I waved my hands between us as if I were creating a magic spell. My heart was beating fast. Joel had to agree. If we told Tristan, he would be crushed. He would never understand. Heck, I didn't understand. I'd never had romantic feelings for Joel in all the years I'd known him. But that kiss . . . It was like I had been possessed.

Joel looked into the woods and said nothing. He rubbed his hand over his face and then took a step closer. My heart stopped dead in my chest. Was he going to try to kiss me again? He bent over, cupping his hands. "Step up. Let's get you back inside."

I let myself take a breath. It was forgotten. It was going to be okay. I stepped into his hands, and from there up onto his shoulders. I could feel the strength of his hands as they cupped my ankles, holding me steady. My hands scrambled to find something to hold on to. I was still a few inches short of the windowsill. The rocks in the walls didn't stick out far enough to make any sort of handhold, and I was afraid the ivy wouldn't hold me.

"I can't reach," I whispered down to him.

"Okay, hang on. Step onto my hands and I'll boost you up farther." He gave a grunt and then raised his arms up above his head. I hugged the wall and stepped up. His arms were shaking with the effort, and I had the image of what it would be like if I fell and broke something. Luckily, the extra lift was enough and I was able to get a hold of the wooden sill for my room. I pulled myself up. Clearly I needed to do more chin-ups in gym, because my arms were screaming from the effort. My feet scraped on the stone wall searching for a bit of extra purchase. I didn't as much crawl into my room as fall in. Once I was inside, I leaned back out the window.

"You okay?" Joel asked.

"Uh-huh. You okay?" I couldn't see his face in the dim light, but I could make out his shape. He nodded. "Thanks for coming to find me."

"You can always count on me."

I wasn't sure what to say, so I waved to him and shut the window. I slid down the wall until I was sitting on the floor. It didn't feel like I could count on anything anymore.

chapter seven

One of things I don't like about Evesham is the shared bath-rooms. There are two per floor in the dorms. It's not like they're nasty. You couldn't charge what Evesham costs and get away with chipped tile and laminate counters. The floors are heated, and there's a wide granite countertop vanity where every-one sits to do their makeup in the morning. It was designed to look like the washrooms they have in Harrods department store in London. My Evesham bathroom was nicer than the bathroom I had at home, and I wasn't even expected to clean it. Evesham has a fleet of janitors who swoop in and mop and polish it as soon as we're done in the mornings. There's never so much as a stray hair in the corner. The problem with the bathrooms at Evesham is that you can never be alone.

I closed my eyes and wished for total silence. It was impos-sible to block out the sounds of the girls who were singing in the shower and the two girls next to me who were breaking down the calorie count of every food item ever known to man. Another girl was standing behind me spraying clouds of some perfume that stuck to the back of my throat like an oily smear of crushed roses. I opened my eyes to glare at her in the mirror.

"I'm sorry, Hailey." She waved her hands around to try to get rid of the smell, but all that did was wave it into my face. "I should do this in my room. I don't know what I was thinking." She scurried out of the bathroom.

I leaned forward to look at myself closely. My foundation had almost completely hidden the scratch on my cheek. All anyone would be able to see was a faint pink line, and they wouldn't even see that unless they were looking really hard. I searched my face. I couldn't put my finger on it, but it seemed as if there had to be something else, something I wasn't seeing, that marked the events from last night. Maybe a giant I KISSED JOEL carved into my forehead. My mind kept replaying the kiss over and over like some demented TiVo.

"You okay?"

I jumped and spun around. "What are you doing here?" I asked. Kelsie's room was on the other end of the floor, and she usually used the other bathroom.

Kelsie stopped short. "Whoa. Someone woke up cranky. I came to bring you a Starbucks. I bribed one of the juniors to make a run. It's my way of saying sorry again for the history project thing." She held out a cup for me.

My mind went blank for a second. I had completely forgotten about our history project. It was like something that had happened in another lifetime. When I'd gotten back to my room the night before, I'd felt like I had run a string of marathons. I had pulled my muddy clothes off, dumped them into the hamper, and crawled into bed without even taking the time to brush my teeth.

I hadn't done a thing on our project. The time line wasn't done. The presentation wasn't even close to done. We were screwed. I opened my mouth to tell her what had happened last night, and then clicked it shut. It wasn't that I didn't trust her. I told Kelsie everything. We'd been best friends since freshman year. It wasn't like she expected me to be perfect, but I couldn't escape the feeling that she wouldn't approve of what had happened. Not that she *should* approve. Even I knew that kissing Joel back was a lousy thing to do. I had lain in bed earlier that morning thinking about it after my alarm had gone off. I liked Joel, I really did. But not like that. He was always teasing how he was crazy for me, but it was just a running joke. He never meant anything by it. If he did, he surely wouldn't have joked about it right in front of Tristan. Besides, even if we did like each other, it wasn't like it would work out. He was best friends with Tristan. The kiss was just a onetime thing. There had been all that emotion, and then Joel had talked about how he felt like an outsider, and things had just happened. Besides, Joel and I had already decided that we were going to blot out the event altogether. If I told Kelsie, even if I told her only part of the story, it would make it real again.

Plus, there was the fact that Kelsie couldn't keep her mouth shut. She was an awesome friend, but she wasn't the kind of person who had a big future ahead of her in keeping secrets. It was safe to say the CIA wouldn't be recruiting her anytime soon. She was just incapable of keeping a good story to herself.

"Earth to Hailey," Kelsie said, interrupting my thoughts.

I blinked a few times and saw Kelsie staring at me with concern in her eyes. "Sorry. My dad and I had a fight last night and it's playing with my head."

Kelsie yanked out the plush stool next to mine and plunked down. "You and your dad never fight. What happened? Was he screaming? My dad yells so hard that the vein in his forehead looks like it's going to pop out of his head. I think it's all the sugar he eats at his job. It makes him really high strung."

"Well, I guess it wasn't really a fight. There was no yelling or anything. In fact, we didn't even talk."

"So this was, like, an imaginary fight?" One of Kelsie's eyebrows went up.

"He sent me an e-mail. He's canceling our summer plans. He's going to England for some conference."

"What about the party? Everybody's already planning on going."

I felt a rush of anger. The party? That was the first thing

she thought of, how it would affect her and her summer plans? "There isn't going to be any party," I spat out.

Kelsie touched my arm softly. "I'm sorry. I know how much you were looking forward to the whole curing lepers thing. On the upside, now you can go traveling with Tristan all summer. Think about how amazing that will be. Be a glass-full kind of person."

"Yeah."

"Wow. Try to keep down the enthusiasm there. Oh, the horrors you have to deal with, a whole summer in Europe with the cutest guy in the world, who's insane for you. How will you manage? The UN should totally step in and do something. Maybe some celebrities could band together and hold a telethon. If you ask me, the big problem you have is telling everyone the party's canceled. People are going to be seriously bummed. I know a few people booked flights and vacations around the plan. I wonder if Tristan can talk to his folks and see if they'll host it. I bet if you asked him, he'd clear it with them."

"I didn't get our project done," I said, changing the subject.

Kelsie's face wrinkled up. "What do you mean you didn't get it done?"

"I had the fight with my dad and I forgot. We'll have to ask Ms. Brown for an extension."

"She automatically drops two grades for an extension. That means at best we get a C."

"What? Is it going to ruin your chances to get into your

acting class?" I yanked my brush through my hair. *Now* she was all worried about our history grade? Where was the concern when she was supposed to be getting the time line done?

Kelsie held up both of her hands. "Don't snap my head off. I brought up the grade because of how you get about it. A C is fine with me. Heck, it's a step up from what I'm getting in French."

I felt suddenly deflated, like someone had sucked all the energy out of my body. "I'm sorry. The thing with my dad got to me."

Kelsie put her hand back on my shoulder. I could see both of us in the mirror. "I bet if you told Ms. Brown what happened, she wouldn't mark you down. You're her favorite by a mile. You're the only one who does the suggested additional reading in that class. It's clear you actually like history. You're the daughter she always wanted to have. Besides, if she doesn't change your grade, you can blame your dad and maybe he'll feel guilty enough to buy you a car for graduation."

I looked at my watch. "We better hurry or we'll be late for assembly."

Kelsie threw her arm around me as we walked down the hall. "Don't stress, Hail. What is it you're always saying? Things happen for a reason."

chapter eight

Evesham starts every day with an all-school assembly. The official reason is tradition. The administration liked to "bring us together as a community" and start the day with a "shared vision." Near as I could tell, the real reason we do it is because our dean, Mr. Winston, likes to be the center of attention. The school is nondenominational, but I'm pretty sure Mr. Winston secretly wants to be one of those evangelical ministers. Every day he starts with an inspirational story or quote, before diving into the various announcements about clubs and the importance of people being careful not to toss their silverware into the trash when they dump their trays in the lunchroom.

Most people would have preferred to have an extra fifteen minutes of sleep, but I usually didn't mind assembly. There's something relaxing about the sameness of it. The pews we sit in always smell like lemon polish, and the large arched windows make the hall feel important, like a cathedral. That morning I almost wished it were a church. I would need to do some serious praying if I were going to be able to get Ms. Brown to give us an extension with no penalty. History was my favorite subject. I felt like it should be science, since that was my dad's thing, but deep down it mattered more to me how I did in history.

Kelsie and I were two of the last people to walk into the assembly hall. We slipped into the back row just as Mr. Winston was taking his place at the lectern. My eyes skimmed over the crowd. Girls and guys sat on opposite sides of the hall, seniors in the back, with the younger grades closest to the front so the teachers could keep a close eye on them. Tristan caught my eye. His hair was still wet from the shower. He winked at me, and I found myself smiling. Then I noticed Joel was right next to him, and my heart skipped a beat. Joel looked at me and then pointed at his watch, shaking his head. Kelsie flipped him off, and I felt the tight band around my chest loosen. It was going to be okay.

Kelsie pulled her iPhone out of her bag and held it in her lap, where none of the teachers would see it. She liked to check celebrity blogs during assembly.

"I'm afraid there is a serious issue we need to discuss this morning," Mr. Winston said.

"Holy shit," someone whispered a few rows in front of me. I looked up and saw Mr. Winston standing with Mr. Hanson, the football coach, who was holding the metal arm from the knight. A few people started to giggle, but stopped as Mr. Winston's gaze fell on them.

"That is priceless," Kelsie whispered to me.

"People, this is not a joke. I see no reason for laughter. This statue is a symbol of this institution. It stands for the values that this school is based upon. It was a gift from a benefactor from the 1950s. This crime is a slap in the face of every student here."

"How the hell did they get the arm off? They must have had a blowtorch," Kelsie said, leaning forward to see the arm better.

I shrugged. I wondered if I'd left any fingerprints on the statue. Would the school have some sort of CSI crew that could dust it? Crime wasn't my usual thing. I had never even stolen a Tootsie Roll from the bulk section of the grocery store. I could feel myself starting to sweat.

"I would like the guilty parties to do the honorable thing and stand up and admit to their crime," Mr. Winston said. People looked around to see if anyone felt honorable. My butt felt glued to the seat. My eyes shot over to Joel, but he was staring around like everyone else. I forced myself to slow my breathing down.

"Very well." Mr. Winston straightened up. "Would Hailey Kendrick and Tristan Johl please come forward?"

I felt everyone in the room swivel around to look at Tristan and me. I wanted to sink into the bench. Kelsie was staring at me with her mouth open. The link between my brain and my legs didn't seem to be working, and I didn't think I could stand. Tristan was standing, but looked confused.

"Ms. Kendrick. Front and center, please," Mr. Winston bellowed.

Tristan came to the end of the row and held out his hand for me.

"Don't worry. We didn't do anything," Tristan said softly in my ear.

I wanted to explain to him that it was complicated, that I had done something, but I couldn't get my mouth to form words. Everyone was watching us, and Mr. Winston was standing at the front like an executioner. I was shaking, but I managed to stand, and we walked to the front. There was a rustle of whispering. I would have turned and run out of the hall, but there was nowhere for me to go. You can't really run away in rural Vermont unless you have your own car.

"Mr. Winston, I'm sure there's been some sort of mistake," Tristan said, turning on the charm.

"Really?" Mr. Winston looked down his nose at Tristan. It was well known that Mr. Winston preferred the kids who came from "old money." He thought kids who were connected to Hollywood were trouble. He seemed almost happy to have finally caught one doing something wrong. "The both of you should know you could be expelled for this prank. Ms. Kendrick, I am especially disappointed in you. I expected far more from you as a member of the student council and a leader in this school. What do you have to say for yourself?"

I stared into his eyes. My mind seemed to have lost the ability to communicate.

"We had nothing to do with this," Tristan said, motioning to the severed arm that Mr. Hanson was still holding.

"I saw you," one of the security guards said as he stepped forward. "I heard something, just after eleven and when I got to the statue, I saw the arm on the ground and you standing there making out. I looked you straight in the face," he said, looking at me. He crossed his arms over his chest.

"But I was in study group," Tristan said, sounding lost.

"Then, who were you with?" Mr. Winston asked, turning to me. I could hear someone in the audience gasp.

"You were with some other guy?" Tristan asked. He looked as if I had slapped him.

"Tell me who else was involved," Mr. Winston demanded.

Out of the corner of my eye I saw Joel starting to stand. The situation was going from bad to worse. If Joel admitted that he was the person I'd been making out with during the Great Statue Destruction, then Tristan was going to be completely crushed. He already looked at if someone had scooped his guts out with a rusty ice cream scoop. If he heard in front of the entire school that it had been Joel I was kissing, he wouldn't be able to cope.

"It was some guy from town," I spit out. "I was with this guy, and we broke the statue as a joke."

"This is true?" Tristan's voice cracked. We were close enough that I could see his lower lip starting to shake. His eyes looked like he was close to crying. He would be gutted if he cried in front of everyone. He didn't even cry sophomore year when he broke his arm in gym class. I felt my face turn red hot with shame. Everyone in the crowd was staring at me like I had grown a tail. Even Mr. Winston looked unsettled. He had thought he had everything tied up, but things were turning out to be more complicated. The chapel bells on campus chimed eight. Mr. Winston glanced down at his watch, annoyed that even time was getting away from him.

"The rest of you are dismissed for classes. Ms. Kendrick, you'll come with me to the office." He took me by the elbow and guided me toward the door. "Mr. Johl, there's no need to stand there. You're going to be late." We brushed past Tristan. I could feel his eyes burning into my back as the dean and I walked out of the hall.

Fifteen minutes before, I had been sure that everything was going back to normal. Now my entire world had blown up and was never going to be the same.

chapter nine

I shifted on the wooden bench. It must have been made out of some type of especially hard wood designed to make people feel pain. I was stuck waiting outside Dean Winston's office in the area that held his secretary, while he spoke to my dad on the phone. Mr. Winston and I had already discussed:

- How what I'd done was vile and on par with kicking disabled kittens.
- That I was on the path to becoming a criminal and likely would spend the rest of my life in jail giving myself homemade tattoos with a needle and a Bic pen.
- That the statue was a work of art, and would I dare to tear the arm off the Mona Lisa? He didn't think so.
- That I was a disappointment to him, my

family, my boyfriend, my fellow students, and likely all of Western civilization.

I watched out the window as people walked past. I wanted to see Tristan to explain, but at the same time I had no idea what I would say. How do you tell your boyfriend that you kissed someone else but you hadn't meant to? Kissing isn't exactly a common accident. I couldn't explain it to myself, so how was I going to explain it to him? I jumped, suddenly noticing Kelsie standing outside looking in. She met my eyes and spread her hands in a universal *WTF?* gesture. I shrugged, and for the first time felt like crying.

"Ms. Kendrick," Dean Winston barked. I spun around. He was standing in his doorway. "Your father would like to speak with you." He held the door open so I could walk past him into the office. His large desk was clean, with only the phone in the center of the highly glossed mahogany space. The red light blinked, indicating the speaker phone was on. Mr. Winston dropped into his leather chair and pointed to the small wooden chair across from him. I had hoped I might be able to talk to my dad by myself, but it looked like Winston was planning to have a front row seat for the discussion.

"Hi, Dad," I said, weaving my fingers together to avoid picking at my fingernails.

"Hailey, can you explain what's happened?" My dad's voice sounded clipped through the speaker.

"It was sort of a joke." My eyes darted over to Dean Winston, and I rushed to finish. "I realize it was a huge mistake and not remotely funny at all. It was one of those things that sort of just happened."

"Things like this don't just happen," my dad said. "This is very serious. If the school wanted to file charges for vandalism, they could. The cost of the statue is significant."

Out of the corner of my eye I could see Mr. Winston nodding along with what my dad was saying. He was most likely wishing my dad would come up with some form of vile punishment, but once your family sends you off to boarding school, there isn't that much more they can do to you.

"I'll pay for it. I can use some of the money in my savings account, and I'll get a job this summer and send the money here," I offered.

"You better believe you're going to pay for it, and you're also going to write the school administration an apology letter." A tired sigh came through the speaker. I could picture my dad at work in his office, rubbing his temples. Discipline wasn't really his thing. My mom used to do it, and after she died, he hadn't needed to punish me. I had been too busy being the perfect kid. We were in uncharted territory.

"There is one other issue still on the table," Dean Winston said, leaning over so his voice would be picked up by the speaker. He was stroking his tie as if it were a cat. The whole thing gave me the creeps, and I had to fight the urge to pull my chair farther away from him. "Hailey has not been willing to give us the name of the"—he cleared his throat—"young man from town that she was with last evening. "

"I don't see why his name matters," I said. "It was just a guy from town."

"I'm sure your father would also like to know about this *guy* from town that his daughter is cavorting about with in the middle of the night, committing acts of vandalism."

"I thought you were dating Taylor. Who is this boy?" My dad asked.

"Tristan. His name isn't Taylor. This was just a guy I met. I really don't want to talk about my dating life," I said.

"This boy is responsible for half the cost of the damages. Non-students are not allowed on school grounds after hours."

"I said I would pay for it," I said again, kissing my hefty savings account good-bye.

"Are you protecting this boy for some reason?" My dad asked. "Is he threatening you? How do we even know Hailey had anything to do with this vandalism? My daughter is not the type to be in trouble. I think it is far more likely that this boy was the instigator."

"Your daughter appeared to our security guard to be a very willing participant."

"What exactly are you trying to say about my daughter? I would think there might be a need to spend less time smearing her reputation and instead looking into how this boy was allowed on what is supposed to be a secure campus," my dad snapped back.

I ground down a millimeter of tooth enamel. I hated how both Dean Winston and my dad were talking about me like I wasn't even in the room. It seemed to me that it wasn't about the statue anymore. Now it was about which one of them was more in charge.

"This guy has nothing to do with this. I was the one who was upset. It was my idea to damage the statue. The guy was just there. Nothing more," I blurted out, shutting both of them up for a beat.

"Hail, why were you so upset?" My dad asked, his voice tuning in to what I was saying for the first time. I felt my throat seize shut with rage. He wanted to know why I was upset? Either he'd completely forgotten that he'd torpedoed our summer plans a day before, or it had mattered so little to him that he couldn't even imagine that I might have been upset about it. I pressed my lips together to hold in what words might come flying out. I felt myself starting to tear up, and I stared down into my lap.

"Mood changes can be a sign of substance use," Mr. Winston said. "If Hailey has fallen in with an unsavory crowd, this might be something we need to investigate."

Dean Winston was about to see a mood change. I pictured how satisfying it would be to sweep my arm across his desk and send the phone flying to the floor. I forced myself to take a deep breath.

"I'm not on drugs. I understand you want to know who I was with, but I'm not willing to get anyone else in trouble for something that was my fault. I'm not going to tell you. I'm not going to tell anyone."

"It's not that simple, Hailey. What happened impacts the safety of the entire school," Dean Winston said. "As you know, we've had security challenges of late with the paparazzi. If there are unauthorized people sneaking onto campus, we need to know."

"If she refuses to tell, I'm not certain what you expect to happen," my dad said. "We can't force her."

"I assure you, Mr. Kendrick, I have extensive experience working with teens. When direct requests are met with resistance, then we take further action. Your daughter will be placed on campus restriction. This means she will not be allowed off campus for any activity. No trips to the mall, no movies, no sporting events. She's not allowed to go down to the store to pick up soda, candy, or those fashion magazines they all seem to love. She isn't allowed to leave the campus grounds without an escort from the faculty until she decides to share with us the identity of who she was with last evening."

What Dean Winston seemed to have forgotten in coming up with a plan that he clearly thought would crush me, is that it wasn't like anyone was going to want to hang out with me. I had to cancel the biggest social event of the year, thanks to my dad, and I'd publically hurt the most popular guy on campus. It wasn't like my boyfriend was going to want to take me anywhere. I couldn't imagine what Tristan thought of me. I could pretty much guess that this morning's assembly had dropped the whole nearly-naked Mandy scandal off the chart. Being stuck in my room by myself actually seemed like a gift rather than a punishment.

"That's fine," I said.

"While it might be fine for you, Ms. Kendrick, I doubt your classmates will share your perspective." Dean Winston leaned back in his chair, crossing his arms. "The entire campus will share your punishment."

I sat straight up. "You can't punish everyone. That's not fair."

"Evesham prides itself on its sense of community. It's been my experience that the pressure from one's peers is more convincing than anything I can do. If I can't persuade you to provide the name of the other person involved, then perhaps a week of no one being able to leave campus will be all the encouragement you need."

Winston looked really proud of himself. He seemed to be getting some kind of perverse pleasure out of the idea of seeing me ostracized by everyone I knew. I was starting to get the sense that he would see waterboarding as an acceptable form of information gathering too.

"Hailey, you should expect a punishment from me as well. We'll discuss it this weekend after you've had a chance to think about what you've done," my dad said. He might have wanted Dean Winston to think he was giving me time to stew, but I suspected the truth was that my dad had no idea what to do in terms of a punishment and couldn't be bothered to take more time away from his job to deal with me. I hadn't given him a lot of practice over the past few years. The worst thing I'd done since my mom had died was forgetting to put the tub of ice cream back in the freezer, resulting in a puddle of French vanilla on his polished marble counter. Destruction of school property was a pretty big step up.

"That's not all," Dean Winston said, interrupting my dad before we could end this call from hell. "We expect Hailey to make reparations as to the cost of the statue, of course. However, we feel that true reparations are more than just taking money out of an account. Many of our students come from fortunate backgrounds, and as a result, coming up with funds often isn't an issue and not a large deterrent."

"What is it you're thinking of?" My dad cut him off before Dean Winston could go ahead and call me a spoiled brat, which is what he was hinting at.

"Hard work. Hailey will be assigned to work with the cleaning crew. Her hours will be tracked and those minimum wage earnings applied to repay the statue."

"You want me to be a janitor?" I had an image of myself in a gray jumpsuit with my name stitched over the pocket and the stench of Lysol following me around like a yellow cloud. After canceling my summer party, cheating on the most popular guy on campus, and getting everyone in the whole school on restriction, being one of the cleaning crew was really going to be the icing on the cake of my newfound leper status.

"When you make a mess, it's important to clean it up," Dean Winston said.

"I agree," my dad said.

"What about school? I have college apps to finish." It wasn't that I thought I was above cleaning, but in the big scheme of things, was it more important for me to scrape gum off the bottom of desks or focus on pulling up my grade in history so I could go to Yale? Seriously, this couldn't get any worse.

"We're hardly planning to make you work around the clock." Dean Winston looked over my shoulder and nodded at someone behind me, before turning his attention back to my dad and me. "But you will be monitored, of course. I've selected a student leader to keep an eye on your participation and encourage you to do the right thing regarding being fully honest about this situation."

I couldn't wait to see who was going to be Winston's lackey. I turned around and saw Joel in the doorway. When he saw me, his face went white. He'd overheard what Winston had said and knew he was my new jailer.

I was wrong. Winston had found a way to make things worse.

chapter ten

I needed to be alone or I was going to lose it. I wasn't sure what losing it was going to look like, but I was willing to bet it would make what had happened with the statue look like small-time. I pictured myself standing in the center of the quad screaming and flopping around on the ground like a two-year-old having a full-on meltdown.

When Winston finally dismissed me, I put my head down and hustled toward my room. I was supposed to go to the last ten minutes of calculus, but whatever. I needed at least ten minutes of silence where I could just sit and pull things together. Everything had blown apart. I felt like I was standing in the middle of the rubble of my life, unsure about what to pick up. My hands wouldn't stop shaking, and it felt like I could throw up at any second. However, I couldn't be alone, because I had Joel stuck to my side like Velcro, and he was following me back to the dorms.

Joel shuffled through the leaves. "What should we do?"

This was the fourth time Joel had asked this question since we'd walked out of Winston's office.

"I don't know. Nothing, I guess." I wondered if people looking out of the classroom windows were watching, and what they thought of me. I couldn't look Joel in the face. I still wasn't sure how to handle what had happened. My plan of ignoring it altogether was now going to be a bit harder, since the entire school knew there'd been a kiss, even if they didn't know who it had been with.

"Do you want me to confess?" Joel asked. "I was going to, right after the meeting. I followed Tristan out of the hall, but then he puked."

I stopped short. "What?"

"He threw up. I've never seen him like that. I was going to tell him that it was me, that I was the one who kissed you, but when I saw him, I couldn't."

I couldn't think about Tristan now. I forced the image of him out of my mind. Tristan acted cool and aloof about everything, but he wasn't. He was used to protecting himself. It came from years of having photographers following him around hoping to capture a vulnerable moment. I remembered him telling me that when he was six, he took a nasty spill off of his bike. His knee had a huge gash, and there was a flap of skin, a triangle of flesh, that was ripped free and hanging. Tristan said it was that flap of skin that had really freaked him out, almost more than the pain. He'd been afraid that if he'd pulled on it, his entire skin would have peeled off his body. He'd started crying, and someone had snapped a picture just as his mom had come rushing up to his side. The picture ended up on the cover of some tabloid magazine, and the kids he went to school with teased him about being a crybaby. He told me that was the last time he ever cried in public. I couldn't imagine what he must have been feeling to be upset enough to puke in the bushes.

"I could get kicked out of school for this," Joel said, snapping my attention back. "I'll lose my scholarship for sure."

"You're not going to get kicked out," I countered, continuing toward my dorm.

"Winston is just big enough of an ass to do it. All the shit he's doing with you, putting the whole school on restriction, the cleaning crew detail, that's all because he can. He loves a power trip. He'd like nothing better than to put someone like me back in my place. He doesn't think I belong here, and certainly not in the Ivy Leagues. People like me are supposed to clean his house and wash his car."

"You're not going to get kicked out, because I'm not going to say anything."

"I can't let you take the heat for this on your own."

"It'll blow over. He can't keep the entire school on lockdown forever. Someone will whine to their parents, who will threaten to pull their donation for a new wing on the science building, and that will be the end of it. We've just got to wait it out." I stopped at the stoop to my dorm and fumbled for my key card.

"Are you sure?"

I wanted to yell in his face that of course I wasn't sure. I'd never been in trouble like this before. How was I supposed to make him feel better when I felt like shit? I spun around to say something, but stopped short. Joel was still pale, and his hands were jammed deep into his pockets. He was scared.

I put my hand on his shoulder and managed what I hoped was a reassuring smile. "It'll be okay."

"I'm sorry I'm the one monitoring your punishment." Joel kicked the stair halfheartedly, unable to meet my eyes.

"I'm not sorry. I'd rather have you do it than someone else. Can you imagine if he'd put Mandy in charge? She'd love to see me tarred and feathered."

Joel laughed. It sounded a bit forced. "When she realizes that you're standing between her and her regular trips to Starbucks, I think she'll demand we bring back burning at the stake."

"I forgot about her caramel macchiato addiction. I bet she ends up with the shakes before the day is over." I gave his shoulder a pat. "That almost makes it worth it."

"You should go. It's one thing to miss the rest of calculus, but you need to be on time for history."

My stomach sank to a new low. Any chance of Ms. Brown giving me a pass on turning in our project on time had disappeared. "So, what happens if I'm late, you'll give me a demerit?"

Joel looked up, his eyebrows squishing together with concern. "I'd *have* to give you a demerit. He's going to be watching me, making sure I enforce everything. It's not that I'd want to, but I can't afford to cut you any slack. He'll say I'm not living up to my role as president."

My hand dropped from his shoulder, and a lump formed in my throat. I hadn't felt this alone since my dad had dropped me off at Evesham for the first time. "I know. I should go. I don't want to be late." I ran up the stairs without looking back.

chapter eleven

I lay on my bed, staring up at the ceiling. I had less than fifteen minutes to get to history. I wondered if this was how people felt after some kind of disaster, like an earthquake or a plane crash. The last time I'd felt like this was after my mom died. My grandma had taken me to the mall to get black dress shoes for the funeral. The mall was full of people bustling around, swinging shopping bags to the bouncy beat of the pop music that pumped through the speakers. The smells of pizza and fresh baked cookies competed as they poured out of the food court. It seemed like everyone was wearing artificially bright colors, like a clown academy had run amok in the hallway.

I'd stopped in the doorway of the mall, and a salesclerk from the nearby department store had seen me hesitate, and had moved in to spray me with a puff of perfume. She'd blathered about how there was a sale and if I bought the perfume I could get a free lipstick. I'd taken the flyer she pressed into my hand

and looked down at it, trying to make sense of what was written on it, but it looked like Arabic. My grandmother took me by the elbow and guided me through the crowd to the shoe store. I felt like I was watching myself, or someone playing me, on TV. It didn't seem it was possible that this was reality. How could everything be going on just the same when my world had stopped? My mom was dead, but to everyone else it was just another day at the mall. They were complaining about jeans that didn't fit, and whispering about boys who were hanging out at the arcade. The salesclerks just wanted another sale or for their shifts to end, and little kids were still tossing pennies into the fountain and making wishes. I remember feeling how small and insignificant my life must have been, that when it came crashing down, it wasn't enough to make a ripple in the rest of the world.

Now it was happening all over again. I had lost Tristan. I was sure of it. He had been one of the constants in my life since moving to Evesham. We went everywhere together. People thought of us as one unit, Tristan and Hailey. His popularity had rubbed off on me. People liked me because Tristan did. They worried about what I thought and copied my hairstyles. I was pretty and smart, but Tristan had been what had made me special. He would never forgive me for what had happened, and I couldn't even explain it to him without hurting him even more.

I rolled into a ball on the bed. By now the announcement would have been made in classes that everyone was on restriction. Anyone who had thought it was sort of cool that Miss Perfect

Kendrick had destroyed the school statue would suddenly be changing their minds. Now my prank was going to cost them their freedom, and that wasn't going to be appreciated. Not at all.

I didn't want to run away. That would mean starting all over someplace else. What I wanted to do was disappear, but that wasn't an option. Neither was turning back time and not getting myself into this situation at all. What had I been thinking? Just like when my mom died, there was no way to change what had happened. I had to get through it. If I got through that, I could get through this. I would do it exactly the same way. I would put my head down and toe the line. I had gotten all wild and crazy for one night, and look where it had gotten me. I was going to follow every rule, guideline, and bylaw. I was going to follow rules that hadn't even been made yet. I was going to be so good I would make Mother Teresa look like an escapee from a *Girls Gone Wild* video. I wasn't sure how I was going to make this up to everyone, but I was willing to try.

chapter twelve

When I walked into history, everyone stopped talking and turned to face me. I ducked my head and slid into my seat next to Kelsie. She had her book open and was pretending to be riveted by the description of the battle of Saratoga. I slid my foot across the aisle and lightly tapped her leg.

"Hey," I whispered. She looked over, and I saw she was ticked. Not just a little angry but seriously pissed off. I pulled my leg back, my face no doubt registering the shock. I hadn't thought she would be one of the people who would be mad.

Kelsie leaned over so that no one could overhear us. "I thought we were friends," she hissed.

"We are," I said.

Kelsie shook her head like she couldn't believe a word that came out of my mouth. "Really? Because I would think that if we were friends, you might have thought it was important to share something like that with me. I don't know. I thought friends told each other stuff. What the hell do I know?" She turned back around and stuffed her nose back in her book.

I slunk down in my seat and did my best to ignore the whispering around me. Ms. Brown walked in and perched on the edge of her desk. She was thin and angular, with a long nose. She reminded me of a heron waiting to pounce. Her gaze swept across the room. She paused at my desk and raised one pencil thin eyebrow in my direction. I could feel her disappointment coming off in waves.

"Hailey, would you and Kelsie like to present first?"

I stood up next to my desk. "Our presentation isn't done. It's my fault. Kelsie finished yesterday, and I said I would get my half done last night, but I didn't." I sat back down, my cheeks burning.

"That's unfortunate. I would ask what was important enough to keep you from your studies, but I trust we've already discussed that topic enough this morning," she said.

Someone in the back of the room giggled, but the sound was choked off when Ms. Brown looked over. I could feel Kelsie eyeing me, evaluating what I'd said and deciding if she would say anything or keep quiet. It might as well have been completely my fault. If I hadn't screwed up last night, the project would be done and we'd be standing up there right now talking about the importance of the French to the success of the American Revolution.

"Very well. I'll expect you two to present tomorrow. We'll discuss the impact of this extension later." She looked down at her grade book. "Phillip, let's have you and your partner start us off."

When the bell rang for the end of class, I sat in my seat while everyone else streamed out of the room. The room was quiet except for the ticking of the clock on the back wall and the sound of Ms. Brown tapping her long fingernail on her desk.

"'Nothing is a greater stranger to my breast, or a sin that my soul more abhors, than that black and detestable one, ingratitude,'" she said.

My forehead scrunched up. I had no idea what she was talking about.

"It's a quote from George Washington during the war," she clarified.

"Oh." I pulled my notebooks together. I didn't know if she was calling me an ingrate, or was implying that Kelsie should be grateful that I was taking the blame for our project, or was randomly spitting out historical quotes. History teachers are an odd breed. Maybe it comes from inhaling all those dusty books. "I'll make sure our presentation is done by tomorrow."

"It's an automatic reduction in your grade."

"I know."

She waited until I was almost out the door. "If you're interested, I may have some extra credit assignments you could do. It might balance out your overall grade. The assignments are of course also open to Kelsie if she wishes."

85

A smile spread across my face and I gave her a nod. The brief upswing in my mood lasted until I got out into the hallway. Kelsie was leaning against the wall waiting for me.

"I have no idea what you're trying to pull," she said, her jaw thrust forward.

"Nothing. The project is my fault. I should have finished it. It was just, with everything that happened, I honestly forgot."

Kelsie sighed. "What kind of sign of the apocalypse is it when Hailey Kendrick forgets to do homework?" She looked around the hall to make sure we were alone. "Who were you with last night, and why the hell did you cut the arm off the statue?"

"We didn't cut it off. It sort of fell off. Not by accident or anything. I was sitting on it. We were trying to get his head off, actually."

Kelsie looked at me like I was speaking another language. "How long have you been cheating on Tristan?"

"I'm not cheating on Tristan," I said firmly. "There wasn't any big secret Romeo and Juliet relationship. It was a onetime kiss. It shouldn't have happened. It was a heat-of-the-moment kind of thing. A bunch of stuff went wrong yesterday, there was the project to finish, and then I got nail polish all over my mom's sweatshirt. Then the thing with my dad . . ." My voice trailed off. "I had to get out of my room and blow off some steam. I was so mad—mad at everything. Then there was the statue, and I happened to meet this guy there, and stuff happened." I shrugged. I knew it sounded crazy. It was crazy, but it was the truth and the only explanation I had.

"What's some townie doing on campus?" Kelsie's nose wrinkled up a bit when she said "townie," as if I had been caught kissing a homeless guy who smelled like cat pee.

"He was taking a walk and ended up on campus. No big deal. There wasn't a big plot or plan. The whole thing was like a weird freak accident. It just happened. You know me. You know this isn't the kind of thing I do."

"Man, when you decide to blow off steam, you sure do it big. Most people just sneak a few beers and throw up."

Throwing up reminded me of Tristan and what Joel had seen. "I have to talk to Tristan," I said.

Kelsie grabbed my hand. "No, you shouldn't. He's really hurt. And ticked."

"I have to tell him my side of things. What if he thinks I've been cheating on him?"

"You did cheat on him. You were making out with some guy. The security guard saw you."

"We weren't making out. It was one kiss. One kiss by accident." Why was that so hard to grasp? "I don't want Tristan thinking that I've been sneaking around behind his back. I feel sick about what happened, Kels. If I could change it, I would, but all I can do is tell him how sorry I am."

"Leave it to me," she said.

"What?"

"Trust me. I talked to Tristan right after the assembly. He's not interested in talking to you right now." She waved her hand in front of my face to stop me from saying anything. "I'll talk to him for you. Try to smooth things over. He's really hurt, and he doesn't want you to see that. You know how he is."

I nodded, chewing on my lower lip. I wanted a chance to explain, but it was quite likely he wasn't interested in talking to me. It might be easier if she talked to him first, gave him a chance to calm down. "Would you do that for me? Explain how I feel terrible, and that it was just a onetime thing."

"I'll talk to him. You might want me to talk to a few other people too. Everybody's pretty ticked about the restriction thing."

"Did you hear what else? Winston put me on janitorial duty."

"Gross. Why?"

"I'm supposed to be learning the importance of cleaning up my own messes."

"I'd have my parents complain."

"My dad thinks it's a great idea. He's still coming up with a punishment of his own."

Kelsie shook her head sadly. "This situation is totally screwed."

I wanted to throw my arms around Kelsie. It felt so good to

talk to a friend, to feel like at least one person was on my side. "Thanks for talking to Tristan. It means a lot to me."

Kelsie hitched her backpack up onto her shoulder. The bell was ringing to let us know there were only three minutes left. "Don't thank me yet. I'll talk to him, but I'm not sure it's going to do any good."

chapter thirteen

When I was a really little kid, I wanted to be invisible. I used to pretend that I had a magic cape that would make me disappear. I loved the idea of slipping in and around what was happening in the world and no one even knowing I was there. I would tie a pillowcase around my neck and slink around the house. My parents would play along, saying in loud voices: "Where has Hailey gotten off to? I don't see her anywhere." Then I would cover my mouth and giggle. Forget flying, or setting fires with my mind—I was convinced being invisible would be the best superpower ever.

Turns out being invisible sucks.

I used to say being popular wasn't important to me. That was before I found out what it was like to be on the other side. Now I realized that being popular had come with significant advantages. The week dragged on—snide comments in the hallways, my toothbrush knocked off the countertop onto the bathroom floor, no one saving me a seat in class or complimenting me on what I was wearing. The bubble of approval that used to surround me, people telling me how great I looked, laughing at my jokes, and agreeing with my views, was busted. What I noticed the most about my new status was how lonely I felt. I realized that before, I had almost never been alone. There was always someone calling out to me when I walked across campus, or stopping by my room to chat, or asking me for advice. If I went out, there was always someone who wanted to come along or a group that would beg me to join them. Now no one wanted me around.

I had never been so glad to see the weekend. All I wanted to do was hole up in my dorm room and pull my covers up over my head; instead I was following Joel to the administration building to begin the next stage of my humiliation.

Parked in front of the building was a beat-up red pickup truck. It looked like the only thing holding it together was the random bumper stickers that were plastered all over it. I'D RATHER BE SKIING. ADRENALINE IS MY DRUG OF CHOICE. FRODO FAILED. ELVIS HAS LEFT THE PLANET. There was dried mud sprayed across the side panels. A guy leaned against the truck reading a paperback. He was tall, at least six feet, with long hair that he had tied back in a ponytail. He seemed to be around my age, maybe a bit older. He looked like a surfer who had gotten very lost coming back from the beach and had somehow ended up in Vermont. When the guy saw us walking up, he carefully folded over the page he was reading, to mark his spot, and tossed the book into his truck.

"You must be Joel," the guy said. He turned to me with a half smile. "And you must be the guilty party coming to scrub your soul and the toilets clean."

I didn't say anything to him, but pleaded with Joel. "I don't see why I can't be assigned a project to do on my own. I could paint a classroom or something."

"That doesn't sound like a team player attitude," the guy said. "You know what they say: Many hands make light work."

Great. I was partnered up with a motivational speaker who smelled like Mr. Clean.

"Dean Winston wants you to work on the cleaning crew, not on your own," Joel said. "This is Drew. He'll show you around and make sure you know what needs to get done." Joel stood there looking at both of us, his face pinched. "Are you going to be okay?"

"Don't worry. She's going to be washing floors, not defusing bombs in a war zone." Drew clapped Joel on the shoulder and started walking, indicating I should follow him. I didn't.

Joel waited until Drew had taken a few steps away. "You know if I could take your place I would. I hate to see you having to do this."

I wasn't sure how it had ended up that I had to be the one to comfort Joel when he was going to be able to go back to bed and I was going to be the one cleaning fly corpses out of the lamps. "It'll be okay. Cleaning is good exercise. It's like a step class, only more productive." Joel squeezed my hand and then left, looking as if he were dropping me off at the executioner.

A disbelieving snort came from behind me. I spun and saw Drew standing there next to a cleaning cart. He rolled it over to me. "Do you want to push the cart? Really feel the calorie burn?"

I pressed my lips into a thin tight line and yanked the cart over. I must have pulled too hard, because the mop flew off and the handle smacked me right between the eyes. Drew gave another snort as he choked back a laugh.

"Do you think that's funny? If that had bleach on it, I could be blind."

"You look okay, Helen Keller. I'm guessing it takes more to keep you down than you think. Let's get going before you amputate a finger with the dustpan. It's got that sharp edge, you know. Careful. There's a feather duster, too. It might be full of bird flu germs."

I shoved the giant Rubbermaid cart ahead of me and walked away before he could make fun of me anymore. One wheel was stuck and wouldn't turn, so I wasn't able to make the dramatic exit I had been hoping for.

I rolled the cart into the first classroom and looked around, wondering where we were supposed to start.

"We need to wash all the desks down with disinfectant, mop the floors, wash the windows, and give everything else a quick wipe down. You do know how to clean, don't you, Prima

Donna? I'm hoping you learned something watching your maid all those years."

I didn't dignify his comment with an answer. It was true I had always had a maid, but it had never struck me as a job that required a lot of experience. I was pretty sure I could figure it out.

Drew bent over and started to pull various bottles and rags out of the cart. "You can pick what you want to tackle. The desks are easy. You might want to start with that and work up to the hard stuff." He looked up at me, and when I didn't comment, he tossed a rag and a can in my direction.

I looked at the can. It was some kind of industrial cleaner, most likely able to eat my flesh off if I got it on my skin. It looked way less user friendly than the organic, good-for-the-environment cleaner that my dad's cleaning service uses. I flipped the can over so I could see the warning label.

"Have you had any formal training for this job?" I asked Drew.

He looked over the mop bucket at me. "How did you know I got my master's degree in this?"

"I'm being serious. You know if you mix some cleaning supplies you can create chlorine gas? It can kill people."

Drew smacked his forehead. "Ah, that explains what happened to everyone else. I thought the death toll was high for this job."

"Have you considered a career in stand-up? Your talents are clearly wasted here," I said. I sprayed the desk closest to me, inhaling the oily stink of the cleaner. I wiped it down and moved to the next.

"Don't worry, Prima Donna. If you start to look faint, I'll drag your body to safety."

"My name is Hailey."

"Okay, Hailey. I'll drag your prima-donna butt to safety, right after I finish my lunch break. Never underestimate the appeal of a leftover Spicy Italian from Subway."

I made a face at him. "Chlorine gas can cause brain damage too."

"You're going to want to make sure you wipe under the desktop as well. A lot of these classy kids drill their noses during class and leave boogers under there," he said, pointing.

"That's disgusting." I pulled my hands away from the desk. I sat in some of these chairs. It had never occurred to me to check underneath them.

"You're telling me. I'm not joking either. Look for yourself if you don't believe me. Some of the desks practically have snot stalactites growing down. You would think instead of a Mercedes they could have bought some manners."

I glanced at Drew as he mopped the floor. I'd met his type in town before. They resent us for who we are. It isn't our fault our parents have money. What did people expect us to do? Give it all away to charity? Did he think I believed for a moment that he would send it all to Afghanistan to build schools if the situation were reversed? Most likely he'd spend it on fast food and

NASCAR races. I wiped the desks with renewed vigor. The last thing I wanted Drew to do was whine that I didn't pull my weight. I really wished I had a pair of rubber gloves to wear, though. The idea of touching someone else's crusty snot grossed me out. Since I was on restriction, I couldn't buy any gloves in town, and I wasn't sure I could bring myself to ask Drew to do me any favors. Maybe I could buy a pair from someone who worked in the cafeteria.

"So, what did you do to land yourself here?" he asked as he moved the mop across the floor.

"What makes you think I did anything?"

Drew's lip raised on one side. "Of course. My mistake. How kind of you to volunteer your time. Or are you planning a career in the cleaning arts and looking to log some valuable practical experience?" He leaned on his mop. "Come on. Fess up. Did you get caught pawning someone's silver spoon right out of their mouth?"

"What is your issue with me?"

Drew laughed. "You should see yourself. Your face is all red."

"You like annoying people, don't you?"

"As you can tell, this job isn't exactly a huge intellectual drain. I have to do something else to keep myself entertained."

"I wouldn't think you would require much to keep you intellectually challenged. Walking and talking, for example."

"I'm remarkably skilled at multitasking, actually. Check this out." Drew grabbed a couple rolls of toilet paper off the cart and began to juggle them. Great. I was stuck working with Bozo the Cleaning Clown.

"You're impossible to insult."

"Years of practice. My ego is armor plated." He tossed the toilet rolls back into the cart and picked the mop back up. "Besides, I knew you'd insult me, so I was able to prepare. Your type never likes the help when we get uppity."

"My type? What exactly do you mean by that?"

"You shouldn't ask. The answer is just going to upset you. In my experience your type is overemotional. Sensitive."

"You think you know everything about me?"

"Not everything, but I'm betting I've got the big picture covered."

"You know what I did to land myself here? I was the one who broke the statue in the quad," I said, putting my hands on my hips. I felt almost proud of myself when I saw his surprise.

"You?"

"Yes, me. I guess you don't know my type as well as you thought."

Drew looked at me as if he were reappraising my character. "I guess not. My opinion of you has just gone up. I wouldn't have pegged you as the vandal rebel-without-a-cause type. Personally, I've always hated that statue. The knight always looks like he has a lance wedged up his ass. I'm impressed you did it. I would have thought you were a by-the-rules kind of person. You don't look like you would cross an empty street without being in an approved crosswalk with the light on your side."

I stopped short. "Crossing the street can be riskier than you think. It can change everything."

Drew tossed me a fresh roll of paper towels. "True. Thing is, Prima Donna, anything can be a game changer. The question is, why do you assume the change has to be bad?"

chapter fourteen

I sat up in bed, using my finger to hold my place in *The Count of Monte Cristo*. I thought I had heard something. I paused for a beat, but when I didn't hear anything else, I went back to Dantes's revenge plans. A door opened down the hall, and a burst of music shot into the hallway. I heard a bunch of girls giggle as they walked by. I waited to see if anyone would drop by my room, but they walked right past. There are few things sadder than doing homework on a Saturday night, not because you're behind but because you have nothing else to do. I opened the book again, but the words marched back and forth across the page without making any sense. I chucked the book to the floor.

This was stupid. I had friends. They weren't just Tristan's friends, but we were never going to be able to hang out as a group if I couldn't make things right with Tristan. He didn't have to forgive me and throw his arms around me, but we couldn't keep up the silent treatment. Every time I stumbled across Tristan, in the hallway for classes or in the dining hall, he would freeze. His entire body would go stiff as if he had been exposed to a nerve agent, and then he would turn away. I tried to smile or even say a quiet hello, but he looked straight past me as if I were invisible. It was time for me to talk to Tristan directly. Kelsie kept telling me to give him more time, but how was time going to help if it was time spent hating me? I looked over at my clock. There was an hour before the dorms were locked for the night. The one good thing about a school-wide restriction was that I knew where to find everyone.

I slipped across the quad into Tristan's dorm. The guys' dorm always smelled like a mix of Axe, sweat, and popcorn. In the front lobby there was a group playing some weird version of full contact soccer, where the sofa seemed to be one goal. There was no clear way to identify who was on what team, and a smaller group was trying to watch a sci-fi movie in the corner, while sitting on the same couch. Our dorm had Ms. Estes, but Tristan's was monitored by Mr. Harrington. Mr. Harrington had served in the military before becoming a dorm monitor. There was a theory that he had some kind of post-traumatic stress syndrome and as a result was on heavy medication that kept him mellow. He couldn't be bothered with enforcing the million small rules in the student guide. I guess if you were used to seeing people blowing themselves up trying to set roadside bombs, you couldn't get too worked up about some fifteen-year-old kid forgetting to tuck in his uniform shirt. I wished I could live there. It was still a dorm, but it felt more like a home.

Tristan and Joel's room was on the second floor. There was an open space near the top of the stairs that was supposed to be a public study area, but it had somehow morphed into being an extension of their room. Tristan had bought a big flat-screen TV that he'd plugged in out there, and no one turned it on without checking with him first. It was a strictly invitation-only public space. As I climbed the stairs, I could hear voices. It sounded like a decent-size crowd was hanging out. I could make out Joel and one of our friends, Aidan, debating if they wanted to order a pizza. They had the hockey game on. I'd practiced on the way over what I would do and say. Making a big deal out of it would only focus everyone on it, so my plan was to act casual. I took a deep breath and got ready to face Tristan.

"This is bogus. I had a date tonight," Aidan said. "Just because Hailey got lucky, I can't."

I froze in place. I peered around the corner. Kelsie was folded into the corner of the sofa, flipping through a magazine. Joel and Aidan were sharing the remainder of the sofa, and Tristan was sprawled on the floor. There were a couple of other guys watching the game, and two sophomore girls wearing way too much makeup were giggling like a broken record.

"Dream on. It's going to take a lot more than a movie and

large popcorn to convince a girl to sleep with you," Joel said, chucking a throw pillow at his head.

"Hey, I was going to spring for the real butter for the popcorn. I was willing to spare no expense. I wasn't looking for a cheap lay, just an easy one."

"You guys are pigs," Kelsie said without looking up from her magazine.

"If you wanted an easy lay, you should have asked Hailey out," Tristan said. "If she'll do a townie, then I guess she'll do anyone."

My heart stopped beating. I couldn't believe he had just said that. Everyone looked embarrassed, but no one spoke up to defend me.

"I don't think it's fair that we all have to be on restriction just because of what she did," one of the sophomore girls said.

Kelsie whacked the girl on the back of the head with her magazine. "You should stay out of it. What do you care about restriction? You weren't going anyplace."

The sophomore blushed and looked down at her lap. I felt like pumping my fist in the air. *You tell that stupid lip-glossed silver-eye-shadowed freak, Kels!* That girl would have licked my shoes clean a week ago if I had asked her to. How dare she suddenly plop down in my group of friends and judge me.

"I still can't believe . . ." Tristan's voice trailed off. His jaw thrust forward, and I knew that meant he was fighting back tears. Suddenly I forgave him for what he'd said. He was hurt and was trying to lash out. I wanted to rush into the room and throw my arms around him and tell him that everything would be okay and that we could work through this.

Kelsie leaned over and gently laid her hand on the side of Tristan's face. He pressed his hand to hers and closed his eyes. It felt like a knife sliding between my ribs to stab my heart. I knew she was just trying to comfort him, but it felt too intimate, too personal. Then I hated myself for thinking anything bad about Kelsie, when she was the only one who had stood up for me since everything had happened.

I didn't want to be there anymore. There was no way I could sit down and act like things were going to be okay. I needed to get out of there. I took a step back and stepped into nothingness.

My arms spun around trying to regain my balance. I must have been closer to the top of the stairs than I'd thought. For a split second I thought I was going to be okay, but then my ankle rolled to the side and I fell.

I screamed as I bounced down the stairs. I rolled down like a tumbleweed, my feet slamming against the wall as I went. I saw flashes of red carpet runner as I spun, and I prayed that I wouldn't break anything.

When I finally hit the bottom of the stairs, my head was throbbing and I had torn a hole in my yoga pants. I could hear people rushing to see what had happened. I tried to sit up, and winced when I put my hand on the floor to prop myself up. It felt like I must have sprained my wrist. In addition to the two nails I had broken cleaning classrooms today, now my pinky nail was sheared off and bleeding. I heard someone gasp, and I looked up. At the top of the stairs Tristan, Joel, and Kelsie were looking down at me.

"Ms. Kendrick," a voice said. I spun around to see Mr. Harrington standing in the lobby. "How nice of you to drop by."

chapter fifteen

Mr. Harrington helped me to my feet. I was shaking from the shot of adrenaline. Everything hurt. It felt like I had been run over by a truck, but I was pretty sure no permanent damage had been done. I looked over each of my limbs. The crowd of soccer players from the lobby was jockeying for position. They seemed disappointed that I didn't appear to have broken anything, my brain wasn't leaking out my ears, and my shirt hadn't popped off. They would have been happy with either guts or boobs, but this wasn't as interesting as they had hoped.

It is a truth universally acknowledged that if you do something embarrassing like fall down the stairs in front of a group of people, you are required to act like you are fine, even if you aren't. Your arm could have a bone jutting out, and you would still try to laugh it off as if everything were hunky dory. *This compound fracture? It's nothing! I like to let my bones out of my body once in a while for fresh air. It's good for them.*

"I'm fine," I said, trying to give Mr. Harrington the impression that nothing important had happened and he didn't need to call Ms. Estes. She played by the book. She would require me to go to the hospital to make sure I didn't have a brain bleed or anything that could be blamed on her. If there were painful medical tests I would have to undergo, she'd love it even more. With my luck she would insist on sleeping in my room so she could wake me up every ten minutes in case I had a concussion. I took a step back from Mr. Harrington so that he could see I wasn't going to fall over. He pulled a Kleenex from his pocket and handed it to me. He motioned with his hand to my mouth. I touched my lip with the Kleenex and saw a bright bloom of red appear. One of my teeth must have cut my lip. Great.

I looked back to the top of the stairs. Tristan was starting to back away. Joel's mouth was hanging open in shock. He couldn't have looked more surprised if he had found the tooth fairy lying sprawled at the bottom of his staircase. He looked down at me and then over at Tristan, as if he weren't sure what might happen.

"Tristan, wait." I started up the stairs after him, wincing and adding an ankle strain to the list of injuries. I slipped between Kelsie and Joel at the top.

"What are you doing here?" Kelsie whispered as I went past.

I didn't bother to answer. I kept my focus on Tristan, who was still walking away. The two sophomore girls were standing in the hall, thrilled to have a front row view of this action. I was surprised they didn't pull out popcorn and Team Tristan T-shirts.

"Stop." I grabbed the back of Tristan's sweater. He whirled around, and I took a quick step back.

"What do you want?" he asked in a hard, flat voice.

"I need to talk to you," I said.

Tristan laughed, and the sound was harsh, nearly barking. "You know what I need? I need to know that I can trust the people in my life. I need to know my girlfriend of four years hasn't been screwing around on me. I need to know when someone is talking to me that they're telling me the truth."

"I'll tell you the truth."

"Who was the guy?"

"I can't tell you that."

Tristan shook his head, crossing his arms in front of his chest. "Well, that's great. This has been a really useful conversation."

"That's not what's important. It doesn't matter who it was. What matters is that it didn't mean anything. It never should have happened, and if I could take it back, I would. I can tell you that it never happened before that night and it wouldn't have happened if I hadn't been in some sort of crazy state." I whirled my hands around my head to indicate just how nuts I was.

"How do you live with knowing what you did? I would never have done something like that to you. Never."

I looked down at my feet. He was right. He wouldn't have. Given the circles his parents traveled in and the fact that he was both good-looking and rich, Tristan was always surrounded by girls who wanted him. They'd flirt with him when I was standing right there, and he always brushed them off. He wasn't someone who didn't have opportunity; he was someone who didn't have that kind of motivation.

"I am so sorry. I'm more sorry than I've ever been in my life. I don't mind being on restriction and having to clean the school. I can even live with the fact that everyone's mad at me, but I hate that I hurt you."

"Do you love this guy?"

"No! He means nothing. The kiss meant nothing."

Tristan looked me straight in the eyes, his stare pinning me to the ground. "That makes it worse, you know. I know you think that somehow it will make me feel better, but it doesn't. You threw away everything, and it wasn't even for someone who mattered."

Tristan turned and went into his room, shutting the door behind him. I turned and faced Joel and Kelsie, who were standing behind me.

"Wow. The guy didn't mean anything to you? That's good to know," Joel said.

I closed my eyes. I seemed to be incapable of making anything go right. "That's not what I meant. This is complicated."

"You don't owe me any explanations." He moved past me to join Tristan in their room.

"You have a wad of Kleenex stuck to your lip," Kelsie said, breaking the silence. "What's stuck up Joel's ass with the whole thing? Why does he think he deserves a bio on the guy?"

I started to cry. I wasn't making a sound, but my shoulders were shaking from the sobs. Kelsie stepped in and hugged me, letting me bury my face in her hair. My ankle and wrist were throbbing with pain, and the metallic taste of blood filled my mouth.

"What are you staring at?" Kelsie said over my shoulder to the sophomore girls. "Get a life. Go do something else somewhere else."

I could hear the girls scuttle off, whispering as they went. They would spread the news of my graceful fall down the stairs and my fight with Tristan to the rest of the student body faster than any emergency broadcast system. With the way things were going for me, they would act it out so that everyone could have the full experience.

"I want to go home," I whispered.

"Let's go." Kelsie grabbed her *Vogue* off the sofa and started to lead me back to our dorm.

When I'd said "home" I hadn't meant the dorm. I'd meant someplace that didn't even exist anymore. The house I used to have with my mom and dad had been sold. My dad's apartment had never been home to me. He'd never asked me what I wanted. Instead he'd had a decorator design a room for me. It was purple. I hate purple. I was a guest. A guest who didn't even rank having the guest room to myself, since my dad kept his treadmill in there too, as if my room were more of a storage closet.

"This is a nightmare," I mumbled as we walked outside. It was raining, and the wind whipped the drops so that they felt like razors hitting my skin.

"I told you it wasn't a good idea to talk to Tristan. He's really upset."

"He's got you to comfort him, though." The words flew out of my mouth. Turns out I was still thinking about her hand on the side of his face.

Kelsie stopped and turned to face me. "What do you want? Yes, Tristan's my friend, and if I can help him feel better, then I'm going to try to do that. I'm the kind of person who tries to think of my friends, which is why I'm standing in the rain with you now instead of upstairs watching the rest of the hockey game. For someone who got caught kissing some random guy, you sound awfully judgmental."

My insides crumpled like a wet tissue. Now I was making the only person who was on my side turn against me.

"I'm sorry. I don't know what's wrong with me. Everything I do or say is exactly the wrong thing. From now on I'm going to listen to your advice. Just tell me how to get through this."

"It won't do much for the situation with Tristan, but things would go a lot easier all around if you would spill the identity of the guy. One week on restriction isn't that bad. It gives everyone a chance to chill out, but if this stretches into next week, you're going to see people getting ticked. You aren't doing yourself any favors."

"I can't tell. I know it doesn't make any sense, but I can't."

"I hope that whoever he is, he's worth it," Kelsie said.

There was no way to explain that keeping Joel out of trouble and not involving him in the situation with Tristan was the only decent thing to come out of the situation so far. That night scared me. Not because of what had happened but because I hadn't thought I was the kind of person who could do something like that. Doing this one thing right gave me the hope that I was still, somewhere deep down, a decent person.

"Any other advice?" I asked.

"Keep your head down and pray someone else screws up even bigger. Who knows, maybe someone will sell a full frontal naked photo of Mandy and people will find something else to talk about."

"Like her third nipple?" I joked.

Kelsie laughed. "You know what she says . . ."

"It's a MOLE," we screamed together, and for a second I felt just a little bit better.

chapter sixteen

I was determined to make my Sunday cleaning shift, if not enjoyable, at least more tolerable. Based on how things were going, I wouldn't be separated from this cleaning job anytime in the near future, so I figured I might as well get along with Drew. While I thought it was unfair of him to lump all of us Evesham kids together as rich brats, it wasn't surprising. We were a fortunate crowd. It was the kind of school where the student parking lot was full of Mercedes and BMWs, and on parents' weekend there was more than one limo parked outside.

The night before I'd even had an idea of how to do something nice for Drew. Maybe if I were nice to someone who annoyed me, the universe would see that I was trying to do the right thing.

We were scheduled to clean the gym, and I was hoping that if I showed him a different side of myself he might let me be the one to run the floor polisher rather than having to pick gum, or god knows what else, out from under the bleachers.

"Good morning!" I said in a positive singsong voice so he would know there were no hard feelings from yesterday.

"Hey," he said, and then he froze in place when he saw me. "What the heck happened to you?"

I touched my lower lip. My flight down the stairs last night had resulted in quite a few injuries. I was so covered in bruises that I looked like a cheetah, including a giant bruise on my temple that looked like I'd colored a dot on my face with a black marker. My cut lower lip had swollen overnight. It looked like what would happen if Angelina Jolie got her mouth stuck in a vacuum.

"This?" I shrugged, trying to turn the whole thing into a joke. "Bar fight."

Drew crossed the floor and gently cupped my chin, turning my face right and left so he could assess the damage. The skin on his hands felt rough, but also warm. "Did someone hit you?" His eyes pinned me into place. "That's never okay. If you need help, you can tell me."

"Are you going to beat someone up for me?" I pulled my chin back, even though I had liked it resting in his hands. It wasn't that I wanted him to touch me, but it felt nice to be touched by anyone, given my current leper status. "How gallant."

"I'm being serious. My sister's ex-boyfriend used to hit her. There's a women's group in town that can help."

"They can't help me." I held up my hand to deflect his argument. Who knew that in the chest of a teen janitor beat the heart of a knight in shining armor? It wasn't fair to compare him with Tristan or Joel, given the circumstances, but they had seen me fall and hadn't offered this much sympathy. "No one hit me. I fell down the stairs."

"Why did you fall down the stairs?"

"Well, it wasn't exactly a well-thought-out plan. It was an accident."

"You don't strike me as the klutzy type. Did something upset you?"

"What is this, the inquisition?" I laughed, but it sounded fake even to my own ears. "No big story. I was rushing around and missed the top step."

"All right." Drew looked around the gym. "You look pretty banged up. I'm not sure you should be going up and down the bleachers bending over to do gum detail. Try to take it easy."

"I could sit over there and supervise," I offered. "Keep you entertained with jokes or something."

"Nice try, Prima Donna, but the best thing when you've taken a fall is to keep moving. Otherwise your muscles stiffen up."

"So you have a lot of experience falling down stairs?"

"I usually manage stairs, but I've taken my fair share of falls. I like to ski and snowboard, and I've wiped out mountain climbing a couple of times."

"Mountain climbing?"

Drew laughed. "You should see your face. It's like I told you I like to swim in sewers."

"I don't see the point in climbing a mountain, just to say you did? It seems awfully risky."

"It's more than bragging rights. It's about pushing yourself. Challenging yourself to do more than you thought you could. Be all you can be kind of thing."

This was a great entry into what I wanted to talk about. I'd even stopped by the computer lab in our dorm to print out a few information sheets I'd found the night before. "It's interesting you bring up the idea of reaching for more." I motioned for Drew to sit down on the bench. "I hope you don't think I'm sticking my nose in where it doesn't belong."

"I find that people who start a conversation like that are just about to stick their nose in the wrong place. It's the same with people who say, 'I don't want to offend you, but . . .'"

I handed Drew the sheets of paper from my jacket pocket. He flipped through them and then looked over at me. "What's this?"

"You're really young, right? You're not that much older than me."

"I'm nineteen."

"There you go, nineteen. That's not too old."

"Too old for what?"

"You seem like you work really well with your hands and you're smart. There are a bunch of local programs where you could train to be an electrician or in another skilled trade."

Drew chuckled. "Wow. Is this your good deed for the day?"

"I'm not being rude. I'm actually trying to help. You act like everyone who has money thinks they're better than everyone else, and what I'm saying is that I think you can do better than what you're doing. I meant it as a compliment." It hadn't occurred to me that it would offend him. Wow. It seemed I could even screw up being nice to people.

"Well, then, I'll take it in the spirit you intended." Drew heaved himself off the bench and plugged in the floor polisher. "Since we're passing around advice, do you mind if I give you some?"

I could tell I wasn't going to like anything he said, but I couldn't very well refuse. "Are you going to tell me to keep my nose out of things?"

"Nope. One of the problems in the world is that people aren't willing to stick their noses in more often. We all ought to look out for each other better. My advice is for you to loosen up a little. For someone who has the whole world on a silver platter, you're wound way too tight."

"I don't have the world on a platter."

"Fine. For someone who has the world on a salad plate, you're wound way too tight. You should step out of the box more often. See what the world has to offer."

"I stepped out of the box the night I broke the statue, and look where that got me."

"Exactly! You had a chance to get to know me as a result. Talk about lucky. Think what could happen if you tried again."

"No, thanks."

"You can't play it safe all the time."

"I don't play it safe all the time."

"Are you telling me that you weren't just calculating how much water on the floor it would take before the electrical cord for the floor polisher becomes an electrocution risk?"

I crossed my arms. He could make fun of me if he wanted. There were 550 accidental electrocution deaths in the United States last year. Most of those took place at work. Call me a fool, but water and electricity don't mix. That's why it isn't advised that you blow your hair dry in the shower. I stepped forward and grabbed the handles of the polisher. Drew raised an eyebrow, but then flipped the switch on the handle. The polisher nearly shot out of my hands. It felt like trying to hold a rodeo bull in place. I spun in a couple wide circles, trying to get it under control.

"Interesting technique," Drew yelled out over the sound of the machine.

"If *you* want to polish the floor, then you can do it your way." I turned my back on him and wrestled the machine to my will. Eventually it began to behave and glided up and down the gym parquet floor in a rough approximation of rows. I would stop every so often and squirt (a safe amount) of the combination liquid wax and cleaning gel onto the floor in front of me. I shot a few glances over at Drew, but he was busy walking up and down the bleachers, using a paint scraper to clean the bottom of each bench, then starting over at the beginning of the row to sweep the trash down to the next level.

It seemed strange not to talk, but the polisher was so loud and the gym so big that it made conversation practically impossible. It wasn't that I wanted to be insulted by Drew, the jolly janitor, but I had realized how nice it was to talk to someone about anything other than what had happened. Drew was right about one thing. As the hour went on, I felt less stiff and sore. My muscles limbered up, and when I turned the machine off, I looked back over the floor and felt a huge sense of satisfaction. I had accomplished something. It might not have been much, but it was something.

Drew was at the far end of the gym gathering all of the trash into three giant black bags. We'd finished sooner than I'd expected, and I wondered if that meant we got to knock off early or if we were expected to tackle some other chore. I had just started to make a dent in the extra credit history homework. I could use the extra time. I began to wind up the cord.

The doors to the outside burst open, and a group of guys spilled into the gym. It must have been snowing outside, because they were covered with a mix of slush and mud. One of them, a junior, gave a whoop when he saw the waxed floor. He took off at a run, dropping to his knees and sliding six or seven feet. He left a long dark smear of mud in the center of my floor.

"What the hell are you doing!" I screeched. I ran out into the middle of the floor waving my hands as if I wanted to scare off a group of wayward geese that were pooping all over my lawn. The guys stopped in place. I looked around. They were all wearing their outdoor shoes, some with cleats and hard soles. They'd tracked in mud, granite-colored slush, and a few random twigs. The floor was ruined.

"Easy, Kendrick. Who made you Miss Clean?" The junior tossed a filthy football into the net box at the end of the gym. "We had to bring the equipment back. What's the big deal?"

"The entire floor has to be done again," I said, pointing out the obvious.

"Isn't that what you have your townie for?" The junior motioned to Drew, who was still standing to the side. "You keep them around for more than just looking at, don't you? Or do you just use them for kissing?" The other guys laughed. Drew crossed over to us in several short strides, and the Evesham guys suddenly bunched together.

"Is there a problem?" Drew asked. He may have been only a few years older than the guys, but looking at them together, it was clear it was the difference between a bunch of boys and a man. Drew was broad through the shoulders, and his face had clean lines, with no baby fat sticking to his cheeks. I could tell the guys were scared that Drew would start something with them, and I liked that. They outnumbered him eight to one, but they were still afraid. I stood behind Drew with my arms crossed. I hoped he would make them wipe up the slush off the floor with their tongues.

"There's no problem, man." The junior rocked back and forth. I think he was trying to look tough, but it looked like he was trying out for a chorus role with a production of *West Side Story*.

"All right, then." Drew stood his ground. The Evesham kids headed out of the gym, darting looks over their shoulders to make sure Drew wasn't following them. I pressed my lips together. I wanted to scream.

"Make sure there aren't any sloppy seconds left behind," the junior yelled, and then they all laughed, slamming the door.

I whirled on Drew. "Why didn't you make them clean that up? How can you let them get away with that?"

"You don't do a lot of meditation, do you?" Drew pulled the mop from the cart and started to wipe up the mess on the floor.

I stared at him, wondering if he'd lost his mind. "What are you talking about?"

Drew motioned to the mess on the floor. "This is just dirt. Save your wrath for something bigger than mud."

"He was rude."

"No, he was an asshole. Me telling him that isn't going to change anything. He isn't suddenly going to fall on his knees and see the light. You know what's going to happen? He's going to run to the dean and say that he was returning the ball when I forced him to clean the gym floor. His friends will back him up, and I'll be the one in trouble."

"But that isn't fair," I said, knowing I sounded like a five-year-old. "I would have backed you up."

"Nothing personal, but I'm guessing Dean Winston doesn't have your picture on the wall for Student of the Month."

My mouth snapped shut. He was right. Winston wouldn't believe me. Even if he thought I was telling the truth, he'd never admit it.

"You can go ahead and get out of here. I've got this covered," Drew said, glancing at his watch. "You put in your time."

I was tempted to take him up on his offer. I still had homework to finish. The smart thing to do would be to thank him and get the homework done. The image of my empty dorm room flashed in my mind. I didn't feel like doing the smart thing.

"It'll go faster with both of us," I said. "Besides, I've started to get the hang of this polisher."

"I noticed. I was just thinking how you were the Princess of the Polisher," Drew said, smiling.

"Master of the Mop," I said.

"Sultan of Shellac," he fired back.

I laughed, and turned my back to fire up the machine. I heard Drew call my name, and I turned around to be smacked with a blob of slush smack in the center of my chest. I stared down at the wet splotch. I looked up, and Drew's face was twitching as he tried to avoid laughing. I bent down and picked up a handful of slush.

Drew held up his hands as if he were surrendering. "I don't know what came over me."

I flung the slush ball at him and missed. "I meant to miss you. I'm showing you what a better person I am."

"Of course."

I waited until he bent over to pick up the mop handle, and

then I hurled another slush ball at him, this time hitting him in the center of his butt. He turned around, wiping the rest of the slush off of his jeans. He raised an eyebrow in a silent question.

"I decided I'm not really a better person," I said.

It didn't take long to redo the floor. Turned out Drew was right, mud wipes right up. I helped put the cart back into the closet. Drew made sure everything was put back in just the right place, and he ticked off the tasks on the to-do list. He made sure the mop was clean before he hung it up to dry. He clearly took pride in his job. Once everything was properly stowed away, he grabbed his jacket off the hook.

"Here, don't forget these." I handed him the printouts of the training programs I'd found.

"Oh, right. Thanks." He pulled a book out of his coat pocket and folded the papers inside.

"What are you reading?" I asked.

Drew flipped the book over so I could see the cover. *Dante's Inferno*. I hadn't expected that. I'd seen him as more of a Stephen King fan.

"Fan of the classics, huh?" I asked, trying to hide my surprise.

"It's on the reading list. I'm trying to get a jump start."

"Reading list?"

"I'm going to Yale next year. I'm working this job to earn some extra money."

"Yale?"

"I got in last year but delayed my start. I wanted to travel a little, earn some extra cash."

I could feel my face burning. "Oh." I couldn't believe I'd given him a bunch of information on vocational programs and had acted like he would be lucky to get in. "I didn't mean to imply that the skilled trades were your only option."

"Don't worry about it. Your heart was in the right place. Besides, I thought it was kind of cool that you noticed I have good dexterity." He waved his fingers in front of my face. "I like the idea of you thinking about what my hands can do." He winked before turning to leave.

I flushed even redder. "I wasn't thinking about your hands," I called after him.

"Sure you weren't."

"I wasn't. I was trying to be nice."

Drew turned around to face me, leaning against the doorjamb. "Admit it. You're thinking about it now." He saluted and left.

I kicked the cart. Darn it. Now I *was* thinking about it.

chapter seventeen

The dining hall at Evesham is decorated to look like one of the halls at Oxford. The long wall has arched cathedral windows, and the ceiling is painted with vines and leaves. There are long wooden tables, and although seats aren't assigned, it's habit that the seniors sit in the back, farthest from the front faculty table. Well, at least most of them do. I'd taken to sitting by myself in the leper section near the trash cans. Out of site, out of mind. Unlike in most cafeterias, we don't wait in a line for food. Each table has menus on a clipboard, and you check off what you want and then one of the servers bring your tray.

I ticked off scrambled eggs and toast and pulled out my math homework to go over my answers one more time. My grades had gone up lately because I'd had way more time to do homework, without needing to spend time talking to anyone. Isolation has its advantages. Kelsie sat down and waved away the server. She never eats breakfast. Or to be more precise, she never eats her own breakfast. Kelsie picked the strawberry off my toast plate and popped it into her mouth.

"So how come I have to hear from someone else that you're assigned to clean with some sort of hunky man model?"

"What?"

"If I had known they hired cute townies to clean, I would have taken an interest in dust long before now." Kelsie looked around to make sure no one was paying attention to us. "Is he the one from that night?"

I rolled my eyes. "No, he is not the one."

"You're going to want to bail on breakfast, by the way."

"Why?"

"Trust me. Make yourself scarce." Kelsie took a piece of my toast and wrinkled up her nose. "I hate this whole grain stuff. The nuts get in my teeth."

"Then, get your own toast." I grabbed the piece back. "Why should I leave?"

"I can take time to explain things, or later we can talk about how next time you should listen to me," Kelsie said, pointing a pink nail in my face.

I opened my mouth to argue the point, but there was a rustle at the front of the room and Joel hopped up onto one of the tables.

"Too late," Kelsie groaned.

Joel clapped his hands to get everyone's attention. "As the student council president I would like to call a town meeting."

I raised an eyebrow at Kelsie, who gave me a look that said I should have made a run for it when I had the chance. Town meetings are an Evesham tradition. If someone has a gripe—ranging from someone playing their music too loud (or playing music someone else can't stand) to the need for more organic veggies for the salad bar—then we are supposed to talk it out over one of our meals. It's supposed to remind us of how we would have talked over issues with our families over a dinner table. The truth is most of Evesham's students didn't have family dinners, unless you count sitting down with your nanny over fish sticks while your parents go to some fancy fund-raiser.

Joel nodded to one of the tables, and I saw Mandy Gallaway get up. She pulled her uniform skirt down and paused long enough to make sure everyone was watching her walk to the front of the room.

"Uh-oh," I said softly under my breath.

Kelsie grabbed the last piece of my toast. "File this experience under, 'Next time I will pay attention to my best friend when she gives me advice.'"

"I wanted to bring up the issue of having to be on restriction." Mandy looked around the room. "I think it's unfair that we're all on lockdown when only one person did something wrong."

There were a few grumbles from other people in the cafeteria. I stared down at my eggs so I didn't have to meet anyone's eyes. Did they think this was my idea? If Mandy wanted to go into town and flash a nipple or her thong at a random photographer, it was fine by me. If they wanted to gripe, they should take it up with Winston.

"Hailey, can you come up here and join us while we talk this out?" Joel asked.

I looked up from my eggs, my stomach flipping over. I pointed a finger at my chest, on the off chance that Joel had another Hailey in mind. He nodded, and Mandy crossed her arms over her chest with a smirk. With everyone's eyes on me, I figured bolting from the room was out. Taking a deep breath, I stood up and walked slowly to the front.

"Dean Winston imposed restriction on all of us as a way to demonstrate how we're connected. What impacts one of us impacts all of us," Joel said in his best presidential voice.

"I don't think Hailey cares how what she did impacts all of us," Mandy said. "She isn't showing Evesham school spirit. I haven't been able to go into town. I know Hailey thinks sticking up for this guy is important, but what I want to do is important too."

I fought the urge to push Mandy into a pile of pancakes. I could picture the syrup running down her face, slicking her hair down to her head.

"Of course everyone has their own unique wants and feelings, and all of those are important. Does anyone else want to share how this situation is affecting them?" Joel offered.

I turned to look at Joel. Was he kidding? I pulled on his shirt so we were closer.

"Why are you doing this?" I hissed into his ear.

"This is a reasonable way to handle the situation. People are unhappy. They want to share how they're feeling."

Joel could act as if he were doing the right thing, but I sensed that the reason he was willing to have me stand up in front of everyone and be humiliated had to due with him being upset by what I'd said to Tristan on Saturday night.

"You can't do this," I whispered to him.

"Mandy went to Winston. This is his idea," Joel whispered back. He shrugged slightly. My lips pressed together. Joel was going to stand there and play the party line. What Winston wanted, he would do.

A freshman in the front row raised her hand. "I think it's disgusting that you cheated on your boyfriend," she said. She shot a look at Mandy, who nodded her approval. I had the feeling the room was stacked with people that Mandy had spoon-fed comments to. We'd be there all morning hearing what a lousy person I was.

"I have to go to the bathroom," I said.

"You can't leave," Mandy said. "You have to stand here while everyone gets their say."

"Fine, but do you mind if I go to the bathroom first? There isn't a rule against that, is there?"

"It's important that you understand how what you've done affects everyone," Joel said.

I clenched my teeth. "I'll be right back."

I stepped into the hallway and crossed to the ladies' room. I shut the door behind me and leaned against it. I didn't plan to stand in front of the whole school while everyone listed out how I was making their lives miserable because they couldn't get to the mall.

I cracked the door open and peeped out. Mandy was standing in the doorway to the cafeteria, watching the hall. There was no way I was going to be able to sneak past her and out of the building. I wondered how long I could stay in the bathroom before they sent someone in after me. I looked at my watch. There was another thirty minutes left until the first bell. Way too long. I felt my stomach turn over again. I felt like I might throw up my eggs. Maybe if I vomited, people would consider it sufficient apology, but I doubted it. They were going to make me stand there and just take it.

A car horn outside honked, and it made me look up. Above the stalls there was a long thin frosted window. I stepped up onto one of the toilets and slid the window open. The window faced the alley behind the cafeteria building. There was a Dumpster directly below. It was insane. Most likely I wouldn't even fit, the window was so narrow. Besides, I would only be putting off the inevitable. Sooner or later I would have to face the music. My heart was pounding. All I wanted to do was escape. I heard Mandy's high shrill laugh from the hall. That decided it.

I pulled myself up onto the ledge and swung one foot out the window, and then the other. I started to lower myself down. My uniform skirt was caught in the window, and I could feel it hitching up. Great. Now my bare butt was on the outside of the window while the rest of me was still inside the bathroom. My feet swung around, feeling for the edges of the Dumpster, but all I felt was empty space. I tried to lower myself farther, but the combination of my skirt and blazer bunched up was keeping me from sliding down any more. This wasn't going to work.

I tried to pull myself back up through the window. My arms were shaking from the effort, but I wasn't moving. Great. I was stuck in the window. What's worse than being called to the front of your entire school and humiliated? Being caught trying to sneak away with your skirt up over your waist and your panty-clad butt hanging out over the cafeteria Dumpster.

"Well, here's something you don't see every day," a voice said in the alley.

My head shot straight up. I knew that voice. "Drew?"

"Hailey?" He sounded shocked. "Looks like you need some help."

"I don't *need* help, but some help would be appreciated."

"Looks to me like you need help. Do you know you're wearing Thursday panties and today's Monday?"

I blushed. "My grandma buys these for me. Stop looking at my butt," I demanded.

"It's sort of a focal point from out here."

"Help me out of here." I wiggled my legs. "Hurry up. I'm in sort of a situation."

I could hear him climbing up onto the Dumpster behind me. "You know, there's a waitlist to get into this place. You don't see many trying to get out. At least this way." His hand was on my leg. "I'm going to heft you up a bit and then pull you out."

"Watch your hands," I warned him.

"I am watching them."

I could hear voices from the hallway. It was just a matter of time before Mandy busted her way in, and then there would be no amount of explaining that would make things right.

Drew held me around the waist, and I felt myself start to slide backward. I held on to the window ledge.

"Rest your feet on the rim of the Dumpster."

I slid until my feet were resting next to Drew's feet and my face was still looking through the window. I used one hand to jam my skirt back down into place.

"Okay. Hang on to the window while I get down, and then I'll help you."

Through the window I could see the bathroom door start to open. I threw myself into Drew, and we dropped to the ground in a heap. I landed on top of him, and he gave a loud "Ooph."

I held my finger over my mouth, indicating he needed to be quiet.

"She's not in here." Mandy's voice drifted down from the window.

Drew raised an eyebrow. He stood and pulled me up. His shirt was smeared with ketchup. He jerked his head to the right, indicating that I should follow him, and I did. His truck was parked at the end of the alley.

When we reached it, he turned back to me. "You need a ride somewhere?" He held up a hand. "I mean, of course, that you don't *need* a ride, but would one be helpful?"

I wiped my hand across my face. I was shaking. I didn't know what to do. I couldn't go back inside.

"I can't leave campus."

"No, you're not *supposed* to leave. But I'm betting you're capable. Rules are meant to be broken."

"I've never skipped school in my life," I protested.

Drew's eyes went wide like a kid who had just spotted Santa Claus. "Really? Your first time? Oh, that's exciting." He rubbed his hands together. "This will be good. Time's wasting. Let's go." He motioned to his truck.

I held back. "I'll get in trouble."

"News flash, Prima Donna. You're already in trouble. There's no death penalty for skipping school. If you're already in trouble, why not go really big? Are you telling me you had the guts to sneak out of a place by jumping into a Dumpster, but then you were just going to go right back inside? Besides, with what they charge for tuition for this place, they aren't going to kick you out for skipping one day. It wouldn't be cost efficient."

My mind raced. I hadn't thought through this plan very well. Everything had been based on the idea of getting away. I heard a burst of laughter, and at the other end of the alley I could see a few Evesham students making their way over to a classroom building. At the very least I needed more time to think of what to do. "I'll go with you," I said.

"Allow me," he said, bowing low and opening the door.

chapter eighteen

I wasn't sure what I'd expected. I'd never snuck off campus before. I guess I thought Drew might race the truck toward the gates while the security team released savage German shepherds and shot up the back window in a blaze of gunfire. Drew had me sit on the passenger-side floor, and he tossed his coat over the top of my head. He eased up to the security gate at the front of campus and casually chatted with the guard—someone named Earl—for a few minutes about football, before we pulled away. There were no alarms, no searchlights, no police barricades. The whole thing was almost anticlimactic.

"You can sit up now," Drew said.

I pulled myself up and clicked the seat belt. The vinyl seats of the truck were patched here and there with duct tape. The truck was old. It had a tape deck. My legs were bare and covered with goose bumps. I pulled my socks up to cover as much real estate as possible.

Drew slammed his hand against the dashboard. "Sorry. The heater is kind of dodgy." He slammed his hand again, and then a rush of hot air whooshed out of the vent. "Are you freezing? There's a sweatshirt in the back somewhere."

Without looking he hooked his arm over the back of the seat and started fishing around in the pile of junk that was in the back of the cab. There seemed to be an array of books, sporting gear, and clothing. Like a magician with a rabbit, he yanked a sweatshirt out of the middle of the pile. There was a Boston Bruins logo across the front. He handed it to me. I held it pinched between two fingers.

"It's clean," Drew said, looking over at me with a smile. "At least, there's no Ebola on it or anything."

"Of course. I wasn't thinking that." I gave it a quick sniff test. It didn't smell funny. In fact it smelled nice, like pine trees. I pulled it on over my sweater. I pulled the length of it over my knees. "Where are we going?"

"Your first skip day." Drew shook his head as if he were over-come by the enormity of it all. "We have to do something good. You can't waste something like that. We'll get some breakfast at Denny's and come up with a plan."

"Who's Denny?"

Drew laughed. "You're joking, right? Denny's? As in Denny's restaurant?"

"Oh, right. Of course."

Drew stopped the truck in the middle of the road. "You've never been to a Denny's, have you?"

"I have been to a Denny's. My family stopped at one once when we were driving to New York."

"You didn't eat there, did you? You went there for the bathroom."

"Don't make a federal case out of it." I pulled my hands up into the sleeves of the sweatshirt.

"Where does your family go for breakfast?"

"Will you just drive? God. We go out. We just don't go to Denny's. There are other places to eat, you know."

Drew put the truck back into drive, and we headed toward town. "Where do you go? Four Seasons?"

"You have some sort of obsession for Denny's, don't you? Were you raised by wolves in a Denny's parking lot?" I shifted in the seat. I wasn't going to tell him, but we did used to go to the Four Seasons for Sunday brunch. My mom used to love their smoked salmon eggs Benedict.

"Your first Grand Slam *and* your first skip day. I feel like we should get a picture taken or something. You could frame it later for your fireplace mantel. A person never forgets their first Slam."

I had no idea what he was talking about. I'd thought a grand slam had something to do with baseball. Was he planning to take me to a game? Did anyone even play baseball this time of year?

We pulled into the Denny's parking lot, and I followed Drew inside. The restaurant seemed to be decorated in orange and yellow surfaces that all could be cleaned with a power washer—

vinyl seats, tile floors, laminate countertops. Given the amount of grease that seemed to be in the air, it probably took a pressure washer to get this place clean. Drew walked right past the WAIT HERE TO BE SEATED sign and grabbed a couple of menus out of the server's lectern, waving at the cook as he walked by. The cook waved back with a spatula. Why was I not surprised he was a regular?

"Hey, darling! I'll bring you some coffee," a waitress called out. Drew slid into a booth and motioned for me to take the other seat. He began to pore over the menu as if it contained the secret of the universe. I sat down and touched the tabletop carefully, looking for any random sticky spots. There were a few places where cigarette butts had burned the laminate, back in the days when smoking in restaurants was legal. The waitress came by, dropping two coffee cups out from under her arm and artfully pouring coffee into them before they had even stopped rattling on the tabletop. Her other hand held a rag that looked like it had last been clean around the turn of the century, and she used it to wipe the table down, no doubt smearing bacteria all over. Drew could mock the Four Seasons if he liked, but there was something to be said for fresh linen tablecloths.

The waitress looked me over, noting my uniform skirt. She raised an eyebrow at Drew. I was impressed she could lift it, given the amount of foundation that was on her face.

"We're going to need a range of things here. I'm not sure we can choose. We'll have the All-American Slam, a Lumberjack

Slam, a side of biscuits and sausage gravy, the smothered hash browns . . . oh, and some pancakes. Are you still doing that stuffed French toast, too? The one with the strawberries?" Drew ran his finger down the menu to make sure there wasn't anything he had forgotten.

"You got it, Drew. You need cream for the coffee, sweetheart?"

I looked down at the coffee. "Do you make lattes?"

"Does this look like Starbucks?" She asked with a snap of her gum.

"Right. I'll have the cream." I considered asking her if they could warm the cream up in the back, but I decided it wouldn't go over well, and with my luck she would spit in my eggs. Drew gave a nod to the busboy as he passed with his tub of dirty dishes.

"Do you know every Denny's employee, or just the ones that work at this location?" I asked him.

"I used to work here in the kitchen, and I still help out once in a while if they're short staffed."

"Can't resist the allure of the food, huh?"

"Can't resist the extra cash. Somehow I managed to misplace my trust fund, so I've got to stockpile as much as I can for Yale."

I wasn't sure exactly how much Yale cost, but I knew it wasn't cheap. I was worried enough about getting in. I couldn't imagine worrying about how to pay for it too.

"Maybe you can get a scholarship," I suggested. "There's all kinds of information about that stuff online."

Drew cocked his head and looked at me. "Careful, or I'm going to start thinking you care. Don't you worry about me. I've applied for loans and grants, and that fancy school of yours pays pretty good to clean desks. I'll come up with the money." He rubbed his hands together. "Now we have to decide what to do with the day."

"Why do we have to do anything?"

"Because this is found time. It's a gift. Where should you be right now?"

I looked over at the yellowing plastic clock that hung on the wall. "Math."

"Now, isn't this better than math?" Drew motioned around the room.

"I'm withholding judgment at this point."

"Now you're just being a snot. If you're going to skip, then you have to do something worthwhile. Otherwise the trouble won't be worth it." Drew snapped his fingers. "We could go skiing."

I looked at him. Was he nuts? "I don't know how to ski."

"You look like you have the capacity to learn. I can spot talent. You look like a natural. Didn't your mom and dad ever take you to Aspen? Maybe doing a bit of snow time with the royal family in the Alps?"

"No." I sipped the coffee. It wasn't bad. "I can't say the queen and I have done a lot of snowboarding."

The waitress was back. She filled the table with plates. "The French toast is still coming."

I poked the gray object on the plate in front of me with my fork. It looked like it might fight back.

"Biscuits with sausage gravy. Looks disgusting, tastes great." Drew jabbed his fork in and held a clump of it out in front of my face. He waved it back and forth in front of my lips. "Open up, or I'm going to start making choo-choo noises."

I opened my mouth, and he popped the food in. I was prepared for it to taste like dryer lint covered in Elmer's glue, but it was actually sort of tasty.

"Ah, not bad, huh?" Drew stuck the fork back in and ate some. "Try the hash browns. Give that Four Seasons palate a good grease wash."

I wasn't crazy about the hash browns—they were too greasy for me—but the French toast when it arrived was beyond divine. Drew clearly took his eating seriously, because he didn't attempt conversation while we ate. He would look up and smile every so often, but otherwise he was focused on his food.

I wondered what was going to happen when I went back to school. The top of Winston's head was going to lift off when he found out what I'd done. Drew was right that there was no death penalty, but Dean Winston was going to come up with something. Something that might make me wish for death. Winston struck me as the kind of guy terrorists call when they're looking for new ideas. I stared out the window. He might expel me, despite what Drew said about the school wanting the tuition money. My grandma would freak out if I got kicked out of school. No one in our family had ever been expelled. And I was pretty sure an expulsion would blow my chances with Yale. It wasn't the kind of school that catered to the juvenile delinquent crowd. I wouldn't be surprised if Winston was already contacting the admissions office, telling them that I was the type to spray paint my name on Yale's Harkness Tower, or beat up the mascot bulldog.

Drew leaned back from the table. "All right. Now tell me everything."

"Why?"

"Because I'm interested, and you want to talk about it."

"No, I don't."

"Liar. You think I won't know how to help you, but that's where you're wrong." He raised his hand to cut me off before I could say anything. "Admit it. You were wrong about me before. I happen to be a keen problem solver. Sometime I'll tell you about the time I had my wallet lifted in the Cairo market, and I followed the guy and won it back in a game of dice, along with an extra hundred bucks."

"You traveled through Egypt?" I had pictured Drew as the kind of guy who didn't travel out of the state, let alone the country. Maybe down South to some kind of barbecue championship event, but exotic travel had never occurred to me. "Did you see the pyramids?"

"That's what you pay attention to? I tell you I managed to infiltrate a den of thieves and win, and you focus on the pyramids?

If you don't mind me being so blunt, that's part of your problem. You focus on the wrong things." He leaned back into the corner of the booth so that his crossed feet hung out into the aisle. "Telling someone who has no connection to a situation gives you a fresh view. You could use a fresh pair of eyes. Now, start at the beginning. You decided to attack the school mascot because . . ."

I looked into his eyes. I *could* use a new perspective. It wasn't like I had any great ideas on my own.

"I'm going to need more coffee," I said. "It's a long story."

Drew raised his finger, and the waitress headed in our direction. I took a deep breath and tried to figure out where to start.

chapter nineteen

When I stopped speaking, Drew leaned back and said nothing. I sipped my coffee to have something to do. I was practically humming with all the caffeine in my system. If anyone looked directly at me, I bet I would be a blur.

"So, as you can see, it's pretty screwed up," I said, wanting him to say something.

"You did a good thing."

"Are you kidding? I haven't done anything right since this whole thing started. It was like I took one wrong turn and now I can't get my life back on track."

"I don't know. Seems like you've done some good things. You took the heat so your friend Joel doesn't lose his scholarship. That shows character. Sad truth is that most people only do the right thing if it doesn't cost them anything."

I shrugged off his praise. "How much character does it show that I kissed my boyfriend's best friend?" I left off the part that really scared me. Not only had I kissed him, but I'd liked it.

"Well, I'll divide my answer to that question into two parts. How much character is Tristan showing? He won't even give you a chance to explain."

"You don't understand. Tristan has issues around trust."

"We all have issues. If you want to worry about issues, worry less about his and focus on why you kissed this Joel guy in the first place."

"I told you. It was a heat-of-the-moment thing."

"Uh-huh." Drew smirked and looked out the window.

"It was," I said.

"If that's what you want to think, that's fine with me."

I crossed my arms and tapped my foot on the floor. "So you think it's something else. You have some explanation for the whole thing. Go on, share your wisdom."

Drew turned around so that his feet were on the floor and he was staring me straight in the eyes. "You kissed Joel as a way to break up with Tristan."

I laughed and looked away. "Are you kidding me? Why would I want to break up with him? Tristan's the perfect boyfriend. We've been together for years."

"You're not in love with him."

"And you know how I feel better than I do? That's amazing." I couldn't believe him. His brain must have been clogged with the amount of grease he'd consumed. He had bacon brain. "You must be some kind of psychic, since you know things about me that even I don't know."

"Tell me why you love him," Drew said.

"You want a list, fine. He's nice. I can depend on him. He's very loyal." I started ticking off items on my fingers.

"You make him sound like a cocker spaniel. That's not love. That's affection. He's a habit. Deep down you want to break the habit, so you did the one thing you knew he wouldn't be able to stand. You kissed someone else, and now you're free. You're scared to be off track, but I think you're sick of always living in the lines. Maybe you wanted to explore what you might find if you wandered away from the tracks just a bit. Best part of being lost, you know, is discovering things you didn't know you were looking for."

Just my luck. In addition to his keen cleaning abilities and skill at rolling dice with Egyptian thieves, he was also a philosopher. "That's absurd. I'm not sick of living 'in the lines' of my life. My life was going just fine before all of this."

"Really? What about the situation with your dad?"

"A person can be disappointed in something without it meaning they want their entire life to be different."

"Why didn't you tell your dad that it wasn't okay for him to ruin your summer by bailing on you?"

"It's not that simple. He has to go. It's his job."

"Ah, slave labor program." He laughed at my expression. "Don't get yourself all riled up. All I'm saying is that people act like they're stuck, when the truth is that they have a choice. Your dad doesn't have to do that job, and you don't have to be the good girl all the time. You don't have to keep dating Tristan just because you did for years. If you want to be happy, then you have to make it happen."

"Well, this has been very helpful," I said, rolling my eyes. "Your words of wisdom will make all the trouble I'm going to get in for skipping worthwhile."

Drew stood up, smiling. He was either ignoring my sarcasm or had missed it completely. "You're welcome, but you're going to get even more bang for your buck. I thought of something we can do."

"I should go back."

"You're already in trouble. Might as well make it count. Besides, you're going to love this." Drew left some money on the table for the waitress and started walking out. He stopped at the counter and said something to the cook. The cook passed him two giant metal trays. They looked like cookie sheets on steroids.

"What are those for?"

"Wait and see."

"Where are we going?" I trailed after him. I felt nervous; God only knew what he had planned.

Drew stopped to hold the door open. "Prima Donna, you cannot even imagine how much fun you're going to have. But first I'm going to introduce you to another place I'm willing to bet you've never been to." He paused for dramatic effect. "We're going to Walmart. You're going to love it. It's like a redneck version of Harrods."

chapter twenty

Five hours later I sat outside Dean Winston's office trying to ignore the glances his secretary kept shooting in my direction. I couldn't tell if it was because she knew how much trouble I was in, or because of my outfit.

Drew had made all my fashion choices at Walmart. He'd decreed that my school uniform was not appropriate for the activity he had planned. I ended up wearing black and yellow striped tights that were a leftover from a Halloween costume that didn't sell. Over those I wore a pair of black snow pants decorated with fake spray painted tags. Across my bum in purple letters with silver trim was the word "RADICAL." There was a "Kilroy Was Here" on one knee, and running down the side was a bright yellow cursive "Anarchy." I was still wearing my uniform blouse with Drew's Bruins sweatshirt over the top. My new red gloves were normal, but after Drew declared my head to be freakishly small, I ended up with a hat from the kid's department, complete with earflaps and a pom-pom on top. It was decorated with various glittery fairy decals. I reached a hand up to touch it. It was the tackiest thing I had ever seen, and I loved it.

My face was windburned. We'd gone sledding. I hadn't been sledding since I was a little kid, and I couldn't remember when I'd had so much fun. I wasn't as fearless as Drew. He liked to get a running start and then fling himself facedown onto the giant metal tray, barreling down the hill. I preferred to sit at the top on the tray and then inch myself forward until gravity kicked in and carried me to the bottom, but I loved the rush of the wind. The air was so cold that it seemed hot and burning when I sucked it in. It felt like it was scouring my lungs clean. As soon as I came to a stop at the bottom, I would pop up and do my best to run up the hill so I could go again. For the first time since this whole mess had started, my mind had stopped spinning around with everything that had happened. I didn't think about my dad, Tristan, Joel, or anyone else at Evesham. I didn't even worry about sledding injury rates. We went sledding until my legs were rubbery from walking up the hill in the deep snow, and the sweatshirt was damp from melted snow and sweat.

As Drew drove me back to the school, he gave me advice on how to handle Winston. "Tell him you felt mentally unstable. That you were so emotionally damaged that you were afraid you might 'do something' so you ran away to clear your head. Trust me. The last thing this guy wants on his hands is a suicidal student. Boarding schools live in fear of that stuff. It's bad for public relations."

"You should let me out here," I said, motioning for Drew to pull over a block or so before the school gates.

"What? Is this one of those things where you're embarrassed to be seen with me?" Drew made a face as if he were deeply wounded.

I smacked him on his shoulder. "I get sarcasm for trying to keep you out of trouble? I save your job, your financial ticket to Yale, and you mock me? This will be the last time I'll take all the heat."

Drew laughed. "I would be happy to be the Clyde in your Bonnie and Clyde lawless adventure."

Bonnie and Clyde were lovers. I wondered if that was why Drew had used that example. As soon as the thought flashed through my mind, I felt myself flush. Apparently, since the Joel incident I was incapable of having interactions with a guy without wondering if he liked me.

"I should get going," I said, cracking the door open. "Thanks for making my first skip day so memorable."

"It's all memorable with me," Drew said with a wink before driving off.

I went directly to Dean Winston's office and told him that my delicate emotional state had snapped in the dining hall. I'd had to walk away before I did something . . . desperate. I made sure my voice had a slight quaver in it. Drew had warned me not to argue but to admit I was in the wrong. Winston glowered at me across his desk. I could see him thinking through his options.

I could tell he wanted to yell, but he was uncertain. He made me wait outside his office while he decided what to do. There was a puddle of slush on the floor by my feet. I'd been at Evesham for four years, and I'd spent more time in Winston's office in the past couple weeks than I had in the entire rest of the time I'd attended the school.

Dean Winston opened the door and motioned me inside. I stood, saying a quick mental prayer that Drew was right and I wasn't about to hear that I was expelled. Drew had kept pointing out that expelled kids don't pay tuition and Winston would be crazy to kick me out over one day of skipping. People like Dean Winston would think through the economics of the situation before doing anything rash.

"The deterioration of your behavior is very troubling to me, Ms. Kendrick."

I looked down at my shoes and watched a rivulet of slush start to wind its way to the thick rug in the middle of the room. He took a step closer and put his arm around my shoulder. I felt myself tense up, and I had to fight the urge to pull away.

"I hope you know you can talk with me if you're going through a difficult time. I know these years as girls grow into young women are challenging."

I stayed perfectly still. Winston sounded like one of those films they showed us in junior high about menstruation and how we shouldn't be scared if hair started to grow on our bodies in new places. I made a noncommittal sound.

"I want you to be honest with me. Did you sneak into town to see the boy? The one you were with the night of the incident with the statue?"

"What? No." I met his stare. "I promise you I was not with the guy from that night."

Winston sat down and guided me into the chair next to him. "It isn't uncommon for young girls to become"—he searched for the right word—"enamored of the 'bad boy.' Maybe it feels daring or exciting, but you need to be careful."

Oh, god. Dean Winston was going to start talking about safe sex. "I'm not dating anyone from town," I said, hoping to cut him off. "I'm not dating anyone now."

"You're a very fortunate young lady, and part of that fortune is that you're being protected from some of the unseemly sides of life. There are people who would want to take advantage of you, to use any relationship for their own gains. Nothing against anyone from town, but they would certainly be aware that you come from a prestigious family."

"So you think anyone from town would only be seeing me for my money?"

Winston patted me on the knee. "Of course not." He waited a beat before continuing. "But this can't be something you're sure about. People aren't always open about their motivations. In general I think you'll find it's best when people stick with their own kind. Not that I'm advocating that anyone is better than anyone else, but you come from different worlds."

"Different worlds," I repeated. "Got it."

"Normally anyone who skips class is placed on restriction. Now, you're already on restriction, so that isn't really an option for us."

"I understand." I really hoped Winston wasn't going to do the thing where he asked me what I felt a reasonable punishment would be.

"If you'll tell me who else was involved in the earlier incident, then I'm prepared to consider things wrapped up and behind us."

"I can't."

Mr. Winston sighed as if I had caused him a deep grievous harm. "There's a difference between 'can't' and 'won't,' Ms. Kendrick. Very well. We're going to continue with your existing punishment. The restriction stands for you and your classmates. You're going to write a letter of apology to each of your instructors for missing today's classes and prepare for me a written report on the history of the school. Also, I'm going to require that you meet with the school counselor."

I nodded. I figured I was going to have to see Ms. Sullivan once I brought up the whole emotional fragility thing. I had zero interest in spending time spilling my guts to the school counselor, but I didn't see any way out of it.

"All right. I've already called Ms. Sullivan, and she's cleared her schedule to see you."

He stood, and I let out a deep breath. I wasn't going to be expelled. There was a tap at the door, and Kelsie stood there.

"I brought over Hailey's things that she left in the dining hall." Kelsie held out my books.

"Very well. Don't dawdle, Ms. Kendrick. Ms. Sullivan will be waiting for you in her office."

I nodded and followed Kelsie out into the hall. Our footsteps echoed on the wooden floors. We walked past the framed photos of various Evesham graduation classes. I felt the eyes of all the past students watching us go by. Ms. Sullivan's office was down a level on the first floor, in a room she'd decorated to look like someone's grandmother's overly fussy formal living room. Kelsie waited to say anything until we hit the stairwell. She shot a look over her shoulder to make sure Mr. Winston wasn't following us.

"Where the hell did you go?"

"You told me to leave. I was just taking your advice."

"Did you seriously crawl out the bathroom window?" Kelsie giggled. "You should have seen Mandy when she figured out you were gone. She was practically foaming at the mouth. No one could figure out where you went. That one freshman girl who is always doing tarot cards actually wondered out loud if you'd disappeared. She thinks maybe the guy from town is a ghost or a vampire or something and that's why you can't tell anyone who he is."

"She's got to lay off watching all those paranormal TV shows."

"She's hoping you're dating the undead, because it gives her hope that all her *Twilight* dreams might actually come true."

Kelsie stopped me on the landing. "Okay, be honest now. Why are you dressed like you're homeless?"

"You don't like the hat?" I fluffed my pom-pom.

"I would burn it before I would let it touch my head."

"Well, don't come begging me to borrow it later when it catches on as a trend."

"Where did you go?"

"I went sledding."

"Sledding?"

"And to Denny's." I broke into a smile. "I had a Grand Slam."

"I have no idea what's going on with you," Kelsie said.

"I know. I don't know what's going on with me either, but I'm not sure it's all bad." I hugged her, took my books, and loped down the rest of the stairs to meet with Ms. Sullivan.

chapter twenty-one

My favorite building on campus is the library. I love the smell of books and how the silence makes the place feel special, almost sacred. The corner of the library is a three-story stone turret room with thin windows. The room is full of several long wooden tables set with green banker lights making puddles of yellow light. Each of the windows is set out slightly, creating a small window seat. I always grab one of those to work in. It isn't as easy as having the table as a desk, but I like to lean against the cool stone and look out the leaded glass windows. It feels like being inside a castle. A castle where you would never run out of things to read. Most of the students at Evesham don't use the library often; they prefer to do their research online. As far as I'm concerned, the fact that it is often empty makes it even better.

My meeting with Ms. Sullivan had gone okay. I think she was excited to have a potential crisis on her hands. Her job had to be pretty boring most of the time, with people only showing up to talk about college admission options, roommate conflicts, and the occasional bout of homesickness. It would be like being a doctor where people only came into the office to have splinters removed or with stuffed-up noses. You'd have to look forward to someone coming in with a lawn mower amputation of the foot or a good cardiac condition. Most likely, thinking I was on the verge of an emotional breakdown had made her entire week. She got almost giddy when she saw a long scratch on my arm that I'd gotten while sledding. Ms. Sullivan thought she might have a cutter on her hands, and I could practically see her lift out of her seat in excitement. I'd hoped I would get away with just the one meeting, but apparently she didn't think my emotionally fragile state could be repaired that quickly. I was going to have to see her weekly until she decided I was stable. I was tempted to make up multiple personalities to keep things lively for her, but I figured if I wasn't careful I'd end up in the psychiatric wing of the hospital.

The librarian had helped me pull information on the history of Evesham. I carried the dusty pile of materials back to my window seat. I'd brought my cashmere wrap with me, and my plan was to curl up and pound out the paper for Winston. I propped my feet up on the bench, tucking my wrap in around my legs. I pulled the first book off the stack and opened it up. It was dark outside, so the windows mirrored back the inside of the room. My eyes caught a reflection, and I saw that there was someone sitting off to the side watching me. Great. Ever since Drew had dropped me back at school, I'd felt like a creature at the zoo.

Every time I walked into a room, everyone stopped talking and stared. The story of my great escape had spread all over campus. I couldn't tell if they were impressed with what I had done or were waiting for me to do something else unexpected at any moment.

I shifted in the seat, turning my shoulder to my new stalker, and tried to focus on the book. I read a few lines, but my eyes kept darting back to the reflection to see if the person was still watching. Finally I turned around so I could see who it was and hopefully embarrass them into moving along.

My eyes went wide. It was Tristan. He sat at one of the long tables, just staring at me. He didn't have any books with him; he wasn't even pretending to do anything else. The book I'd been holding slipped out of my hands and smacked loudly onto the marble floor, making me flinch. Tristan stood and shuffled over. I pulled my knees up so there was room, and he sat across from me in the window seat, our feet lined up in the middle and our knees making two mountains to separate us.

"You okay?" Tristan asked, his voice low and quiet even though we were the only ones in the library.

I nodded. "You okay?" My heart was beating fast. We were having an actual conversation. No ignoring each other, no screaming, just talking.

He shrugged and looked out the window, his reflection staring right back at him. "Some people are saying you snapped this morning and Dean Winston found you wandering around and brought you back."

"Not exactly. I couldn't handle the dining hall meeting thing, so I bolted. I went into town for a while to think. I came back on my own."

"You skipped classes?"

"Can you believe it?" I asked, trying to make him laugh, or at least smile. Tristan used to tease me about being a rule follower. He would say there was never a guideline I didn't embrace.

"These days there are a lot of things about you that I can't believe," he said, looking at his lap.

So much for trying to lighten the mood. "I'm sorry. I really, really am."

"What do you want to happen now?" Tristan picked at the hem on his sweater, pulling a thread loose. "Do you want to be with this guy?"

"No." My heart sped up, and I was glad I wasn't hooked to a lie detector test. I didn't want to date Joel. I was almost sure of it, but I couldn't deny there had been something that night, and that meant I was attracted either to Joel or to the idea of kissing someone else.

"Do you want us to get back together?"

My heart skipped a beat. I couldn't tell if he was asking me out of curiosity or if he thought he might be able to forgive me. Suddenly I had an image of Drew sitting at Denny's telling me that what I really wanted was to break up with Tristan. I shook my head slightly to clear his voice out of my mind. Getting back together with Tristan would be a huge step forward to getting my life back.

"I never wanted us to be apart," I said softly. I touched his wrist. He didn't pull away, so I left my finger resting there. I could feel his pulse just below the skin. "I want to be able to explain, to give you a good reason for everything that's happened, but I don't have a good reason. I screwed up." A tear ran down my face, and I wiped it away quickly. I didn't want him to think I was relying on guilt.

"You want me to say it's okay, that I forgive you, but it's not that easy. I always felt I could trust you, and then this happened. Everything feels upside down."

"I know."

"What do we do now?" Tristan asked.

I felt a brief flash of annoyance. Why did I always have to be the one to make decisions? What was I supposed to say? Was the choice over whether we got back together really in my hands? I always picked the movies and where we went to eat. Wasn't this one of the decisions Tristan should make on his own?

"What do you want to happen?" I asked.

Tristan didn't answer. I couldn't tell if that was because he didn't want to tell me, or if he didn't know himself. Maybe he was trying to keep me on my toes.

"Are you and your dad still fighting?" Tristan asked, changing the subject. He saw the confusion on my face. "Kelsie told me everything, about him bailing on your summer plans."

"I was counting on him, on our plans. Then, with everything that's happened, he's not exactly pleased with me these days. I feel like he and I need to hash things out."

"What good does that do? Do you think he'll change his mind?"

I slumped against the wall. "No." My dad and I still hadn't talked since the call with Dean Winston. He'd sent me an e-mail that he was out of town for a business trip and that he was still trying to determine what punishment he wanted to add over the whole statue incident. I hadn't bothered to write back. What would I say? He'd perfected the fine art of ignoring me the past few years. It only seemed fair that I do the best I could to try ignoring him for a change.

"Not having the end-of-summer party won't be that big a deal."

"Mandy practically considers it the crime of the century. You would think I'd canceled her birthday." I sighed. "It's not really the party that matters."

"I know. It's your dad's loss, not having the summer with you. You can't get time back."

"Thanks."

"I keep thinking that we won't be able to make up time either. We already didn't have much time left," Tristan said. "Just the rest of this year, and then you're gone for the summer, and then college for you after that."

I didn't say anything. Tristan and I had never talked about

what would happen after senior year. I knew he wasn't happy that I was going away for college, but he also knew it wasn't reasonable to ask me to not apply to the schools I really wanted to go to. I knew there were millions of high school couples facing the same issue, but it was different for us. We'd spent almost every day of our lives together for the past four years. We were like a married couple that just happened to live in different dorm rooms. Our parents weren't around to tell us to take things easy. We spent more time with each other than with our families. It had a way of making things more intense. We'd dealt with the end of school by ignoring it altogether. Maybe Drew was right. Maybe I had wanted to bring things to a definite end rather than let them slowly die out in a painful long-distance relationship.

Tristan stood. "I want things to go back, but I honestly don't know if they can. That's what I came to tell you. I hate that we're not talking. A million times a day I go to tell you something, that my dad got the part in the movie he wanted, or that I heard there are those brownies you like on the menu for dinner, or to ask you what you think I should do for my senior thesis project in government, and then I remember all over again what happened."

"I don't think we can go back," I said. Tristan looked down at me. "We either go forward or we don't, but there is no going back. I'd understand if you didn't want to, but if you do, I'm here."

chapter twenty-two

I sat straight up in bed. I looked at my clock and saw it was six a.m. I couldn't figure out what had woken me up. After Tristan had left the library, at first I didn't think I'd be able to focus. I wondered if there was something else that I should have said. There was no telling if I was going to get a chance to talk with him like that again. I could have thrown myself into his arms or begged for him to take me back. I suspected that was what he'd expected me to do. Then in the middle of worrying, my mind cleared out and I was able to bury myself in the history of Evesham. I stayed at the library until it closed just before eleven, and brought a few of the books back with me to my room. I'd actually found myself caught up in the project and hadn't turned my light out until after one a.m. I was exhausted, and now, for some reason, I was awake.

I closed my eyes and lay back down. I pulled my pink comforter up over my shoulders. I didn't have to get up for another hour. I could push it to an hour and half if I was willing to skip breakfast. After my Denny's gorging session yesterday, I wasn't sure I'd be able to face breakfast for a long time anyway. Then I heard it, a scratching sound. I pushed the covers off and crawled out of bed. I walked over to my door and leaned against it, pressing my ear to the wood. Then the sound happened again.

I unlocked the door and cracked it open to see what was causing the noise. Kelsie slid inside, looking behind her to make sure no one had seen her. Suddenly my best friend was James Bond.

I stood there in an old pair of Tristan's boxers and a T-shirt I'd bought on vacation to New York a few years ago. I rubbed the sleep out of my eyes. Kelsie wasn't normally an early bird. In fact, I couldn't remember the last time I had seen her up at this hour. Last year we had a fire drill for the dorms first thing in the morning, and Kelsie refused to get up for it. When Ms. Estes tried to get her in trouble for not evacuating, Kelsie did research to prove there was such as a thing as a "right to burn."

"What's up?" I asked.

Kelsie pulled a stack of magazines out from under her arm. "I bribed one of the maids to pick these up last night at the 7-Eleven. It hit the Web on TMZ."

"What are you talking about?"

Kelsie thrust the magazines in front of me. On top was *In Touch*, the cover story something to do with a reality star who had been caught with someone else's husband. I looked down at it and then over at Kelsie. I was a fan of reality TV as much as the next person, but it didn't strike me as the kind of thing that was worth waking up at dawn for. I searched my mind to see if the star was someone related to anyone at Evesham. Kelsie grabbed the magazine out of my hand, flipped through it, and handed it back to me.

Spoiled Heiress Breaks Hollywood Hearts—Boarding School Girl Goes Wild! There was a large photo of Tristan, posing in between his parents outside of some premier, then an inset photo of him turning away from the camera. I couldn't tell when or where the photo had been taken, but it was framed to make it look like Tristan was upset. Knowing Tristan, he could have been joking around, or hungry, or ticked about the Yankees losing, but the photo was captioned: "The brokenhearted heartthrob." My heart stopped. At the bottom of the page was a grainy photo of me. It was a picture taken at Evesham. I was walking on campus, and my mouth was open in a way that looked like I was sneering. There was also a small inset picture, my photo from last year's yearbook.

I felt the blood drain out of my face. I sat down quickly on the bed. "Are you kidding me?" I flipped through the pages. I couldn't focus on the words. They seemed to shimmy and dance across the page. Tristan had been in the tabloid magazines dozens of times because of his parents, but this was my first time. Unless you count a picture that was in *People* a couple years ago, where I was blending into the background at a party at his parents' house.

Someone more famous had their elbow in front of my face in the shot. You wouldn't even have known it was me unless someone told you.

"They're spinning you as a real ball breaker. How you told Tristan you were cheating on him in front of the entire school. They also make the statue thing into some kind of political statement you were making."

"What sort of political statement am I supposed to be making?"

"It's not really clear, sort of an anticapitalist thing. Down with the man, blah, blah, blah." Kelsie plunked down onto my bed. She pulled the magazine back and flipped through it. "The photo of you is a nasty one. You look like a mouth breather."

"How can they spin me as some sort of rich spoiled heiress on the one hand and an anticapitalist terrorist on the other?"

"Look, these magazines aren't the *New York Times* or *Newsweek*, you know. They aren't known for their journalistic integrity." She flipped a few more pages. "Hey, I hadn't heard this. Did you know these guys had broken up? I always thought she could do better. He always looks like he needs a shower." She turned the magazine to show me a large glossy photo of a rock star and his model girlfriend. Or ex-girlfriend. I pulled the magazine out of her hand. Unwashed musicians were not what I was interested in.

"My family doesn't even have that much money. Mandy's an heiress. I'm just"—my brain scrambled to find the right term— "like, ordinary rich. Maybe not even rich, just well to do."

"They talk about your vacation home on the lake."

"That's not a vacation home. It's my grandparents' place."

"I know that. I'm telling you what the articles say."

"Articles?" My question came out in a shrill high voice.

"Oh, yeah. There's a version of the same thing in both of these." Kelsie tossed the other magazines onto the bed. "Same picture of you too. That's unfortunate. At least *Star Magazine* used a shot of you from one of the student government meetings where you have your mouth shut."

I flopped facedown onto the bed and buried my face in my pillow. Just when I thought things couldn't get worse. "Has Tristan seen these yet?" I asked, my words muffled by the pillow.

"I called Joel last night when I saw it online and told him to give Tristan the heads-up."

"How exactly did you get the magazines?"

"You know the maid who does the bathrooms? The woman with the ring in her eyebrow that Dean Winston made her take out?" She waited for me to nod that I knew who she was talking about. "Everyone buys their weed from her, so I got her number from one of the girls on the floor and asked her to pick up something legal for a change. Even so, she charged me a hundred bucks to drop them off first thing this morning. Talk about a markup, but what are you going to do?"

"If no one can get off campus, maybe no one will see them," I said.

"I doubt it. I heard Mandy talking about it in the bathroom last night. That's how I knew to look for it. If I can get copies of the magazines, you better believe she can get her hands on copies."

"What is her problem with me?" I rolled over so I could look up at the ceiling.

"Well, first off she's a bitch in general. That's her natural state. Then you add on top of it that you were more popular than her and that you were dating Tristan. She always had a thing for him."

"She likes Tristan?"

"I don't know if she really likes him, but he's the most popular guy here. She likes the idea of them as a couple. I'm not sure she's capable of actual emotion; it's more a thing of how a relationship can benefit her. Dating him would double her star power."

"I don't even know why she's famous to start with. She's stinking rich and pretty. That's it. Oh, and she's willing to flash her hoo-ha to anyone who wants a peek. There's a real claim to fame. She should stick a disco ball between her legs and put down a dance floor, there's so much traffic through there."

"Maybe that's why she vadazzled her snatch last year." Kelsie and I both snorted. Mandy glued Swarovski crystals all over her waxed crotch and then acted surprised when a photographer got pictures. Whoever glues crystals on themselves is clearly doing it with the goal of someone seeing it.

"I still can't believe, with everything happening in the world these days, that my life counts as news."

"Tristan's a big deal. He's news."

"What does that make me?" I asked.

"Collateral damage. If you want to look for the positive, your life drama is most likely helping to support someone on the Evesham staff. It's sort of like sponsoring a kid in a third world country."

"You think the security guard that sold the picture of Mandy sold this story?"

"Someone did. The pictures of you are from campus. The story is all over this place. It might not be the security guard. It could be a maid, or someone from the cooking crew. Then there's the guy you're cleaning with. He'd have an inside track."

"Drew? You think Drew would do this to me? That's so unfair. You think he would do that just because he's from town. Everyone here is always judging everyone else." I felt like pushing Kelsie off the bed.

"Easy. Don't get your panties all knotted up. I'm not saying he did anything. What I said is that he *could* have sold the information. You act like he's your best friend now. Lately everything is all 'Drew says this' and 'Drew does that.' You've known this guy for like a week."

"Why would anyone do this?"

"Why not? Money, most likely. Maybe it's one of those staff people who don't like us because we go to Evesham. You heard about the maid who got canned two years ago because she was caught trying on Stephanie Wild's clothes? They clean our floors, wash our dishes, and make our meals. You have to figure sometimes they look at us and think it's unfair. Heck, maybe it is unfair. It's no wonder there are stories leaked out of here all the time."

I crumpled the cover of one of the glossy magazines. I didn't want to think Drew would do something like this, but I had told him everything that day at Denny's. He'd admitted that he needed to make money for school in the fall. Selling Evesham secrets would be a fast way to make a buck, and he hadn't exactly made a secret of what he thought of Evesham students in general. I think I had hoped it was different with me. My stomach clenched, filling with sour hot acid.

"I can't believe this had to happen now. Things with Tristan were just starting to get better."

"What do you mean?"

"He came to see me last night in the library." I almost laughed when I saw Kelsie's face. "You don't have to look that shocked. We dated for four years, after all. Did you think he'd really never speak to me again?"

"So are you guys getting back together?"

I shrugged. "I don't think he knows what he wants."

"You don't have to make him sound like a child who doesn't know what to do. The situation really threw him. He trusted you."

I leaned back, surprised at how angry she sounded. "I know. I didn't mean to make it sound like he was doing something wrong. You know how he is. He can't decide what he wants for dinner half the time."

"You always do that. Make snide comments about him. If you don't want to be with him, then don't date him."

"Do I have to do nothing but create poems in his honor? He's a guy. He's got great qualities and he has flaws. Why does everyone assume I don't want to be with Tristan?"

"Oh, I don't know. Hmm, let me think." Kelsie placed her finger on the side of her chin in an exaggerated gesture. "It could be because you were caught kissing some other guy. Or it might be that you make fun of him, or it could be because suddenly you're acting all strange, sneaking off campus, breaking stuff, hanging out with some townie instead of your friends."

I cut her off before she could say any more. "Maybe I'm not hanging out with my usual crowd because just about everyone in it is making me into the campus pariah. Everyone is acting like the fact that they can't get off campus is some great hardship. No one from student council has had anything to do with me, and even you only hang out with me when it works for you."

Kelsie stood up, her face flushing red. "Do you know how many times in the past week I've stood up for you? You act like everyone is blowing you off, but you're blowing them off just as much. You don't come to any of your regular activities. You isolate yourself and then blame us. I gave a hundred bucks to a drug dealer to get you these magazines. What do you want?"

"You're supposed to stand up for me. We're best friends." I reached a hand forward to touch her arm. I couldn't understand how I kept screwing things up with the people that mattered. My dad was mad, my best friend was mad, my boyfriend didn't even know if he wanted to be with me. My best guy friend wanted to be with me, but I didn't know if I wanted to be with him, and someone on campus, possibly the only friend I felt like I had left, was selling out my secrets for a few extra bucks. "I don't want to fight with you, too. I don't want you to be mad. All I was trying to do was explain what's going on for me."

"Whatever. I have to go." Kelsie crossed my room and flung the door open. "You can keep the magazines, and you might want to give some thought to the idea that while stuff is going on for you, the rest of us also have a life."

The door swung shut softly, separating us with a click.

chapter twenty-three

I didn't wait for Drew. By now I was becoming a seasoned pro. I didn't need him to hold my hand. I dragged the cart out from the closet and started on the first classroom. If I didn't get into Yale, I could always apply to work as a janitor. Someone had written notes on the white board with a regular marker. I rubbed it harder, but it didn't make a dent. I pulled out the oily cleanser I'd seen Drew use.

"Hey, Prima Donna. I was waiting for you outside," Drew said.

I didn't look behind me and kept my focus on the board. "I want to finish up early if we can. I have a lot of homework."

"That's a shame. I was going to suggest sneaking you out of here after work and doing something fun."

I made a noncommittal noise. My elbow was starting to hurt from the rubbing. I wasn't built for manual labor. I wouldn't make it long term as a janitor. Yet another future opportunity lost to me. "You know what I would consider fun? If you stopped calling me Prima Donna."

"What? It's Italian for 'first lady.'"

"It means 'stuck up,' and you know it." I glared at him over my shoulder.

"Wow. Someone woke up on the wrong side of the mop and bucket today. Better not let anyone see that expression. They're going to start calling you Cruella De Vil on top of America's least favorite heartbreaker."

I dropped the cleanser. "What do you know about that?"

"Just what I read online. You didn't mention that the boyfriend in question was some famous Hollywood star."

"He's not a star. His parents are."

"I don't know. I figure if the people on *Entertainment Tonight* have you on a first name basis, you count as a star."

"What journalists do you know on a first name basis?" I asked, crossing my arms.

Drew raised an eyebrow. "Is this a trick question?"

"Do you find it tricky to answer?" I held my breath while I waited for him to respond. I searched his face, looking to see if I would be able to tell if he was lying. His eyes didn't shift away, and he didn't blush or act like I had caught him. It could mean he had nothing to do with it, or that he was a good liar.

"What are you getting at?" Drew asked.

"Did you sell my story to the magazines?"

Drew took a step back, his face registering shock. "You think I would do that?"

"Someone did."

"Someone is also responsible for that ten-car pileup on the highway, but that also wasn't me. Last I checked, I also didn't start the war overseas, or have anything to do with the banking scandal or global warming. On the whole I've kept my nose pretty clean. If you're looking for a full accounting, I'll admit that when I was twelve I stole a Snickers bar from the local grocery. I've been known to speed in a school zone on occasion, and I've had a few underage beers, but never while driving. My mom would be right that I'm the guy who drinks almost the last of the milk from the carton and then sticks it back in the fridge, and she thinks I should make my bed." Drew stopped, as if he was thinking about it. "I also once dissected my kid sister's teddy bear. She considered it a case of murder, but I honestly wondered what was in there. I'd call it scientific curiosity gone awry. I thought I could put it back together. I was only eight, if that makes a difference."

"When I was that age, I once dug up all the tulip bulbs my mom had buried in the garden. I put them in my closet. I think I thought they might grow in there," I confessed.

"There you go. Neither of us is coming to this situation with clean hands." Drew crossed the room so that our faces were mere inches apart, his eyes locked to mine. "I haven't told anyone what you told me, and I wouldn't. Not for money, not even if they asked me nice."

I felt myself slump with relief. "Okay. I didn't mean to accuse you." All I needed was for him to be mad at me too.

"Nothing wrong with asking. Who else do you think could have done it?"

"One of the security guards sold a picture recently. It might have been her."

"Ah, the Mandy Gallaway scandal."

"You know about it?"

"Are you kidding? The whole staff was pulled into a meeting where we got our asses handed to us. We were all warned that if the administration finds out anyone is selling pictures of the golden children, there will be hell to pay. I'd be surprised if it was anyone on staff after that. I can't think anyone would risk their job over you." Drew pulled out the rag to wipe down the desks. "Is the story a problem? I would think people here would be used to that kind of thing."

"People like Mandy might be used to it, but I prefer to keep my private life private. Half the stuff in that story isn't true anyway."

"Do you really have a bunch of homework you have to do tonight?"

"Yes. I'm sure it seems like all we 'golden children' need to do is manage our media events and look good, but some of us have academic goals too."

"I never doubted you were smart." Drew looked over. "Crazy as all get out, but smart."

I tossed a roll of paper towels at his head, and he ducked.

"Careful. Those are the double thickness towels. Nothing but the best. You could make a baby diaper out of those. You waste supplies, and they take it out of your check."

"Seriously?"

"You think they don't watch our Windex usage? You better believe it. Winston is always convinced people are stealing. He caught a secretary a few years ago taking home a pack of Post-it notes, and you would have thought she was embezzling gold bars instead of some office supplies."

"What were you thinking of doing later?" I asked.

"I thought you had all that homework, not to mention those academic goals."

"I'm not saying I want to go. I'm just interested to know what you're doing. That's what friends do, take an interest."

"What if I won't tell you? Then you'll have to come to find out. It's a surprise."

"I don't like surprises."

"You're missing out. Surprises are what make life interesting."

"Isn't that supposed to be a Chinese curse, that you live in interesting times?"

"I'd take interesting over dull any day."

"So are you going to tell me what you've got planned?"

"Nope. Either you come or you don't. Your choice."

I bustled around emptying the trash cans as if I were too

busy to even consider his plan. Without even glancing over at him, I knew he would be smiling. Smirking, most likely. He was a big smirker. Sneaking off campus was a bad idea. I might have been able to convince Winston once that I was an emotional wreck, but if I got caught again, he wouldn't go so easy on me.

I sprayed the windows with Windex, perhaps a bit less than I might have used in the past, now that I knew there was a cleaning supply Nazi keeping track. I wiped the glass, watching groups of students walking across the quad. I spotted Tristan walking with Kelsie. I raised my arm to wave and catch their attention. Kelsie jabbed Tristan and he pushed her back, and she fell onto her butt on the ice. She threw her head back, and I could see she was laughing. Tristan tried to pull her up, but she used her weight to cause him to fall into the snowbank. I stood frozen, watching them. Tristan got up and tried again to help Kelsie. They were both laughing now. He finally settled for picking Kelsie up like a bag of laundry and throwing her over his shoulder to carry her off. I stepped back slightly so that if they looked at the window they wouldn't see me.

Drew was standing right behind me. He looked past me out the window. "That's Tristan, isn't it?"

I nodded, watching as he and Kelsie headed back toward the dorms.

"Who's with him?" Drew asked.

"Her name's Kelsie. She's my best friend." I pinned Drew in place with my expression, stopping him before he could say anything. "The two of them are friends too. They're always joking around like that. Tristan says Kelsie's the annoying younger sister that he never wanted."

"Fair enough." Drew turned away to go back to the mopping.

I kept an eye out the window, waiting to see if I would spot them again. "I'll go with you after work," I said suddenly. "I feel like a surprise."

chapter twenty-four

I swallowed hard to keep myself from throwing up. I knew I didn't like surprises. I had assumed Drew would have planned some sort of physical activity. Something that he thought would scare me. Bungee jumping off a bridge, ski jumping, or walking over hot coals. Now I realized there was something worse than putting myself in a life-and-death situation.

Karaoke.

A woman on the stage was singing some Top 40 song. The sound coming out of her was what I imagined would come out of livestock if you hooked them up to a car battery. More people would have been laughing at her, except she was doing this bump and grind number that was too hard-core for most porn movies, so the men in the audience were distracted. The bar wasn't like anyplace I'd been before. I'd been to a few of the nightclubs in LA with Tristan, but they were all red-rope affairs where you didn't get into the building if you weren't already on the A-list. This place looked to be a bit less discriminating. There were a few people in the back of the room that I suspected didn't even have a pulse. They appeared to be passed out in their beers. While the clubs I'd been to spent millions on décor and imported glass and marble from Europe, this place had a décor that seemed to be themed around plug-in beer signs.

I shifted in the seat. My glass of Diet Coke was making a puddle of condensation on the table in front of me. Drew jammed another nacho into his mouth. He'd ordered them with triple jalapeño peppers. It was a wonder his mouth didn't start shooting flames. He pushed the laminated pages back over to me.

"You still haven't picked a song," he said with salsa in his teeth.

"I'm not sure there's anything I like." I held the song list between two fingers. There was something sticky on the pages. I had no desire to even think what it might be.

"There's over two hundred songs on there. You can't find anything? I'm all for being discriminating, but at some point it becomes picky."

"I'm not sure I should be singing at all. My throat's been a bit sore. I might be coming down with something." I held my hand to my throat and tried to look wan.

Drew laughed. "Do not go into a life of crime. You suck at lying. You're not sick, and your throat is fine. Either you pick a song or I pick a song for you. If you want to pick a duet, I'll do it with you if you're too nervous to be up there by yourself. Or I could pick something super-embarrassing and sing it to you."

I slouched down in my seat, pouting. I pulled the list over and began looking through it again. Most of the duets were love songs. No way was I going to stand up in that bar and sing "Endless Love" with Drew.

"I don't see why I have to do a song at all. Why can't we just watch other people sing? That's fun." I gestured to the group of guys who had taken the stage and were belting out "You Shook Me All Night Long" by AC/DC. One guy was attempting to use his leg as a guitar. He fell over a stool, but popped right back up.

"Don't you want to be a part of things?" Drew's hand tapped the table to the beat of the music.

"Not if being a part of things means humiliating myself."

"There are two kinds of people in this world. People who are a part of what happens and people who sit back and watch other people make it happen. Life isn't supposed to be a spectator sport. It's supposed to be messy." Drew took my hand and leaned closer. His hands were rough with calluses. "Tell me the truth. When you were a kid, did you always color inside the lines?"

I went to pull my hand away, but he held it tighter. His hands were warm. I looked around to see if anyone noticed us touching. With my luck there would be some magazine reporter in the bar who would take a picture. "Coloring in the lines is the whole point. That's why they have lines," I said.

"That's where you're wrong. The lines are there just to hold you in. Like a prison. Think what you might have created if there hadn't been any lines. To quote my friend Thoreau: 'I wanted to live deep and suck out all the marrow of life, . . . to put to rout all that was not life . . . and not, when I came to die, discover that I had not lived.' Now, there was a guy who didn't color in the lines." Drew raised his glass to the ceiling as if to salute Thoreau, dropping my hand. He was able to quote poets. There was no end of random information he knew.

"I'm not sure we should be taking life advice from him. Thoreau lived in the woods, like some kind of crazy hermit," I said.

"Call him crazy if you want, but the guy is immortal because of what he did. He took risks. Did you know he was part of the Underground Railroad that helped sneak slaves north toward freedom? This was a guy who marched to the beat of his own drum. How many line followers are immortal?"

"How many people who don't stay in the lines cross into oncoming traffic and end up getting hit by a car?" I countered. This was something I knew from personal experience.

Drew rolled his eyes. "Singing in public isn't going to kill you. It won't even maim you. The only thing that's going to get bruised is your ego." Drew pulled the song list back over to his side of the table. He used the pencil on the table to scribble a song number on a sheet of paper. He pulled me up from my chair. "There you go. Now it's done. Come on. We're up."

"Wait, what song did you pick?"

"It's a surprise. I know how you love surprises." Drew

winked. He pulled me by the arm toward the stage, handing our slip of paper over to the DJ running the music.

"What if I don't know the words?" I dragged my feet, trying to slow our process.

"That's why they have them on the TV." Drew motioned to the small screen to the side of the stage. "You haven't been going to that fancy school for this long without learning to read. All you have to do is follow along. Now, once we get going, I expect you to belt it out."

The DJ called our names, and Drew jumped up onto the stage as if he couldn't wait. He handed me a microphone and took one for himself. A few people in the crowd hooted while we waited to start. I prayed that there would be some kind of natural disaster. A small earthquake would work, anything that would stop what was about to happen. All I needed was for the ground to split open and swallow me alive. It would also work if Drew were swallowed alive. Either option was fine with me.

The music started. Drew had picked "What a Wonderful World" by Louis Armstrong. I'd heard the song before, but I had to follow the lyrics on the TV to sing along. At least it wasn't as bad as some things he could have chosen. Looking out at the audience made me feel like I was going to pass out, so I focused on a flashing Budweiser sign at the back of the room. Drew stood next to me, throwing his arm around me so that we could sway in tandem back and forth for the final verse. Drew motioned to the crowd, and they yelled along with us, "I think to myself, what a wonderful world!"

Everyone cheered for us when we were done. Drew held my hand, and we bowed to the audience. Drew waved to the people in the back. I was starting to think I was going to have to drag him off the stage. I found myself smiling and taking a few extra bows while pulling him toward the stairs.

When we sat back down, some people a few tables over bought us a round of Cokes. Drew leaned back in his chair and put his feet up on the chair next to me.

"Admit it. You had fun." He shook his finger at me.

"It wasn't as bad as I thought it might be."

"Not bad?" Drew waved off my comments. "Coming from you that's practically a giddy endorsement."

"Unlike you, I'm not a karaoke pro. It would take more than one song to make me feel comfortable."

"I'm not a pro. I've never done this before just now."

The chip I was eating fell out of my mouth. "What do you mean?"

"I mean I've never done it. I saw the flyer at the Laundromat that they do karaoke here, and it sounded like fun." Drew noticed my expression. "You've heard of Laundromats, right? It's where the average people go to air their dirty laundry, instead of in tabloid magazines."

I looked down my nose at him. "Ha, ha. Yes, I've heard of Laundromats. I'm just surprised you haven't done this before. You jumped up there like the stage was your second home."

"I'm a big believer in faking it until you make it. If you're going to do something, you can't always sidle up to it. You have to jump in with both feet."

"No guts, no glory, huh? Not everyone has that kind of courage. Some of us have a normal sense of fear."

"You know what courage is, don't you? It's not a lack of fear. It's being scared and doing it anyway." Drew put his feet back on the floor and leaned forward. "Like asking your friend what's up with her and Tristan, instead of letting it eat you up inside."

I choked on my Diet Coke. "Now you've lost your mind. There's nothing going on between them."

"You don't need to convince me. You're the one bothered by it."

"I'm not bothered by it," I yelled. The people at the tables near us turned to see what was going on. Hanging out with Drew was turning me into one of those people who hangs out in cheap bars and has screaming matches in public. I pressed my mouth into a smile, lowered my voice, and repeated myself through clenched teeth. "I'm not bothered."

"I can see that." Drew pulled the straw out of his glass and chugged his Coke.

"I'm not."

"Okay. You're not. My mistake." Drew took another long drink. "All I'm saying is that life is too short to sit back and wait to see what happens, what everyone else decides. You're in charge of your own life. If your dad is ticking you off, then you should tell him. If you don't want to see Tristan anymore, then break up with him. If you think your friend is dating your boyfriend, then ask her."

I shook my head. "You're reading too much be-all-you-can-be poetry. That, or all that sucking the marrow out of life has resulted in an oxygen shortage. It's not that simple. In polite society we don't always do whatever comes into our head." I glanced down at my watch. "I should get back. I need to sneak back into my room before eleven."

Drew shrugged and pulled his coat on. I followed him out into the parking lot. The silence seemed jarring after the loud music in the bar. I could hear the squeak of my shoes in the fresh snow.

"I suppose you always do what you want," I said. "You go out and seize every day like some sort of motivational speaker."

Drew pulled on my jacket to make me stop. "If you don't seize the opportunity, how do you know what will happen? Sometimes you have to take the chance."

I started to disagree with him, but Drew leaned in and kissed me. Not a friendly peck on the cheek, but a full-on tongue-in-my-mouth face-sucking kiss. My mind went completely blank. Before Tristan the only person I had kissed was Wilbur Trent in seventh grade. Wilber sat behind me in class, and his mom had invited me to his birthday party, where he kissed me in the living room while we were supposed to be watching a movie. He had tasted a bit like the Juicy Fruit gum he was always chewing. There was no tongue with Wilbur. That summer his dad was transferred to Colorado and our young love affair never had another chance. Once at Evesham, I started dating Tristan the fall of freshman year and hadn't kissed another soul until Joel had planted one on me that night by the statue. Now Drew was kissing me out of nowhere. I couldn't tell what was going on in my life that suddenly people felt the urge to kiss me without being invited. I must have been giving off some kind of hormone scent that made people think I was easy. I could feel the sharp brush of Drew's stubble as it ground against my face. He pulled back and stared at me. I knew he was waiting for me to say something. I waited for the words to form, but my brain was blank.

I slapped him hard across the face. The crack of my hand against his skin sounded unnaturally loud in the quiet parking lot. Drew's face went bright red in the perfect shape of my hand.

"Well, that answers that question," Drew said.

"How dare you." I forced myself to take a deep breath and calm down. "I don't know what gave you the idea that that was something I wanted. I've enjoyed getting to know you, and I appreciate all the help you've given me over the past few weeks, but I don't have those sort of feelings." I hoped he wouldn't leave me in the parking lot, but what did he expect? You can't just kiss people.

"Easy, Prima Donna. It was a kiss. It wasn't an unending declaration of love or a marriage proposal. I took a chance, and not all chances can turn out as good as karaoke."

I didn't know if I should be relieved that he wasn't upset, or ticked that he was comparing kissing me to karaoke. "What do we do now?" I asked.

"Well, if we're going to get you back to the dorm on time, we should leave." Drew climbed into the truck. I watched my exhaled breath fog in the cold air. For someone who was always advocating that people should talk about things, he'd picked a fine time to go silent. I climbed into the passenger seat and slammed the door. Men.

We drove back to campus in silence. Drew pulled the truck to the side of the road behind the administration building. He got out and trudged up to the stone wall that circled the campus.

"You coming?"

If he thought playing it cool was going to upset me, he was wrong. I'd perfected acting like nothing was wrong for a good part of my life. I stomped through the deep snow. Drew bent over and cupped his hands. I stepped into his palm, and he hefted me up onto the wall. I sat on top and spun my legs around so that I could drop onto the campus side.

"Thanks for bringing me back to campus," I said. I dropped to the ground, the pile of snow cushioning my fall. I took a quick glance around to make sure no one had seen me.

"Hey, Hailey?" Drew's voice drifted over the wall.

I considered pretending that I hadn't heard him and just walking away, but I couldn't do it. "Yeah," I called back softly.

"I still think it's a wonderful world."

chapter twenty-five

Joel was sitting outside my door in the dorm hallway working on his math homework when I got back. I wondered how long he'd been waiting. When he saw me, he stood.

"Where were you?"

"Studying," I said, before I realized I didn't have any books or notes with me. Joel looked me up and down, noting the clumps of snow on my socks. "I took a walk to clear my head."

"Through the snow?"

"It's winter. Sort of hard to avoid the snow. Besides, I like fresh air." I unlocked my door and went in, leaving the door swinging behind me. Evesham allowed people of the opposite sex to visit the dorms, but you had to leave the door open. It was supposed to prevent people from having sex. Clearly the administration didn't have the imagination that the student body did. Evesham was full of places where couples could hook up. "What's up?" I asked, sitting down on my bed so I could pull my wet socks off. My legs were red from the cold. The bright red skin made me think of Drew's face. I shoved that image out of my head. I wasn't prepared to deal with Drew right now. I was having a hard enough time figuring out what to say to Joel. I was suddenly aware we hadn't spent much time in each other's company by ourselves since the whole statue incident.

"I tried to call you, but you didn't pick up your phone," Joel said. "You're supposed to keep it on so that I can get in touch with you. I'm responsible for making sure you're meeting the conditions of your punishment."

"I didn't think about it." I shrugged.

"I needed to talk with you about your punishment."

"That's good. I needed to talk to you, too."

"Dean Winston is getting flack from people's parents about the restriction rules."

"He can always decide to lift it." I pulled on a pair of hot pink fleece socks that my grandma had given me for Christmas last year. I wiggled my toes to get the blood moving.

"He isn't going to give in," Joel said.

"If you're worried that I'm going to tell on you, I'm not. It's up to him what he chooses to do about that. He can keep me on restriction for the rest of the year if he wants."

"I feel bad," Joel said.

I pushed down a wave of annoyance. I couldn't remember if Joel had always been this passive or if this was something new.

Wasn't it enough that I was the one in trouble? Did I also have to make him feel okay about it? I couldn't imagine Drew ever talking about how he felt bad. If he felt bad, he would *do* something, not just talk about it.

"If you want, you can help me out with something else," I said. "I need you to get me off the cleaning crew. Isn't there something else I can do? Wash dishes in the café? Maybe shelve books in the library? I like the library."

"I don't think Winston's going to change his mind about the cleaning. I think he would see the library as too easy."

"Can you get me assigned to work with someone else?" I avoided Joel's eyes. "That guy, Drew . . . He and I aren't getting along. I don't want to work with him anymore." It wasn't that I disliked Drew, but I had more awkward friend-kissing situations than I could handle already.

"How well do you have to get along? You're cleaning classrooms. I didn't figure the two of you would become friends or anything."

"He hit on me, okay?" My voice came out flat. "It's a bit awkward working with him." I stood up and began bustling around my desk. I stacked my books and folders back in order. I'd forgotten about an essay due for English. I was going to be stuck staying up late.

"Oh." Joel sat staring at his math book. "I can see what I can do. It's completely inappropriate for him to try anything with a student. He's asking for trouble. You would think he would know enough not to take advantage of the situation." He touched the back of my hand.

My hand froze in place, and then I yanked it back to dig through my backpack, looking for my book. "It's not that he's creepy or anything. I don't want to get him fired. It's not that big a deal. It's just uncomfortable. He likes me and I don't like him. That's all." I pulled the book out and flopped into my desk chair. "Like, today, he said this bizarre thing trying to make me jealous. Get this. He said he thought Tristan and Kelsie were seeing each other." I snorted to show how absurd I thought the whole thing was. "Talk about a transparent bid to get my attention."

Joel was silent. His face was frozen as if I were pointing a pistol at his head instead of just looking at him. His Adam's apple was bouncing up and down. My stomach sank to the floor.

"What's going on?" I whispered.

"It's not really my place to say anything." Joel wiped his hands on his pants.

"Don't pull that 'I'm neutral' act with me." I crossed the room in two steps and grabbed hold of Joel's sweater. I was prepared to shake the truth out of him if I had to. "Are they a couple?" I held the sleeve tighter in case he had any plans of making a run for it.

"I don't know." He held up his hand as if he thought I might hit him. "I swear, I don't know. Right after everything went down, Kelsie was around a lot. More than usual, or maybe it seemed like more because you weren't there too. Tristan was really upset, and, I don't know. They've been hanging out. Doing stuff just the two of them. You know Kelsie's always had a case of hero worship for him."

"And Tristan?"

"I think he likes that Kelsie likes him. She's always telling him how great he is and building him up," Joel said.

I let go of Joel's sweater. "I don't get it. I never even imagined the two of them together." I pushed down a feeling in my gut that I had imagined it before, that some part of me had suspected for a while.

"They have a lot in common, you know. Kelsie wants to go into acting, and Tristan's a part of that world, with his folks and all." Joel shrugged as if he were overcome by the destiny that was pulling Kelsie and Tristan together.

"That's a lot in common? That's one thing. What about the fact that Kelsie's a vegetarian and Tristan's favorite food is a rare steak? He never met a living animal that he wouldn't kill and grill. He would eat a kitten burger if it came with pickles. Or how about the fact that Kelsie can spend hours debating the shape of her eyebrows and Tristan hates that high maintenance stuff? Oh, wait. I forgot they both have a connection to acting." I smacked myself in the forehead. "How stupid of me not to see that they're meant for each other. I feel so foolish having stood in the way of true love all this time."

I realized I was crying, which made me mad. I dragged my sleeve across my face to wipe away the tears.

Joel touched my shoulder. "Don't be upset."

"I'm not upset!" My voice snagged in my throat, giving a hiccup sob. The tears came faster. Joel put his arm around me and had me sit on the bed. He knelt on the floor in front of me. Tristan and Kelsie didn't have much in common, but Joel and I did. We were both overachievers, we liked to watch the news and debate the issues, and we both preferred books versus anything on TV. In theory he and I were perfectly matched, but I'd never thought of him that way before that night. Now I couldn't tell if I was confused because I did like him, or that I liked that he liked me. Maybe I was only afraid of being left alone, especially if Tristan was picking Kelsie.

"I don't think Kelsie or Tristan want you to be hurt," Joel said.

"They should have told me. I know I'm in no position to be angry with Tristan, given what happened, but sneaking around means they think it's wrong too. If Kelsie thought dating Tristan was fine, she would have said something. She and I are supposed to be best friends."

"She's hurt that you didn't tell her who you were kissing that night." He cut me off before I could protest. "I know why you didn't tell her, but she doesn't understand. Neither of them knew what to say, so they didn't say anything."

I sniffed. My nose was running. "Why didn't you tell me? You could have warned me. I shouldn't have had to hear that from Drew."

Joel took both of my hands in his. He was on his knees, and I had the sudden fear he was going to propose.

"You're right. I should have told you, but it was complicated. What happened between us that night? It wasn't an accident. I've been in love with you for a long time. I should have told you about Tristan and Kelsie, but I think part of me wanted them to get together. I didn't want to get in the way of it. I hoped that if they were a couple, you wouldn't spend any more time worrying about him. I figured you wouldn't feel bogged down with guilt. That maybe you would see me with new eyes."

My heart sped up. I wanted to pick up my wet socks from the floor and shove them into Joel's mouth to keep him from saying anything else. "We've been friends a long time," I said, trying to remind him. Weren't the best relationships supposed to be based on friendship? Was that enough?

"You know freshman year? I liked you even then. I remember how your dad had ordered the wrong size uniform for you. Those first few weeks you were always having to hitch your skirt back up and roll the sleeves on your sweater up until your new uniform arrived."

"You never said anything to me. You never acted like you liked me," I said.

"The first time I got up the guts to talk to you, you asked about Tristan, my roommate."

I flinched. "Sorry."

"Can't say I blame you. Tristan was already, you know, Tristan, and I was such a dork back then. I weighed, like, eighty pounds. Remember how everyone called me the beanpole?"

I smiled, but if I had been honest, I would have told Joel that I didn't have a lot of memories of him from freshman year. I'd been so homesick at first. I'd felt lost among all these people who seemed totally comfortable living without their parents. I hadn't wanted to screw anything up, and then suddenly in the middle of all of that there was Tristan. He always seemed so confident and was so good-looking. Tristan always teased me about how hard to get I'd been in those first few weeks, but I hadn't been playing at anything. It had never occurred to me that he would actually like me. The fact that he'd been flirting with me had sailed right over my head.

"I never knew," I said. "You never said anything, even after what happened at the statue."

"I guess I hoped you'd realize it wasn't an accident. Then when you didn't, I didn't want to push things. I hoped that eventually you would look around and notice me." Joel shrugged. "I think I was hoping you'd think it was destiny."

"You can't do that. You can't sit back and wait for life to happen to you. You should have said something." As the words came out of my mouth, an image of Drew flashed into my mind. I touched my lips lightly as if I expected to feel the burn of his mouth on mine.

"I couldn't do that. Not to Tristan. What was I going to say, 'Hey, guess what? I have a crush on your girlfriend.' I always figured you guys would eventually break up and then after a decent amount of time I would step in. Who would have thought you guys would stay together for all of high school?"

The idea that Joel had been spending the past four years just waiting for something to happen made me sad.

"So when Kelsie and Tristan got together, you didn't mind at all. It must have looked like your opportunity was finally here."

"I swear I never planned it." Joel raised his hand as if he were taking the Boy Scout pledge. Joel was a good guy. I suspected he was right. He never would have done anything to try to get a chance with me. He would have sat back and waited forever if he needed to. He wouldn't have wanted to upset anyone.

"Hailey, I love you. I've loved you for a long time. I know this must seem sudden to you, but it's not. You're right. We have been friends for years. Maybe now we can see if it might grow into something more."

"You don't love me," I said, pulling my hands back, suddenly sure.

"How can you say that?"

"If you loved me, you would have taken the chance. You would have risked having everything go wrong because the slim chance that it might go right would have been enough to make it worth it. Love is risky."

Joel leaned back on his heels. He was like one of those giant inflatable parade balloons that had sprung a leak. "You want to be with Tristan," he said.

I sighed. "Not everything is a competition between the two

of you. I thought I wanted to be with Tristan, but I don't know. Maybe I wanted to be with Tristan because it's easy." I shrugged. "It might not even be up to me. It sounds like he and Kelsie are an item now."

"I bet he would drop her if he knew you guys could work it out."

"Then, that's a shame. Kelsie deserves better than that." I touched the side of Joel's face. "You do too. You deserve someone who's crazy about you."

"But that's not you," he said, his eyes filling up.

"No, it's not me."

chapter twenty-six

I stared at my copy of *The Count of Monte Cristo*. For some reason writing an essay for English on the effects of betrayal seemed a bit too close to home. I considered calling Kelsie, but I wasn't sure how to start the conversation. How do you ask your best friend if she's seeing your boyfriend?

Kelsie and I hadn't become friends right away at Evesham. I'd thought she was too wild. Freshman year I was known for having color-coded file folders that matched my notebooks, and she was known for having the largest collection of lip gloss. She'd gotten in trouble at Halloween for wearing a cat costume to the masquerade party that would have made a stripper blush. She hung with the party crowd, and I hung with the nerds.

Kelsie and I had been assigned to do a project together for biology. She refused to touch the worm we were supposed to dissect, on ethical grounds. She was already a member of PETA and threatened that if our teacher made her touch "the innocent wildlife victim," then she would arrange a protest march that would shut down the science wing. Our teacher decided that I would handle the dissection portion of the project and Kelsie would write up our results. I could tell ten minutes into the project that if I wanted to keep up my A average, I was going to have to write the paper too. I based this on the fact that Kelsie wasn't interested in writing down anything I was doing with our worm. She was more interested in creating a chart that listed the calorie burn and fitness potential for a range of activities, so that she could get the maximum burn in the least amount of time.

"It's genetics, you know. My grandmother was Italian, which makes me predisposed to plump up. It's all the carbs." Kelsie shook her head as if she couldn't believe this cruel twist of fate.

"I'm pretty sure this part of the worm is the esophagus," I said, pointing and trying to pull her attention back to what we were supposed to be doing.

Kelsie didn't even look over into the tray. "You know the other issue I have to worry about? Facial hair. Italian women are very prone to those long black chin hairs." She wiggled her fingers at the end of her chin as if to demonstrate how all the hair would look waving in the wind.

"I didn't know that," I said. If I thought I was going to have a beard, I wouldn't tell anyone. I wasn't sure if I was supposed to be impressed or repulsed.

"It's true. You can tell I'm going to be hairy by looking at my eyebrows." Kelsie pointed with a perfectly manicured finger to her face.

I inspected them, leaning in close to get a better look. "They look fine to me."

"Well, of course they do. Do you think I would show up in public unless I'd been waxed? I've been plucking since I was ten. I remove enough hair per week to make wigs for at least two kids with cancer."

"Wow." I looked back at our worm corpse.

"I'm guessing you don't have facial hair issues, huh? Nordic heritage?"

"Me? No. My family's originally from Ireland." I touched my eyebrows with one latex-covered finger.

"You're lucky. You can't beat good genes. No wonder Tristan likes you."

I chopped our worm in two, shocked at what she said.

"Are we supposed to make two worms?" Kelsie asked, leaning in.

"Why would you say Tristan likes me?" My voice was high and a bit screechy. I whirled around to make sure he was still sitting across the room and hadn't heard what she said. He looked up from his worm tray and smiled. I spun back in case he thought I was staring at him.

"What's the matter? He's cute. I wish someone like that liked me," Kelsie said.

"He doesn't like me." I pushed the worm ends back together,

hoping either the worm would spontaneously heal itself or our teacher wouldn't notice what I'd done. "He's just nice."

"Are you blind?" Kelsie tapped me on the back of the hand. "You might know science, but I know boys. He's been flirting with you."

I casually scratched my back so I could turn enough to have Tristan in my view again. He was still glancing toward our table. I backed up quickly, and my lab chair fell over, making a loud clang on the tile floor. Our science teacher scowled. She wasn't fond of clowning around in her lab.

"He's staring at me," I whispered out of the side of my mouth to Kelsie. "What do I do?"

Kelsie smiled. "You're in luck. In addition to being plump, and the chin hair thing, Italians are naturals with love and romance. I can totally help you. Romeo and Juliet were Italian, you know."

I thought about telling her that Romeo and Juliet were created by Shakespeare, who was British, but I decided I wanted her advice more than I wanted to make a point.

Her advice worked too. It wasn't hard advice to follow. It consisted mostly of meeting his eyes instead of looking away, flipping my hair around like I was having some kind of seizure, and wearing lower-cut shirts. By the end of that week Tristan and I went from shameless flirting in the cafeteria, to talking after class, to kissing while hidden in the stacks of the library, to being a full-fledged established couple. In addition to gaining a boyfriend, I'd gained a best friend. Kelsie and I hadn't been separated since that time.

Now I needed to know what to do, and the person I usually went to for advice was the one person I couldn't ask.

I looked at my watch. It was an hour earlier in Chicago; it wasn't *that* late. No one would consider it the middle of the night. Weren't parents supposed to be the ones we went to when there was trouble? Adults were always telling us that we should go to them. I pulled my cell out of my bag and hit the number before I had time to overthink the situation. He picked up the phone before it finished ringing the first time.

"I thought we said we wouldn't talk again until morning," my dad purred into the phone.

"Dad?"

"Hailey?" His purr was gone. "What's wrong? Are you okay?" He gasped slightly. "Your not in jail, are you?"

"No, I'm not in jail." I couldn't keep the annoyance out of my voice. Jail? Really? I'd been in trouble exactly twice in my high school career, and because I called at ten p.m. the first thing that came into his mind was that I must have been picked up by the cops?

"Why are you calling?"

"Who did you think was calling?" I narrowed my eyes as if I could see through the cell phone into my dad's eyes.

"I'm not having this conversation with you now."

My heart stopped. My dad was dating someone. "You have a

girlfriend?" Logically I knew there was always the chance that my dad would see someone at some point. It wasn't that I expected him to be alone forever with a shrine to my mom above the gas fireplace in the living room, but he'd never said anything. This felt sneaky and wrong.

My dad sighed. "This isn't something I planned to talk about on the phone."

I held off from pointing out that since he was always out of town and we never saw each other, the phone was pretty much our only option. Maybe he'd been planning to save this discussion for graduation, or maybe he'd never planned to tell me at all. There'd been a lot of that going on in my life lately.

"I've been seeing someone. Her name is Linda." His voice sounded nervous. "She works with me. I think you'll like her. She's smart and funny. She's an engineer. I thought maybe you could meet her this summer up at Grandma's."

"Huh." I kicked at the floor with my foot. "How do you know you'll still be dating her in the summer?"

"I knew you wouldn't be happy about this. Seeing Linda doesn't change how I feel about your mom."

"How does Linda feel about you being gone all summer?"

There was silence on the phone. "Linda will be in London with me. The project over there is hers."

My throat narrowed. "Linda's project is in London." I felt my breath come low and shallow. "That's why you changed our summer plans. You wanted to go with your girlfriend on vacation." My voice stretched out the word "girlfriend," making it sound slimy.

"It isn't that straightforward."

"All I wanted for graduation was to spend the summer with you. You told me we could, and you let me plan a party for all my friends."

"I know canceling your party was a disappointment, but this workshop in England is very important. I would hope you could understand that, especially given your age. You're not a child."

"Well, I'm glad you noticed I'm growing up. And for the record, it wasn't some little party; it was a chance for me to spend one last time with my friends before we all go our separate ways. That might not seem like a big deal to you, but these people have been my family for the past four years. You know, family, what you used to be a part of."

"This isn't like you. You've become belligerent and angry. It's not becoming. I don't know what's gotten into you."

"Then, ask me! It's not a big secret. I was calling to tell you. I don't even know who I am anymore. I'm not sure what I want. I feel like you don't want me in your life. Tristan and I broke up. Kelsie, who's supposed to be my best friend, is dating Tristan on the sly. Joel likes me, which is totally awkward, because we're supposed to be friends. Then there's this other guy, who sort of drives me nuts, but then I kinda like him at the same time." I took a deep breath, but before I could go on, my dad cut me off.

"This is a hard time, with graduation coming and all. I'll call Dean Winston tomorrow and arrange for you to talk to someone. They must have a counselor there given what they charge."

"I don't want to talk to Ms. Sullivan. I want to talk to you."

"Girl problems aren't my thing. If your mom were here, she'd know the right thing to say."

"There isn't a right thing, Dad."

"Now, look, I'm going to call the school tomorrow, and we can talk again later, when you're not so upset. Or you could give your grandma a call. She'd love a long chat with you."

"I don't want to talk later, I want to talk now, and I want to talk to you." I hated how my voice sounded whiny.

"Take care of yourself, pumpkin. You know I love you."

"Dad, wait." I hated these conversations on the phone.

"Sleep tight." He clicked the phone off.

My dad hung up on me. He *hung up* on me. Maybe he thought because he said he loved me before he did it that it wouldn't count, but a hang up is a hang up. I might only be seventeen, but I know a hang up when it happens.

I picked up the phone to call him back. My finger hovered over the button. What if he didn't pick up? He would glance at the call display this time. He would know who was on the line. I chewed on my thumbnail. It would almost be worse if he did pick up and did the platitudes thing where he told me how everything was fine without actually listening to a word I said and then told me to call someone else.

I bet he was on the phone talking to Linda already, telling her how hard it was for him to deal with a difficult teenage daughter. Maybe London Linda was offering to come over and rub all that tension out of his back. She'd giggle and tell him how she was a real handful when she was my age. He'd pull her into his lap and say she was still a handful.

Gag.

I paced back and forth in my room. I'd taken psychology class. I knew that my dad had a hard time dealing with me because I reminded him of my mom. Heck, what was it Drew had said? We all had our issues. He was still my dad. Just because it was hard didn't give him an excuse to bail out. My mom had died, but my dad was just as absent from my life. I might as well have been an orphan.

I couldn't believe he had chosen going to London with his new girlfriend over spending the summer with me. After he'd promised! Of course, for all I knew, Linda wasn't a new girl-friend. He could have been dating her since I started at Evesham. I couldn't decide what was worse, that he had a girlfriend he'd kept secret for years or that he was chucking our plans over some-one he'd met only a few months ago. I pictured him and Linda walking through the London streets. Maybe she liked antiques like my mom.

My vision narrowed to a small dot. He didn't want to hear what I had to say, but if I was in his face, he wouldn't be able to hang up. He'd have to listen to me then. It might not change what was going to happen. Most likely he'd still go to London, and if I was honest, I wasn't sure I even wanted to spend the summer with him anymore. What I did know for sure is that I wasn't going to sit back and wait for the chance to tell him how I felt.

I flipped open my laptop.

I was going to Chicago.

chapter twenty-seven

I was awake before my alarm even went off at five forty-five. I'd stayed up late last night getting everything together, but I was still humming with adrenaline, so I didn't even feel tired. I wanted to be ready to go as soon as the clock rolled over to six. My credit card had just enough left on the limit to cover the ticket and cab fair to my dad's place. I'd packed a small duffel bag to take with me. I wouldn't need much. I wasn't planning to stay for long.

I'd struggled with what to do about everyone at school. When I didn't show up in class, someone would come looking for me. I didn't want them to think I'd gone missing and there was some mystery to be solved. There was nothing that CNN and the tabloids loved more than a missing white girl. I'd have Nancy Grace all over my butt before the day was out. I needed to leave a note so people would know I was okay, but not give them any information so they could find me. It took me a while to come up with the perfect wording. The note was pinned to my bed so it would be found when they came to look for me.

Once I was over the fence, I'd call Drew and see if he would pick me up and drive me to the airport. There was the chance he wouldn't talk to me after what had happened, but I was counting on him sticking with playing it cool. If he wouldn't come, I'd have to walk. I didn't want to do that, but I would if I had to. There was only one hitch in the plan. I needed my passport.

Airline security required photo identification. I'd searched everywhere for my driver's license. I didn't have a car at Evesham, so I almost never needed my license. The last time I could remember having it was Christmas, when I'd used it to drive to the mall with my grandma. I had a sinking feeling that it was still in the dress coat that I'd worn over the Christmas holidays. The coat that would be hanging in my grandparents' front hall closet. I wasn't willing to wait for my grandparents to FedEx me my license, not to mention that they would want to know why I needed it right now. My only other option was my passport. There was no way an airline was going to let me through security with only my school ID.

Evesham had kept our passports in the administration building ever since two juniors ran off for an elicit weekend in Paris a few years ago. This is the problem with people having a lot of money but not always a lot of sense. People could still get into a lot of trouble, but with our passports locked up, I guess the theory was that we wouldn't get too far. Dean Winston's secretary had them in a giant lateral file cabinet behind her desk. The janitorial staff started unlocking buildings on campus at six a.m., but in most cases staff and faculty didn't start the day until closer to seven or seven thirty. All I needed to do was get into the building and up to Winston's office, liberate my passport, and get out before anyone knew what I'd done.

I pulled on sweats and my sneakers. My story if anyone saw me wandering around campus this early was that I'd wanted to go for a run. It would still be a bit odd. This time of year most people either ran on the treadmills in the fitness center or at the track in the gym, but it was the best story I could come up with.

I shut my door behind me and passed a couple of girls in their bathrobes shuffling their way to the bathroom. I crept downstairs and saw Ms. Estes in the lobby. I stopped and did some exaggerated stretches trying to look fit and sporty. I bounced on the balls of my feet and swung my arms around to get the blood moving. I jogged in place for a beat, and then left the building. I could feel her eyes on my back. There wasn't anything she could say; at six a.m. I wasn't breaking any rules by leaving. I jogged down the path in case she was still watching, and waited until I had rounded the corner of the dorm before I stopped running and headed off across the quad to the administration building.

The front door to the administration building clicked open. The hallway was lit, but the doors to most of the offices were closed. My wet sneakers made a loud squeaking noise on the tile floor. It seemed like with each step my shoes were screaming out *I'm doing something I shouldn't!*

I ran up the stairs toward Winston's outer office. The only person I saw was one of the maids using a floor buffer way down the hall. She didn't even look up when I went past. I tapped lightly on the door in case his secretary had come in early. The door creaked open a few inches. I peeked my head inside. Winston's private office door across the room was closed, and I was willing to bet it was locked, too. The outer office had two sofas where visiting parents or important people could wait. Directly outside Winston's office were two hard-backed chairs and a bench where those of us in trouble were relegated to wait for our fate. The secretary's desk was almost directly in the center of the office, with the file cabinet right behind it. I took a few steps forward. My heart was beating fast. Up until this point I would still have been able to make an excuse as to what I was doing there, but soon there would be no amount of explanations that would make things okay. My hands were shaking. I either had to take the plunge or go back to the dorm and forget the entire idea.

I let my mind slip back to the phone call with my dad the night before, and that was all the motivation I needed. I wasn't done with that conversation. I crossed the rest of the way to the file cabinet. I pulled on the center drawer labeled *G* through *K*. I yanked harder. It was locked. I wanted to scream from frustration. I wondered how hard it would be to pick the lock. Growing up, I'd taken hundreds of courses in gymnastics, ice-skating, crafts, and swim lessons, but I'd never learned anything really useful like lock picking. If I ever had kids, they wouldn't waste their time gluing Popsicle sticks together. I'd make them learn skills that would come in handy later in life. I kicked the cabinet, in case the drawer might fly open like in the movies. Nope. I'd come this far, and I'd been beaten by a two-dollar lock. My brain scrambled to think of a way around the problem; maybe I wouldn't need my passport. I tried to think if there would be any way to sneak onto the plane without my photo ID, but with my luck I'd be caught and accused of being a terrorist.

I stood there feeling defeated. Unless I was willing to start whacking away at the cabinet with a stapler, I was screwed. I took a couple steps toward the door. I'd have to go back to the dorm and take my shower and try to pretend it was like any other day.

A jolt ran through me. My heart skipped a beat. I had an idea. I stepped back to the secretary's desk and slid the top drawer out. My fingers ran over a collection of pens and pencils, pads of Post-it notes, and a pack of cigarettes. Huh. I wouldn't have guessed she was the type. There was a box of paper clips, and I stuck my finger in, saying a quick prayer. Bingo! There it was, a small silver key.

I pulled it out and fought the urge to dance around in circles with the key held above my head. I slid the key in and jiggled the lock a bit, and it popped right open. The file drawer slid out smoothly. My fingers ran over the folders. They had color-coded tabs on the top for each year. I found my folder and yanked it out. There was a slip of paper clipped to the front that held my dad's contact information and all sorts of "in case of emergency" details. There was a copy of my transcripts with all my grades. Four years at Evesham, and it amounted to little more than five or six sheets of paper. My passport was tucked into a pocket of the folder, and after a small shake it slid out into my hands.

I heard a shuffle outside the door. I froze in place, not even breathing. The steps moved down the hall, and my heart started to beat again. My eyes shot to the clock. It was time to get out of there. I shoved the passport into my bra and shut the cabinet drawer. I took a couple steps before I realized I had forgotten to lock the drawer. My fingers fumbled with the key and I dropped it onto the floor with a curse. Then the lock clicked and I slid the key back into the paper-clip box.

I put my ear to the door to see if I could hear anyone in the hallway. It was quiet. I pulled the door open a few inches and peeked out. No one. I stepped out into the hallway and headed toward the stairs. I'd only made it about three or four steps when I heard Dean Winston. He was talking to someone as he came up the stairs. Why did he have to pick that day of all days to choose to come into work early? My eyes darted around the hallway. There was a long wooden table against one wall, but there would be no way Winston would miss me crouching under there.

I ran past Winston's door and down the hall. At the very end of the hall there was a door that led to a second-floor balcony. I could hear Dean Winston getting closer. Any second he was going to turn the corner on the landing and see me. I hit the latch on the door, and it flew open, spilling me out onto the deck and into a pile of snow. I stood quickly and shut the door. The balcony had a picnic table and a few chairs sprinkled around. They were covered in snowdrifts. Near the door was a coffee can filled with sand and cigarette butts. This must have been where the administration staff came to take their smoke breaks. I waited to see if Winston had heard the door and would come to investigate, but after a minute it was clear no one was coming. All I had to do was wait a few minutes to be sure Winston was tucked away in his office, and then I could slip back into the hall and get out of the building.

I made myself count to sixty, five times. I bounced on the balls of my feet, trying to stay warm. I didn't want to move too close to the end of the balcony, in case anyone on the ground would look up and see me. When the time was up, I went to open the door, but the handle didn't budge. I let go of the handle. I refused to believe it was locked. I closed my eyes and took a deep breath. I took hold of the door and gave it another yank. It didn't even rattle in the frame. Then I saw it, a wooden block leaning up against the brick wall. The kind of block that would be handy to prop open a door that had an automatic fire door lock.

I was locked outside. I wanted to throw myself onto the balcony and have a meltdown, complete with screaming, kicking feet, and flailing fists. I'd managed to break into Winston's office and steal my passport, and now I wasn't going to be able to get away with it because I was stuck on the terrace. I'd either freeze to death or have to beat on the door until someone came to let me out, and with my luck it would be Winston. Even if it wasn't him, there was going to be a whole bunch of questions about what I was doing there.

I leaned against the door. My body was still humming with energy. I didn't want to give up. There was a tree near the corner of the balcony, its branches hanging over the railing. I walked over and looked down, and then back up at the branches. They were thick and sturdy, close to the balcony, and at least the thickness of my thigh.

People climb trees all the time. It is practically an American pastime. Baseball, apple pie, Boy Scouts, and climbing trees. Cats can climb trees, and they aren't even that smart. Statistics about how many people fall out of trees flashed into my brain, along with the odds of impaling myself on a branch if I fell, but I pushed these thoughts out of my head. Sometimes the payoff is worth the potential risks. My brain started going through the geometry, the angle of the branches, the distance to the ground. It looked easy. If I stood on the banister of the balcony, I would be able to reach one of the larger branches. Then just a few hand-over-hands and I would be near the tree trunk. It looked like I would be able to climb down, to the ground. It was basically a jungle gym with sap and bark.

I was going to have to make a decision soon. I needed to get off the balcony, pick up the duffel bag that I'd dropped outside my dorm window, and then get over the fence before too many people were up and around. Hopefully Drew would be around to give me a ride, but I had to leave time to walk to the airport, just in case.

I could do this. I would do this. I glanced down to make sure no one was walking through the quad below. I stepped up onto the brick banister that ran around the balcony. It hadn't looked that high up when I'd been standing next to it, but being an extra three feet up suddenly made it seem a lot higher. I wouldn't have been surprised to see a plane shoot past my ear. I reached up and grabbed the branch. I gave it a shake to make sure it wasn't rotted, before I let my weight hang on it. I also figured this would flush out any rabid squirrels. All I needed was some rodent chewing on my fingers. With the way this breakout plan was going, I wouldn't have been even remotely surprised if one did. The branch seemed stable, and no squirrels came rushing out in attack mode. I took another quick look down to make sure no one was around, and then when I saw it was clear, I took a step off the banister.

The branch held. My legs swung free and I decided not to look down again. My hands shuffled along the branch. I felt a splinter run into my pinky finger. I hummed the theme song that went with the army commercials and pictured myself in camo being all I could be. My hands shuffled a few more feet, and then my feet, found the branch beneath me. Almost there. I took a step onto the branch, bringing me closer to the trunk.

Then my foot slipped on an icy patch on the branch and slipped off. The sudden shift of weight put me way off balance. I felt my fingers slide on the branch above me. There was a beat when I convinced myself it would never happen, and then I fell. I felt the branches break beneath me as I plummeted toward the ground.

Then it went dark.

chapter twenty-eight

My eyes struggled to open. Everything hurt, even my eyelashes. I stared up at a white ceiling. My mouth tasted funny, like I had been sucking on rusted nails. My tongue seemed to be stuck to the roof of my mouth. I couldn't tell where I was. I turned my head to the side. It felt as if the entire world slid off the axis and my stomach flopped over. I closed my eyes quickly, trying to get my sense of balance back. My eyes opened again, and I saw there was an IV pole. I followed the plastic tubing down from the pole to where it was connected to my arm.

IV. White. Hospital. I had to be in a hospital. Then the fall from the tree came rushing back to my memory. I'd fallen. There was a bright flash of pain in my leg. I glanced down. There was a giant cast that went from above my knee all the way down, with just my toes peeking out the end. Looked like the fall hadn't ended well.

"Hail?"

I turned my head slowly to the other side. Kelsie was sitting in a chair next to the bed. Her eyes were red and her face splotchy. She'd been crying.

"Can you hear me?" she asked, her voice shaking.

I tried to nod, but moving my head up and down made the sickening bed spins start again, so I stopped.

"Oh my god. I'm so glad you're awake." Kelsie grabbed my hand.

"Is there anything to drink?" I asked, my voice coming out raspy.

Kelsie leapt into action. She poured a glass of water from the pitcher on the rolling table next to the bed and jabbed the bendy straw into the glass. She held it out, and I took a sip. The cool water tasted better than anything I could imagine. I took another sip, but Kelsie pulled the glass away before I could finish.

"Careful. Not too much. Do you want me to get your dad? He's downstairs talking to one of the doctors."

"My dad's here?" My brain tried to find something to hold on to that made sense. I'd been trying to get my passport so I could see my dad in Chicago. What was he doing in Vermont?

"The hospital called him right away. He flew in last night. He's super-worried about you."

"Last night? How long have I been out?"

"A day. The doctors said it was a concussion. There have been a few other times when you seemed to come around, but you didn't make much sense. Mostly just mumbling and stuff."

"Huh." I closed my eyes. My stomach was starting to feel better. At least I didn't feel quite so much like I was going to throw up at any moment.

"Hail, you have to know I am *so* sorry. I have never been so sorry in my whole life." Kelsie started crying again.

I patted her hand absently while I searched my memory to figure out why she was sorry. Right. She'd been seeing Tristan. Maybe it was the fall, but I couldn't remember why it had made me so upset to start with. They would be good together. This could be what they meant by having sense knocked into you. Why had I been so concerned about the relationship with Tristan? I didn't love him. "It's okay," I mumbled.

"I never thought you would do something like this. I just feel sick," Kelsie sobbed.

"Something like what?"

Kelsie stopped crying for a beat and looked at me. "Suicide," she whispered.

I tried to sit up, and then froze when every muscle in my body screamed. "Suicide? I fell," I explained.

"Everyone is saying you tried to kill yourself when you heard about Tristan and me."

"If I'd wanted to kill myself, I would have jumped off the top of a building, not from the second floor." I couldn't decide if I was more offended that people thought I was the kind of person who would kill myself over a boyfriend or that I was apparently too stupid to know how to do it right.

"Ms. Sullivan gave a talk at the morning assembly and said your kind of attempt can be seen as a cry for help." She sniffed. "It's like when someone takes only a few pills or does superficial cutting."

Great. It sounded like Ms. Sullivan had finally found something to keep her busy. She was most likely giddy with all the excitement I'd caused. "It wasn't a cry for anything. I was trying to get out of the administration building," I tried to explain.

"Why didn't you use the door?"

"It's a long story." I could tell that she didn't believe me. She acted suddenly fascinated by a microscopic-size chip in her fingernail polish. "It was an accident, Kels."

"Then, why did you leave a suicide note?"

"What! I didn't leave a note." Then my mind flashed to the note I had meant to keep people from coming after me when I left for Chicago. I wanted to pull the covers up over my head.

"There was a note. I saw it; someone leaked to the Web already." She slapped her hand over her mouth. I guessed she wasn't supposed to upset me further by telling me that my latest adventure had also made the tabloids.

"Can I see your phone?" I said. Kelsie opened her mouth to protest, but I held my hand out. She passed me her phone, and I did a quick search on the Internet. The story popped right up on one of the celebrity sites. I skimmed past the headline and story and read the note again, to see if it sounded as bad as I'd feared.

Please don't worry about me. I have to go away. No one is making me do this. Please don't blame anyone. This is my decision. I know my leaving will upset people. I don't want anyone to be hurt or angry, but this is something I have to do. Please try to understand.

I closed my eyes. It sounded worse than I'd imagined. I might as well have ended the note by writing *GOOD-BYE, CRUEL WORLD!* and drawing a skull or a black heart.

"It'll be okay." Kelsie patted my arm like it was a kitten.

"I jumped off the balcony because I didn't want to get caught for having broken into Winston's office. I needed my passport for identification for the plane, so I took it out of his secretary's file cabinet. My plan was to go to Chicago to see my dad. We had another fight and I wanted to see him."

"We thought you had your passport on you so your body could be identified."

"I was jumping from the second story, not into a farm combine. I would have been identifiable."

"Unless you landed on your face," Kelsie pointed out.

Our eyes met, and we started to giggle. "Good point. Never land on the face."

"Well, I suppose the silver lining is that you don't have to travel to Chicago. Your dad's here. Not to mention you don't have to take a cheap discount airline. If you're going to travel, go first class, or don't bother going."

"Whew. Saved from the horrors of low-cost coach travel. All I had to do was break my leg and knock myself out." I laughed again.

"I am sorry about Tristan, you know," Kelsie said. "I was going to tell you a thousand different times, but then I never could bring myself to do it. At first I excused it by telling myself nothing was happening. We were just flirting, joking around. Then when it was more, I didn't know how to stop."

"Do you love him?" I asked.

Kelsie's eyes filled back up with tears. "I know I shouldn't, but I think I always have."

"It's okay. You'll be good for him. He always needed someone who would keep him more on his toes."

"He still cares for you."

"I care for him, too. I never stopped. We were good together, just not meant to be a couple forever. I think both of us stayed because we loved how comfortable it felt. Stability is a good thing, but not everything."

"You still must have been mad that I didn't tell you. You shouldn't have heard it from someone else."

"I wasn't exactly making myself easy to talk to," I admitted.

"You pulled away from everyone. Not just Tristan, everyone. It was like you put yourself in exile. It was like you didn't want to be our friend anymore."

"I know. At first I was sure it was everyone else, but I think you're right. I did exile myself. Maybe I needed the space to figure things out, figure me out."

"Did you?"

"Nope." We laughed. "But I'm making headway. At least I'm doing something about it instead of waiting for someone else to figure it out for me. I'm not sure where life is going to take me, especially when Dean Winston figures out I broke into his office and wasn't suicidal. But at least now I feel like I'm going somewhere," I said.

"Can I come with you?" Kelsie's voice was serious.

"Can't imagine going anywhere without my best friend," I said.

Kelsie threw her arms around me. "As long as you know that if I'm going, we're going first class."

chapter twenty-nine

After Kelsie left, I closed my eyes, and I must have fallen asleep, because when I opened them again, the room was dimmer, the late afternoon light turning silver gray. I saw a figure standing in the doorway, but with the bright light from the hall, I couldn't make out who it was.

"Dad?" I asked.

"He just left. He went down to the cafeteria to get something to eat. Watching you sleep can wear a man out." Drew stepped into the room.

"I was just dozing." I ran my fingers through my hair, trying to make it look decent, or at least not horrid. I wiped my tongue over my teeth. They felt a bit furry. No one had brushed them for me while I was out cold. My breath probably smelled like dirty gym socks.

"Dozing, huh? You always snore like a truck driver when you doze?"

"I wasn't snoring," I insisted.

"Oh, I'm sorry. You weren't snoring. You were simply choking to death on a live ferret."

I pressed my lips together to keep from laughing. Drew pulled the chair closer to the bed and sat. Great. He was close enough now to see the smell waves coming out of my mouth.

"Just so you know, typically, bungee jumping works best when you wear the bungee part." Drew motioned to my leg. "How are you feeling?"

"A bit rough. You know what they say. The fall went fine right up until the very end." I picked at a loose thread on the blanket. "About the last time we were together . . ."

"You want to apologize."

I met his eyes, surprised he knew what I was going to say.

"The thought of not having a chance to kiss me again made you throw yourself off a roof. I should be more careful. I know the effect I can have on women."

I threw one of my pillows at him, then winced from the effort. He caught it before it even came close to his face.

"I was going to apologize for hitting you. There was no excuse for that. And I didn't throw myself off the roof—for you or anyone else." I had the feeling I was going to be explaining this to people over and over for weeks. I paused, trying to find the words to explain to Drew how I felt. I couldn't explain it to myself, so I wasn't sure how to tell him.

"I know you didn't try to kill yourself. You're crazy, but not that kind of crazy. Besides, now that you've seen the glory of Denny's, you've got too much to live for."

"The stuffed French toast was pretty amazing."

Drew poured a glass of water. "I brought you some more ice while you were out." He held the glass so I could have a drink. "I figured you'd be thirsty. I've been knocked out a few times in hockey. I always wanted a giant glass of water when I came around."

"Thanks. It was nice you came."

"I keep telling you, I'm a nice guy." Drew looked around to make sure we were still alone. "In addition to checking on you, I came to tell you something."

"Sounds very top secret."

"I know who's leaking all the stories to the tabloids."

I sat up, ignoring the flash of pain. "Who?"

"Mandy Gallaway."

My mouth fell open. "Why would she sell stories to the press? She hates the tabloids. And it's not like she needs the money."

"You might be wrong about that. I asked around. Turns out her grandfather controls the purse strings and he thinks some of her shenanigans make the family look tacky. Sounds like he's limiting her allowance. Now, she still is getting more money than the average family of four, but with her tastes she's going to need any extra coin she can get her hands on."

"Did you actually just use the term 'shenanigans'? Are you channeling your inner eighty-year-old?"

"I think you're focusing on the wrong thing again."

"Are you sure that it's her?"

"I'm sure. She's ticked off a lot of people on staff. It's one thing if she wants to do her own thing, but letting that security guard take the heat was low. The guard was put on unpaid suspension for two weeks. The maid who cleans her room saw the leaked photo of Mandy on her laptop and did some poking around. Mandy's doing it under a fake name, of course, but she's definitely the leak."

"Should we tell the police?" I asked. I enjoyed the image of the cops coming and taking Mandy down, maybe handcuffing her in the middle of the morning assembly, or perhaps they could set the police dogs loose on her.

"Selling out your friends isn't a crime, just disgusting. The police aren't going to do anything."

"She's not my friend."

Drew leaned back. "That's true."

"What should I do, then?"

"Up to you, but if she blames anything else on the staff, I'm going to make sure it comes out." Drew shuffled his feet. "I should go, let you get some sleep."

"No," I said quickly. "I mean, I'm not tired. You could hang out if you want."

Drew smiled. "Looks like the only thing you needed to enjoy my company was a hit on the head."

"That's not true." I could feel my face flushing.

"It's okay. I'm teasing you. Don't worry about what happened before. I was the one out of line. I shouldn't have kissed you like that. We'll just pretend it never happened. Friends?"

I opened my mouth to tell him I didn't want to be his friend. What I wanted was for him to kiss me again. Preferably when I was out of the hospital and had a shower.

"Hey, there."

Both Drew and I whirled to face the door. My dad was standing there, holding a take-out container of Baskin-Robbins ice cream. I was willing to bet it was mint chocolate chip, my favorite. As he came into the room I saw he hadn't shaved, and his shirt was missing a button.

Drew stood up. "Hello, Mr. Kendrick. She's awake now. I think her snoring finally woke even her up."

My dad smiled.

"I wasn't snoring," I repeated.

Drew and my dad shook hands, ignoring my protests.

"Thanks for keeping an eye on her while I ran out. Would you like some ice cream?" My dad asked Drew, holding up the bag. I hoped he had another flavor in there, because I wasn't planning on sharing my pint.

"I should be going. Besides, I'm sure you'll want a chance to catch up." Drew grabbed his jacket by the door.

There was still a lot I wanted to talk about with Drew, but I didn't want to have that conversation in front of my dad. If I hadn't been hooked to an IV, with my leg in plaster, I would have followed Drew out into the hall.

"See you soon?" I asked, hoping I didn't sound too needy.

"I'm like gum under a desk," Drew said. "Next to impossible to get rid of."

chapter thirty

My dad bustled around finding spoons and bowls for the ice cream, making the entire process seem more complicated than pulling together an entire Thanksgiving dinner for a family of twenty. He was constantly in motion, a blur in the room. A blur who kept avoiding my eyes. The entire time he was getting things ready, he kept up a nonstop stream of chatter. He told me about how the airline had lost his luggage and he'd had to buy a sweatshirt from the hospital gift shop, and how the ice-cream store had been out of butter pecan, so it wasn't really thirty-one flavors, only thirty.

"Dad?" I didn't say anything else until he finally stopped moving and looked at me. "I wasn't trying to kill myself."

His face turned gray, and his eyes shifted away. "Of course not. I never thought that."

I could see he had thought it, that he was still thinking it. "I was upset about our conversation," I said, trying to explain what had happened.

My dad turned back to dishing out the ice cream. "We don't need to talk about that now. I thought maybe when they spring you from here we could take a small vacation. Maybe go someplace warm."

"I don't want to go on vacation."

"If this is about Linda, then you don't need to worry, she won't be coming." He passed me a wad of napkins. "She and I are going to take a break."

"You broke up with her?" Great. Not only was I ruining my own love life, but now I had managed to ruin my dad's, too. "I didn't want that."

My dad patted my leg. "It's nothing you need to worry about. All you need to focus on is getting better. A vacation will do us both some good."

"I can't go on vacation. I've got school." I could feel my frustration growing.

"You let me take care of school. I'll talk to your teachers and we'll work something out. They can give you some projects to work on long-distance."

"I don't want you to take care of it." My hands were balled into fists at my side.

His face fell. I could see he was hurt. "Okay. If you don't want to go anyplace, we don't have to." He stared at his bowl of ice cream, then perked up with a smile. "Heck, you're right. Who wants to deal with airlines and traveler's tummy? We could go up to your grandparents'. We can rent a bunch of movies and hunker down, maybe play some board games. Remember how you used to kick my butt at Monopoly? I bet if we ask nice, we can even get your grandma to make her famous spaghetti and meatballs."

"I don't want to go to grandma's, either. What I want is for you to listen to me! For once don't try to solve the problem or shove it out of the way. Just listen!" I yelled.

My dad went silent, his face still for the first time. A nurse peeked in to see what the fuss was about, but backed out when she saw my dad. "I listen to you, Hailey," he said.

"No, you don't. You hear what you want to hear, or you end any conversation you don't find comfortable."

He rubbed the palms of his hands on his pants. "I should have told you about Linda. I realize now how wrong I was about that. I didn't want you to think I was being disrespectful to your mom."

I flopped back down onto the pillow. "This isn't about Linda. And it isn't about Mom, either. It's about us."

"What about us?"

"Just that. There is no us anymore. I don't even know if you like me."

My dad grabbed my hand. "Of course I like you. I love you. I love you more than anything else in my life."

"Then, why is it you never want to be around me? First it was school, but then it was all the time. You're always too busy. There's always a good reason why you have to run off. Then you changed our summer plans. You say you love me, but you don't even know me anymore."

"That's not true, Hailey." He ran his hands through his hair. "I get distracted with work, but I've never taken my focus off of you."

"Really? What's my favorite subject?"

"You like science." He looked relieved, as if I had asked him an easy question.

"It's history. I act like it's science because you like science. I figured it would give us something to talk about. I'm not even sure I want to major in it anymore."

"But you get straight A's in science." He sounded confused.

"I don't care!" I used my ice-cream spoon to point at the door. "Who was the guy that was here?"

"Drew?" My dad looked at the door as if he were hoping Drew would reappear and provide some answers. "I assume he's one of your friends from school. Isn't he the one dating your friend Kelsie?"

"Kelsie is dating my boyfriend, Tristan. Drew works the janitorial crew at Evesham."

"A janitor?"

I could see my dad's brain spinning, trying to figure out why a school janitor had shown up at the hospital to visit me. "Remember how Dean Winston assigned me to a cleaning crew as part of my punishment? That's how I met Drew. He's going to Yale."

His eyebrows drew together as he tried to sort out what

direction the conversation was going in. "He got a janitor job at Yale?"

"No. He got accepted there," I said. "He's going to major in English."

"Oh. That's good."

"I think I like him."

My dad nodded very seriously. "That's good too. He seems like a very nice young man."

"Except I blew it. He kissed me and I slapped him, and now he doesn't want to be with me. All he wants is to be friends." I grabbed my dad's hand before he could say anything. "Please don't tell me how you don't know what to tell me and that mom is the one who would have handled this kind of boy-girl stuff. Mom is gone. I wish she wasn't, but she is. You're the only parent I've got left."

My dad got up and moved so he could sit on the bed next to me. He had tears in his eyes. "I'm sorry, Hailey. I let you down. I let your mom down. If she could see what a mess I've made of things, she'd be so disappointed."

"I think she'd be pretty ticked at me, too," I said.

"We'd both be grounded."

"Remember how when she was really mad she would give herself a time-out?" I said.

My dad laughed. "She used to crawl back into bed with a book. She said life would be better if everyone took a time-out when they needed one."

"I miss her." My eyes spilled over. With all the crying I'd been doing lately, I was going to have to increase my water intake or run the risk of dehydration.

"I miss her too. She was a hell of a woman. You remind me of her."

I wiped my eyes. "How?"

"Your mom was persistent. She used to say it didn't matter if she won the race but that she kept going even when she fell down. She wasn't a quitter. That was one of the reasons I was crazy about her. I was always worried about what other people thought of me. I didn't ever want to look stupid. Your mom didn't worry so much about other people. She kept her focus on not letting herself down. I can tell you've got that same focus. You're going to go far. She'd be the first person cheering you on."

I smiled. I had a memory of her being at one of my school recitals in elementary school. She'd been the only parent giving a standing ovation. Maybe that's how you know someone loves you; they make you want to be a better person by believing in your effort, not just your accomplishments.

My dad handed me my bowl of ice cream. "Okay, let's get back to the issue. If you like Drew, why did you hit him when he kissed you? Was it that bad of a kiss?"

I laughed. My leg was broken, I had a concussion, and I was most likely in the largest amount of trouble I'd ever been in at school, and suddenly it felt like things had never been better.

chapter thirty-one

I shifted in the wheelchair. I had wanted to walk out on my crutches, but the hospital had some sort of policy against it. You would think they would want people to walk out. It would make it look like people got better in the hospital, but no. I was parked in the lobby waiting for my ride.

I'd sent my dad home yesterday. He'd offered to be the one to take me back to school, but I knew he needed to get back to work. The past three days we'd talked like we hadn't in years. We'd made plans for spring break. We were going to go down to North Carolina, just the two of us, but on the way back my dad was going to arrange for me to meet Linda. He'd offered to cancel his summer plans in London, but suddenly it didn't seem as important as it had earlier. We'd talked about how London was full of history and maybe I'd spend at least part of my summer with him over there. I didn't know what else I would do with my summer, but I was okay with that.

Finally the car pulled up to the hospital doorway. The nurse who was pushing my chair through the doors let out a gasp when she saw who it was. She was so focused on him, there was the very real chance she would have let me roll into oncoming traffic.

Tristan opened the passenger door of his car. "Your chariot awaits," he said, bending low.

"My chariot is late," I pointed out.

"Not just late, fashionably late." Tristan put his hand on my back as I crutched my way into his car. "Watch the ice. You don't want to end up back in there five minutes after getting out."

Tristan turned on his charm for the nurse as he gathered up my bags and took the discharge papers. If she asked him for an autograph, I was going to push her down with one of my crutches. He climbed in and waved to the crowd that was gathering near the door. I was starting to feel like we were in a parade. Tristan jacked up the heat in the car before taking off. We drove in silence out of town toward school.

"Thanks for picking me up," I said.

"What are friends for?" Tristan glanced over and smiled. "Kelsie wanted to come too, but Dean Winston wouldn't let both of us leave campus. She's looking forward to seeing you. I should warn you, I think she's planning some sort of welcome back party."

"I'm not sure Winston's going to approve a party." My dad had met with Dean Winston after my accident. I was still on restriction for the next three months, and I'd been moved to working in the library so I could still help pay for the statue as long as I was in a cast, but everyone else was off restriction. My dad had hinted that Dean Winston's actions had been designed to ostracize me and no doubt had led to the amount of stress I was under. Winston was probably worried that we would sue him for emotional distress that resulted in me throwing myself off the administration building. My dad had clarified that I'd been after my passport and not trying to do myself in, but clearly my decision-making had been impacted by all the stress. I was willing to bet Dean Winston couldn't wait for spring to come and for me to graduate. However, he had decided to allow me back at school, and there wasn't going to be anything on my permanent record either.

"It won't be a wild party. No strippers or Jell-O wrestling. More of a friends-welcoming-a-friend-home party. How can he have a problem with that? If it makes you feel better, we can say the party is a going away party for Mandy." He glanced over quickly to see my reaction.

"She's leaving?"

"She may have already left. She wasn't around this morning. The official story is that she wants to move back to New York to be closer to her half sister."

"I didn't think she spoke to her sister."

Tristan shrugged. "I'm not sure she's even met her half sister before. Her mom has been married more often than most people change their underwear. I don't think anyone buys the story, but if it makes her feel better about things, it's no skin off my nose."

In the hospital I'd debated how to handle the Mandy situation. Drew had been right; it wasn't illegal, so the police wouldn't care. I could have turned her in to Dean Winston, but I wasn't interested in helping Winston out in any way. I could have confronted her myself, but ending up in a catfight with her didn't seem like a good plan. She struck me as the kind who would fight dirty. She was probably a hair puller. Then I'd end up with a bald spot in addition to the cast on my leg.

In the end I went to the person who had the most experience with the tabloids, Tristan. He'd come to the hospital, and we'd had a chance to talk. Being able to focus on the situation with Mandy let us get over what was between us. Seeing him reminded me how much I liked him. I didn't love him, but I did want him in my life. If he was going to be dating my best friend, there had to be a way for us to be friends.

Tristan and I discussed the idea of leaking our own story to the tabloids that would out what Mandy had done. The public would eat up the idea that she was so desperate for attention that she'd placed her own stories in the news. I could picture the headline PAY ATTENTION TO ME! in a giant font smeared across a picture of Mandy running from a pack of photographers. While that was an appealing image, I didn't like stooping to her level, and Tristan wasn't keen to help the tabloids sell any magazines.

In the end Tristan met with Mandy. He let her know we knew what she had done, and if a single story about anyone on campus came out, we would make sure stories about her flooded the press, and they wouldn't be stories she wanted. Tristan said that she had started off by crying, but had ended up yelling that everyone was jealous of her fame and then storming out. When he'd told me that, I'd felt sick. I'd hoped the whole situation would be resolved, but it seemed like Mandy might make things worse.

What neither Mandy or I had counted on was the reaction of everyone else at Evesham. The night after Tristan met with Mandy, we filled in Kelsie and Joel, and word started to spread that Mandy was the leak. People stopped speaking to her. They shunned her. Tristan said it was like people thought she had leprosy or a really nasty STD. Apparently it was all too much for her. I shouldn't have been surprised. Mandy didn't mind if people liked her or loathed her, but she couldn't stand to be ignored.

"There's something else I should tell you before we get back to school," Tristan said. "Joel and I talked last night."

"Oh? What about?" I fidgeted in the seat, avoiding Tristan's eyes. The last thing I needed to do was spill my guts, only to discover they had been talking about baseball statistics.

"He told me what happened that night, that he was the one you were kissing."

So much for hoping it had been a random sports discussion. "I can explain . . ."

"You don't need to explain. Joel told me he was the one who kissed you and that you kept it a secret to protect him. He would have lost his scholarship if you'd told. Not that any of that excuses the fact that he's my best friend and he kissed my girl and then lied to me about it."

"Are you mad at him?"

"We're guys. I punched him, he hit me back, and then everything was fine. We went out for ice cream after."

I rolled my eyes. Men.

"I can't blame the guy for wanting to kiss you," Tristan said.

"I never wanted you to get hurt," I said.

"I know." Tristan paused, chewing on his lower lip. "If you guys want to go out, date or whatever, that would be okay with me."

I touched his shoulder. "I like Joel. He's always been one of my closest friends, but that almost works against us. It's almost too comfortable. There's no spark." I shrugged. I didn't know how to explain it. Logically Joel would make a great boyfriend, but sometimes the heart isn't logical. "I don't think he and I are meant to be, but I still appreciate you saying it."

"Feel good to be back?" Tristan asked as we pulled through the school gates.

I watched the line of trees that lined the driveway march past until we came into the quad. I looked up at the library, the gray stones covered in ivy. To my left were the dorm buildings. From the outside I could spot the windows for my different rooms over the years. I realized how well I knew this place. I knew how the second sink on the right in the bathroom never had really hot water. I knew the best place to sit in the library, and how the toffee chocolate chip cookies in the cafeteria were worth every calorie. I knew which stairs creaked and how if you wanted extra towels, you could bribe the maids by bringing them Starbucks from town. I hadn't wanted to go to Evesham, but in its own way it had become home.

"I can't believe I'm going to say this, but I think I'll miss this place after graduation."

"You know what they say: Loyalty, Duty, and Honor."

"That saying used to drive me nuts."

"I guessed that, after you went all whack job on the Tin Man."

I shoved Tristan in the shoulder. "I feel bad about that now. I think I was missing the whole point. It's not about blind loyalty and doing what you're told. It's about being loyal to yourself and those you respect, and about doing what you have to do, even when you're afraid."

"For graduation maybe all of us should get tattoos with the logo on it." Tristan pointed to his bicep. "Right here. That way we'll never forget our time at Evesham."

"Or each other."

"I got to tell you, you're not the kind of person that is easy to forget. Besides, we're all going to stay in touch. There isn't going to be a chance to forget."

chapter thirty-two

W e were late. The morning assembly had already begun. The drama teacher was at the lectern talking about a field trip to New York to see some productions. Parents would have to pay the costs, but those who went and wrote a paper had a chance to earn some extra art credits. Dean Winston's eyes narrowed when he saw Tristan and me slip in the back. It was hard to be subtle, since I was on crutches. Tiptoeing in wasn't an option. Then there was the fact that Kelsie was waving at us like we'd been separated for years instead of a couple of days. She slid over on the bench to make room for me. Tristan made sure I made it safely to the row, and he made a funny face at Kelsie. She started giggling. At this point everyone was looking at us; even the drama teacher had stopped talking. From the back I could see the vein in Winston's forehead starting to throb.

I sat down as fast as I could and let my cast stretch out into the aisle. Joel had saved Tristan a seat a few rows ahead on the guys' side. Joel turned around and smiled. He mouthed the words "Welcome back" before turning back around.

The drama teacher picked up where she'd left off. The school would book rooms at the Library Hotel for three nights. I could hear a few people whispering. Weekends in New York were always popular. I wondered if the drama teacher believed that everyone who signed up was really interested in the plays. She must have thought Evesham was full of theater geeks.

Dean Winston got up as soon as she sat down. "For those of you considering the trip, be aware you'll be expected to sign the code of conduct agreement before you go. This means you will be held to the expectations of an Evesham student." His eyes swept the room as if he could tell already that people were planning to sneak out of the hotel and try to get into the clubs. "Evesham students should always demonstrate the highest standards of quality."

Kelsie poked me in the side with her elbow, and I pressed my mouth down to avoid giggling. I went to poke her back and accidentally hit my crutch, which fell into the aisle with a loud clang. Kelsie snorted, and I bit my lip to stop smiling.

Dean Winston stopped mid-word and froze me in place with his stare. "Is there something you find funny about this, Ms. Kendrick?"

Everyone turned around to look at me. "No, sir." I made a vague gesture with my hand to the crutch. "It just fell."

"Ms. Kendrick, will you please step forward?"

"Oh, shit," Kelsie whispered under her breath.

I picked up my fallen crutch and went up the aisle until I was standing just in front of the lectern.

"This school is founded on principles, Ms. Kendrick."

"Yes, sir." I could feel everyone's eyes on me. My face was burning hot.

"You've been doing some research on the history of the school, haven't you?"

"Yes, sir."

"Then, perhaps you'd like to share with the group what you've learned thus far about the principles that are the cornerstones of this institution?"

The last thing I wanted to do was share, but I had the sense that he wasn't really asking it as a question. He twirled his finger, indicating that I should turn around to face the audience.

I turned to face everyone and cleared my throat. "Evesham is named after one of the two main battles in thirteenth-century England. It was part of the Barons' War. The school's founder, Simon Kenilworth, started the school in 1911 with the idea that it would provide an opportunity for privileged young men to complete their education, with a focus on also developing their character. He'd attended boarding school in England and felt that there should be a school of equal caliber here in the United States. The school started admitting girls in the 1960s."

"Thank God," someone in the crowd said. Winston searched the crowd to see if he could tell where the comment had come from.

"And do you believe in the principles this school was founded upon?" Winston asked me.

"Yes and no," I answered honestly.

Winston's nostrils flared in annoyance.

"I've come to realize that the school is only a collection of buildings. History teaches us that nothing is permanent, but I do believe in this place, if by 'school' you mean the people who have gone here."

"If this school is so important to you, Ms. Kendrick, perhaps now you would be willing to share the name of who you were with the night you destroyed the statue that represents the principles you say you hold so dear."

I opened my mouth to tell him again that I wasn't going to tell. Not now, not even if he dragged me up in front of a million assemblies.

"I was the one with her," a voice called out.

I looked up. Drew was standing in the back. He walked down the center of the aisle until he was standing by my side.

"I was with Hailey that night. It was my idea to destroy the statue," he said.

"I hope you realize this means you're fired," Dean Winston said.

"What are you doing?" I whispered to Drew.

"It doesn't matter that I wasn't there. I wish I had been," Drew whispered back. He smiled, and I felt my heart turn over. "I'd choose to be with you anytime, anywhere." He squeezed my hand, and we turned to face Winston together.

"It wasn't him. I was the one with Hailey!" Joel yelled out.

Joel was standing up. I could tell he wanted to throw up, he was so scared, but he was standing up for me.

"Actually, it was me," Kelsie called out, and she stood as well. She gave me a thumbs-up.

"Nope, it was me," Tristan said as he stood.

I felt my eyes start to fill up. There were squeaks and rustles as more and more people started to stand in the hall.

"It was me."

"I was there."

"I was with Hailey."

"I did it."

Soon more than half of the student body was standing up. Everyone from my old crowd was standing, and even a bunch of people that I didn't know that well.

Dean Winston looked like he was ready to have a stroke. His entire head had gone red, and the vein in his forehead was thumping like it was laying down a club beat.

"Everyone return to their seats. Right now," he yelled. He pointed at me. "Return to your place, Ms. Kendrick."

Drew walked by my side until I got back to my seat. I smiled at everyone as I walked past. They might have been mad at me, but they'd never abandoned me. If it wouldn't have gotten me into more trouble, I would have stopped to hug each and every person as I went by.

"You can leave now," Dean Winston directed Drew.

Drew winked at me. "I'll catch up with you later." He walked out of the assembly with his head held high. A few people, many of them girls, turned to watch him leave.

"Oh, now, he's dreamy," Kelsie whispered. "You should hang on to him."

"I plan to," I whispered back.

chapter thirty-three

Winston ended the assembly just a few minutes later. He was deflated like a helium balloon the morning after a birthday party. There was a sense in the room that things had changed. Or maybe it just felt that way to me.

Instead of running to class when the assembly was over, almost everyone stopped to tell me how glad they were to see me back. Tristan had his arm draped over Kelsie's shoulders, and she was busy inviting everyone to the party she was planning.

"Oh! Maybe we should do costumes! We could make it a theme party, dress up like your favorite past Evesham student," Kelsie said, her eyes sparkling. "Or people could just pick a time period they like, anytime since the school started." She never met an event that wasn't made better by dressing up.

"I bet my parents could snag some great 1920s costumes," Tristan suggested.

"I love those flapper outfits!" Kelsie squealed. A few of the girls surrounding us started to buzz with ideas for food and decorations. It was rapidly changing from a small welcome back party to an A-list event.

Joel touched my elbow softly. "I'm sorry," he said, so quietly that only I could hear him.

"Me too."

"I should have owned up to Tristan long ago. I never should have left you hanging. I didn't exactly come across as a real knight in shining armor."

"You stood up for me when it mattered. And you told Tristan when you didn't have to. Besides, I think, since I tried to behead one, I'm not all that keen on shining armor types anyway."

"Even without the armor, I'm guessing there isn't going to be a you and me, is there?" Joel asked.

I shook my head. "Someone's going to be lucky to get you, though."

We hugged. "There will always be room for you to visit at the White House," Joel said.

"Visit? What happened to my ambassadorship?"

Joel snapped his fingers. "Right, I almost forgot. You wanted someplace like the Arctic, right?"

I pleaded that I had to go, leaving everyone else to plan the party. It was going to take me time to get across campus to class with my crutches, and I wanted to go back to my room first to pick up my things. Kelsie offered to come with me, but I waved her off. When I stepped outside, the sun was shining. There were still splotches of snow around, but there were also shoots of green popping up from the mud. Spring was coming.

I'd hoped Drew would still be around, but I didn't see him anywhere. I started heading toward the dorms. A horn beeped, and I turned to see Drew sitting in his truck parked in the lot. I smiled and headed over. He got out to meet me halfway.

"You've got some nice friends there, Prima Donna."

"I do."

"I'm glad things are working out."

"Yeah, about that. Some things haven't worked out." I took a deep breath and reminded myself, no guts, no glory. "I need to tell you something. I don't want to be friends with you."

Drew blinked. "Sort of wish you had said something before I opened my big mouth to Winston and lost my job."

This wasn't going the way I'd expected. I tried to figure out how to explain everything. That I liked him. I wanted to be with him. I'd only slapped him because I hadn't been expecting the kiss. I'd been confused, but I wasn't confused anymore. I knew what I wanted. My brain scrambled for the words that would make all of this make sense and leave Drew with no choice but to throw his arms around me, but I couldn't think of a thing.

I dropped one crutch and grabbed Drew by the shirt and yanked him close and kissed him. The entire world shrunk down to the point where our mouths met. I felt off balance, and not just because I had only one good leg. The air outside was cool, but I wasn't remotely cold. I felt like my entire body was thawing out. The kiss lasted forever, but eventually we both pulled back. Drew was quiet.

"Aren't you going to say anything?" I asked. He remained silent, so I kept going before I could lose my nerve. "I like you. I was afraid to say anything, but something you told me stuck with me. How being brave is about being scared but doing it anyway. That's why I kissed you. You may not want to be with me anymore, and I can understand that. I'm high maintenance, and it apparently takes me a long time to sort out what I want. Sometimes I come across as stuck-up, but it's more because I only know my own world. I'm bad about trying new things unless someone pushes me. I'm a lousy cleaner."

Drew put his finger over my mouth. "You also talk too much." He leaned in and kissed me again. He pulled back and cupped my face in his hand. "It also took you long enough to figure this out."

"You're saying you knew I liked you?"

"Oh, yeah. Written all over your face. I figured you just needed to get to the answer on your own."

"Is that right?"

"Yep. You were crazy about me from the start. You needed some shaking up, and I was just the guy to do it."

"You got me. As soon as I saw your prowess with the floor buffer, I was yours."

"Chicks dig men with mechanical skills. Evolutionary."

I rolled my eyes. "I'll have you know I don't need anyone to buff my floors."

"Very true. That's one of the things I like about you." Drew smiled. "I always went for the independent type. That, and I find plaid skirts and knee-highs hot."

The bell tower chimed the hour. A few Evesham students started to rush for class.

"I have to go."

"I know. You better buckle down. If I'm going to show you all the dive bars that offer karaoke around Yale, you're going to have to do your part and keep your grades up so you get in."

I took a few steps toward the dorm, but then turned back. Drew was still standing by the truck. It reminded me of how my mom would always wait to make sure I got inside safe when she dropped me off someplace. An idea came into my head.

"Hey!" I called out to him. "You want to come to a party later? My friends are throwing a thing, and I want you to meet them."

"Sure. Count me in."

"By the way, you're going to have to wear a costume."

Drew's eyebrows pulled together. "Dress up? Like what? I don't know—"

"What's the matter? Are you afraid?" I held my arms out, using my crutches to wave around the quad. "You gotta live life, suck the marrow from its bones!"

Drew laughed. I headed back toward the dorms. It was going to be a busy day, and I didn't want to miss a moment of it.

I didn't plan to miss another moment of the rest of my life.

acknowledgments

A writer without a reader is a lonely thing, so the first thank-you goes to you for reading this book. With so many good books and not nearly enough time to read them all, I appreciate your taking the time with mine. I want to say a particular thank-you to two of my teen readers, Valentina Misas and Abi Coale. Not only did they read my books and write to tell me they liked them, they spread the word to all their friends on Facebook and in school hallways. I couldn't ask for a better promotion team. I think you guys are awesome. To everyone else who wrote to tell me they liked my books—thanks. You made my day, sometimes the entire week.

I am so fortunate to have a great team behind each of my books. My agent, Rachel Vater, picked me out of the slush pile and has cheered me on since. The entire team at Simon Pulse is fantastic. Thanks to Cara Petrus (cover design goddess), Annette Pollert, Anna McKean, Amy Jacobson, and Emilia Rhodes. Special thanks to my editor, Anica Mrose Rissi, who is not only an editorial genius, but shares my love of shoes and dogs. Thanks for all your guidance, insight, and willingness to put up with me and my tendency to use Canadian spelling and stick *u*'s into every other word. I hope I can write books with this team for years to come.

My friends and family continue to support my dream of being a writer and are just darn fun to have around. Big thanks to Avita Sharma, Shannon Smith, Jamie Hillegonds, Serena Robar, Alison Pritchard, Laura Sullivan, Shanna Mahin, Joelle Anthony, Brooke Chapman, Joanne Levy, Carol Mason, Robyn Harding, Lynn Crymble, Jeanette Caul, and Melissa Mills.

I couldn't do any of this without my husband, Bob, who not only provides technical support, cooks meals as needed, and is never jealous of my legions of imaginary friends, but can also always make me laugh. This journey wouldn't be nearly as much fun without you. To my dogs, stop chewing my shoes.

getting revenge on lauren wood

chapter one

L ast night I dreamed I dissected Lauren Wood in Earth Sciences class. She was wearing her blue and white cheerleader outfit, the pleated skirt fanned out and the sweater cut right down the middle. She lay there, unmoving, staring straight up at the ceiling tiles. She was annoyed. I could tell from the way her jaw thrust forward and her lips pressed together in a thin line. I opened up her chest, peeling her ribs back like a half-opened Christmas present, and the entire class leaned in to get a good look.

"As I suspected," I declared, "no heart." I pointed with my scalpel to the chest cavity, where nothing but a black lump of coal squatted in the lipstick-red center. The class leaned back with a sigh, equally appalled and fascinated. The mysterious inner workings of Lauren Wood exposed for all to see.

"Earth to Helen."

My Earth Sciences teacher, Mr. Porto, was staring at me,

waiting for an answer. Someone behind me snickered. I hadn't heard the question. I had been reliving my dream from last night and must have spaced out. I looked at my desk in case the answer was there, but the only thing on my page was a doodle of an anatomically correct heart. I didn't think Mr. Porto would be impressed with my artwork at this particular moment. I prayed for time to speed up and make the bell ring, but the clock kept on ticking one second at a time.

"People, I know vacation begins in a few days, but at the moment you still need to worry more about your final exam than about your summer plans. Can anyone else list for me the six kingdoms of the scientific classification system?" Mr. Porto asked.

He looked around the room for a victim. I slouched down in my seat and attempted to resume my train of thought and natural state of invisibility.

Before the incident there hadn't been a single moment of my life without Lauren in it. We were born in the same hospital, her the day before me. They placed us side by side in the nursery, our first sleepover. Helen Worthington right next to Lauren Wood. Even alphabetically, Lauren came before me. Lauren was in every one of my birthday photos—from age one, when she has her fist buried in my cake, to fourteen when we are both posing supermodel style for the camera, Lauren's outstretched arm covering part of my face. Looking back, I can see how she always had to be front and center.

Speaking of needing to be front and center, Carrie Edwards

must have been running for star biology student. She wa[s]
arm like she was flagging down traffic until Mr. Porto called on her.

"Eubacteria, arche bacteria, protists, fungi, plants, and animals," Carrie spouted off. She paused as if she expected applause. I drew a cartoon of a cheerleader on my paper. I gave her a giant mouth. My eyes slid back to the clock and watched it tick over the final seconds. The bell rang out, and everyone stood up together and jostled toward the door.

"Be sure to look over chapter twenty-two before the exam! I don't want to hear anyone saying they didn't know they were supposed to know the material. Consider this your last warning," Mr. Porto yelled to everyone's back. The volume in the hallway seemed even louder than usual. Everyone was excited to see the year come to an end. Next year we would be seniors, on top of the world. I slipped through the hallway by myself. A few people nodded in my direction, but nobody said anything to me.

It had been the end of the school year when it happened three years ago, only a few days after my fourteenth birthday. Sometimes I look at the photo from the party to see if I can find any clues. Lauren and I are both smiling. My smile is easy to explain—I didn't know what was coming—but Lauren would have known. She had already put pieces of her plan into action, but there isn't a sign of regret on her face. No hesitation at all, just her wide smile. I suppose she expected me to be grateful that she let me have my birthday before she brought the world crashing down around me. It was the least she could do. After all, what are friends for?

chapter two

THREE YEARS AGO—SPRING, EIGHTH GRADE

I never should have worn my jean skirt. I wasn't fat, but I was definitely pushing the chubby border. I wanted to wear the skirt because I thought it looked good, but I quickly regretted it. It was too warm for tights, and my bare thighs had been rubbing together as I walked, and they felt like they were going to blister. I shifted again on the bleacher, trying to give my legs their own breathing space.

"What's the matter with you?" Lauren asked. "Stop moving around."

"I'm hot."

"I know I am, but what are you?" she said with a smirk and a raised eyebrow.

"Ha. Lauren Wood, stand-up comic extraordinaire."

Lauren took a regal bow. It was good to see her joking around again, even if it was a lame joke. The idea of starting high school seemed to freak her out more than me. For the past few weeks she'd been in a rotten mood, and everything set her off. That week alone we'd had at least four fights, one where she didn't speak to me for a full day because she thought I was making fun of what she had brought for lunch. Lauren was a huge fan of the silent treatment when she was ticked at you. I would end up begging her to forgive me, even when I was pretty sure I hadn't done anything wrong. It had been established years ago that Lauren was the drama queen and I was the diplomat. I had pleaded with her to stop being mad about the lunch fight. I even declared I was sincerely sorry if her Oreos had suffered any emotional distress on my account. I didn't care about sacrificing my pride. Keeping my best friend happy was worth it.

"Do you see that guy over there?" Lauren yanked her head to the left. I leaned forward to look, but she rammed her bony elbow into my side.

"Don't look at him."

"How am I supposed to see him if I don't look at him?"

"I mean look, but don't *look* like you're looking. God."

I leaned forward casually and then let my eyes drift over the crowd. The gym was packed. Lincoln High was huge, with at least seven hundred students in every grade. Students came from different middle schools all across the city. Each spring the school did a welcome event for the incoming freshmen so that we could bond as a class. We had already been given a tour of the school, taken to an extracurricular "fair" so we could see all the clubs and teams we had to choose from, and subjected to a hot lunch from the cafeteria. Now we were rounding out the day with a rah-rah school spirit rally. All of this was supposed to help keep us from freaking out next fall, as if not knowing how to find our way to our lockers was the problem. If schools really wanted to reduce the anxiety level, they would distribute student handbooks with useful information like which bathroom belongs to the stoner kids, and how the sink in the biology lab always sprays water, and how under no circumstances should you order the hot lunch on the day they serve "shepherd's pie" because it's leftovers from last week with boxed mashed potatoes on top. They never tell you the useful stuff. That you have to figure out on your own.

Lauren was taking the whole thing very seriously. She scribbled down notes during the fair, grabbed handouts from each table, and ranked activities in preference from best to worse. I suspected that later her mom would help her turn it into a spreadsheet complete with social acceptability ratings.

My eyes scanned the rows of people. At first I couldn't figure out who had caught Lauren's eye, but then I saw him. Lauren usually went for the Mr. All-American type, blond, fresh off the country club look. This guy was different. He was leaning back, his elbows on the bleacher seat behind him. He was wearing what looked like a vintage T-shirt. Not some shirt from Old Navy that was meant to *look* like a cool vintage shirt, but really wasn't—his was the real thing, pale and soft from years of washing. He had red hair that was cut short in the back, but a little longer in the front. I was staring at him when he looked over and met my eyes. He gave a smile and then a small salute in my direction.

"Oh my God, he saw me." I yanked my head back and Lauren leaned forward to see the situation for herself.

"He's waving," she whispered. She looked at me and we burst out laughing. "Is he looking at me?" Lauren asked.

"I'm not looking again. You look."

"No way. You look."

I leaned forward again and risked a quick glance. He was staring over. He gave another wave. I found myself smiling and then figured what the hell, and waved back. Lauren grabbed my arm, practically snapping it off at the elbow, and yanked it back down. I leaned back so fast I nearly fell off the bench, my legs kicking out.

"What are you doing?" Lauren asked. She looked around to see if anyone had noticed that she was stuck sitting next to me, the dork.

"Well, it's not like he doesn't know we were checking him out. We can't act casual now."

"Oh God, he's coming over here. Do I look okay?" Lauren gave her teeth a quick wipe with a finger in case there was any hot lunch caught in there. I looked her up and down. She looked the way she always looked to me.

"Hey." The good-looking waver guy stood at the end of our row, his hands in his pockets. He smiled and I felt my stomach turn over slowly, but in a good way, not in a hot-lunch-gone-bad kind of way. Lauren giggled but didn't say anything.

"Hey," I answered back as it seemed one of us should say something.

"I'm Tyler."

"Helen, and this is my best friend, Lauren," I said, and Lauren gave another giggle. She was doing this thing with her eyes like she had something in them; they were fluttering up and down spastically. It must have had a hypnotizing effect because Tyler was staring at her with a sort of vacant smile on his face. With everyone identified we seemed to have run out of things to talk about. I looked down at his T-shirt and felt myself break into a smile. It was the logo for the Sundance Film Festival.

"Movie fan?" I asked.

"Yeah, you?" he asked, breaking eye contact with Lauren.

"Uh-huh. I love old movies best, all the *Bringing Up Baby* or *The Philadelphia Story* stuff."

"I'm into more current stuff. Sort of edgy. The Coen brothers . . . stuff like that."

"Curtiz was better," I countered.

"Who?" he asked.

This guy thought he was into film and he didn't know Curtiz? Puh-leeze.

"Director of *Casablanca*," I answered.

"*Casablanca*? Could you pick something more out of date?"

Lauren interrupted. We both looked over at her. She gave her hair a toss.

Tyler laughed as if she had said something profoundly amusing.

"So what kind of movies do you like?" Tyler asked Lauren.

"Romances," she said, doing the fluttery eye thing again.

"How can you say you're a film nut if you don't like *Casablanca*? That's like saying you love ice cream except for vanilla."

Both of them looked at me, but neither spoke. It seemed like everyone had agreed to act like I hadn't said anything at all.

"Nice to meet you, Lauren." Tyler smiled at her and then looked at me blankly.

"Helen," I reminded him. "Nice to meet you too." I felt my face flush. Someone at the front of the gym was testing the microphone, calling out for people to take their seats.

"I should go." Tyler leaned over and took my pencil from my hand. "Here's my number. Why don't you guys give me a call if you want to catch a movie sometime." He scribbled his number on the top of my sheet. I looked at it like I had never seen a phone number before. I certainly had never seen one that a boy had given me. I might have to frame it.

"Yeah, okay," I mumbled, my face turning bright red.

"We'll see you around," Lauren added, and he gave her a nod before heading back to his friends. I watched him walk away. I turned around to see if Lauren noticed how nicely his jeans fit, and she was staring at me with her lips tight and thin. Uh-oh.

"God, Helen, why don't you throw yourself at him?"

"What?"

"You knew I liked him, but you practically attacked him when he came over."

"You like him?"

Lauren cocked her head to the side and then looked away. "Whatever."

"I was just talking to him."

"You like movies? Why, I *love* movies. Let me bore you with all the stuff I know about stupid old movies," Lauren said in a high squeaky voice.

"Sorry." I tried to think of where I went wrong. I could tell she was annoyed with me, but it wasn't like I brought up movies out of nowhere.

"Just forget it." Lauren crossed her arms and stared out at the gym floor. "You have to cut that out."

"Cut what out?"

"Acting like a total dork all the time. We're going to be in high school, so it wouldn't kill you to act normal once in a while. I mean, it's one thing to like all that weird stuff, but you don't have to brag about it any time we meet someone."

"Old movies aren't weird. It's not like I like taxidermy or something."

Lauren sighed. "Talking about taxidermy is weird too. It's like you don't even know what normal is." We sat there not talking until the band began playing the Lincoln school song and the assembly officially started. I risked glancing over at Tyler one more time. He was staring in our direction, and I turned away quickly as if I had been caught doing something wrong. I don't know why I bothered. He was looking in our direction, but the only person he saw was Lauren. People always liked Lauren. I was the bonus item, what people got for free when they hung out with her.

The assembly went on forever. If one more person got up to tell us how many opportunities awaited us during the next four years I was going to stick a sharpened pencil in my ear.

"I have to go to the bathroom," I whispered to Lauren.

"Thanks for the update."

"Seriously, I have to go. Come with me."

"Not now." Lauren pointed toward the stage. Lincoln's cheerleading squad was doing a routine. "We should try out in the fall." She rummaged through the stack of handouts for the one that gave the details on the cheer squad.

I looked at Lauren as if she had announced that she wanted to take up cattle roping. We weren't exactly cheerleader material. Cheerleaders do not have thighs that rub together, and Lauren, who didn't have the same thigh issues, suffered from near terminal clumsiness. She couldn't do a cartwheel without falling over.

"Are you kidding?"

"What? We could be cheerleaders."

"Have you ever noticed that the cheerleaders are the most popular girls in school?"

"Yeah."

"We're not the most popular girls." I hated to be the one to point this out to her, but you'd think she would have noticed by now.

"My mom says high school is completely different. It's like a fresh start."

I rolled my eyes. Fresh start, maybe. Complete life do-over? I don't think so.

Lauren went back to watching them intently, as if her life depended on memorizing the dance routine. I slipped past her, leaving her to her cheerleading daydreams.

The bathrooms under the bleachers doubled as the girls' locker room. The room smelled like a mix of chlorine, mildewed towels, and Secret deodorant. I pushed a stall door open and sat down. As soon as I was seated the stall door started to creep back open. I kicked it shut and it flew right past the latch and swung out into the bathroom. Great, one broken latch and now I was on display for the entire locker room. This was exactly the kind of thing that schools should give you a warning on but don't.

Suddenly I heard someone laugh. I finished as fast as I could and yanked my skirt back down, trying to look casual. I waited there for a moment, but no one came into the bathroom. I took a few steps toward the sinks, and the voices and laughter got louder. There was a door leading to the pool, bolted from the locker room side. I pressed my ear against the door. The voices were coming from there for certain.

I slipped the bolt open, the click sounding very loud in the empty bathroom, but the voices on the other side didn't change. They hadn't heard anything. I pulled the door open slowly and peered through the crack.

Holy. Shit.

There were soap bubbles everywhere; bubbles spreading like a foamy blob across the tile floor. The swimming pool was covered in a frothy concoction, like a giant latte. At the back of the room near the diving board a group of seniors stood pouring bottles of lemon yellow dish soap into the water. They were laughing, and Matt Ryan, who I knew from the local paper as the school's star athlete, was standing back trying to capture the whole thing on his camera phone. He was the one who saw me. He winked at me then pressed his finger to his mouth, in the universal symbol for *shhh*, and I knew I should pretend I never saw a thing. I shut the door quietly and slid the bolt closed.

"What are you doing?"

I jumped and whirled around to face Lauren.

"There are a bunch of seniors dumping soap into the pool."

"Get out!" Lauren walked past me and slid the bolt back on the door.

"I don't think we're supposed to know about it."

"Duh." Lauren pulled the door open and peered through the crack. She gave a tiny squeal and shut the door. "It must be the senior prank."

Senior prank was a long-standing Lincoln High tradition.

Each class tried to come up with a way to outdo the class before. I figured by the time we were seniors we would have to come up with something worthy of making CNN, like kidnapping the prime minister of Canada.

"They must have dumped at least a dozen bottles of soap into the pool," I said.

"We should go. The assembly is almost over, and we don't want to be caught down here." Lauren took off. Once we were in the hall I looked behind me. There was a wall of bubbles pressing against the frosted glass window in the door that led directly to the pool. I jogged after Lauren.

The whole thing seemed funny. It was a prank after all, a joke. Just good clean soapy fun. I thought I was pretty cool to be in on it, especially considering I wasn't even officially a freshman yet.

The school administration took a dimmer view of the situation. Apparently dish soap and pool filters are a bad combination. Then there was the fact that one of the school janitors slipped on the soapy pool deck and fell, pulling his knee all out of whack. Rumor had it he was suing the school in some kind of worker's compensation case for millions of dollars, but that part might not have been true. What was a fact was that the school administration was on a mission to find out who was behind the whole thing.

The day after my birthday party an article appeared in the Sunday paper saying the seniors responsible had been caught.

The paper showed a photo of Principal LaPoint looking stern with his arms crossed over his chest. He was quoted as calling those caught the "ringleaders," like it was a major crime versus a senior prank. He was forbidding those four students from attending either prom or graduation. He wanted to withhold their diplomas altogether, but apparently the school board wasn't willing to go that far. There were quotes in the paper from people around town, most of whom thought the punishment was too severe, although there were a few who seemed to think the death penalty might be in order.

The first hint I had that anything was wrong, that the story would involve me at all, was on Monday morning. I was wearing a new soft white short sleeve sweater that I had gotten for my birthday. I was in a good mood until I got to my locker. *SNITCH* was written in black marker across the door. It was underlined three times. I walked up slowly, my finger extended. The ink looked still wet, but it was dry. It didn't smudge. I heard someone laugh and turned around to see a group of girls looking over from across the hall before they scurried away, still laughing. As I walked to math class I noticed it—everyone was staying far away from me. An invisible force field between me and the rest of the world. No one got closer than a few feet. It was like I had developed leprosy over the weekend.

I was walking into the classroom when someone bumped hard into my back. My book and papers went flying to the floor. I whirled around and Bill from my math class stood there looking at me.

"What?" he asked, his voice flat. I could hear his friends laughing.

I bent down to pick up my stuff. No one said anything to me in math. I hadn't been the social butterfly before, but this was different. I felt people staring at me, but when I looked around, no one would meet my eyes. My stomach felt hot and tight, and I wanted to throw up. Even Mr. Grady, our teacher, seemed annoyed with me. The whole morning was like that. I kept trying to find Lauren, but she wasn't in English or at her locker between classes. When I saw her standing in the lunch line getting her food I had never been so glad to see anyone in my whole life. I had to fight the urge to run over to her.

"Where have you been?" I asked.

Lauren looked at me like she had never seen me before. It was like I was stuck in a weird sci-fi movie.

"What do you want?" she asked holding her tray between us like a barrier.

"What's with you? I need to talk to you." I touched her elbow. Lauren yanked away and her tray lurched, slopping orange red ravioli sauce onto my new sweater. We both looked down at the spreading stain. Everyone else in the cafeteria was gaping at us.

"Don't touch me."

"Lauren? Why are you mad at me? Why is everybody mad at me?"

Someone standing in line gave a disbelieving snort.

"I didn't think you would ever do something like that," she said.

"Like what?"

"Tell on the seniors. I mean, it isn't just you; by telling, you make our whole class look like a bunch of losers. We all have to fit in at Lincoln High next year, and now we're going to be known as part of the class that ratted out the most popular seniors. Everyone will connect us with what you did. It was just a prank, Helen." Lauren's voice was so loud I was pretty sure everyone in the cafeteria could hear her.

"But I didn't tell," I said softly.

"There's no point lying about it now. Everyone already knows."

I felt a hot rush of tears in my throat choking off what I was going to say. I walked stiffly out of the cafeteria as kids yelled things after me. I didn't even stop by my locker; I walked straight out of the school and went home. I peeled off my ruined sweater, stuffed it under the bed, and crawled in. When my mom came home I told her I was sick.

I stayed home sick for the entire week. It wasn't even lying. I felt awful. I didn't want to eat anything and even though I was tired, I couldn't sleep. On Friday I went over to Lauren's house. I had to find a way to make things right. I could live with everyone else being mad, but I couldn't stand to be on the outs with my best friend. Lauren was in the backyard with a guy I didn't recognize. They were both wearing sweats. I stood at the gate and watched. He was spotting her, helping her learn how to do a cartwheel.

"Keep your legs up, nice and straight."

"I'm trying."

"You can do it. It's just a confidence thing. You think you'll fall, so you do. Just believe, and then up and over."

Lauren turned a perfect cartwheel. She gave a squeal and jumped into his arms. That's when she saw me.

"Helen."

We stood awkwardly looking at each other.

"This is Mark, my gymnastics instructor. My mom hired him."

Mark made his excuses and left.

"Still thinking of trying out for cheerleading, huh?"

"Mmm-hmm."

"I didn't tell anyone, Lauren. You have to believe me." The words came rushing out in one breath. My eyes burned and threatened to spill over. Lauren crossed her arms and sighed.

"Don't start crying again," she said, her voice sounding tired.

"Someone else must have told on them, or maybe one of them got cold feet and ratted out the others. Maybe together we can figure out who did it." Lauren loved mysteries. I was hoping to convince her that this would be a fun one to solve.

"God, just give it up. No one else told."

I looked at her and felt my stomach ice over. I felt things fall into place.

"You . . ." My voice trailed off.

"Me."

"Why?"

"Do you remember when Principal LaPoint talked about how many opportunities we'll have in the next few years?"

I nodded.

"I'm taking one of them."

"What are you talking about?"

"Did you know Emily Watson called me?"

"Who?"

"Emily Watson. She's a junior. She'll be a senior next year. She's captain of the cheerleading squad. She was very appreciative that I was willing to tell who ratted out her friends. When I told her how I was scared that I wouldn't have any friends since you were my best friend, she told me that I don't have to worry. She'll make sure I meet lots of people next year."

"I didn't rat out anyone. You did."

"Yeah, but that wasn't a problem. The truth isn't important. What matters is what people *think* is the truth. If I'm going to be somebody, then I need people on my side." She looked over at me. "People who are in a position to get me what I want."

I sat down hard on the ground, the air whooshing out me.

"But why?"

"There isn't always a big reason why. It just is."

"But you're my best friend."

"And you're happy with good enough. You don't care about dressing the right way or being invited to the right parties. You're happy to rent movies on a Friday night. Not even new movies. You want to rent stuff no one has seen in like a hundred years. I want to go out. I want to be invited out. We were always second string, but now I have a chance to make the A-list."

"And that matters so much?"

"Of course it matters." Lauren tossed her hands in the air and paced back and forth. "My mom tells me that the friends you have in high school determine who your friends are in college, and then who your friends are for the rest of your life."

"Well, my mom says you can't buy friendship," I countered.

"And your mom is a hippie who doesn't even use deodorant."

"She does too. It's just that rock crystal kind."

"Whatever."

"So you're just done with me? That's it?" I could hear my voice getting tight and high. This wasn't going the way I had planned. I had figured my problem would be convincing her I hadn't told. I wasn't prepared for this conversation at all.

Lauren sat down next to me and pulled a few strands of grass out of the lawn. We sat there quietly for a minute. "Nothing is forever, you know. Once I'm popular, we can be friends again and then you'll be popular too. It will all be worth it."

"What makes you think I'll want to be your friend?"

"What makes you think you'll have other options?"

chapter three

The last two weeks of eighth grade were vile. Someone mashed spoiled tuna fish through the vents in my locker so that everything I owned stunk. A person in my English class smeared glue on my chair. No one talked to me, but everyone was whispering about me behind my back. People left mean notes in my books, and the janitor stopped even bothering to clean my locker door, since every time he did, someone else would write SNITCH across it. I stopped eating lunch in the cafeteria after someone spit on my food tray. For those last two weeks of school I sat in the back of the library during lunch and pretended to study. During gym class someone dumped my clothes on the wet shower floor, so I had to wear my gym uniform for the rest of the day. I cried every night. My parents talked to the school administrators, who said there was nothing they could do. I would have to "ride it out."

My mom tried to convince me that it would be better next year and I would make new friends, but I wasn't buying it. The way I figured it, high school would be worse. Instead of having one hundred fifty classmates trying to make me miserable, I would have seven hundred. Unless you counted the other grades, in which case I would have thousands of people dedicated to making my life hell. I was certain that my reputation as a ratfink had spread to every school across town.

My parents are huge believers in karma. Actually, they're huge believers in a bunch of stuff: chi, feng shui, the benefits of being vegan, the superiority of natural fabrics. They believe in everything from Buddha to fairies. Most of the time I shrug off what they say. They kept telling me that somehow things would just magically work out and the universe would take care of things. I was preparing for the idea that I may have to run away from home, when it turned out my parents were right. My dad was offered a job in New York. Thank god for karma.

Technically it wasn't New York City, it was some town just outside the city, but it was still good enough for me. Heck, I would have gone anywhere, including remote Alaska. I just wanted to be as far away from Terrace, Michigan, as possible. We were moving. I was so happy, I didn't even mind doing the packing. For once the universe seemed to have noticed what I needed.

From the time school ended until we moved at the end of July, I didn't hear from Lauren once. I guess she was too busy focusing on mastering the intricacies of the perfect cartwheel to find time to say good-bye to her best friend. She might have forgotten all about me, but I certainly never forgot about her. Not for one single day.

chapter four

I'd be lying if I didn't admit that over the next three years, even from New York, I thought about getting back at Lauren somehow. But it was never anything specific. Once I dressed up a Barbie doll in a cheerleader outfit and tossed it into the giant wood chipper in the park. I grinned as the flesh-colored plastic sprayed out in tiny half-moon crescents onto the ground. Although I thought about it all the time, I didn't think I would ever really do anything about the situation. Logistics alone would make it impossible. I lived halfway across the country from her. Revenge by mail didn't seem that satisfying. Not to mention there are laws against sending anthrax. I hoped my parents were right, that karma would balance things out and Lauren would have some (or preferably all) of the following things happen to her:

1. She would be permanently disfigured by a virulent acne condition.

2. She would suffer some type of cheerleading accident involving choking to death on a wayward pom-pom.
3. Her hair would fall out due to a shampoo manufacturer's defect.
4. All the lies she told would come back to haunt her by turning her tongue black.

But none of these things happened. I watched her from a distance by stalking her Facebook page. I told myself I didn't care, but I couldn't stop checking to see what she was doing. I kept waiting for something to go wrong for her, but nothing did. For the next three years she went from one success to another. She mastered the cartwheel the summer before freshman year and made the cheerleading squad. She started dating Justin Ryan, the younger brother of the popular Matt Ryan of soap bubble fame. Justin, like his brother before him, was the star of every team at Lincoln High and looked like an Abercrombie & Fitch ad. Lauren was always posting pictures of the two of them, arms wrapped around each other. She was active with the drama club and a shoo-in to get the lead for senior year. She was always getting tagged in smiling groups mugging for the camera. She would be right in the middle, her giant, white horse teeth reflecting the camera flash. Her friends were always posting notes on her page about how she was their "BFF!!" and how her "party last night rocked!" Her friends used exclamation points for everything. She was at the top of the social ladder at Lincoln High.

It wasn't like I didn't have my own life. Things weren't bad or anything. I loved New York. I wasn't popular in my new school, but I wasn't unpopular either. To be honest, I was one of those people that no one noticed. When I first moved I didn't want to make friends with anyone. I felt like my whole life was one exposed nerve, and I couldn't stand to have anyone close enough to touch me. By the time I wanted to make friends, everyone else had moved on. I already had the reputation of being a loner. I wore a lot of black but didn't quite go far enough to be Goth. I didn't play sports or an instrument. I liked art, but drawing isn't exactly a group activity. I didn't really put an effort into changing things. Once you've been classified into a certain role, it's hard to make a change. Or maybe it just seemed easier to be by myself. I was friendly with a lot of people, but I didn't have any true friends. Sometimes it sucked that there wasn't anyone to talk to about things, but on the bright side, no one was close enough to screw me over either.

The only picture of me in this year's yearbook was my standard school photo. No clubs, no sports teams, no student government. No shot of me surrounded by friends. In fact, it would be easy to forget I existed at all.

Three years after she stabbed me in the back, Lauren was the queen of Lincoln High, and the fact that she lied and destroyed my life to be popular didn't seem to matter to anyone except me.

Sometimes karma does a shitty job of evening the score.

chapter five

I was lying on my bed reading my history homework. We were studying the French Revolution, and I was doodling Lauren's giant teeth on the picture of Marie Antoinette being led to the guillotine. I sat up when my dad tapped on the door. He and my mom stood in the doorway.

"Hey, poppet," Dad said, scratching his arm. My parents' latest thing was clothing made from hemp. It was supposed to be super-renewable and great for the planet, but my dad was having some kind of allergic reaction to the whole thing. He kept breaking out in these red hives, but he continued to wear it. Saving the planet wasn't supposed to be easy.

Dad looked at what I was reading and broke out a big smile. "Ah *liberté, egalité, fraternité.*" He took the book from my hand and flipped through the pages. He had majored in French in college, one of those degrees that might have been useful if, for example, we lived in France. My mom took a step forward so she was standing right next to him. She tucked her hair behind an ear. It was so curly that it instantly sprung back out.

"What's up?" I asked.

"We have some good news." Dad rubbed his hands on his pant legs and my mom gave him a reassuring nod. "The school has approved my research grant."

"Dad, that's awesome!" The alternative school where my dad taught was always out of money, so for them to support anything was a big deal. Also, research wasn't completely their thing. It was more of a live-and-let-live kind of place. His eyes shifted over to my mom.

"Your dad will have a chance to look into the role of meditation in healing. He might even have time to write the book he's always talked about."

"Okay." I drew the word out slowly so that it was more of a question. My dad has talked about writing a book on alternative health care for as long as I can remember. He should be thrilled, and instead he seemed like he had come to break the news to me that he was going off to war or something.

"We'd be living at the Shahalba Center," Mom continued. "It's a chance to learn meditation techniques from the very best in the world."

I had sudden insight into what was up. My parents wanted us to pick up and move to some granola hippie camp where everyone would be praying to their muse, chanting, and eating a strict vegan diet. Great. Why couldn't my parents be happy in the suburbs like everyone else?

"What's the school like?"

My dad looked confused. "There isn't a school."

"How am I supposed to finish high school?" My parents are really smart, but not great at the common sense stuff. Maybe they thought colleges would accept me based strictly on how Zen I was, no high school diploma needed.

My mom sat down next to me on the bed and petted my knee. "The Shahalba Center is in the woods of Maine. It's completely off the electrical grid." My mom seemed thrilled by the self-sufficiency of the place, but I could already picture it was going to be a problem if I wanted to bring a hair dryer. My mom was a big fan of the all-natural look, but I didn't go anywhere without my flat iron. "The center has a small farm and grows most of its own food. The closest school is almost fifty miles away."

"So are we going to get an apartment or something halfway?"

My mom and dad exchanged another look, and my stomach went into a sudden free fall. I knew what they had in mind.

"No way."

"We've talked to your grandmother and she would love to have you stay with her for the year," my mom said, as if it were completely reasonable for me to consider moving back there.

"Do you remember what happened, what they did to me?

Do you honestly expect me to go to school there? Why don't you ask me to move in with Lauren?"

"All this negative energy isn't good for you."

"It's not random negative energy, Mom. I hate her. I hate Terrace. I don't want to live there."

"And that may be exactly why the universe is bringing you this opportunity. It's a chance to heal, to come full circle." My mom made a large circular motion with her hands, her silver rings flashing in the light.

"This isn't the universe. This is you and dad deciding you want to chant for a year."

"It's more than chanting," my dad said, as if that was the point. Both my mom and I gave him a look, and he stopped talking and went back to scratching his hives.

"Your grandmother is really excited," my mom said.

"What about what *I* want?" I gave a noisy sniff. I wouldn't let them treat me like a five-year-old—easily distracted. *Sure we're ruining your life—but look over here, a shiny grandma!* Hell no. I wasn't falling for it.

"This is a huge opportunity for your dad and me. Living at a center like this is something that we've always wanted to do, and now the school is offering the funding to make this possible. You don't need to be afraid of Lauren."

"I'm not *afraid* of Lauren," I said. I loathed her, but I wasn't afraid. What else could she possibly do to me?

"You should walk back there with your head high. Heck, I

doubt any of those kids would even recognize you now," my dad said.

"Nice way of saying I used to be fat." I turned and faced the wall resting my head against the cool plaster. Trapped.

"I didn't mean you were fat. It was more your old nose I was thinking about," my dad said.

"Great, so I was fat with a big nose. This conversation is doing wonders for my ego."

"What your dad is saying is that you've grown into a lovely young woman. The only power Lauren has over you is what you give her. Hating her just feeds the negative energy. I'm asking you to think the situation over. Grandma is going to give you a call tomorrow morning to talk about it, but if you want my advice, you go back there and you show them that they may have knocked you down, but you didn't stay down."

"What if I think about it and decide I still don't want to do it? What if I want to skip the whole holding my head high thing and instead stay right here and feed my negative energy?"

My mom gave a tired sigh, no doubt thinking I had been switched at birth and somewhere out there was her real child who loved natural fibers, didn't shave her legs, and wasn't difficult about keeping her energy positive.

"We love you. You're the most important thing in our lives. If this is something that you absolutely can't do, then we'll turn down the grant. But before we do that, I want you to think about it, okay?" My dad patted my back a few times before slipping out of the room. My mom took a deep cleansing breath and walked out after my dad.

I could hear my bedroom door shut quietly behind them. Great, a one-way ticket to Guilt Trip. I could either ruin my parents' dream or move to hell's backyard.

I glanced at the full-length mirror on the back of my bedroom door. All around the edges I had taped different pictures— fashion ads from *Vogue*, copies of old vintage movie posters, and some of my pencil drawings. In the upper-right corner, half buried under other photos, was taped a picture of Lauren I'd printed off her Facebook page. I stood up and looked closer at her photo. Lauren hadn't changed much, aside from the black mustache I had drawn on with a Sharpie. She had the same wide smile and strong nose. If you asked me, she was bordering on a horse face. Her hair was longer than in eighth grade, but otherwise I would know her if I saw her.

I looked at myself in the mirror. It had been only three years, but I'd changed a lot. I'd lost thirty pounds the summer I moved. The silver lining of having my life ruined was the stress just melted those pounds off. In New York I walked everywhere and took up yoga. Although I hadn't lost any more weight, what remained, shifted. My braces were gone and I had stopped chewing my fingernails a year or two back. My old nose, as my dad called it, had been a bit beaklike. A year after we moved to New York, I fell down a flight of stairs and landed on my face. I was pretty out of it when they took me to the hospital, but I still had the wherewithal to beg the doctor for a better nose before he put me under for surgery. I may have been raised in an all-natural household, but on my own I had discovered the idea of better living through chemistry—or at least better hair. My former white-girl 'fro of frizzy short hair was now shoulder length, straightened, and highlighted. I had bought a bunch of vintage clothing over the past few years and had my own style. My boobs had also finally showed up. I wouldn't go so far as to say I was hot, but I looked pretty darn good.

I stood straighter and pulled my shoulders back. It was quite possible that my old classmates wouldn't even recognize me, especially since they weren't expecting to ever see me again. Out of sight, out of mind.

chapter six

There is nothing normal about my family. You would never see a picture of us in the encyclopedia under "typical family." My parents don't worry about normal parent stuff, like what time I come home at night or my grades. They worry I might buy clothing made in sweatshops and that my love for meat is some kind of character flaw. When I first got my period my mom threw me a "welcome to womanhood party," where she and her hippie, non-armpit-shaving girlfriends got a little drunk on homemade red wine and sang songs about the cycles of the moon. I was the kid in third grade who, instead of bringing cookies to school on my birthday, brought all-natural organic zucchini cupcakes made with applesauce instead of refined sugar. Even the teacher couldn't choke one down.

My grandma doesn't fit the typical grandmother mold either. She doesn't knit or wear sensible shoes. She paints her toenails bright red and wears high heels. She drinks scotch neat and cuts her hair supershort and styles it so it's spiked up in different directions. She looks less like she should be at a bingo parlor and more like she just stepped off a set for MTV. She couldn't be more different from my mom if she tried. You would never know they were related except for the fact that we have the family pictures to prove it. My grandma was the one who got my ears pierced and convinced my parents that a hot dog or two wouldn't kill me.

I sat on the kitchen counter the next afternoon, talking to her on the phone. My parents were in their room so I could have privacy, but I could hear them practically pressed up against the wall trying to hear what I was saying.

"So your folks are going to go off and stare at their navels, huh? I never did get that 'learning how to breathe' thing. Comes natural to me, in and out, regular as clockwork. Given how dumb some people are, you would think more people would just keel over dead if breathing had to be learned."

"Yeah."

"Come on now, I know this place isn't as great as New York, but I've got cable and I'll let you order pepperoni pizza. We'll even get real cheese instead of that soy crud your mom buys."

"It's not that. It's school."

"Is this about that snot Lauren?" she asked. One thing I like about my grandma is she doesn't worry about negative energy; she just calls things as she sees them. "I never was crazy about her. She was a pushy kid, even as a toddler. And her parents? They're so busy social climbing it's a wonder they don't have nosebleeds and a fleet of Sherpas trailing them."

"My parents say the universe is giving me a chance to come full circle, that this is an opportunity."

"Might be on to something."

"Huh?" My mouth dropped open. Was my grandma finally going hippie? Had my mom worn her down with all the talk of chi over the years?

"Look, I don't think the girl is worth another thought, but it's clear she's still stuck in your craw. If she's bugging you that much, then you should do something about it instead of stewing. You'll be going away to college soon. You need to lighten your load."

"Get her out of my craw, so to speak."

"Exactly. Maybe the universe wants you to come back here to teach her a lesson. Lord knows the girl could use it. You know I'm crazy about your mom and dad, but I'm thinking karma could use a helping hand. "

I didn't say anything. I just thought about what she'd said. That was the first time it occurred to me that instead of just thinking about revenge, dreaming about it, I could actually make it happen. Lauren would never see it coming. She would never expect it.

I hung up with my grandma and went back to my room. I pulled the picture of Lauren off my mirror and stared into her face. Revenge didn't have to be a daydream. It could be reality. All it would take was a bit of planning. I could screw her just the same way she screwed me. Maybe my parents were right and it was time to move back. I crumpled up Lauren's picture and tossed it into my trash can. Nothing but net. I went back out to tell my parents the news. Well, part of the news. I kept the bit about the revenge plan to myself.

chapter seven

I planned my move back to Terrace with the same level of care and detail employed by nations going to war. My parents, who never met a self-help book they didn't like, were huge fans of goal setting and visualizing your perfect future. How would the universe send you your heart's desire if you weren't clear about what you wanted? I forget which book my mom had gotten it from, *The Secret*, or maybe *Energy for Life*, but she was big on writing down what you wanted. Somehow this was supposed to help the universe bring it to you. The universe apparently has short-term memory loss issues. It needs things written down. My mom was always saying, "The difference between wishing and goal setting is that goal setters have a plan." I wasn't sure I bought into the whole theory, but why take the chance? I thought about every facet of my plan very carefully. I made lists and diagrams. I kept a three-ring binder with all of my notes separated by color-coded tabs. On the first page of my binder I wrote my new mission statement in large block letters so that the universe would be sure to see it, even if the universe had bad eyesight:

GET REVENGE ON LAUREN WOOD

Revenge is a tricky thing. I wanted Lauren to pay, but pay in a very particular way. For example, it might be momentarily satisfying to do one of the following:

1. Push Lauren out in front of a speeding dump truck
2. Slather her with BBQ sauce and set a herd of hungry pit bulls on her
3. Pour honey in her hair and then tie her down on an anthill
4. Dress her in a bathing suit made out of herring and then push her into shark-infested water

However, all of these things would be over quickly. I'll admit it doesn't sound nice, but I wanted her to suffer a bit longer. I wanted her to know what it felt like to have everything taken away. Then there was the added factor that it would be difficult to make a bathing suit out of tiny stinky fish, and I was pretty sure you could do some heavy jail time for pushing people into shark-infested water or into the paths of speeding dump trucks. I wanted Lauren to pay, but I wasn't looking to spend the next forty to life wearing an orange jumpsuit. Orange is so not my color.

No, my revenge plan was going to have to be more creative. Plus, I wasn't even sure where I could find a pack of hungry pit bulls.

I made a list of the things that were important to Lauren:

1. Being popular
2. Her boyfriend
3. Getting the lead in the school play
4. Her status as a cheerleader

Once I had the list, the basics of the plan were already framed out. I had to become more popular than she was. I had to steal her boyfriend out from under her, ensure someone else took the lead in the play, and get her kicked off the cheerleading squad.

Now I just had to figure out how to make those things happen.

The popularity angle was going to be the easiest to tackle. High schools have a social structure more strict than a Hindu caste system. By the time you get to your senior year everyone knows exactly where he or she belongs compared to everyone else. You could try to change your status—you could get a new wardrobe or take up a new sport, for example—but it would only take a few days before everyone would shove you back into the place where they felt you belonged. There might be a few people who shifted ranks, but it was highly unusual. I would have the advantage of being a new kid. No one would know exactly where to put me, but they would be trying to sort it out from the first moment they met me. I had to stack the deck. I couldn't *become* popular at Lincoln High. I had to *be* popular from the moment I walked through the front door. I spent hours thinking about what made one person more popular than another. When I was done I taped a list to the mirror in my bedroom so I could study it. It was a thing of beauty.

The Popularity Scale

Attractive: Assign yourself up to 10 points, depending on your level of hotness, zero points being seriously ugly and 10 points being supermodel hot. Bonus 2 points for being fit and in shape versus merely thin. An additional 2 points for hair that looks like a shampoo ad. Minus 1 point if you flip it around way too much. Bonus 3 points for big boobs. Minus 5 points for being attractive but too slutty. Plus 1 point for good use of makeup. Minus 2 points for mild disfigurement such as bad skin, crooked teeth, or bad breath.

Sporty: Assign yourself 5 points for general athletic ability as defined by ability to run without falling over and catching a ball without getting smacked in the face. 5 bonus points for being on key school teams such as football, cheerleading, basketball, or soccer. Minus 2 points for being on dorky teams such as archery or fencing. Bonus 2 points if you have a leadership position on a team. Minus 2 points if you never play and instead always sit on the sidelines.

Rich: Assign yourself 10 points for being filthy rich, 5 points for possessing mere wealth, zero points for being middle class, and minus 5 points for being poor. Bonus point for each item of designer clothing that you own or for accessories such as handbags that cost more than a small used car. Minus 5 points for purchasing your wardrobe at Wal-Mart. Give yourself 2 points if you shop at a funky vintage shop, minus 2 points if you buy your underwear at a thrift store. Some things should never be secondhand.

Cool: Award yourself up to 10 points for exotic factors such as being from a cool place (large city, anywhere in Europe or Hollywood), knowing famous people, having a good car, being in a band (but not *the* band—wearing a uniform that makes you look like a hotel bellman is never cool), or demonstrating artistic ability.

I was going back to Lincoln High, but not as Helen Worthington. I was going to be remade into the destined-to-be-popular Claire Dantes.

I was named Helen after my mom's great aunt. Ever notice you don't meet a lot of Helens these days? That's because it's an old lady name. Thankfully, my middle name is Claire. My mom's maiden name was Dantes, and since I would be living with my grandma it made some sense to borrow it. My mom was ticked that I wanted to register for school under a different name. She said she didn't feel it was necessary for me to hide myself like I was spending my senior year in the witness protection program, but I could tell she was just hurt that I didn't want to use the name she had given me.

In the end my mom backed down. Either my grandma talked her into it or, more likely, the guilt of abandoning me kicked in. No matter the reason—I didn't care—Helen Worthington ceased to exist. Claire Dantes officially registered at Lincoln High. Step one of the plan was in place.

chapter eight

It was my grandmother's idea for me to skip the very first day of school. She pointed out the importance of making an entrance. On the first day everyone is hyperexcited, wearing their best new school clothes, squealing when they see people, like they had been separated by the war instead of the summer. She said if I started on the second day, more people would be likely to notice me.

It took everything I had not to skip into the building. My outfit was killer. My hair looked perfect. My plan—foolproof. I could tell just from people's appraising glances as I walked down the hall that I could count on being recognized as destined for popularity before the day was over. I was so excited to finally be doing something versus just thinking about it. I couldn't believe that I had ever hesitated to move back to Terrace. Thank you, universe. I sat in the office waiting for the secretary to give me my locker combination, my foot tapping on the floor.

"Okay, here we go," the secretary said, with that fake cheery voice people use for small kids and the demented elderly. I took the locker combination out of her hand and started to turn. "Wait a minute. Your buddy isn't here."

"Buddy?"

"We provide a buddy to all new students here at Lincoln. She'll make sure you find your classrooms, introduce you to people, and help you feel at home," the secretary said in the same singsong voice.

"You know, I think I'm fine, so I don't need a buddy, but thanks anyway."

"Oh, here she is now. Brenda, this is Claire. You've lucked out, Claire. Brenda is one of our star students here at Lincoln."

Brenda may have been a star student, but I was willing to bet she wasn't popular. Her hair had no layers and came down at an angle, making her head look like a fuzzy, brown Christmas tree. She didn't wear any makeup, and her glasses made her eyes look buggy. She dressed like she borrowed her clothes from a frumpy elderly librarian who had a fetish for the color beige. I had a sneaking suspicion her favorite show was something like *NOVA* or another PBS series. I'm sure Brenda was a lovely person, but she was going to be a big barrier to my popularity project. I needed to ditch her ASAP.

"Here you go!" The secretary stuck a name badge with bright red letters on my shirt: HI! MY NAME IS CLAIRE AND TODAY'S MY FIRST DAY! Brenda was wearing a badge that proudly declared:

LINCOLN HIGH BUDDY! SAY HI TO MY NEW FRIEND, CLAIRE! I stared down at the label on my boob as if some type of disgusting insect had landed there. "You have a great day now," the secretary chirped.

I followed Brenda out of the office. She didn't seem to mind the giant name tag at all. Maybe she thought it was an accessory—fashion didn't appear to be her thing.

"Your locker is down this way," Brenda said as she took off down the hallway. She walked as if she were heading into a windstorm, head down, shoulders squared, her torso thrust slightly forward. She plowed through the crowds of students, a woman on a mission. While she walked, her hands made spastic gestures as she pointed out different things and offered advice: "The gym is down that way. There are water fountains in every wing and also bathrooms. Cell phones aren't allowed in class, so if you have one, you should leave it in your locker. The only class we have together is biology. Do you like science?"

"I guess," I mumbled, trying to look like I wasn't actually with her.

Brenda stopped suddenly and I nearly slammed into her back.

"It's my absolute favorite subject," she stated as if she thought I was going to argue with her, maybe debate the merits of science versus English lit. "What's yours?"

"I don't know. Art, I guess."

Brenda's eyebrows scrunched together. I should point out

that her eyebrows didn't have far to go to meet in the middle. I suspected she didn't consider art to be a real subject. When I didn't say anything else, she headed back down the hall.

Brenda stopped in front of my locker and then stood to the side as if she were my Secret Service agent, prepared to take a bullet for me. Nice girl, but Brenda had to go.

"You know, I appreciate your helping me find my locker and all, but I don't need a buddy."

"The buddy code says that we stick with you for your first week. We give you a tour, make sure you find your classes, help you meet all your teachers, introduce you to our friends, and eat with you at lunch." She ticked each item off on her fingers.

"There's a code?"

"I don't want to get into trouble or anything."

"You're not a big rule breaker, are you, Brenda?"

"No, not really."

"Here's the thing—I think I'll do better on my own." Brenda's eyes widened. I suddenly had the feeling that when she got the call about me coming to town and her chance to be a buddy, it had been the most exciting thing to happen to her in months. "I mean it's not you; it's totally me. I'm the independent type. I'm not really a buddy kind of person." She had no idea how true it was that being buddies didn't come easy to me.

"It's not just the buddy code. I'm also hoping to put this on my transcript so I can show some community service activities. The problem is, we don't get a lot of new students, so if I don't get to help you, then I can't really put it on my applications."

Great, now I was standing between Brenda and her college dreams. Why couldn't she feed the homeless or something? There must be a diseased kitten farm or something where she could volunteer.

"Okay, look, you can show me around and stuff, but we don't need to do the full buddy program thing. Like the name tags, for example."

"You don't like the name tags?" Brenda fingered the edge of her tag.

"No. I hate name tags. It feels like a label. I hate to label people. Isn't part of the buddy code making sure I feel at home?" Brenda nodded. "I don't feel at home in a name tag."

"I guess we could get rid of them."

I ripped the tag off my shirt, crumpled it, and tossed it into my locker. Brenda looked around as if she expected a SWAT team to come and take me down for name tag violations. I pointed at her chest and the offending tag. She sighed and pulled it off. The morning bell gave its first warning.

"Okay, I should get going. I've got French." I dumped a few things in my locker, slammed it shut, and started to head off. "I'll catch you later."

"Wait a minute. How do you know where to go?"

I stopped short. Shit. This was supposed to be my first time in the building. The revenge plan wasn't going to go very well if I couldn't even fool buddy Brenda.

"Just a guess. It felt like French would be that way." I motioned vaguely down the hall.

"Well, you guessed right." Brenda looked like she wasn't sure if she should believe me or not. "Do you want me to walk you down there?"

"No, I'll be fine."

"So, I'll see you later?"

"You bet, buddy!" I gave her what I hoped was a friendly smile and started down the hall. I shot a look behind me and noticed that she was still watching me. What kind of person volunteers to show new people around? With any luck she would settle for giving me a quick tour and then go back to hanging out with her own friends, who no doubt included the president of the chess club.

I slipped into the classroom and gave a quick look around. At the back of the room sat Bailey and Kyla. I recognized them from Lauren's Facebook page as two of her best friends. Of course their matching blue and white cheerleader skirts were also a giveaway. Cheerleader outfits are like gang colors, a sure way to identify who belongs and who doesn't. I didn't talk to anyone, just sat down in an empty desk and stared straight ahead. I had practiced this cool and aloof expression in the mirror until it was perfect. I was wearing a vintage lace shirt under a short black jacket with slim black pants. I'd used a skinny plaid men's tie as a belt. I'd done my best to modify my wardrobe to ride the line between edgy and popular. I peeked down to make sure there wasn't any sticky glue from the name tag still on my shirt.

"*Bonjour*, everyone," Mrs. Charles said tapping on her desk for attention. She looked over at me with a smile. "We have a new student joining our Lincoln High family. I'm sure everyone will welcome"—she paused to look down at her class register— "Claire Dantes. It says you're from New York City. This must be quite the change for you."

I heard people in the room perk up, just as I knew they would. Someone from New York was infinitely cooler than someone who moved from Wisconsin or North Dakota. Granted, we hadn't lived right in the city, but it was close enough. Plus, I didn't plan to mention that we lived in the 'burbs. I gave Mrs. Charles a smile.

"This is senior French. We can test you later to see how what you learned in your old school compares to here, but I'm sure the students here can help you if you need anything."

"*Merci, Madame Charles. J'attends avec impatience vraiment cette classe.*" I looked out over the room. "*J'ai hâte aussi de recontrer tout le monde.*"

Mrs. Charles's mouth dropped open in surprise.

"You speak lovely," she sputtered, looking down at her class notes as if there would be some additional information there, like that I was secretly a French exchange student or former Bond girl.

"My family spends our summers in France," I said with a

shrug. This was not technically true, but we did spend two weeks there one summer. My dad was fluent, and he and I used to practice by speaking French at dinner. I was willing to bet my French was better than Mrs. Charles's. Besides, summering in France was worth several bonus points on my Popularity Scale with a triple bonus score for being fluent in a cool language.

"You spend your summers in Paris?" Bailey asked, leaning forward on her seat.

"Usually just a few days at the beginning and the end of the trip. You know how it is; Paris is so hot and gross in the summer," I said. Bailey nodded. "We spend most of our time on the Riviera." I gave Bailey and Kyla a smile and turned around so they couldn't see me rubbing my hands together in evil glee.

When class was over I took my time getting my stuff together. As expected, Bailey and Kyla were waiting for me by the door. I tossed my purse over my shoulder, making sure they got a good look.

"Is that a Fendi bag?" Kyla said, eyeing it as if it were sirloin and she was starving.

I spun the bag around and looked at it as if I was noticing it for the first time.

"This? Oh yeah. I got it in New York." I left off the part where I bought it as a knockoff from a street vendor. Let her think I had a few spare thousands to spend on handbags, and that it was the real thing.

"It's gorgeous!" Bailey cooed, running her finger down the side of the bag like it were a baby's cheek.

"Thanks."

"I like your whole outfit," Kyla said.

"London flea market," I tossed off casually.

"You're going to hate shopping here. There's, like, nothing but a total fashion wasteland out here," Bailey offered sadly.

"It's just a year. I'm moving right after graduation."

"Back to New York?"

"Probably, or I'll take a year and backpack through Europe."

Bailey and Kyla looked at each other. I had the feeling they were planning on being roomies at Michigan State, then being the maid of honor in each other's wedding, and most likely would buy houses on the same block. Even though this is what they wanted, they *wanted* to want something else.

"Do you have first or second lunch?" Bailey asked.

"First."

"Awesome. We usually sit over by the windows. Come find us and we'll introduce you to everyone."

I felt a smile slide across my face. It was even easier than I'd hoped.

"Why, that would be just great."

chapter nine

I felt nauseated as soon as I walked into the cafeteria, and not just because of the way it smelled. This would be the first time I saw Lauren. Although I was pretty sure my former BFF wouldn't recognize me, I still wondered. We certainly had enough past history. We spent thousands of nights at each other's houses as kids. Her family took me with them on summer vacations. We knew all of each other's secrets. I felt like she should know me even if I looked completely different, and yet at the same time I was counting on her not recognizing me.

The cafeteria at Lincoln High was a mini–solar system of popularity. The most popular kids sat by the windows near the fresh air and light. Even the tables and chairs were nicer in that section. Circling out from there were the hangers-on, the second tier, those who didn't set the trends, but who were the first to carry them out. Then the third tier, those who weren't popular, but weren't unpopular either. And in the final ring, the untouchables, the geeks, the dorks, the stoners, and the losers. Everyone knew their places as well as if there were assigned seats or name cards.

At the very center of the universe, where no doubt she felt she should be, was Lauren. She was the sun; everyone basked in her light. They would be nothing without her. People circled around her like satellites.

I grabbed a salad (popular girl food) from the café lineup and tried to work up the guts to go over to Lauren's table. Kyla saw me and gestured that I should join them. I noticed Lauren still talked with her hands. They waved around as if she were directing an orchestra or guiding in low-flying aircraft. I could see that her nails were painted neon pink. I walked over and stood at the end of their table.

"Hey, there you are! Good thinking not getting the hot option. It's disgusting," Kyla said, making room for my tray.

Lauren was looking at me. I felt my throat tighten. Her head tilted slightly to the side as she inspected me.

"Lauren, this is Claire. She's from New York!" Bailey seemed to be the social secretary in charge of introductions.

"Hey," I said.

Lauren gave a hair flip. I flipped mine. Lauren's nose was scrunched up slightly as if she was considering something very profound, or maybe she was trying to figure out why I seemed familiar to her. I reminded myself to breathe.

"Sit down," Kyla said. "I was just talking about how I have

Mr. Weltch, who everyone calls Mr. Wretch, for anatomy and phys ed. I swear he gets off on cutting stuff up for class. I bet if the police raided his place, they would find a basement filled with the corpses of tortured frogs. He even breathes heavy when he talks about dissection."

"Anatomy is gross," Bailey added to the discussion.

"Yeah, but Tony Mathis is in my class, so things aren't all bad." Kyla turned to me. "Total eye candy. I'll point him out later."

"Do you have a boyfriend?" Lauren asked, finally speaking to me.

"Today's my first day, give me a week or two." For a beat no one said anything, and then Lauren laughed.

"I meant back in New York," she clarified.

I shrugged. "I dated a few guys who went to Columbia, but nothing long-term. I hate to be tied down."

"Well, then don't go out with Mike Weaver, I hear he likes the tie-down thing," Kyla offered, and we all laughed. "If you have any questions on the guys here, just ask us."

"There was this one guy hitting on me, but I don't know. He seems sort of white bread," I said.

"White bread?"

"Looks good, but no substance," I said.

"Who was he?" Lauren asked.

I looked around the cafeteria and spotted my victim.

"There he is, over by the soda machine." I pointed out Justin. An awkward silence fell over the lunch table. I widened my eyes and tried to look innocent. "What? Does he have a reputation, or a disease or something?"

"Uh, no. I mean, he's, uh . . ." Bailey's voice trailed off.

"That's Justin. He's my boyfriend," Lauren said, her lips set in a firm line.

"Oh, sorry." I picked at my salad for a beat. "I'm probably blowing the whole thing out of proportion. Most likely he was just being nice."

"Justin is totally nice," Bailey stressed. Kyla nodded her head in tandem.

I popped a cherry tomato in my mouth and chewed. Poor Justin. Nothing erodes a relationship like some distrust. I mentally placed a check next to the boyfriend-stealing column.

"There you are," a voice said behind me. Kyla's nose wrinkled up like she smelled something bad. I turned around and Brenda was standing there holding her lunch tray, which looked like it had an extra heaping portion of the beef stew. "We're supposed to eat lunch together. I waited for you by your locker."

"Oh, sorry," I said.

"We can still eat together if you want." Brenda looked at the other girls. "I'm her assigned buddy."

"Wow. Assigned friends. Neat," Lauren said.

"It's one of our service programs," Brenda explained. She looked like she couldn't tell if Lauren was making fun of her or not.

"Lincoln High should be proud," Lauren said. "It's students like you who make us such a happy family."

"Thanks," Brenda said. I wanted to crawl under the table on her behalf. Why in the world did she come over here? Kyla gave a quiet snicker.

"I guess you don't want to eat lunch together then, huh?" Brenda asked.

"You know, I'm almost done so it doesn't make much sense." We both glanced down at my tray still piled high with salad, a full drink cup, and an apple.

"Yeah," Brenda murmured, shuffling off, her head down again. She walked as if the lunch tray weighed at least a thousand pounds.

"Catch you later," I said softly, but she didn't turn around.

"God, there's a buddy program? How could I guess that Brenda Bauer would sign up for it? It's like her best chance to make friends." Lauren broke off a piece of her rice cake to eat it.

"She doesn't have any friends?" I asked. I had assumed she had her own crowd.

"She used to hang with some other nerdy girl, I can't remember her name, who moved away at the end of last year."

"So she just hangs out on her own?"

"Her and the voices she hears in her head. She's seriously weird if you ask me," Lauren said.

"What is with her hair anyway? How is it possible to have hair that bad?" Kyla added. "It's like she must deep-fry it to get it that dried out."

"She's been really nice to me," I said. I mentally kicked myself under the table. Sticking up for Brenda was not part of the plan.

"Oh, I'm sure she's really nice," Lauren said, before dismissing Brenda's existence altogether. "So, Claire, are you going out for any school activities?"

"I'm not really sure. At my old school my friends and I didn't do a lot of organized activity stuff." I gave a hair flip, trying to look like I was above school activities. Let them think I hung out at nightclubs or other big-city diversions that weren't even possible here.

"Well, if you're interested, you should check out the drama club. The school musical is huge. We go all out with professional sets and costumes. We're doing *My Fair Lady* this year. It's going to be great."

"You are going to make the best Eliza," Bailey told her, and then looked over at me. "Lauren has had a major part every year, even freshman year when no other freshman was even in the play."

"There's no guarantee on anything," Lauren said. "I don't know who else might try out." She looked over at me with a raised eyebrow.

"Well, you don't have to worry about me. I can't sing. I sound like a reject audition for *American Idol*. You know, the ones they air just for laughs?"

"I can't sing either," Bailey said softly, as if to assure me that my lack of ability was okay, in fact preferred, so that there would be no chance of getting in the way of Lauren.

"Do you want to be a professional actress?" I asked, facing Lauren.

"Oh, I don't know. I mean, it's fun, but the business is so difficult if you want to pursue it as a career." Lauren waved her hand dismissively.

"But you're so good! I mean you are way better than most of the people on TV. I can totally see you walking the Oscar red carpet," Bailey gushed. I wondered if her lips chapped from the amount of ass kissing she did.

"Duh, Bailey, theater stars don't go to the Oscars, they go to the Tony Awards," Lauren said, and I saw Bailey's face flush red hot in embarrassment. "Anyway, I'm not sure about making acting my career. I've thought about majoring in theater in college and giving myself more time to think about it. It's important to keep my options open, but I would never skip college and go straight to Broadway. I wouldn't want anyone to think I went into acting because I couldn't get through college."

Right. God forbid you follow your dreams—what if people think that's the best you could do? I only half listened to Lauren talking about the pros and cons of different theater programs and instead looked around the cafeteria to see if I could spot Brenda. There was no way she could have eaten all that stew so quickly.

I pushed back from the table. Lauren stopped talking,

looking surprised. I had the sense she was used to people hanging on her every word. Well, it was time for her to get used to a new reality.

"Sorry, I've got to go." The three of them looked up at me. My brain scrambled around for a good excuse. "I told my friends in New York that I'd give them a call. We used to have lunch every day at this sushi joint near Times Square, and this is the first time I won't be there." I give a halfhearted shrug. "I told them I would let them know how things are going here."

"God, it must suck having to start over senior year," Bailey sympathized.

"I was really hating it, but I have to say I feel so much better after meeting you guys today. I was afraid I wouldn't meet anyone cool."

Lauren's smile spread slowly across her face and both Bailey and Kyla sat up straighter. Flattery will get you everywhere. Add this to the secrets of popularity: Popular girls are insecure. They act like they aren't, but they are, and a bit of kissing up never hurts.

"Give me your number. We go out all the time. We'll text you and let you know where to meet up with us next time if you want," Kyla said.

"That would be great." I scribbled my number down and passed it over to them. I could tell the people at the tables around us were paying attention to the exchange. Lincoln High's caste system was looking to slot me where I belonged. The way I was dressed helped, and being from New York was a bonus for sure, but what was slotting me into place more than anything else was the fact that the three most popular senior girls wanted to hang out with me. It wasn't even the end of lunch and the popularity project was already a success.

chapter ten

I pushed open the bathroom door and heard a juicy sniffle and then silence. I peeked under each of the stall doors. Only the last one had anyone in it—brown, lace-up shoes that looked like they belonged on an orphan in a Third World country. I knew it.

I heard the smothered sound of a choked-back sob. There is no dignity in having a good cry in a public bathroom. My stomach sank as I remembered what the last two weeks of my eighth grade year had been like. I tapped on the stall door with a fingernail.

"Brenda?" I asked softly. She didn't say anything, but I heard another sniffle from behind the stall door. "Brenda, I know it's you. I recognize your shoes. Are you okay?"

"Uh-huh."

My eyebrows went up in disbelief. Brenda was a lousy liar.

"You're not okay. You're crying."

"Just leave me alone."

"Look, I'm sorry about the lunch thing. I should have waited for you at my locker."

Brenda didn't say anything.

"I met those girls in one of my classes and they invited me to eat with them."

"And you would rather eat with them than me. It's fine. I understand. I totally understand."

"You don't understand. There is way more going on than you're imagining. It has nothing to do with you."

"It never does," she said, and then gave a loud blow on her nose.

"Look, come out of there so we can talk."

"No."

I tapped on the door a bit more firmly this time. "You have to come out, classes are going to start."

"I don't have to do anything," she said.

"You're supposed to be my buddy, Brenda. Locking yourself in the bathroom and refusing to talk to me is almost certainly against the buddy code."

"Stop making fun of me."

"I'm not making fun of you. I'm trying to apologize, but it's sort of hard to do talking to a bathroom door."

"Fine, you've apologized. You can go now."

I backed up and leaned against the sink, thinking over my options:

1. **Leave Brenda**. I just met the girl. It wasn't my responsibility to make sure she was okay. I was here for revenge, not to be the Mother Teresa for unpopular girls.
2. **Do something nice**. It wouldn't kill me to be nice to her. It wasn't that long ago that I was the one crying in the bathroom. Besides, no one could see us in here. It wasn't like she was going to derail my popularity plan.

I sighed and got down on my knees, then lay down on the cool tiles and slid my head under her stall door. Brenda looked down at me. Her eyes were red and swollen.

"What are you doing?" she sputtered. For a second I thought she might step on my face as if I were a bug, but instead she scooted over so she was as far away from me as she could get without climbing onto the toilet.

"You don't think I'm serious. I really am sorry. I'm lying on a disgusting bathroom floor so I can show how sorry I am. My hair is touching the floor, Brenda."

"What if someone comes in here?"

"Then no doubt they will call us weirdos for the rest of the year. I'm taking a lot of risks here."

"What do you want?"

"Come out of the stall so we can talk."

Brenda gave me another long look and then unlocked the stall door. Thank God. I stood, brushing off my pants. I went over to the sink and washed my hands. Brenda leaned against the towel dispenser, a long trail of toilet tissue clutched in one hand. She gave a hiccupping sigh, and as she exhaled, a giant snot bubble grew at the end of her nose. It just sat there like a soap bubble perched at the end of her nostril. She didn't seem to notice it was there. It was the saddest thing I could imagine. I took the tissue out of her hand and blotted her nose and then tossed it in the trash.

"It was wrong of me to blow you off today. I never meant to make you feel bad."

"They like you. I could tell. They're the most popular girls in our school."

"I figured. They got the look, you know?"

"Yeah." Brenda went back into the stall and grabbed another wad of tissue, giving her nose a huge blow. She washed her face in the sink and I handed her some paper towels. She tucked her hair behind her ears.

"Wait a minute," I said fishing around in my bag. I pulled out some MAC lip gloss and handed it over. She looked at it as if she had never seen such an item before.

"Put some on."

"My mouth?" She peered at the end of the wand with distrust.

"I don't have rabies or anything. Trust me, it'll look nice."

She put a quick smear on and handed it back. We both looked at her in the mirror. She looked better; the shiny pink lip gloss gave her some color. Of course she was bound to look better without the snot bubble; everything else from there was a bonus.

"Thanks. I guess we're back to being buddies, huh?"

I chewed my lip and tried to figure out how to explain things.

Brenda looked down. "Forget it. This is stupid." She pushed open the bathroom door and left.

I considered going after her, but then I remembered. This was war. There are always risks of civilian casualties.

chapter eleven

I'd checked off establish popularity on my to-do list. Now it was time to move to stage two: active destruction.

I had done as much research as possible on Justin, Lauren's boyfriend. I studied his Facebook page as if it held the secret to immortality. I had a piece of paper where I scribbled down every number I thought could be important to him and different combinations of those numbers: Lauren's birthday, their anniversary, his football jersey number, the number of his favorite player on the Detroit Lions, his best track time, and his top score on Grand Theft Auto. I waited until math class was under way with a riveting lecture on the importance of polynomial algebraic functions, and then I raised my hand to request the hall pass.

The halls were empty. I stood outside Justin's locker and wiped my sweaty hands on my jeans. Lincoln High lets you reset your locker combination to anything you like as long as you give the number to the janitor. I was counting on the idea that Justin would pick something he could easily remember. He struck me as the kind of guy who doesn't have a lot of spare storage space in his brain. I tried Lauren's birthday first, nothing. Then their anniversary, nothing. I tapped my foot, thinking what my best chance would be. I'd only known the guy a couple of days. There were zillions of combinations of numbers he could've picked. I worried it would take all year to try them all, and my math teacher would have someone come looking for me long before then. I dialed in his birthday, hoping Justin was a keep-it-simple kind of guy. I spun the lock around, then said a small prayer, and pulled down. Nothing. Shit. In frustration, I yanked harder and then it clicked, popping open. It sounded really loud in the empty hallway and I flinched, waiting for classroom doors on either side to fly open with people pouring out to ask me what the hell I was doing, but nothing happened.

I pulled open the door and took a step back. Ick. At the bottom of Justin's locker was a pile of gym clothing and football gear that smelled like he last washed them sometime around sophomore year. The odor waves were nearly visible to the naked eye. It was possible that there were a few lunch leftovers buried in there too. Something had a vague banana-past-its-prime smell to it. I held my breath and started rummaging around in his jacket pockets. Nothing.

Lincoln High forbids students from having cell phones in class. I was certain Justin would keep his in his locker like everyone else. I gave another quick look around. I didn't have time to do an archeological dig in the compost pile at the bottom of the locker. How did he manage to get so much stuff in here already? I reached my hand up and tried to feel around on the shelf, hoping that I wouldn't grab a hold of anything too nasty since I couldn't see what he had up there. I felt his keys, a tennis ball, and what I desperately hoped was not a jockstrap even though that's what it felt like, and then—BINGO—his phone. I snatched it off the shelf and fought the urge to do a celebration dance. I snapped it open and dialed my own cell number, waited for the call to connect, and then hung up. I slid it back onto the shelf and shut the door.

I made it one step before I snapped back, nearly falling to the floor. It felt like someone had grabbed me around the neck. Shit. My scarf was shut in the locker.

I gave my scarf a tug, but it was caught. I could hear someone walking down the other hall. They were going to round the corner any second. I turned around the best that I could, given that the locker had me in a choke hold, and gave the scarf a yank. It didn't budge an inch. I tried to figure out if I could lean against the door and look casual. Nope. My fingers flew over the lock, spinning in Justin's birth date. It clicked open and I yanked my scarf out, shutting the door an instant before the janitor came around the corner. He looked at me with my hand on the lock and sweat pouring down my face.

"Wrong locker," I said with a nervous laugh. "They all look alike from the outside. How's a person supposed to tell which one is theirs?"

"They're numbered."

I looked at the lockers like I had never seen them before. "Well, look at that, they *are* numbered. That's handy."

The janitor gave me a look and kept going, pushing the AV trolley. I went back to Justin's locker during biology, English, and study hall, and did the same thing, minus the whole getting-my-scarf-caught part. Karma was clearly on my side, because not once did anyone ever see me in his locker and the timing was perfect. When I went back to my locker at the end of the day there was a text message from Lauren letting me know they were meeting up at Bean There Done That after school. I also had a long list of calls from Justin's phone. Perfect.

chapter twelve

Bean There was a classic Starbucks knockoff—squishy brown sofas pulled up close to a gas fireplace and clusters of scarred wooden tables with tiny bistro chairs scattered around. There were stacks of papers folded open to the entertainment and sports sections on all the windowsills, and the smell of coffee and high-calorie muffins floated through the air. The barista had his black hair tied back and a row of silver hoops marched in lockstep up the side of his ears. He called out the drinks in a singsong voice.

"One large capp-uchiiiiiiiiiii-no." He slid the cup across the counter, confident that it wouldn't go hurling off the edge, and I saw a harried-looking junior girl lunge to grab it before it could slide too far.

I found Lauren and the others at the back of the café. The tables in the back were up a small riser, just slightly higher than the rest of the café. Leave it to Lauren to find a stage wherever she went. Lauren had her feet up on a chair to hold a space for me. Although other people were standing around waiting for tables, I noticed no one even tried to take the chair away from her. I watched them while I waited for my drink. The student body of Lincoln High wandered in and out of Bean There, acting as if it were a privilege to be able to see the great Lauren Wood sip her coffee. And Lauren knew it too. She laughed just a bit too loud and had all these exaggerated hand gestures so that even the folks at the far side of the café wouldn't miss her performance.

"Medium, no foam, skinny, chai laaaaaaaaaaa-te!" I grabbed my drink and after a quick sip, gave the barista a salute with the cup. Always acknowledge perfection. I wove my way through the tables. When Lauren saw me she paused for a second before taking her feet off my chair, just long enough to emphasize what a favor she was bestowing on me. I flopped down and gave everyone a smile. Lauren looked over at my drink.

"Dairy?"

"Chai tea. Want some?" I pushed the drink in her direction, and she pulled back as if I were offering her a nice steaming cup of hemlock.

"I don't touch dairy. It clogs up my vocal cords." She shrugged as if this were a hardship she was used to enduring. "I've still got voice lessons tonight. I'm practicing my song for tryouts."

"So you stick with plain black coffee then?"

"Hot water with lemon."

I nodded and took a long sip of my throat-coating milky tea, fighting the urge to gargle it in front of her.

"Where did you get those boots?" Kyla asked, nearly falling to her knees when she noticed them.

I turned my foot from side to side so everyone could get a good look.

"I think I got them at one of the Manolo sample sales. All the designers in New York do these trunk sales and you can get amazing deals." I bought them at a thrift store, but whatever. Lauren's eyes looked down at them.

"I never liked Manolos. I think they're a bit flashy," Lauren said.

I shrugged. The only thing she didn't like about Manolo shoes was that she didn't own any.

"You can order some great shoes on Zappos online," Kyla said.

"Yeah, but I hate to buy shoes without trying them on, especially when they're expensive, you know?" I said, and we all nodded, acknowledging how it was less than ideal. I pulled my phone out and placed it on the table.

"Waiting for a call?" Bailey asked.

"Someone has been calling all day and hanging up, or worse, sort of breathing heavy. I swear to God, it's driving me nuts. I want to catch it next time it goes off. It's the same number so I know it's the same guy."

"Someone has a secret admirer," Bailey said, and everyone laughed. "Do you know who it is?"

"No idea. On one message there was this 'um . . . um,' like he was trying to say something, but in the end he still hung up."

"You should call him back and ask him if he's worked up the balls to ask you out yet," Kyla suggested.

"Here, give me your phone and I'll call him," Lauren said, snatching my phone off the table. "He might be cute, you never know. I'll tell him you never talk dirty to someone who doesn't speak up."

"Woo!" cheered one of the sophomore boys sitting near us. "You can talk dirty to me anytime." His friends high-fived him.

"In your dreams, Sutherland—you're just a baby. I don't do kiddie porn," Lauren fired back, making everyone laugh.

Lauren flipped her hair and smiled. She looked down at the phone and I watched the blood drain out of her face when she recognized the number. Bailey and Kyla were still swapping comments with the sophomores and didn't notice. Lauren started jabbing at my phone. Kyla yanked her chair closer to the table as if story hour were about to begin and she wanted to be right in the first row.

"So call him. We're ready."

"Don't be a child, Kyla." Lauren tossed the phone back down on the table. "I wouldn't really call him. I don't play games with people. God. Sometimes you act like you're still in junior high."

Kyla pulled back as if she had been slapped. Bailey looked back and forth between Kyla and Lauren like a small kid watching her parents fight. I picked up the phone and looked at it.

"You deleted the number," I said.

"What, you were going to call him?" Lauren asked.

I shrugged as if I couldn't care less.

"We were just joking around," Kyla said.

"Whatever. If you want to act like that, maybe you should start trolling the junior high so you can find a guy with your sense of humor." Lauren's chair legs squealed on the floor as she pushed away from the table too fast. "I gotta go. I've got to get to my voice lessons." Lauren tossed her tote bag over her shoulder and left without another word.

"Whoa. Who peed in her cornflakes?" Kyla asked.

"She's probably just getting nerves over the whole play thing," Bailey said, looking out the window to watch Lauren walk away. "Tryouts always freak her out and this is her senior year, so the lead means the world to her."

"It doesn't mean she has to take my head off." Kyla took a deep drink of her coffee and then winced from the heat. Her foot bounced up and down.

"Oh, you know she doesn't mean it. Don't be mad. Look, anyone want to share a muffin? I'm starving." Bailey didn't wait for us to answer and instead popped up and headed to the bakery case.

"For what it's worth, you totally didn't deserve that," I said, once Bailey was out of range. Step two: divide and conquer.

"Oh, Bailey's right. Lauren doesn't mean anything by it. It's just sometimes, she's . . . you know . . ."

"I know. A bunch of my friends in New York acted just like Lauren. I mean, they don't call them drama queens for nothing."

Kyla met my eyes with surprise, and then we both burst out laughing.

"Hey, what size shoe do you wear?" I asked, pointing at her feet.

"They're huge aren't they? They're eight-and-a-halfs."

"I have flipper feet too—curse of being tall. Do you want to borrow these boots? You can have them for the weekend if you want."

"Are you serious? You would lend them to me?"

"Of course. They're just boots. It's not like I'm giving you a kidney or anything."

I bent over to slide one off and passed it over. "Try it on and see if it fits."

Kyla gave a squeal, kicking off her shoe and pulling on the boot. She held her foot out in front of her, turning it this way and that. Bailey came back with a muffin cut in three equal pieces. I had a suspicion Bailey would end up working as a nursery school teacher in the future.

"Check it out—Claire's lending me her boots!"

"Oh my God, that's so nice."

I gave them both a smile. That was me. Nice.

chapter thirteen

B renda called the next night. She'd used her buddy status to weasel my phone number out of the secretary. So much for privacy. She said she wanted to check in on me and make sure I was settling in okay. I admire tenacity in other people. However, I had my own project that required my focus. On the other hand, being nice to Brenda (at least when no one was watching) would balance out my own karma just in case my parents were right on that angle. I would destroy Lauren, but maybe if I built up Brenda, then in some way the whole thing evened out. I went ahead and accepted her invitation to come over.

Brenda's room was painted an icy blue. Her bed was shoved off in the corner, and the bulk of the room was taken up with a large desk and floor-to-ceiling bookshelves. I stood in front of her closet, sliding the hangers back and forth, hoping for her sake that she was hiding the good stuff in the back.

"I dress more for comfort than style," Brenda said, picking at her cuticle. I took a swipe at her hand.

"You don't say. Did you buy every item of clothing you own from Eddie Bauer?"

"What's wrong with Eddie Bauer?"

"Do you ever look at their catalogs?" I asked, and Brenda nodded. "When you look at the pictures do you notice a lot of hot people our age cavorting about?"

"No." She lifted her hand toward her mouth and saw me staring so she put it back down on the bedspread.

"Correct. You see pretty middle-aged women with good skin. Eddie Bauer's target audience is the suburban mom who wants to look nice, but needs pants that don't have to be ironed and repel stains. Eddie Bauer spends zillions of dollars on advertising. They're telling you in their ads who they are trying to attract. It's not the youth market."

"I'm not the kind of person who wears skintight jeans and crop tops."

I gave a sigh and sat down on the floor in front of her. "You are aware that there are options other than a khaki collection or slut wear?"

"I'll keep it in mind if I ever decide to redo my wardrobe."

"If you're thinking redo, you should tackle your hair first."

Both Brenda and I turned so we could see her reflection in the mirror above her dresser. Her hair seemed to come straight out of her head, giving her the overall appearance of a triangle.

"Where do you get your hair cut?"

"Supercuts at the mall."

"Here's some free advice. You don't have to spend a lot of money to be popular, but you have to spend your money wisely. For example, don't spend wads of cash on underwear. Most people won't see it, and anyone who does will be trying to get you out of it so they won't care. You can buy underwear at Target. However, your hair is a different story."

"What makes you think I need advice on how to be popular?"

I raised an eyebrow. "It's not about being popular, it's about how to play the game."

"I don't care about that stuff."

"Yes you do. Trust me. Everyone cares. Your hair is a giant billboard on your head. Your billboard is saying: 'I've never heard of deep conditioner and I spend seven dollars on haircuts.'"

"They cost fourteen dollars."

"Still not impressed. Toss me the phonebook and I'll make you an appointment."

"I hate fancy salons."

"Tough. With your type of hair, you've got two options: You get a good cut and then use a straightening iron in the mornings and avoid damp weather conditions, or you get your hair cut in layers and let it curl up a little. Trust me, I understand bad hair. You should have seen mine before I did a major intervention on it. How much time do you spend on your hair in the mornings now?"

"I don't know. I take a shower and stuff."

"Basic hygiene doesn't count. I think we should go with curly. It'll be easier for you to keep up. And we need to lose some of the length, something fun and flirty."

I made a call to the salon and asked to talk to the stylist directly. I described exactly the look I had in mind, as I could tell this was not the kind of thing to leave in the cuticle-chewed hands of Brenda.

She was looking into the mirror when I got off the phone, pondering her reflection.

"Look, popularity is a science. It's not as shallow as it looks."

"Really?" Brenda crossed her arms.

"Popularity is a mathematical formula based on desirability criteria. High schools are a classic anthropological case study, and getting people to respond in the way you want is psychology. All science. It's just not the type of science that you're used to."

"I can't figure you out. You don't seem like the other popular girls I know."

"God, I hope not. I'm shooting to have a bit more depth. Lauren is as shallow as a kid's wading pool with a leak."

"I don't get it. If you don't like her, why do you want to be her friend?"

"It's complicated." I looked at my watch. "I gotta go. You'll get your hair done on the weekend and then you'll see: science."

As I bounced out of the house I felt my karma balance out with what I was going to do tomorrow.

chapter fourteen

"Your parents sent you something," my grandma said as I walked in the house. She was in the kitchen drinking a glass of wine and flipping through *Bon Appétit*. "Should we make a cake or something? There's a recipe in here for turtle brownies."

"Sure." I sat down at the counter and opened the box from my folks. The box had large grease stains on it. Inside was a square of some type of baked good. It looked like it had twigs baked into it, and it weighed a zillion pounds. I gave it a sniff. It was hard to describe the smell, but the word "good" wasn't even close to making the list.

"What is that?"

I looked at the note my parents included. "It's a sugar-free high-fiber protein bar. It has fish oil in it." We both looked down at the box.

"Who makes brownies out of salmon?"

"You want to make them out of turtles," I countered.

My grandma laughed and then looked at the box again. "You going to eat that?"

"Are you going to make me?"

"I'm pretty sure that would count as child abuse. I'm too old to do prison time. Do me a favor and don't put it in the kitchen garbage; take it directly to the garage. That's the kind of smell that sticks around." She started pulling things down from the kitchen cupboards. "You look mighty happy with yourself. I take it the whole going to school with Lauren thing is working out okay?"

"So far so good. I'm putting stage two of my revenge plan into place."

My grandma looked at me over her shoulder with her eyebrows raised. "Revenge plan?"

"Yeah. Basically I'm going to ruin Lauren's life, like she did mine."

"Honey, she didn't ruin your life."

"She sure tried. High school is supposed to be the best time of my life and look at me. Do I look like I'm having the time of my life?"

"I never trust people who had the best time of their lives in high school. That's not the point. If you haven't done what you wanted with your life then it's up to you to change it."

"I'm working on changing it."

"Sounds like you're working on changing *her* life, not yours."

I stood up, pushing the box from my parents away from me. The day had gone perfectly and now this.

"You were the one who gave me the idea. You said I should seize the opportunity."

"I meant come back here and show them who's boss. Prove to yourself that you're fine. You're pretty, you're smart, and you have more artistic skill in your little finger than most people do in their whole bodies. I didn't mean that you should go around trying to put some kind of half-baked revenge plan into place."

"It's not half-baked!" I yelled, and both my grandma and I took a step back in surprise at my voice.

"Okay." My grandma wiped the already clean counters. "Look, sit down again for a minute."

I sat down with my arms crossed.

"Maybe what I said when we talked about you moving out here got lost in translation. That's the problem with doing all your deep talking on the phone." She ran her hands through her hair. "Lauren is what my generation used to call 'a real piece of work.' She doesn't deserve to polish your shoes, and I never knew what you saw in her. You can do much better in the friend department. I have no problem with you going back to school with a clean slate and a different name. I think it makes more sense than trying to deal with all that baggage, but the point of a clean slate is that it's clean. If I knew you were going to drag all this mess with you, I wouldn't have gone along with the plan of registering you under another name."

I opened my mouth to protest, but she held up a hand and cut me off.

"You don't have to like her. You don't have to have anything to do with her, but trust me when I tell you that trying to hurt her isn't going to do anything but hurt you."

"You don't think she deserves it?"

"I can think of few people who would deserve it more than she does, but that's not the point. The point is whether you should be the avenging angel. People like her usually get what they've got coming."

"What if they don't?"

"There is usually more going on in people's lives than we know. Maybe her life isn't as good as you think."

"She's popular; she has friends and a boyfriend. She's in the drama group and destined to star in the play. She's captain of the cheerleading team. It's not fair after what she did to me to get there."

"You want revenge? Be happy. Live your life. Make some friends, good friends. Push your talents. Make yourself even better."

"Fine." I picked at the tape on the box and didn't meet her eyes.

"One of the benefits of being an old lady is you get some perspective. I'm not trying to rain on your parade. If I thought destroying her would make you happy, then I'd jump right in and help out, but it won't."

"Okay," I said. I didn't say anything else, as I was pretty sure that if I tried, I would start crying. Instead I pulled the long strip of tape off the greasy box and breathed slowly through my mouth.

"All right then. You get rid of that thing, and I'll get the stuff together, and we'll make ourselves some proper fish-free brownies. I think *Casablanca* is on TV tonight. Chocolate and Bogart, it doesn't get better."

I walked out to the garage and dumped the box into the trash. It wasn't that I didn't appreciate what my grandma was saying; it was just that I thought she was wrong. It could be better than chocolate and Bogart. I wasn't giving up on the revenge plan. I was just getting started.

chapter fifteen

B renda's hand kept wandering up to touch her hair as if she expected to find it gone. The salon had done a great job. They cut her hair about six inches shorter, so it hung just below her ears with layers all over. With the length gone, her hair had bounced right up into great curly waves—it was a pixie cut with moxie. They put in a semipermanent color just a shade or two warmer than her own natural brown along with what must have been industrial conditioner designed to tame hair that had survived a nuclear blast. I'd also convinced her that wearing lip gloss and mascara would not put her at risk for looking like a Cover Girl dumping ground.

"Stop touching your hair," I said as I paused to look at one of the window displays. Bailey hadn't been kidding when she said this place was a fashion wasteland. It was one chain store after another.

"It's pretty short."

I turned to give her a look. "You cannot tell me that you don't like it."

She reached up to touch it again, tucking a small piece behind her ear. The corners of her mouth pulled up slightly. Then I saw it across the hall.

"That's it, over there." I dragged her by the arm behind me. "This is a guy store."

I pointed at the crisp, white shirt in the window. "One of those."

"What's wrong with the white shirt I already own?"

"Wrong style." I wandered past her and into the store. I held the shirt out in front of her. "We're going for an Audrey Hepburn–inspired look. You already own about six zillion capri pants, so that's a start, and we'll add a nice black skirt. You've got a great figure—why not use it? We'll make some of your Eddie Bauer cardigan collection work until you can afford to replace them. You need a few men's-style button-down shirts and ballet flats. That should give you enough to mix and match so you have stuff to wear. "

"I don't know." Brenda looked at the shirt doubtfully.

"You're supposed to trust me. Plus the shirt is half off," I said, pointing at the hanger tag. "They are practically giving it away. The Hepburn look suits you. You have similar body types."

"I don't look anything like Audrey Hepburn."

"That's because you're always hunched over. You have lousy posture. You never saw Audrey all hunched up. That reminds me of something else. We need to stop at Best Buy."

"I already asked my dad to rent the movies you recommended. I don't need to buy them."

"First of all, watching Hepburn movies is not a chore, so stop making it sound like I'm making you do chemistry problems."

"I like chemistry," Brenda said.

"You'll like Hepburn. She exudes charisma—that's nature's chemistry," I said, extending my arms for drama.

"I know what charisma is."

"Stop sounding so grumpy. What I want is for you to buy a yoga DVD. It will be good for your posture."

"Yoga?" Brenda rolled her eyes.

"Trust me. Yoga leads to great posture. Now get the shirt."

Brenda took the shirt and marched over to the cash register. If she decided against a career in the sciences she could consider the military with that gait. However, the hair alone was starting to make a difference. Her shoulders were back just a bit, and she looked into the clerk's face instead of at the floor. Progress.

Brenda came back swinging her bag slightly, which for her was practically giddy girly behavior.

I linked arms with her and we headed out into the mall as if we were starring in *The Wizard of Oz* and the yellow brick road led to Best Buy. We were laughing when I saw the flying monkeys.

"Shit," I said, stopping short and ducking into Claire's behind an earring rack. Brenda took a few more steps forward before she realized I wasn't next to her. She stood in the middle of the hallway looking around to see where I went. A few steps away at the Baskin Robbins stood Kyla, Bailey, and Lauren.

"What are you looking at?" Kyla asked.

Brenda pointed to her own chest with a finger.

"Yeah, you," Kyla said, pinning her in place with her words.

"Nothing. I was, uh . . ." Brenda looked around again.

"Great. All I need is people staring at me. Call the circus, my life is a freak show," Lauren cried. A few people in the mall turned around to see the drama.

"Here, have a smoothie," Bailey said, passing over a giant pink concoction.

"I might as well. What does it matter if I gain a thousand pounds? Then I can be fat and alone instead of just alone."

"You guys will work it out," Bailey said, stroking Lauren's arm as if she were a prized Siamese kitten.

"He's a dumb fuck if he doesn't realize what an ass he's being," Kyla offered.

"Is everything okay?" Brenda asked.

"Nothing that concerns you," Kyla said with a hand on her hip.

"She might as well know, because it's going to be all over school on Monday. Justin and I broke up. It's over!"

I nearly sucked in a pair of silver hoops. They broke up! Yes! The plan had worked. I would have done a celebration dance except for the fact I was hiding.

"Justin Ryan the football player?" Brenda asked.

"Duh," Kyla said.

"Three years. You know there are Hollywood marriages that haven't lasted as long as our relationship." Lauren gave a giant suck on her straw, making an unpleasant slurping sound. "Do you know how many other people I could have been going out with in that time? Plenty. Guys ask me out all the time and even guys who haven't asked—I can tell they totally would if they thought they stood a chance."

"Totally," Bailey assured her.

"I'm sorry he broke up with you," Brenda offered.

Lauren spun around and Brenda took a step back.

"Let's be really clear about something, Justin did NOT break up with me. I broke up with Justin. I caught him lying to me and the one thing I will not tolerate is lies." Lauren punctuated each word with a point of her finger. I noticed even from across the hall that her manicure was chipped and one nail was broken off completely.

I gave a snort; apparently she was fine with tolerating her own lies. Karma's a bitch, bitch.

"If you can't trust them, dump them," Kyla offered, and then gave her head a shake before grabbing her own smoothie off the counter. "I still can't believe it. He worships you. What the hell is worth so much to him that he would lie about it?"

"It doesn't matter what he lied about. The point is, he lied. The individual lie is unimportant. Would you stop trying to pump me for information? All anyone cares about is the nasty details." Lauren chucked her smoothie at the trash can. The cup hit the side, bounced off, and crashed to the floor. It spread pink smoothie goo across the floor. "My pain is not for everyone's amusement."

I couldn't speak for the others, but I was finding her pain quite amusing. Lauren stomped off without a look back. The three of them watched her go for a beat and then looked down at the oozing pink smoothie. Bailey was the first to act, grabbing a fistful of napkins from the counter and sprinkling them onto the floor, tapping them down with the toe of her shoe. Kyla took a step back as if she didn't want to be connected to the mess. Brenda asked the counter attendant for a roll of paper towels and began helping Bailey.

"We're supposed to be her best friends," Kyla grumbled. "Wanting to know why she broke up with her boyfriend of three years is not exactly pumping her for information. She acts like I was trying to waterboard her."

"She's just upset," Bailey said, tossing a wad of soggy napkins and paper towels in the trash.

"There's being upset and then there's being a bitch."

I nodded behind the earring rack. Kyla was starting to catch on. I could have told her stories that would make her think calling Lauren a bitch was a compliment.

"We should go after her," Bailey said.

Kyla tossed her hair. "No thanks. I can think of better ways to spend a Saturday. I'm going to go look at makeup. Are you coming?"

Bailey chewed on her lower lip, looking down the hall where Lauren had disappeared.

"Forget it," Kyla said, and started to walk in the opposite direction. Bailey looked ready to cry. Brenda finished mopping up the rest of the smoothie, throwing another large handful of paper towels into the trash, and then wiped her hands off.

"Well, I'll see you around," Brenda said.

Bailey looked at her as if she had forgotten Brenda had been there at all.

"Thanks for helping me clean up," Bailey said.

"No problem."

Bailey started to walk after Lauren and then stopped.

"Did you get a haircut or something?" Bailey asked, looking at Brenda as if she had never seen her before. Brenda's hand wandered up to give her new hair another pat and then nodded.

"It looks nice," Bailey said before heading off after Lauren. I waited a few seconds and then came up behind Brenda. She jumped when I touched her arm.

"Where did you go?" she asked, whipping around.

"Sorry. I didn't want to run into them."

"Well, thanks for letting me wander into that little scene by myself."

"She liked your hair. Did you notice that?"

"You're changing the subject."

I stood looking down the hallway for a beat. There was something about the whole scene that felt wrong. I should be thrilled Lauren and her boyfriend were busted up. She could say she was the official "breaker upper," but the fact was, from her perspective, Justin cheated on her. He picked someone else. She should be unraveling, falling apart.

"Did you notice Lauren wasn't that upset?" I said.

"She threw a smoothie."

I waved my hand, dismissing it. "Drama. Lauren is an actress. She knows the importance of a good use of props."

"That smoothie was no prop. She seemed upset to me, and her best friends think she's upset."

"One of her friends thinks she's upset. The other one thinks she's being a bitch." I chewed on the inside of my cheek. "Did you notice that she wasn't even crying? Her eyes weren't red either. No stuffy nose. And if they thought she was really upset, would they have brought her to the mall? Doesn't that seem weird?"

"What seems weird is how you're acting about the whole thing," Brenda said.

"What? Admit it, Lauren Wood can be a real cow. Isn't there even a teeny-tiny part of you that sort of enjoys that things are falling apart for her?" I held my fingers and thumb close together and squinted through the hole.

"She's not a friend of mine, but I wouldn't want to see something bad happen to anyone."

I rolled my eyes. "She's not your friend because she would never be your friend. She can't get anything from you, which renders you useless in her book. She wouldn't do a thing to help you out if you needed it, and if she had something to gain by hurting you, she'd do it so fast you wouldn't even see her sneaking up with the knife."

"What did she do to you?"

My lower lip started shaking and out of nowhere I felt like I could burst into tears right in the center of the mall food court. "It doesn't matter." I gave my eyes a wipe. "Let's go get the yoga DVD."

"Sort of seems like it does matter."

I took a deep breath and looked up at the ceiling, trying to pull the tears back into my eyes using willpower. "Forget the whole thing," I said. Brenda had crossed her arms and was looking at me. "As a friend, I'm asking you to drop it."

"Lauren isn't my friend, but it doesn't seem like you're much of a friend either. You don't tell me what's going on, you don't tell me what's important to you, and you don't even want to be seen with me. As soon as we run into someone, you run off. In fact, the only thing you tell me is what to do."

"That's not fair. It isn't that I don't want people to see us together, it's just . . ." My voice trailed off. She was right. I couldn't afford to be seen with her. My popularity was still too tenuous.

Brenda looked away from me and then started to gather up her shopping bags. "Thanks for coming with me to get my hair cut and all the shopping advice. I should head home."

"What about getting a yoga thing?"

"I can manage it on my own. You don't have to hold my hand every step of the way."

"Oh. Okay. I guess I'll see you around."

"And if I'm really lucky you'll even be able to acknowledge that you know me."

"It's not like that," I protested.

"Just because you don't want it to be like that, doesn't mean that isn't exactly what it is." Brenda hiked up her bags, then turned away.

chapter sixteen

When we were in third grade, Lauren and I had a thing for Nancy Drew books. We would pretend to be Nancy and her best friend Bess, the crime-solving duo. (Care to guess who got to be Nancy and who was stuck being boring Bess?) We decided we didn't have to pretend. We would open our own detective agency, Wood & Worthington Incorporated. Her name had to go first. After all, she pointed out, it was only fair to go in alphabetical order. We made agency letterhead and business cards on Lauren's dad's color printer. We passed out our cards to neighbors and posted a sign at the Meijer's and waited for the cases to pour in. Not too bad for being eight and a half. Our first mystery, the Case of the Missing Library Book, came from my mom.

My mom was missing a copy of *Veggie Fun*, a vegan cookbook. It was a high-stakes case, because every day that it went unfound the library was raking in another day's fine. Lauren leaned back in my desk chair, balancing one of her pink, glitter spiral notebooks on her lap.

"We should make a list of suspects," Lauren said, spinning the pen between her fingers.

"It could be Ms. Tarton's dog, Peanut. He's always burying stuff in the backyard."

"Mmm-hmm." Lauren wrote Peanut down in her notebook with a big number one by his name. "Does Peanut have any history with books? Any witnesses who might have seen him chewing on a book or something?"

"Not sure." We went back to thinking. Crime solving was a lot more work than it looked like in the books.

"Has he bitten anyone?"

"Peanut? No. He's a really nice dog. Plus he's a wiener dog so he's only like six inches tall. I'm not sure he could bite anything important. He goes to the hair salon most days with Ms. Tarton, so he's not even around most of the time."

"Remember what Nancy says—just because someone looks like they're innocent doesn't mean they are." Lauren waved her finger in my direction. I tried to picture Peanut as a hardened criminal. We each went back to trying to think of another suspect. One thing our neighborhood was missing was nefarious characters. "Maybe we should do a stakeout and try and see if there are any clues."

A stakeout seemed way more fun than hanging out in my room, so we went prowling around the neighborhood. We ended up in the park that backed up to the Tartons' backyard. Peanut was wandering around the yard, barking at birds as they flew through the sky. Peanut was nothing if not an optimist. We got down on our hands and knees so we could sneak up closer to the fence and observe him at close range. It was possible that if he didn't know anyone was watching, he would disclose the secret lair (or hole) where he had hidden the library book.

The leaves rustled as we crawled forward. Lauren looked over her shoulder and gave me a face to be quiet. I almost started giggling because she looked just like her mom did when she would stomp down the hall to Lauren's room and beg us to "Please keep down the volume. This is a home, not a trailer." We weren't really sure what being in a home versus a trailer had to do with anything, but we would always shush up. Lauren's mom wasn't the kind of parent who liked to tell you something twice. That was when it happened. I took another crawl forward putting my hand down in a pile of mud brown leaves. I felt a sudden hot pain in the palm of my hand.

I yelled out and yanked my hand back. Peanut let out a howl and ran over to the fence near us, barking his alert. Sticking out of the palm of my hand was a large carpenter nail buried into the flesh. I knew it was bad, but I knew it was really bad when I saw Lauren's face. Her eyes were wide and she looked a bit nauseated. I pulled the nail out with my other hand and blood welled up and poured down my wrist.

"Oh my gosh," I cried, looking at all that blood, my blood.

Lauren whipped off one of her shoes and scrambled to get her sock. She wound it around my hand, squeezing slightly. I'm not sure they covered sock triage in Girl Scouts, but it worked.

"It's going to be okay. We'll go get your mom."

"She's going to be mad at me."

"No she won't."

"Yes she will," I said, somehow sure this would be the case. I started to cry in tandem with Peanut's howls. I felt a fresh wave of pain with every beat of my heart. Lauren looked around on the ground, kicking at the piles of leaves and then bent down to grab the nail. Without hesitating she stabbed herself in the palm. Her wound wasn't as deep as mine, but it was longer and it started to bleed instantly. I stopped crying and looked at her in shock.

"Now we're in trouble together," Lauren said, grabbing my hand, the bloody sock between our palms giving a squishy noise as we shook. "And we're also blood sisters. That's better than real sisters because we did it by choice instead of just being born that way. So you don't ever need to worry about stuff, because I'll be there. I'll figure out something with your mom. And then someday you'll do something for me."

I remember thinking at that moment that there was no one cooler than Lauren. I was sure she would be my best friend forever. Heck, we were blood sisters. Of course, in fairness, at that age, I thought Pop-Tarts were the height of good cuisine, so it's clear I wasn't a great judge of quality.

My mom drove us both to the emergency room for tetanus

shots. Lauren was in the front seat telling my mom this elaborate story to explain how we both managed to puncture our hands at the same time. My mom didn't seem to be buying it, but she wasn't mad either. She had washed each of our hands out at home and wrapped them in clean dishtowels for the trip to the hospital. I was hoping for stitches because I thought they would make me look cool. I sat in the backseat holding my arm in the air the way my mom had told me too. My mom braked quickly when someone cut in front of her in traffic, and the missing library book slid out from under her car seat.

Case solved. Whatever happened between Lauren and me was still a mystery.

chapter seventeen

I lay on my bed, tossing a tennis ball up into the air and catching it. Just another exciting Saturday night. I couldn't tell if the plan was working. Lauren didn't seem to be unraveling as much as I had hoped. I wasn't looking to put her in a bad mood. I had total destruction more in mind. I rolled over on the bed and clicked through my phone list. I hit the speed dial for Kyla. She picked up almost instantly.

"Hey, what's up? I heard that something happened at the mall," I said.

"Lauren threw this fit in the food court. I mean I love the girl, but sometimes, the drama, you know?"

"So what happened?" I asked.

"Lauren and Justin broke up."

"Really?" I tried to get the right amount of shock in my voice. "So was she really upset? Brokenhearted and all that?"

"Sort of."

"Just sort of? Haven't they gone out forever?"

"Yeah. Maybe that's it. She's bored of him. She seemed more ticked about the fact that he lied to her about something than the fact that they broke up. Lauren doesn't like it when people don't sort of fall in line."

"But still, it's her boyfriend. I would have thought he was super important to her. Shouldn't she be crushed?"

"I don't know, I guess. Maybe she likes someone else."

"Who?"

"Got me. She's never said anything about anyone else, but she also doesn't rave about Justin either. He was more like an accessory, you know?"

"Huh," I muttered. That put a kink in my plan. What was the fun of breaking up Lauren and her boyfriend if she didn't even care? I chewed on the corner of my thumbnail for a second.

"So are you going out with us tonight?"

"I made other plans." I could tell Kyla wanted to ask what other plans, but she didn't want to let on that she was out of the loop on any possible social options at Lincoln High. I was too tired to deal with Lauren's drama and needed the time to come up with how to take the plan to the next stage given this disturbing Justin news. I was just staying home, but if Kyla thought I had better plans, I was willing to let her think it.

"Would you mind if I borrowed your boots through the rest of the weekend? I'll polish them up before I give them back."

"Sure." I said absently while I tried to figure out the next step.

Kyla squealed. "You're the best. I really appreciate it."

"No worries. You know, if you want, you can keep them. Just let me borrow them once in a while," I said.

There was silence on the other line for a second.

"Oh-my-god-are-you-serious? That-is-so-awesome," Kyla said, stringing all her words together. "Anytime you want to borrow them, I mean any time, you just say the word."

"Deal. Look, I gotta run okay?" I said, but Kyla hardly noticed because no doubt she was already plotting new outfits. I punched the phone off and leaned back against the bed.

Getting revenge was more complicated than it had looked blocked out in my binder. In theory everything was going exactly according to plan. Lauren's two best friends were finding themselves more and more annoyed with her. I, the mysterious New York City girl, got way more stealth glances and blatant kiss-up compliments from random peons in the hallway, at least for now. Her status as top of the social heap was starting to erode. She was still up there, but the ground beneath her was unstable. I had known I would never steal her boyfriend out from under her. Justin wasn't the type to actually cheat, he was too all-American, but I had even found a way around that. I didn't have to steal him, I just had to make Lauren think that she might not be the center of his universe. She would never take the chance that he would break up with her. How would that look, after all? No, I knew Lauren would dump him first. And she did, just the way I expected. Well, except for the part where she didn't seem to care. I had expected that to go differently. I didn't necessarily think she would be gutted, but I had hoped for a bigger reaction.

I pulled my binder out from under my bed. I flipped through the pages. I was popular, her friends were starting to like me more than her, Lauren's relationship was over, but it wasn't enough. It wasn't anywhere near enough. I looked at the other two bullet points under Lauren's name. It was time to move on to the next stage of the plan.

chapter eighteen

The rest of the evening was frustrating. I made a list of ways to get Lauren off the cheerleading team. It wouldn't be enough if she quit. She had to get kicked off. Unlike the situation with Justin, there needed to be no mistaking the fact that quitting wasn't her choice. It needed that added dimension of humiliation. I made a list of possibilities in my binder:

1. Some type of tragic cheerleading injury due to negligence (Is drunken cheering illegal?)
2. Busted for taking pictures of elementary school kids in compromising positions
3. Doing something very unsportswomanship-like, such as beating up our school mascot
4. Failing all her classes (perhaps declared functionally illiterate) and thus losing her sports eligibility
5. Caught starring in a cheerleaders-gone-wild video

None of the options I came up with seemed very workable. It was going to require more research. I decided to go with just making her life generally miserable until I had a better plan.

Sunday mornings the Wood family could be counted on to go to church no matter the weather. If a once-in-a-century blizzard struck the area, then you could bet Mr. Wood would purchase a dogsled team and mush his family there to prove their commitment to being upstanding members of the community. It wasn't that they were particularly religious—they never prayed over dinner and their house didn't have any Virgin Mary statues planted in the front lawn or anything. If I had to guess, Lauren's favorite saint would be Judas, patron of betrayers. I never heard either of Lauren's parents mention God, unless you counted the times her mom would say, "For the love of God, turn down the TV." Like many things the Wood family did, they went to church because it looked good. It was one more check box on their list proving what an all-American family they were.

To me it didn't matter if they were in church for a true religious calling or if they were faking it. The point was, I could count on all of them being out of the house for at least an hour. I parked a block or two down from their house and waited until I saw their car pull out of the driveway. I got out of my car and walked quickly over to the house and slipped open the gate to the backyard. I stood there waiting. This was the first part of my revenge plan that, if you were going to be technical about things, was illegal.

Lauren's older brother, Josh, had his bedroom on the first

floor. He was off at college, but I was counting on the fact that his window would still be unlocked. Years ago, when Josh was in junior high, he had broken the latch so that it looked locked, but with a good push it would slide right open so he could sneak out and in whenever he wanted. I wandered through the backyard trying to look casual in case any of their neighbors were looking out from their houses. The screen popped right off and I placed it on the ground and gave a quick look around. I yanked on the window. It slid open ridiculously easy; it practically flew off the track. I waited for the sound of sirens, or perhaps a neighbor yelling, but nothing.

One quick jump and a pull, and my front half slipped through the window. Where Josh's bed used to be was now a desk and I slid onto it, knocking a stack of papers to the floor. Shit.

Apparently after Josh went off to college Mrs. Wood had redone his room. I would have thought she was the type of mom to keep her kid's room a shrine to his childhood long after he left, but as it turns out, she was more the type to turn his bedroom into a den. I wonder what Josh thought of the forest green duck theme that was going on. The bookshelf was littered with wooden duck decoys. Their eyes looked a bit desperate to me. I had to fight the urge to stuff them into my bag and release them back into the wild. I picked up the papers on the floor and tried to tell if there had been a specific order. When I couldn't figure it out, I shuffled them back into a tidy pile and hoped no one would notice.

As I slipped through the house, I could see that Mrs. Wood had been busy with redecorating since I had been there last. It seemed to be done in an English country cottage style, heavy on the chintz fabric and overstuffed furniture. Something about the decor made me want to sneeze, as if I were allergic to bad floral design. The staircase wall was a gallery of family photos. There was a giant 14 x 16 of Lauren in her cheerleader outfit near the top. I paused to make the frame hang on a crooked angle. I would have colored in her teeth with a marker, but that might have been a bit too obvious.

Lauren's room was the same Barbie pink it had been when we were kids, but the canopy that had hung over her bed was gone, as were most of the stuffed animals. Most likely she had them put down when she no longer had a use for them. The bedspread was a floral and the furniture was all painted a soft distressed white. The room looked like Laura Ashley had thrown up all over everything. No time to look around. Lauren may not care that much about Justin, but her wardrobe was a different story. I went over to Lauren's closet and pulled out her favorite pair of shoes. I took the left shoe and shoved it into my handbag. I liked the idea of her looking for it, holding the remaining shoe and thinking that the other one had to be there somewhere. I rifled through her hangers, grabbed a few things that I knew she liked, and sat down on the bed. I pulled a seam ripper from my bag and went to work. On one blouse I loosened all the threads that held the right sleeve, I took off three buttons on another. I took the hem out on one of her pant legs. Her jeans took me the most time. I cut every third thread on the seam in the butt.

I shot a look at the clock on her nightstand. Time to get moving: They would be home before too long. I sat down at Lauren's desk and jostled the computer mouse. Her computer was on hibernation mode so it fired right to life. Open on the screen was a paper she was writing for English. On the desk was a copy of Cliff's Notes. *Tsk tsk.* This could count as cheating. I looked around in case anyone was sneaking up on me and then hit delete. One term paper—gone. Consider it a form of academic discipline: If she really wanted to write a paper on the theme of *The Color Purple*, then she should start with reading the book. I rifled through the papers on her desk but didn't see anything that would help me. I opened her desk drawers at random. I crouched down and slid my hand between her mattress and box spring. When we were kids this is where she had kept her Disney Princess locking diary. She had either given up journal writing or had found a more creative hiding place. I looked around for evidence that would give away any secret crushes. If Justin wasn't the love of her life, maybe there was someone else. But the pictures that sat in frames on the dresser were mostly her, Bailey, and Kyla.

I stood in the middle of the room and looked around. What was I missing? I gave the clock another look. Shit, church would be over soon. I reached into my purse and took out the Ziploc bag I had brought. I scooped out the tablespoon of tuna fish inside and dropped it into the heat duct. That should fester after a day or two. I stepped into her bathroom. Lauren appeared to have every possible goo and potion. I picked up her perfume bottle, Clinique Happy. I gave a quick squirt onto my wrists. My hands slid over her things: eye shadow, lip liners, pressed powder, lip sticks, glitter gloss, eye liners, toners, creams, and bronzers. Finally I found it, black mascara. I caught a glimpse of myself in the mirror. I was giving an evil smile that reminded me of Dr. Seuss's Grinch. I pulled a package out of my bag. It was one of those lip-plumping lip glosses. My mom hated those lip glosses and had pointed out to me that they contained capsaicin to make your lips swell. Capsaicin is an extract from chili peppers. I took Lauren's mascara brush out of the tube and swabbed it into the lip-gloss two or three times and then shoved it back into the tube. Victory. Nothing like a little chili pepper to the eye to put a smile on a girl's face.

I took my time leaving the house. I wanted to make sure I didn't leave anything behind, not a speck of dust could be out of place. I peeked out the window before I climbed out, but the coast was clear. The window slid shut, giving a satisfying click as it closed. I did my best to walk slowly back to my car, but it was hard to avoid skipping.

I could hardly wait for Monday.

chapter nineteen

Before school started, the popular kids hung out on the back staircase into the building, provided that the weather was decent. Although there was nothing posted, everyone else knew this area was off-limits unless you were in the upper echelon, in the same way they knew the stoner kids owned the wooded strip at the back of the parking lot where they could smoke weed and pretend no one could see them. Monday morning, I sat next to Bailey and Kyla on the cold cement steps, sipping our Starbucks coffee and talking about our respective weekends. I saw Lauren first; she was walking toward the door from the parking lot, her pace slow.

"Hey, you okay?" Bailey asked, as Lauren drew closer. It was clear Lauren was anything but okay; her eyes were red and swollen. Chili pepper in mascara: one; Lauren Wood: zero.

"I know it's early in the day, but use your brain. Do I look okay?"

Bailey's mouth snapped shut; I could hear her teeth click together.

"I heard about you and Justin. I guess the breakup got to you more than you expected, huh?" I said trying to sound suitably sympathetic. Lauren's mouth pressed together until her lips almost disappeared.

"I haven't been crying. I had some kind of allergic reaction or something." Lauren gave a sniff as if to prove her point.

"Of course you did," Bailey offered. "There can be all kinds of weird pollen and stuff in the fall."

Lauren's nostrils flared and she looked around to see how many people were listening. For once she didn't want to be the center of attention.

"You should get that checked out. Maybe you've got shingles," I suggested.

"Are you saying I've got some kind of disease?"

I placed my hand on my heart as if shocked at her attack. "I didn't mean like a sexually transmitted one or anything. Shingles is like chicken pox. I guess it could also be pink eye."

"Just drop it, okay?" Lauren said, giving her watery eyes another swipe.

"Do you want some of my latte?" Bailey offered.

"Lattes have milk, Bailey. Think about it."

"Sorry."

"Sorry for being stupid or sorry for the latte?" Lauren asked with a snarl.

Bailey's lower lip started to shake and her eyes welled up to match Lauren's.

"Somebody woke up on the wrong side of the bed," a voice behind Lauren said, and we all turned to see who it was.

I hadn't seen him before, and I certainly would have noticed if I had. He was tall and lanky with dark, curly hair. His lower lip was larger than the top and it gave him this sultry pout. His jeans were faded and looked as if they would be as soft as flannel to the touch—and oh, I wanted to touch.

"Bailey knows I'm just joking," Lauren said with a toss of her hair, her voice suddenly light and playful.

He looked over at Bailey who was still staring at her shoes. "Quite the sense of humor you got there," he said to Lauren.

I gave a tiny snort that I instantly tried to turn into a cough.

"Don't be mean. You should know me by now." Lauren cocked her hip at an angle. "I'm a tease."

"That's what I hear," said the mystery boy.

Bailey looked up at him with a smile and he gave her a wink. He looked closer at Lauren and then pulled back.

"Looks like you need to lay off the heavy drinking," he said, motioning to her eyes.

"It's an allergic reaction to something."

"Hope it clears up before tryouts next week. Nobody likes an Eliza Doolittle who looks like a crack addict."

"It'll clear up. What's this I hear—you'll be filming the whole thing?" Lauren asked.

"It's for an independent study. I'm doing a documentary."

"Cool," I said.

He gave a shrug and started to move up the stairs. He looked over at me and then looked down at my chest. The corner of his mouth turned up into a slight smile.

"Nice shirt," he said, lifting his gaze to meet my eyes.

With him looking at me like that I couldn't recall what I was wearing. I was too involved in a fantasy where the two of us were wearing far less. I glanced down at my shirt. It was a T-shirt with a print of the 1949 *Wizard of Oz* movie poster. I looked at Judy Garland's face and tried to think of something smart to say.

"Thanks," I mumbled.

"So which character are you?"

"Dorothy, I guess. Strange girl in a strange place."

He looked at me carefully, cocking his head from one side to the other. "No, Dorothy doesn't suit you. I think you might be more complex. I'm thinking lion—bluff and bluster, but a softie inside. See you around Oz, Lion Girl," he said, moving past us and walking up the stairs. I watched him until he went through the doors.

"Who was that?" I asked, spinning back around.

"Christopher Morgan," Kyla said. "Lincoln High's official rebel without a cause."

"Don't bother. He never dates anyone here," Lauren said. "He's totally focused on his art. Unlike other people around here, he's a real artist."

"What makes you think I want to date him?"

"Apart from the fact your tongue was hanging out when you talked to him?" Lauren sniffed. "Anyway, Chris is going to be a serious filmmaker."

"He's nice," Bailey offered.

"You think everyone's nice," Lauren grumped, plunking down on the stairs next to Kyla. Lauren looked over at Bailey who had gone back to staring at her shoes and chewing on her lower lip. "Don't be ticked at me, I'm having a lousy morning. The whole day was craptacular before the thing with my eyes started. I got completely dressed and then I couldn't find my other shoe so I had to change outfits. Then my new shirt was missing a button. So I had to change all over again. The whole thing was a nightmare. Besides, you know me, I just say stuff."

"I'm not stupid," Bailey said.

Lauren rolled her eyes at Kyla. "Of course you're not stupid." The first morning bell rang and everyone around us started to move toward the doors. "I'm going to run to the bathroom and try to do something with my face." Lauren stood and gathered up her things.

"I'll meet you guys in French," Kyla said, moving up the stairs. "I have to drop off my brother's medication with the nurse first."

Bailey gave a slight wave to Kyla. I stayed in place to watch Lauren walk away. The seat of her jeans was split all down the center seam, and as she moved up the stairs, you could see a wink of her bright pink thong and plenty of white Lauren butt cheek. Bailey's eyes grew wide.

"Lauren!" Bailey cried out. Lauren turned around and I grabbed Bailey's arm, giving it a squeeze. She looked over at me, her eyebrows crinkling together in confusion.

"What?" Lauren placed a hand on one hip.

"Nothing. We just wanted to say we'll save you a place at lunch," I said.

"Okay, whatever." Lauren gave her hair another toss and bounced up the stairs, pink and white flashing in the gap in the back of her pants. Bailey waited until she was gone and then looked at me for an explanation.

"She must know it's there. After all, someone would have to be stupid not to know there was a huge hole in her pants," I said, keeping my face serious. I could see the wheels turning behind Bailey's eyes.

This was a calculated risk on my part. Bailey was most likely the nicest person alive. With her long blond hair, blue eyes, and Mary Poppins approach to the world it was possible she would think I was a vile person to let Lauren be embarrassed. She could race after Lauren and stop her from going any farther. She could even let Lauren in on the fact that I had been willing to let her flash the entire school. On the other hand, maybe, just maybe, part of her was sick of Lauren's crap too. Was it possible that Lauren could drive even Mary Poppins to being a conspirator to my evil deed?

Bailey's lips quivered and a shy smile snuck out. She glanced at me and then away. She looked back and had a huge smile on her face.

"Come on, we should get to French," she said, linking arms with me.

"Why, I would be delighted to attend French with you," I said, giving her a warm smile back. We marched down the hall in tandem. It said a lot about Lauren that she could make a Mary Poppins clone want to do her harm.

"Now tell me more about this Christopher fellow," I said. "Just how nice is he?"

chapter twenty

Brenda practically danced into biology class; her new look clearly agreed with her. Her hair looked great and she was wearing one of her new outfits—slim black pants, ballet flats, and the white shirt starched stiff. She was even walking less Lurchlike. She looked surprised to see me sitting at her lab table. She raised an eyebrow in question and slowed her pace.

"I asked Melvin to change with me," I explained. "You don't mind having me as a lab partner, do you?"

"I don't know. Melvin's a whiz with a Bunsen burner. Besides, people will see us together. Will your reputation survive?"

I didn't say anything and instead passed her a pencil drawing I had done over the weekend.

"It's Einstein," I said in case she didn't recognize him. Brenda took the picture and looked it over.

"Thanks. You're really good."

I shrugged. I never knew what to say when people compli-
mented me on my art. I was just glad that Brenda wasn't going
to demand that I change back with Melvin. I liked her despite
myself, and if we were lab partners, we had a great reason to hang
out, all without blowing my reputation. With her makeover she
looked pretty decent. Besides, there is a long and glorious tradition of popular people being friendly with the smart types when
there are grades on the line.

"Nice hair," a girl said as she walked past our table to the
supply closet. Brenda blushed and mumbled her thanks.

"I take it the new look has been a hit." I crossed my arms.
"Guess maybe I was onto something with the idea that looks
matter."

Brenda shrugged. She turned away from me to pull her
things out of her bag, but I could see a hint of a smile on her
face. "I'm not sure it's exactly earth-shattering news to admit that
people are obsessed with appearances."

"No, the earth-shattering part is that you're paying attention."

"It's an experiment."

"Anything for science."

Mr. Wong, our biology teacher, rapped on his desk to get our
attention. He had a project for the class. He was sending us out
to collect swabs from different surfaces in the school so we could
discover just how much bacteria was thriving in the building.
We were to write up our expectations and then let the swab gunk

grow in some petri dishes for a couple weeks to see what came up. Who says science can't be fun?

Brenda considered where to collect our swabs with great care. She had a future as a health department inspector if she wanted; she took her bacteria very seriously.

"I'm thinking we should do some from the bathroom and then some from the cafeteria tables. The assumption would be that the bathroom would have more bacteria, but my money is on the cafeteria. Have you ever seen them wash down the tables? They use the same nasty rag and a bucket that I am sure is an open sewer of disease." She chewed her lip, thinking things over.

"Mmm, nothing makes me hungrier than talk of sewers and bacteria," I said. We walked down toward the cafeteria. I had an idea. "We should collect a swab from the girl's bathroom and another one from the guy's along with the cafeteria."

"That's a good idea." Brenda looked over at me, surprised.

"What? Just because I look good doesn't mean I don't have a brain." I gave a disgusted snort. "And here you act upset about people judging people by their looks. Pot, kettle, black," I said with a singsong voice.

Getting the swabs from the girl's bathroom and the cafeteria was easy. With those secured Brenda and I stood outside the boy's bathroom.

"Maybe you should go in and get it," Brenda suggested. "I'll stand out here and make sure no one goes in."

"You're the scientist, shouldn't you go? It will be like field-work. You can be the Jane Goodall of the men's room." We both peered up and down the hall. "Look, I'll do it, but you're coming with me. We don't have all day." I shoved open the door and pulled Brenda in behind me by her wrist.

"It doesn't look that different," she said with surprise.

"What you were thinking? Wood paneling, maybe some animal heads mounted on the wall?"

Brenda walked over to the stall wall and started looking over the varied things scribbled on it. Her nose wrinkled up. "This is disgusting."

"Yep. The bathroom wall, where poets leave their finest work. It's amazing how many words rhyme with fart." I surveyed the space. "Where do you want to get the swab from?"

"Floor by the toilet. It should be the same as the girl's room. That way we can use it as a comparison."

"Fair enough. I'll swab, you stand by the door and hum or something so no one wanders in."

I pushed the stall door open and gave a quick look behind me. Brenda was by the door. I whipped out a Sharpie and wrote quickly on the wall: LAUREN WOOD PUTS OUT. Then I paused. Would that be considered a bonus? Would it have been better to put down LAUREN WOOD IS FRIGID? What would she see as the ultimate insult? Then it came to me. I added, BUT WHO CARES?

As I bent to get the sample, Brenda started singing in an effort to scare off any rogue bathroom users. Her voice was clear and strong as it bounced off the tile walls. I stopped thinking about Lauren, revenge, or biology swabs. I backed up so I could see her. She was leaning against the sink as if her singing was no big deal. She was singing a song I didn't know. It sounded sort of sad and mournful, but something about her voice made you feel like things would be okay. She turned around and noticed me staring at her.

"What?"

"What are you doing?"

"You told me to sing." Brenda's face flushed red. There was no way she was ever going to go into a life of crime; she looked guilty when she hadn't even done anything.

"That was amazing. What was it?"

"It's an Irish folk song."

"You're really good."

"I sing at my church. I've been in the choir for a few years."

I waved my hand dismissively. "Skip church. You should be singing on the radio. You could be on *American Idol* or something."

Brenda raised one eyebrow.

"Okay, maybe *American Idol* isn't your style, but I'm serious. You're really good," I said.

"Thanks. Why do you look so surprised?"

"I don't know. It's just unexpected. If you had memorized the entire periodic table it would be amazing, but not that surprising. You're a woman of mystery, no doubt about it."

"Did you get the sample?"

I held up the swab and Brenda clicked the plastic top over the tip, preserving our carefully gathered bacteria. She fanned out the three swabs in her hand and looked at them closely as if she could see the microscopic creatures already breeding on the tips. She looked satisfied with a job well done.

"Once we get a good look at them through the microscope we should do up some graphics. You're the art guru—you can make up some color sketches."

"Well, with all this extra credit fun I can see Melvin is going to be upset you're not his lab partner anymore."

Brenda smirked and yanked open the bathroom door, heading back to Wong's class. The idea came to me in a flash; it was so perfect, it took my breath away.

The door closed behind Brenda, and I stood there looking at it, while taking short, shallow breaths. The door opened back up and Brenda peeked her head in.

"So, you coming or are you planning to stay here?"

I stepped out after her into the hallway.

"Brenda?" She turned to look at me. "Have you ever considered trying out for the school play? With a voice like yours, you could take the lead."

chapter twenty-one

Lauren wasn't at lunch. Apparently she made it to third period before anyone told her about her pants. To me this proved that I wasn't the only one who couldn't stand her. Lauren had gone home to change. Kyla started laughing when she told the story, and then we all agreed that of course it wasn't really funny. We were simply laughing with her, not at her.

I left lunch early so I could find Ms. Herbaut, the drama teacher. Rumor was that Ms. Herbaut had been on the verge of fame and glory on the stage when she gave it all up to move to middle-of-nowhere Michigan to marry her one true love. Although this story had a lovely romance novel–like quality, I was more skeptical. My hunch was that Ms. Herbaut got sick of living in a dumpy studio apartment, waiting tables, and hustling to audition after audition, where, if she was lucky, she would end up earning the role of "peasant number two" in an off-Broadway production of Shakespeare.

Ms. Herbaut's room was near the auditorium, and she'd decorated the walls with various playbills and those annoying kitty just-hang-in-there type posters. I wonder if adults really think we're going to get to the end of our ropes, ready to hurl ourselves off a bridge somewhere, and the sight of a cute kitty will turn us around. Saved by big-eyed kittens. Speaking for myself, I don't want to settle for just hanging in there.

Ms. Herbaut wasn't in the room even though this was supposed to be her assigned office hour. I wandered around, stopping at the giant bulletin board at the back. She had pinned up pictures from the film version of *My Fair Lady* and slips of paper with the song lyrics. In the center of the board there was information about the upcoming auditions. I pulled a scrap of paper out of my bag and made a few notes. Brenda still wasn't sold on the idea, but I was working on her.

"So, Lion, we meet again. What has you so far off the yellow brick road?"

I spun around and Christopher, the good-looking guy from this morning, was leaning against the doorjamb. I felt my tongue dry out and I swallowed deeply.

"I'm Claire."

"Cowardly Claire?"

"Courageous," I shot back. He gave a half smile and my stomach fell into a free fall to the floor.

"What makes someone move from New York to this neck of the woods?"

"How do you know I'm from New York?"

"I asked about you." He took another step closer, and I felt my heart pick up its pace. It was slamming around in my chest like I was sprinting uphill.

"What else did you find out?"

"Not much." Christopher motioned to the bulletin board. "You planning to try out for the play?"

"I'm more of a behind-the-scenes person. I was going to check with Ms. Herbaut to see if I could volunteer to stage-manage or something."

"Ah, you like to be the power behind the throne, huh?"

I gave a high and squeaky laugh that made me sound like I'd been sucking helium. I cleared my throat and tried to say something smart. "I hear you're a filmmaker. I wouldn't think you'd want to be involved with a school play."

"So you've been asking about me too?" His smile grew wider. "I'm going to do a documentary short on the play, a sort of drama-behind-the-drama kind of thing. I want to be a director."

"You like Hitchcock?" I asked, hoping that he wouldn't say something like "Hitchcock who?"

Christopher's face lit up. "I love Hitchcock. The man was a master. *Strangers on a Train*? Brilliant."

"I love the costumes in those black-and-white films."

"Old movies are boring," said a voice behind us, and we both turned around. It was Lauren, wearing a new pair of jeans.

She walked over and stood close to Christopher. She looked at me with her nose scrunched up. Her eyes were better, the puffiness was gone, but they were still red.

"What do you think?" Christopher asked me. "Do you have a Hitchcock favorite?"

"*Vertigo*. Hands down. Didn't do well when it was released, but no doubt about it, it's one of his best."

Christopher gave a slight appreciative nod. "Some critics call it one of the best movies ever."

"Did you know they only had like sixteen days of on-site filming?"

"That's cool—I didn't know that." Christopher gave me an appraising look.

"More than just a pretty face," I said.

Christopher opened his mouth to say something, but Lauren cut him off. "So, I thought you said you weren't trying out for the play." Her face was still squished up as if she smelled something bad. She took a slight step forward as if she were trying to use her body to create a wall between the two of us.

"You made it sound like so much fun, I decided to see if I could help out," I said.

"Oh." Lauren greeted the news that I would be involved with the play with the same level of excitement that others use to greet news of impending dental work. Her nostrils were flaring in and out. Mr. Ed grows annoyed.

"So you like old movies, huh?" Lauren's eyes narrowed.

Uh-oh. Helen loved old movies. Claire was supposed to be a completely different person. Showing off for Christopher was going to cost me.

"No. I mean, well, yeah. I mean, I just like movies in general. An ex-boyfriend of mine was in film school in New York. I could take it or leave it."

"Oh," Christopher said, sounding disappointed. "Here I thought I found a kindred spirit."

I shrugged, wishing I could throw myself under a bus. "Sorry."

"Well, Lion, I'll see you around then." Christopher gave Lauren a quick smile and shuffled toward the door. He didn't simply walk, he moseyed.

"Are you headed to gym?" Lauren called after him. Christopher nodded. "I'll walk with you. I was going to ask Ms. H. a question, but I bet you can help me."

Lauren was looking up at Christopher, and I could see it in her face. She was crazy about him. Over-the-moon crazy. Disney singing wildlife, *fa-la-la-la* kind of crazy. Christopher was everything that Lauren's mother would hate—family from the wrong side of the tracks, earring, too-long hair, career plans that didn't involve wearing a suit and earning obscene amounts of money. Even though they were opposites, it was clear from the way she looked at him she was head over heels. No wonder she wasn't that sorry about Justin. Maybe she thought it was time to throw caution, and herself, to the wind . . . and at Christopher.

Doing my best to woo Christopher away from her grasp wasn't even going to feel like work. This wasn't revenge; it was a public service. No one that good should be with someone so bad.

chapter twenty-two

Grandma looked at the half-cooked carcass. She gave it a poke with her fork. "Do you think those onions are caramelizing? They don't look caramel to me. They look soggy."

I peered at the chicken that was squatting on a bed of sliced lemons, fennel, and onions. She didn't really need my opinion; she could make a gourmet meal out of nothing but a soft carrot from the bottom of the crisper drawer, a slice of toast, and the spices no one ever uses, like coriander seed.

"I think the recipe called for too much broth. The onions are just boiling in there, practically floating." She shook her head at the tragedy.

I gave a sigh. Chicken advice I didn't need.

She looked at me. "Sorry about that. Tell me the problem again."

"My friend Brenda doesn't want to try out for the play."

"Maybe the play isn't her kind of thing."

"It's not. She's not good at the spotlight. She's more of a books and laboratories kind of person."

"Well, then there you go." Grandma drained some of the broth and chicken fat into the sink. "So if she doesn't want to do it, why does that frost your cookies? Just because you're doing the play doesn't mean she has to do it with you. Friends can have different interests."

I rolled my eyes. Grandma was usually pretty good at this, but every so often, usually if she had been watching too much *Dr. Phil,* her advice got all cheesy. Of course, I couldn't tell her the real reason I needed Brenda to try out for the play. Grandma was out of the revenge loop.

"It's not that. I can do the play on my own. It's that I think she would be really good. It seems like a waste to have all that talent and then not use it."

"Not like you and art."

I sighed again. Grandma was on my case to pull together some kind of portfolio so I could apply to college art programs. It wasn't that I didn't like to draw, but I hated the idea of sticking my stuff in between plastic sheets so everyone could *ooh* and *aah* and decide if it was any good. I wasn't even sure I wanted to go to college, which was fine with my parents who are all about "finding yourself," but Grandma is all about the value of a college education.

Grandma had always been the sane one in my family. She stayed in the same house versus moving from apartment to apartment. She remembered to pay her property taxes, and you would never catch her out in the backyard naked at midnight chanting at the moon. I loved that her linen closet was full of towels and sheets as opposed to ours, which was always full of plants and herbs my mom was drying out. I used to love to visit my grandma's because it seemed like what a home was supposed to be, but now that we were living together, I was discovering the downside. Grandma believed in regular mealtimes and lights out by eleven. My parents never gave me a curfew because they felt that to learn responsibility I had to have freedom. Grandma was more of the "be home by midnight, Cinderella, or turn into a pumpkin" kind of guardian. She wasn't keen on the whole "letting life unfold" thing. She wanted me to have a plan for my future. She was becoming borderline annoying about the whole art school thing.

"You can't talk someone into something they don't want to do," Grandma said. "All you can do is point out what you think is in it for them. Not why you think they should do it, but what might appeal to them." She brushed her hair out of her eyes and I laughed. "What's so funny?"

Her hands must have had grease from the chicken on them because her hair now looked like she last took a shower in the early summer. I pointed at her head and she reached up, giving a curse when she felt the oil.

A flash of inspiration came to me. I stuck the chicken back in the oven for her while she went to wash up and hummed a victory tune. Grandma was still helping me with my revenge plan, even if she didn't know it.

chapter twenty-three

Brenda cared for our bacteria with a love and affection that some people don't show their flesh-and-blood children. She would sneak in between classes to coo encouragingly at them, cheering on their growth. We had swiped two petri dishes per swab, and one of our dishes that had been swabbed from the girl's bathroom had died after only two days. It wasn't clear what had happened, but Brenda was devastated. She worried that it would throw off our entire paper. I pointed out that we weren't trying to find a cure for cancer and that it is somewhat unnatural to be that upset over dead bacteria. I wouldn't have been surprised to find out she had a small ceremony for them before she dumped the petri dish in the garbage.

A week after collecting the samples, we were at Brenda's, working on our paper. Brenda sat at her computer, her face set in a serious expression. She was looking through the rough sketches I had done for our project. I was lying on her floor, in theory studying for our test, but there is only so much information I can absorb about the life span of bacteria and viruses. In my mind I replayed the day's victory. While Lauren had been in gym class, I went to the locker room and poured olive oil into her hair spray. Knowing her affinity for excessive product use, I had not been surprised to discover that her hair ended up with so much oil that it basically repelled water. It hung from her head in greasy clumps. She tried to wash it out, but she couldn't get it all. As a result she had to go through the rest of the afternoon looking vaguely homeless and smelling like an Italian restaurant.

"I don't think the color is quite right," Brenda mumbled, breaking into my happy flashback. She was holding the picture close and then far away. "I think they look too pink."

I rolled up into a sitting position and scooted over toward her desk.

"What's wrong? Those are lovely bacteria. Did you see what I did with their tails? Very chic."

"Tails?" Brenda raised an eyebrow. "Flagella would be the term you're looking for."

"Right." I watched Brenda as she scrolled the mouse over the computer screen looking at the various shades of pink available in the color wheel and holding up the drawing to compare. She leaned back to get a better view. "You really like this stuff, don't you?" I said.

"What, science?"

"Yeah. Who else cares what color pink their bacteria end up being?"

"What's strange about liking science? I like knowing how things work," she said.

"I can totally see you being a CSI, working in a swanky glass lab down in Miami."

"That show is total bunk, you know. They make it look like you can run a DNA sample in the time it takes to do a Google search."

"What? TV lies? Tell me it isn't true!" I threw my hands up in the air.

"Ha ha. I don't want to be a CSI, even if it means a fancy lab."

"So what are you going to do with all this science know-how?"

"I want to be an astronaut," she said with a solemn voice.

I started to laugh and then realized she wasn't joking.

"Serious? You want to be a space ranger?"

"I was thinking more something with NASA but, yeah, I'm serious."

"When you go to Mars will you paint my name on a rock up there or something? Maybe bring me back some kind of tiny alien I could keep in an aquarium on my desk?"

"I'm pretty sure NASA frowns on those kind of things, but I'll see what I can do. What about you?"

"I could never be an astronaut. I throw up on roller coasters, and I'm pretty sure being shot into space is more traumatic than that."

"I was being serious," Brenda said.

"So am I. When I was nine, my dad took me to Six Flags. I sprayed down a group of Korean tourists with half-digested Fruit Loops and soy milk. Trust me, those Koreans will always remember their American experience. I bet they never got the smell out."

"I meant, what do you want to do for a living?"

"I don't know," I said with a shrug.

"You're really good at art. You could do graphics or something."

"Mmm, the thrill of designing ads for feminine products, much more meaningful than your shallow goal of exploring space for humanity."

Brenda rolled her eyes and turned back to her computer. She chewed on the end of her pencil.

That was it! Grandma's advice to the rescue again. Suddenly I knew my angle. "You know, I bet it's hard to be an astronaut. I suspect NASA only takes candidates from the best schools and stuff, huh?" I asked.

"Well, it's not like they recruit from the vocational programs if that's what you're asking."

"Yeah, come to think of it, you never see any job postings for astronauts in the classified ads. No wonder you worry so much about your grades."

Brenda looked over at me. "What's your point?"

"I'm just thinking you want to make sure your college apps are killer. Give yourself the best chance to get into the best schools."

"Uh-huh."

"Important to be well-rounded though too. They look at more than just grades, you know." I shook my head knowingly.

Brenda pulled her chair back with a yank. "Not again."

"What?"

"You're bringing up the school play thing."

I snapped my fingers as if the connection just came to me. "That's brilliant! Being in the school play is exactly the kind of thing that can round out an application. Gives you an edge— shows you've got the artsy side and the science side."

"Why do you want me to do this so badly?" Brenda asked. "What does it matter to you?"

"You're amazing. You shouldn't keep that kind of talent to yourself. It's, like, criminal. Besides, it would be good for you."

"Like eating broccoli."

"No, like pushing yourself to try new things. Admit it, you like to sing, right?" I asked.

"Yeah, but I don't like being up in front of huge crowds of people, I don't like being the center of attention, and when you round those things out with the fact that I haven't done a single play in my entire life, it seems like maybe going out for the show isn't the best plan ever."

"That's the very reason that you should do it."

"How do you figure?"

"You think NASA wants astronauts who shy away from a challenge?" I pushed.

Brenda tapped her pencil and looked out the window.

"I wouldn't know how to go about trying out even if I wanted to," she admitted.

I scooched up closer. We had moved from no to logistics.

"You sing one song—I'd recommend something that shows your range—and then you do a short monologue. I can help you pick one out and practice."

Brenda's foot bounced up and down as she thought it over.

"You would help me learn the monologue?"

"Totally. Look at it this way: Worst case scenario, you don't get a part. You don't have a part now so, really, no big loss."

"Except for the part where I could make a total ass of myself."

"No guts, no glory." I waited a few beats. "Captain Kirk would go for it."

Brenda shot me a look. "Captain Kirk?"

"I can't remember the name of the woman captain. Star Trek isn't really my thing."

"Captain Janeway," Brenda said.

"There you go. Janeway would try out for the play."

"What about you?"

"What about me?"

"What can I help you do, if you're going to help me with this? What is it you want to do?"

"I'm really not holding out on you. I don't know what I

want." I picked at the carpet. There was no way to explain that what I wanted was to make Lauren's life miserable. More than miserable. I wanted her to think miserable would be a step up from where her life had sunk. I needed her to lose everything that mattered to her: her boyfriend, her friends, her popularity. She sold me out to get those things and I planned to take them back. I hadn't really considered what I would do after that. It almost felt like if I had another goal, the universe would decide I was too greedy and not give me either thing I wanted.

"You must have some idea of what you want to do with your life long-term."

"Not really."

"So what are you going to do after graduation?" Brenda sounded shocked.

"I figure I'll sort it out when I get to college." I could see her eyes widen. "What, a lot of people don't know what they want to do. College is meant to be a time of self-discovery and all that. Don't you read the college catalogs?"

"Okay, forget it."

"If you want to help me, you can help me pass biology."

"Deal." Brenda held out her hand to shake on it.

"So you'll try out for the play?"

"Yes, I'll try out."

I jumped up and pumped my fists into the air. "Yes! Enough coloring cytoplasm. Let's figure out a song for you to sing. Then we can go online and find a good monologue, nothing too over the top. If you ask me, that's where people go wrong. They get too dramatic. Understated will win them over every time."

"Hey," Brenda said, and I stopped pacing and planning to look at her. "I really appreciate this. You're a good friend." She gave me a warm smile.

And just like that, I went from feeling great to feeling like shit.

chapter twenty-four

I started babysitting in seventh grade. Our next-door neighbor back then was Mrs. Kile. She had a son, Jordon, who was four. That kid was equal parts smart and destructive. He took their TV apart and blew the power grid for our whole neighborhood when he stuck something, no one knew what, into the power socket. It was clear that Jordon couldn't be without constant supervision.

It started with his mom calling me to come over when she needed to get something done. I would hang out in their living room and keep Jordon from accidentally building a thermo-nuclear device using LEGOs and Pop Rocks. The Kiles always had Doritos or string cheese or those plastic pudding cups. I would have done it for the trans-fat snacks alone, but Mrs. Kile insisted on paying me. It was the first money I ever made on my own, unless you count my allowance, which I didn't because it was so small.

There isn't much to do in the summer in Terrace. If I made the mistake of complaining to my parents about being bored they would sign me up for some cheesy day camp and I'd spend the rest of the summer making "art" from nontoxic glue, yarn, and Popsicle sticks. Instead, I would head over to Lauren's and we would hang out at the mall all day. The mall was air conditioned, frequently contained packs of other preteen kids, and had a food court. It was as close as we were going to get to an amusement park. We would go into the stores and talk in loud voices about how we had a very important party to go to and then try on the fancy cocktail dresses. The salesclerks hated us. Once we had tried everything on and eaten at least $10 worth of Dairy Queen we would go to Hudson's Department Store and hang around the makeup counter.

Lauren had strong feelings about makeup. Her mom wore only Chanel cosmetics. She had lotions that were made from ground Peruvian berries, cost more than a small used car, and in theory would stop her aging. My mom, when she wore makeup at all, leaned toward some weird organic brand she bought at the health food store.

"This is the kind of lip gloss I want to get," Lauren said one day the summer before her betrayal. She smoothed on a thin coat from the sample container on the display. The salesclerk, who wore a white coat like she was a doctor working in a research lab, not a peddler of eye shadow, didn't even bother to help us. She leaned against the counter chewing her gum and talking about her boyfriend to the perfume salesclerk across the aisle.

"It looks nice," I said.

"It's not just 'nice.' This lip gloss is made in Paris. Everyone knows that the French do the best lipstick."

"They do?"

"Duh? Why do you think they call it French kissing?"

I wasn't sure she was right, but I also wasn't sure she was wrong. I took the tube from her and inspected it. I put a small bit on my pinky finger and smeared it across my lips just like Lauren had.

"How does it look on me?"

"Good. Try a darker color too." Lauren pulled another sample off the display and passed it over to me. "My mom says that she won't get it for me because she's afraid I'll lose it. As if."

I didn't say anything, but Lauren's mom was right. Lauren was the only person I knew who traveled with her own personal black hole. She was always losing stuff.

I looked at the darker lip gloss on my face. It wasn't me at all. Plus my mom would freak out if she saw me in it. She didn't feel I should wear makeup at all until at least ninth grade.

"I think I'll get a tube of lighter stuff," I said, reaching for the display.

"That stuff costs $25 a tube," Lauren said, her tone pointing out that this type of lip gloss was far from the three-for-the-price-of-two sales at Walgreens.

"It's okay, I've got the money." I pulled my babysitting cash out of my pocket. It lay on the counter sort of crumpled and damp-looking. Lauren looked at me and then down at the money. "I started babysitting for Ms. Kile," I added, my chin thrusting up in a proud way.

"You really should get the darker shade. It goes better with your hair color."

"I like the lighter one better."

"Fine." Lauren turned away with her arms crossed.

"What's the matter?"

"Nothing."

I wasn't sure exactly what was wrong, but I was sure something was. Lauren has a PhD in pouting. No one pouts like her. She could teach lessons to toddlers.

"Are you mad I'm getting the lip gloss?"

"I just think it's rude that you would get the color you know I want."

"But you said your mom wouldn't get it for you."

"Well, that's what she says now, but I would have talked her into it. She would have gotten it for me. Or I would have bought it myself."

"You could get it too. What's wrong with us having the same color?"

"Duh, Helen. If you don't understand, then I don't know how to explain it to you."

"Forget it. I won't get the lip gloss," I said.

"No, go ahead. You want it. It doesn't matter that I wanted it first, so just go ahead and do what you want."

"No, I don't want it anymore. I'll get something else." I hated when Lauren was mad at me. It would ruin the whole day. If she was really ticked, the cold shoulder could last all week. I jammed the money back in my pocket.

"No. Get it." Lauren grabbed a tube of gloss from the display and practically tossed it at the salesclerk. "My friend wants to get this."

"No I don't."

"Yes she does."

Now in addition to Lauren being annoyed with me, the salesclerk was too. "Do you want it or not?" the clerk asked, no doubt already counting down the minutes until summer ended and packs of kids stopped trolling the mall.

"We could share it," I offered. "I can pay for it now, and then we can both use it."

Lauren stopped and turned around so she was facing me. There was a hint of a thaw on her face.

"You would share it with me?"

"Of course. What are best friends for?"

Lauren gave a happy squeak. The clerk did her best to avoid rolling her eyes and wrapped up the tube in tissue before placing it in a tiny glossy shopping bag with the logo of the makeup company in thick, raised gold foil.

"I'll carry it," Lauren said, grabbing the bag as if she were doing me a favor by carrying such a heavy item. We went straight to the ladies' room and each applied a coat of the lip gloss and looked at each other very carefully in the mirror. Once we decided we were suitably fabulous we went back out into the mall. Lauren had a new bounce to her step, and she swung the bag to make sure it attracted the maximum amount of attention.

"It might be better if we kept the lip gloss at my place," Lauren said.

"Why?"

"You know how your mom is. If she sees it she'll have a fit. She'll think you should have sent the money to some group that is saving whales or something stupid like that."

"It's not like I would tell her how much I spent on it. Besides, she pretty much stays out of my stuff."

"Yeah, but whenever we go somewhere we almost always get ready at my place, so if the lip gloss is there, then we'll have it. Otherwise you could forget."

And just like that, it went from my lip gloss to hers. I was like a dad after a divorce with limited visitation rights. Of course the whole thing didn't matter much since about three weeks later Lauren lost the tube of lip gloss altogether. She didn't care as much. She had started babysitting too by that time and was earning her own money. She bought another tube, but there was never any discussion of us sharing it. Later, after the whole "incident," I realized that Lauren did stuff like this all the time.

Turned situations around until I ended up apologizing for nothing at all and she ended up with whatever she wanted in the first place. At the time I had thought Lauren was just more sensitive than me, someone who needed to be treated carefully. Later I realized that she manipulated me and used me all along.

The situation with Brenda was completely different. I wasn't using her. Okay, I was using her a bit, but it wasn't like I was using her to get something for myself. She was being used to get justice, for the greater good. Besides, being in the play was going to benefit Brenda in the long-term. In some ways you could see it as me helping her, encouraging her to be all she can be and that kind of thing.

I lay in bed looking up at the ceiling. I wasn't like Lauren. This situation was nothing like the stuff she used to do to me, the stuff she still pulled with Bailey and Kyla.

Even if it was a less-than-ideal situation, there wasn't a choice. I hadn't come this far to settle for merely giving Lauren greasy hair and torn jeans. It was time for her to pay.

chapter twenty-five

Bailey, Kyla, and I took Lauren out for dinner the night before auditions for good luck. Why we picked dinner was a mystery, as the list of things Lauren wouldn't eat was a mile long. She had to avoid anything that might impact her voice or—God forbid—result in her looking bloated on the big day. It was clear she was nervous.

Unlike Lauren, I was really looking forward to the auditions. I couldn't wait to see her face when Brenda started singing. I was going to have to fight the urge to break into song myself. "*Ding-dong*, the witch is dead . . ." Then there was the added bonus that I would have a chance to talk to Christopher again. I tried to keep the focus on getting closer to Christopher as a means of making sure he didn't fall under Lauren's spell. However, I was willing to admit that the idea of spending time with him was the best part of the revenge plan so far.

Lauren sat there picking at a salad that had anything that

might be considered tasty left off. It appeared to be nothing more than iceberg lettuce with lemon juice on top. I took a big bite of my cheeseburger and tossed it back with a slurp from my milkshake. Lauren glanced at me, disgusted. It was becoming clear that Lauren didn't know quite what to do with me. Due to my nonstop scheming and strategic butt kissing, both Bailey and Kyla loved me. Everyone at school thought I was cosmopolitan and cool. Freshman girls copied how I wore my hair. Lauren was stuck with me. I was like a flea on her otherwise perfectly groomed lapdogs.

"So what does your voice coach say about the audition?" Kyla asked, sticking to safe topics, which included anything focused on Lauren.

"She thinks I'm ready. We've practiced the song since last spring." Lauren stabbed another piece of lettuce. I noticed that the skin around her fingernails was ragged, like she had stuck them in a garbage disposal. Plus, despite a heavy smear of concealer, I could see a flock of small red pimples clustered around her forehead. It looked like my daily sabotages were starting to get to her. I took another satisfied slurp on my milkshake.

"You're going to be great," Bailey said.

"Grrrrrrreat!" I roared in a Tony the Tiger voice. Lauren's eyes narrowed. Bailey and Kyla laughed.

"All I can say is nothing better go wrong," Lauren said, tossing her fork down on her plate to indicate that the five calories she'd consumed had rendered her full.

"Nothing will go wrong," Bailey soothed.

"What could go wrong?" I asked.

"Lately, everything is going wrong."

"Everyone has their ups and downs," I said, as I dragged another fry through my river of ketchup.

"I don't."

That pretty much killed the conversation for a few minutes until Bailey resurrected the thrill-a-minute discussion of how great Lauren's hair looked. I managed to refrain from pointing out that the olive oil had perhaps done some good.

Bailey excused herself to go to the bathroom and Kyla tagged along, leaving Lauren and me sitting across from each other in the booth.

"I don't know what your story is, but I don't trust you," Lauren said.

"What are you talking about?" I managed to meet her eyes, but just barely. After years backing down from Lauren, it was ingrained.

"Ever since you started school here, I've had nothing but bad luck."

"What, you think I have it out for you? Why?" I tried to sound casual, but there was a part of me that almost hoped everything would come to a head, that she would realize who I was and realize just what she had done. I felt a slick of sweat sprout up in my armpits.

Lauren looked around the restaurant, her nostrils flaring

in and out. She really needed to do something about that facial tic.

"This is my senior year and I worked really hard to be where I am," Lauren said, as if that explained anything.

"It's my senior year too. Come to think of it, it's also Bailey's and Kyla's and, oh, give or take a few hundred other people's senior year."

"Whatever." Lauren managed to avoid saying out loud what I was sure she was thinking, which was that our hopes and dreams for our senior year paled in comparison to her own.

"I'm sorry that you don't like me, but for what it's worth, I hope you get the senior year that you deserve," I said with a smile on my face. I popped another fry dripping bloodred ketchup into my mouth.

chapter twenty-six

Auditions were held in the school auditorium. I sat with a clipboard and my grandma's cat's-eye reading glasses, trying to look official. I was supposed to keep track of everyone who tried out, what song they sang, and what scene they performed. Ms. Herbaut would make all the casting decisions, but she said she wanted to get my input as her official assistant director. There were about forty people ready to try out, a small core group of drama nerds who were busy doing scales and murmuring lines under their breath and everyone else who was trying out either for a lark or as a joke.

"Okay, we're ready to hear from . . ."—Ms. Herbaut looked down at the sign-in sheet—"Brenda Bauer."

For a second no one moved and I was afraid I would have to go over and drag Brenda up onto the stage, but then she stood and marched up, reverting to her lumbering, trademarked Frankenstein walk. She stopped in the center of the stage and blinked from the bright lights. I shot her a thumbs-up gesture and prayed she would get through the song without bolting from the stage. I was counting on her NASA dreams overpowering any nerves she had. If she wasn't afraid to be shot into space, then she ought to be able to handle this.

"Go ahead," Ms. Herbaut prodded as Brenda continued to just stand there. Brenda swallowed hard and then handed her music to the pianist at the side of the stage. When the music started she shut her eyes.

After much debate we had picked the song "I Don't Know How to Love Him" from the musical *Jesus Christ Superstar*. It had a sort of tragic-dreamy quality that worked well with Brenda's voice and had the added bonus of being a song I didn't think anyone else would pick. Brenda's voice wavered a bit when she started, but soon she hit her stride. I saw the pianist look up in surprise, and even the other students in the auditorium stopped goofing around and listened. When Brenda finished everyone fell silent. I could see her fidget on the stage.

"Who was that?" Ms. Herbaut said, shuffling the papers in her lap.

"Her name is Brenda Bauer." I paused, wanting to brag that I had been the one to convince her to try out, but I couldn't. As far as the rest of the school knew, we were nothing more than lab partners.

"Where has she been hiding for the past four years?" Ms. Herbaut whispered to me. "Brenda? That was lovely. Very lovely.

Would you mind doing another song for me, one from the show? I'd like to hear you do a duet with one of the other actors. Brian? Would you please join Brenda?"

Brian, one of the long-term drama nerds, gave a gallant nod and hopped up on the stage. It was then that I saw Christopher slouched down in a seat toward the back making notes. Ms. Herbaut had forbidden him to film any of the auditions as she thought it would make people too nervous. My stomach did a light flip when he looked up and met my eyes. I tucked a piece of hair behind my ear and tried to look official.

"I'd like to hear you two do 'On the Street Where You Live,'" Ms. Herbaut said to Brenda and Brian.

"I don't know the words to that one," Brenda said.

"I know them," Lauren said, standing up. "I've memorized the whole score. If you want to hear a duet, I can do it with Brian."

"Thanks, Lauren, but I want to hear Brenda right now. Brenda, why don't you and Brian go out into the hall and run through it, then come back when you're ready."

"No problem." Brian gave Brenda a reassuring smile and directed her through the wings, his hand on her elbow.

"I could do the song now," Lauren said again. I tried not to smirk when I heard Ms. Herbaut give a tired-sounding sigh.

"Okay, Lauren, how about you do your song while we wait for them to return?"

Lauren scampered up the steps and presented the music to

the pianist as if it were a royal decree. She took center stage, cleared her throat a few times, and then gave a solemn nod to the pianist to indicate she was ready.

Lauren sang well, but she should have waited. She should have gone after someone else who was merely mediocre so that she would stand out. Going right after Brenda only highlighted that her voice lacked something. Technically it was fine, she didn't miss a note, but it had no spark, no vitality. Partway through the song, you could see that she knew she was falling short so she sang louder and resorted to grand sweeping gestures with her arms when she felt it was needed. She bowed low when the song was over, and the group of devoted drama students gave her a quick smatter of applause even though they weren't supposed to.

"Thanks, Lauren," Ms. Herbaut said.

"I can do something else if you like," Lauren offered. "If you want to see my range, I can do one of the songs from the beginning. I've been working on a cockney accent too."

"We've got a lot of people to go," I reminded Ms. Herbaut. She surveyed the auditorium, calculating just how many renditions she was going to hear of "The Rain in Spain" before the afternoon was over.

"You're right. We're going to move along for right now, Lauren. I'll let you know if I need to hear another song."

Lauren pressed her lips together and her horse nostrils flared in annoyance. Not her best look. She caught me smiling and glared. I held my hands up and gave a silent clap. I'd let her take that any way she liked. I went back to riffling through my stack of papers to find who was supposed to go next. Ms. Herbaut called out for an Erin Legualt. One of the freshman girls jumped up and squealed as if she had been called as a contestant on *The Price Is Right*. As she ran for the stage she tripped over her own feet and fell. She popped right back up as if she were made from rubber. Ms. Herbaut massaged her temples. I'm guessing teaching drama at the high school level wasn't all Ms. Herbaut hoped it would be.

"Claire, can you take a bottle of water down to the pianist? It's going to be a long afternoon."

I gave her an "aye-aye, captain" salute and wove my way down the far aisle. I saw Brenda in the wings of the auditorium and I tried to give her a secret thumbs-up.

"HELEN!" Someone yelled out.

I spun around at the same time as another girl, both of us answering at the same time.

"What?"

The other Helen looked at me annoyed. Shit. I wasn't supposed to be Helen anymore. I could feel my face flushing red. Brenda looked at me strangely.

"I thought she said my name," I said to no one in particular. The girl next to me gave me an odd look, no doubt wondering how hard it was to tell the difference between the names Helen and Claire.

I practically tossed the water bottle at the pianist, fled for the safety of my seat, and smacked directly into Lauren. She was looking at me closely. I could see the wheels turning behind her eyes. Had she overheard the whole Helen thing?

"Excuse me," I said, as I moved past her. I could feel her eyes following me up the aisle. Shit. Shit. Shit. This is how things fall apart, stupid mistakes. Once I sat down I could see Lauren talking to one of the other drama kids, and the girl passed over a Tupperware container. Lauren marched back down the aisle and stood at the end of my row. I clutched my hands together so she couldn't tell they were shaking.

The Tupperware container was full of fruit diced into bite-size pieces, squares of cantaloupe and pineapple tossed with quartered frozen strawberries. Lauren thrust out the container in front of me.

"Have a piece of fruit," she said, her voice stern.

"No, thanks," I said.

"You should have some." Lauren pushed the Tupperware forward again so that it bounced against my chest. "Claire." I could feel my heart beating a thousand times faster. I was allergic to strawberries. Well, my Helen self was allergic and Lauren knew that. She had been with me when I had one of my worst allergic reactions as a kid. In fact, she caused it.

When we were nine or ten Lauren had the idea to do a science experiment where I tried strawberry-flavored gum to see if I would have a reaction, and then when I didn't, we tried a strawberry Fruit Roll-Up. The Roll-Up did me in, and I ended up throwing up with all the force of a fire hose. My mother had been livid. She couldn't believe I ate the Roll-Up just because Lauren asked me to when I knew I was allergic. She had no idea that at the time I would have done anything Lauren asked me. What's a little vomit between good friends?

I reached out and tentatively picked up a cantaloupe square.

"Have a strawberry," Lauren insisted with an impatient shake of the container.

Shit. She knows, or she thinks she knows.

"I actually love cantaloupe, it's my favorite," I tried.

"The cantaloupe isn't ripe. Have a strawberry. They're the best."

My fingers hovered over the berry and then before I could think about it too much I popped it into my mouth and swallowed it whole without chewing. Maybe chewing releases the allergic stuff; maybe if I swallowed it my stomach acid could kill it.

"Mmm, you're right. Those are great," I said.

Lauren's face fell. I could tell she thought she had me, but now she wasn't sure. I gave her a small salute with my clipboard and then made a vague motion indicating that she should head back to her seat. She walked back with her shoulders slumped. Once she sat down, she turned around every few moments and looked at me as if waiting to see what would happen. Christopher looked back and forth between us. I wondered what type of notes he was taking about us.

I pulled my purse up on my lap and started to rummage

through my stuff, hoping I might have some Benadryl in there. Nothing. I wondered if my throat would start to swell and if Brenda had covered enough in her science classes that she could do a trache on me using only a ballpoint pen if I needed one. I rubbed my fingers together, noticing that the tips that had touched the berry felt a bit hot and the skin tight. My stomach did a slow rollover. Uh-oh. I stood to make a run for the bathroom, and Lauren spun around again to look at me. I sat back down. If I went to the bathroom she would follow me—I knew it. She would know I'm allergic to the strawberry and she would know I'm not really Claire. The jig would be up, and I wasn't even close to reaching my goal of complete and utter Lauren destruction.

"Claire? Are you okay?" Ms. Herbaut touched my shoulder.

"Mmm-hmm." I smiled with my lips pressed together. I had the very real fear that if I opened my mouth to say anything that strawberry was going to come flying right out.

"I'll get us a couple of Diet Cokes. These auditions can be exhausting." She slid out of the row and down toward the cooler that was at the front. She motioned to the stage for things to continue.

Shit. Shit. Shit. The music started up for someone's tryout. The pianist was loud. My stomach rolled over again. I swallowed hard, trying to push the berry back into place. I broke into a cold, sticky sweat all over. My body was clearly planning to evict the berry and, from the way it felt, at a high rate of speed. I looked around for a solution. I gripped the handles of my purse. Then I glanced down. No way. I couldn't. I looked up again and saw the back of Lauren's head. I couldn't give up now.

Desperate times, desperate measures, I chanted to myself. I thought about how sometimes you need to sacrifice for what you really want. I dumped the contents of my handbag in my lap and then threw up in the purse. The piano drowned out the sound of my yakking. I sat back and wiped my mouth with a tissue. I even managed to smile at Lauren when she turned around for the millionth time.

I zipped the bag closed and placed it carefully back down onto the floor.

Maybe this would prove to the universe how serious I was about the whole thing.

chapter twenty-seven

G randma tapped on my door.

One of the downsides to having a grandma who used to be a social worker is that she's really into talking. She's not happy unless I'm blathering on about my feelings. She's always coming into my room so we can have these heart-to-heart talks. It's not that I don't appreciate it, but with my Lauren issues off the table for the discussion, I think she wanted me to have some new and interesting problem she could sink her teeth into. Sometimes I thought about making something up, like telling her I'd been considering a gender reassignment, just so we'd have something new to talk about. Grandma tapped on the door again and leaned her head into my room.

"There's someone at the front door for you."

I sat bolt upright in bed. "Someone for me?"

"Yes, it appears someone has discovered your lair despite your hermitlike existence."

I rolled my eyes and loped downstairs, hoping it wasn't Lauren. She would recognize my grandma for sure. Brenda was on the stoop holding a basket. She held it out.

"I made you cookies," she said.

I took the basket and looked inside. Chocolate chip, from the look of things.

"Why?"

"For helping me out, with the play and stuff. Plus I needed to talk to you. Ms. Herbaut called me at home. She's offering me the role of Eliza," Brenda said, fidgeting back and forth.

"Oh my God, that's great!" I did a small dance on our front step, mentally checking off another box on the revenge plan. This news was soooo worth the berry spew. I couldn't wait to see Lauren's face when she heard the news.

"I told her I wasn't sure if I wanted it," Brenda said, and my dance stopped mid-jig.

"You would be an amazing Eliza. What aren't you sure about?"

"It's just that drama means so much to some people, you know. Drama is their *thing*. I don't really care about it—it's just something to put on my transcript."

"So that you can be an astronaut, which *is* your thing," I pointed out. I took a bite out of a cookie and tried to think of a logical argument that would appeal to Brenda. "What made you worry about this anyway?"

"Christopher. He interviewed me for his film after tryouts

and he kept talking about how important it was to some people, how it was their dream, and I started to think maybe it doesn't matter if I do the play or not, or I could do a small part."

"Are you worried about Lauren? Trust me, she wouldn't worry about you." I wondered what Lauren had said to him during her interview. I bet she did that thing where she licked her lips when she talked. I hoped he was smart enough not to fall for that, but with guys you never know. They don't always do their thinking with their brains.

"Doesn't mean I shouldn't still do the right thing. Ms. H. says if I don't want the lead, she would want me to be the understudy for Eliza. I would still have something to put on my transcript, so it sort of meets my goals."

I didn't say anything. One more person who could play second fiddle to Lauren. I was so close. I had thrown up in my purse, for crying out loud, and now she wasn't sure she wanted this? My mind scrambled around trying to think of a reason why Brenda should take the role that didn't involve admitting that the whole thing was about Lauren.

"I think it's cool you're thinking of everyone else," I said. Brenda broke into a huge smile. "But . . ."—my voice trailed off and Brenda's face dropped—"I have to ask if you're sure you're turning down the part for the right reasons."

"What do you mean?"

"You've admitted that you hate being in front of groups. Are you sure you aren't backing down because you're scared?"

"Yeah, being in front of all those people freaks me out. But it's more than that. Why should I do it if the whole thing isn't that important to me?"

"Because challenging yourself is the important thing. I mean, don't take this the wrong way, but you're the kind of person who stays in your comfort zone. Look, you weren't sure if you wanted to cut your hair, right? You didn't care about it, so why bother? Right?"

"Yeah, I guess."

"And now that you cut it, are you glad you did?"

"Yeah."

"Well, this is like the haircut. Sometimes you aren't always sure why a challenge will make a difference, but you won't know until you take the leap."

"Take the leap, huh?"

"Full speed ahead, captain. If it turns out you hate doing the play, it's not like you have to do theater again, but how will you know if it's your thing unless you do it? Push yourself, gain the confidence." I realized I was starting to sound like one of those tacky motivational speakers so I shut up and hoped it worked.

"Do you really think I should?" Brenda asked.

"One hundred percent."

Brenda took a deep breath. "Okay, I'll do it."

"You will?"

Brenda laughed. "Don't sound so surprised. I trust you. If you think it's a good idea, I'll do it." The cookie I had eaten moments ago suddenly felt too big for my stomach. I tried to give her a reassuring smile. "I suspect Christopher will also be thrilled," she said. "I think 'science nerd-girl takes the lead' is good for his documentary."

"Not nerd girl, science-whiz woman," I countered.

"He asked me about you."

"What?"

"Well, that got your attention," said Brenda.

"Seriously, did he ask about me?"

"Yes, seriously, he did." Brenda picked a cookie out of the basket and began to nibble daintily on it. I tried to act like I didn't care what Christopher said. I managed to hold out for about three seconds.

"Are you going to tell me what he said?"

Brenda broke into a smile. "He thought it was cool you helped me with the audition. He wanted to know more about you, that kind of thing."

"What did you tell him?" I asked.

"I told him you were an international spy living undercover."

"What?"

Brenda laughed. "No, I didn't say that. I told him that you were a hard person to figure out. Complex. You're like a black hole or the space-time continuum."

"I've never been compared to a celestial event before."

"You defy typical comparisons. He also mentioned that the theater on the strip runs classic movies on Tuesday nights. He goes every week. In case I knew anyone who, you know, might be interested."

I felt my heart pick up speed. "He did, huh?"

"Yep." Brenda stepped down from the stoop. "I have to get going. I need to call Ms. H. back."

I sat on the stoop after she left. There was a part of me that wanted to drop the revenge thing—stop the lies and all the sneaking around so I could hang out with Brenda, have fun with the play, maybe watch some classic movies with Christopher.

I closed my eyes and remembered the moment I knew it was Lauren who had told the lie about me. I remembered how she looked in her backyard, her hair pulled back in a ponytail and the smug expression on her face. I remembered the instant that our friendship ended and that she hadn't cried a single tear over the whole thing. I thought about how she spun from one success to another and never took the time to think about the knife she'd stabbed in my back. It was time to put the heavy artillery into action. Lauren deserved to pay. What I wanted for my life wasn't important. Justice was on the line.

chapter twenty-eight

The theater was in the middle of what Terrace called downtown. The year I moved away, the city council had decided that what the downtown needed was a makeover. Although it was no more substantial than a Hollywood set, the downtown now resembled a quaint New England town with fancy lampposts and lots of brick and wood storefronts.

I was surprised the movie theater was still around. It was small, built in the 1950s. Most of the big blockbuster movies were shown at the multiplex that was near the mall. My grandma told me the theater tried showing art films for a while, but Terrace isn't a town that is chock-full of people who go to see art films. Now it seemed to get by on showing second-run movies for cheap and, apparently, classic films on Tuesday nights. I had been looking forward to the movie all day. It was the cherry on top of an already almost perfect day.

Ms. H. posted the cast list outside the drama room first

thing that morning. I had meant to get there early, but one of my grandma's friends had broken her hip the day before. Grandma had responded by pulling together a giant get-well basket that included tea, homemade muffins, a casserole, a few books, a couple of trashy magazines, and a card. She wanted me to drop it off at her friend's house before school. The package weighed approximately the same amount as a small hatchback car. I ended up missing all the action, but I certainly heard about it.

Once Lauren saw the cast sheet, she ran into the bathroom and refused to leave. She had the role of Henry Higgins's mother and—even better—was Brenda's understudy. Apparently people were all gathered outside the bathroom because they could hear Lauren crying and kicking the stall doors. When the school counselor heard about the fit she went into the bathroom, but Lauren wouldn't even talk to her. She stayed locked in a stall. Bailey and Kyla were called out of class to try and talk her down. They didn't have any luck with her either so someone called her mom. Mrs. Wood showed up in one of her fancy power suits in under ten minutes. She marched down the hall with a snarl on her face that she may have thought looked like a smile. The counselor cleared the bathroom and Lauren and her mom had a discussion. Kyla told me that you could hear Lauren's mom yelling from the hallway. Her mom was shouting at her to "pull it together" and "stop humiliating the whole family."

Fifteen minutes later, Lauren came out with her face washed clean, wearing a brittle smile. By the time I saw her at lunch she was insisting that she thought things had worked out for the best. Not having the lead would give her more time to focus on cheerleading—after all, she was the captain. You could almost believe her except for the fact that her face was completely frozen and her eyes looked a bit wide. She also kept giving a really high, loud laugh whenever anyone said anything, regardless of whether it was funny. She kept shooting glances over at Brenda, who was sitting surrounded by a bunch of the drama kids. Bailey and Kyla kept glancing at me behind Lauren's back when she wasn't paying attention. Kyla cocked one eyebrow, which I took as the universal sign for "whoa, look who's taken a one way trip on the *woo-woo* train."

I still hoped to see Lauren break down later in person, but she seemed to pull it more and more together as the day went on. I may not have liked her, but I had to give her credit. Lauren was a lot tougher than she looked.

I looked up at the marquee. For this week's classic film they were showing *The Thin Man,* starring William Powell and Myrna Loy. I had seen it on TV a few times. A great detective story set in the 1920s full of high society, martinis, and fabulous outfits. I paid for a ticket and went into the lobby.

The refreshment stand had all the usual snacks, but they were also selling vintage candy that you don't see anymore: Charleston Chews, Bottle Caps, Zagnuts, Necco Wafers, and Slo Pokes. Most of the people in the lineup seemed to be the senior set.

There wasn't anyone my age to be seen unless you counted the harried-looking girl with a metal hoop through her left nostril who was running the refreshment stand.

I slipped into the back of the theater and waited for my eyes to adjust to the dim lights. The movie was just starting and the light from the screen bounced off the faces of the people sitting there. The first face that I made out clearly was Christopher's. I slipped down the row and sat next to him. We both looked up at the screen and not at each other. He didn't say anything for a few minutes.

"Junior Mint?" He asked softly, shaking the box. I held my hand out, palm up, and he poured in a small pile of mints. He picked a mint out of my hand, and I could feel every nerve in my palm light up as his fingers touched me. When the mints were gone and my hand empty it seemed somehow right for him to fill it with his own hand. We held hands for the rest of the movie, and it was a good thing I had seen the movie before because I found it a bit difficult to concentrate. This was due in part to the proximity of Christopher and the fact that he was holding my hand, and in part to the elderly couple in front of who us kept whispering back and forth to each other. It appeared they shared one hearing aid. The elderly man spent the whole movie loudly whispering to his wife, "What did they just say?"

The only thing that would have made the night more perfect would have been if Lauren could have seen me with him. I loved old movies, but I almost wished we had gone to see something newly released. That way there would have been a greater chance of someone seeing us together and word getting back to Lauren. It was unlikely anyone here was going to spill the beans to her unless her grandma was in the audience.

When the lights came up, Christopher didn't rush to leave. He was a true film nut, the kind of person who wants to know every name on the lighting crew. When the final credit went by, we were the only people left in the theater.

"Have you seen the sequel?" he asked.

"*After the Thin Man?*"

"Creative titles weren't their specialty back in the 30s."

"As opposed to now, when we come up with the ever-unexpected *Spider-Man 2*," I pointed out.

"Touché." Christopher stood and began to lead us back out into the lobby. Everyone who worked at the theater nodded at him as we wove our way through. I had the sense he was a frequent visitor.

It was cold outside and Christopher let go of my hand to zip up his jacket. I stuck my hands in my pockets because it seemed sort of strange to let them just hang there in the freezing weather. Apparently, Terrace was skipping fall and moving directly into winter.

"I wasn't sure if you would come," Christopher said.

"You didn't exactly invite me," I countered.

"Then can I officially invite you for a cup of coffee?"

"No," I said, and then paused. "I'm more of tea drinker. Coffee makes me jumpy."

Christopher laughed. "We wouldn't want you jumpy."

We went in his car to the Bean There Café. The car was an ancient Honda that looked like it was held together with duct tape. What impressed me was that he never apologized for it the way so many people would. It was his car, and if you didn't like it then I suspect he would tell you to get out. When we walked in the café, another couple was just getting up from the two battered leather chairs that flanked the fireplace.

"Grab those seats and I'll get us some drinks," Christopher said. I reached into my pocket to pull out some money. I was going to have to get a new purse soon. I still hadn't replaced my bag since the whole projectile-strawberry incident. I had hoped if I washed it out well and used some Febreze it might somehow survive, but it was a lost cause. Not that I was complaining—the payoff had been worth it. I held out some money, but Christopher waved my cash away. "I think I can swing the tea."

I kicked my shoes off and folded up into the chair, my legs tucked under me. The fireplace was gas, more for show than anything else, but it did put out a bit of heat. The door swung open and a wave of cold air rushed into the room, but it was her voice that gave me the shivers. Lauren.

Bailey saw me first and waved like she was a plush Disney creature at the doorway to the Magic Kingdom and I was a guest from the Make-A-Wish Foundation. If they could bottle what Bailey had it would be better than Prozac. You usually didn't find people this happy unless there was serious medication support. Kyla held out her leg, and I couldn't figure out what she was doing until I realized she was wearing my boots. I shot her a thumbs-up. Lauren looked right past me.

"Hey, I tried to call you earlier," Bailey said, as they drew close. "We decided to go out and have a girls' night." She looked at me meaningfully and then over at Lauren. I'd missed out on a chance to cheer up Lauren, not that she needed cheering up—after all, she was just fine. She didn't want the part anyway, *blah blah blah*.

"My phone was off. I was at the movies."

Christopher turned around from the counter with our drinks. He walked over slowly and gave everyone a nod of recognition.

"Christopher!" Lauren said, her voice bright. "I guess you can't get enough of me—I see you everywhere these days. If this keeps up, I'm going to think you're following me."

"How could anyone ever get enough of you, Lauren?"

"Is that for me?" Lauren asked, gesturing to the extra cup he was holding in his hand. "How did you know I wanted hot tea?"

"It's for Claire."

Both Bailey and Kyla looked down at me. Kyla raised an eyebrow and I felt my face flush. Bailey looked so excited I thought she might levitate for a moment. I grabbed the tea and took a deep drink, the hot water searing my mouth. Lauren looked at Christopher and then at me. I suspect most people wouldn't know how upset she was, but I could see her nostrils flare out and the hitch in her chest as she tried to get a deep breath.

"Oops, sorry. Didn't mean to bust in on your big date," Lauren said, pausing to see if either of us would correct her.

"No worries." Christopher sank into the seat next to me.

"How are you feeling?" I tried to force my face into an expression that looked sympathetic.

"I'm fine." Lauren bit each word off.

"You sure? I know you must be disappointed. I think it's great you could go out with your . . ."—I paused to let the next word sink in—"girlfriends, and get your mind off of everything." Lauren's nostrils were nearly rippling with agitation. I touched the side of Christopher's hand to drive home the point that some of us weren't going to settle for being out with a girlfriend. Some of us had a date.

"Thanks for asking, but like I said, I'm fine." Lauren stomped over to the counter to order. Bailey and Kyla trailed after her. Bailey gave me an obvious okay sign with a wink that she must have imagined Christopher was incapable of seeing. Christopher waited until they had walked off.

"You know what I can't figure out?" he asked. "Why you and Lauren are friends."

I shrugged, not sure what to say. I couldn't bring myself to think of a single nice thing to say about her that would explain why anyone would be friends with her. I couldn't tell what he thought of Lauren. Did he think I was lucky to be in her sacred circle or an idiot to hang out with her? It was my duty to get him away from her clutches, before he fell under the Lauren spell that infected everyone else. He seemed flip with her, but I couldn't tell if it was meant to be friendly teasing or sarcasm tainted with disdain.

"I'm more friends with Bailey and Kyla."

"Sort of breaks up the holy trinity though, doesn't it? Those three have been thick as thieves since freshman year."

I shrugged again. At this rate he was going to think I was a conversational retard with shoulder spasms.

"What about you?" I said.

"What about me?"

"What do you think of Lauren?"

Christopher pulled back, surprise on his face.

"Lauren?"

"Yeah, do you like her?"

Christopher didn't say anything. He just looked at me. I felt someone else's eyes on me and turned to the side. Lauren, Bailey, and Kyla were sitting at a table. Bailey and Kyla were having a discussion, but Lauren was staring at me. If looks could kill I would have been six feet under with an ax in my head.

"I mean, I was just wondering," I added, turning back to Christopher. I touched his shoulder, making sure Lauren would get a good look.

"I don't think I'm her type," he said.

I took my hand off his shoulder. I noticed that he didn't say she wasn't his type.

"You don't seem to hang out with anybody," I said, dropping the whole Lauren topic altogether.

"Maybe I'm the kinda guy who likes my own company."

"Ah, a loner." I took a sip of my tea.

"Something like that," Christopher said, staring at me. I brushed the end of my nose to see if anything was there. He was staring so intently it felt like he had X-ray eyes, and I wasn't sure if I wanted him to see what was under the surface.

"What?" I asked finally.

"What do you mean?"

"I mean, why are you staring at me?"

"I thought girls were supposed to like it when guys looked into their eyes."

"Have you been reading *Cosmo*?" I teased.

"Nah, that magazine is trash. Besides, last time I read it, it promised '25 Ways to Drive Him Wild,' and I'm pretty sure only twenty-two of them would work."

I tried to laugh casually like I was used to joking around about sexual tricks with attractive guys, but the only thing that came out sounded like what would happen if someone stepped on a poodle.

"You okay?"

"Mmm, tea must have gone down wrong," I said. Christopher smiled and I had the sense that he knew I was lying. I couldn't tell if I wanted him to bring up the *Cosmo* article again or not. Part of me wondered, if I read the article, if I would be able to guess which three things out of the list didn't work for him.

"I can't quite figure you out," he said.

"Complicated, that's me."

"Something like that." He stared at me again for what seemed like forever. "You just don't fit into any single category."

"I tried to fit into someone else's definition once, but it didn't work out."

"Well, then you should stay unique." He leaned back in his chair so that we were sitting side-by-side facing the fire. His hand reached over and traced lazy figure eights on the side of my arm. Oh God, I hoped Lauren was catching a peek of this. Clearly if I was going to start a 25 Things to Drive Me Wild list, this would be in the top five. I wondered what would happen if I let out a moan right there in the coffee shop.

When my cell phone rang, I nearly jumped out of the seat. I yanked the phone out of my pocket so quickly that it flew out of my hand and landed in Christopher's lap. I grabbed it back without thinking. Christopher evidently wasn't expecting me to lunge at his crotch (I'm guessing that maneuver didn't make the *Cosmo* list), and he jumped up, splashing his coffee onto the floor. Everyone in the café turned to see what was going on. Lauren had already been looking over, only now I had given her something to smile about. I clicked the phone on. *It had better be an emergency.*

"Helen!" Grandma's voice bellowed into my ear. She sounded

surprised to hear me on the line, as if she meant to call someone else.

"Gram." There was a pause while neither of us said anything for a beat. I shot Christopher an apologetic smile. He was mopping up the coffee with a stack of napkins.

"I'm checking to see when you were planning to come home. It's a school night," Grandma said.

"I'll be home soon."

"Define 'soon.' It's already after ten."

"Gram."

"Helen."

I rolled my eyes at Christopher as if to explain the craziness that is my family. "I'll be home in an hour."

"Half hour."

"I'm a senior. In a year I'm going to be living on my own."

"Then in a year you can stay out as long as you like."

"I can take you back to your car now if you have to go," Christopher whispered.

"I'll be home in a half hour." I clicked off the phone before my grandma could begin her "the importance of boundaries" lecture.

"Sorry," I said, not sure if I was apologizing for the fact I had to go home or the fact that I'd grabbed him when the phone rang.

"No worries. I've got family too."

"I note yours doesn't call to check on you like you are a

five-year-old. It doesn't help that she used to be a social worker and worked with all these juvenile delinquents."

"What's her name? Maybe I know her."

I looked up, shocked.

"Joke. I'm joking."

I laughed to show that I knew that the whole time.

"Why does your grandma call you Helen?"

I choked on my tea when my throat seized shut. Christopher gave me a few whacks on the back.

"What?" I asked. Maybe if I stalled for time he would forget what he asked me, or maybe I could swallow my own tongue. I'd settle for a natural disaster, a small earthquake perhaps, anything to change the topic.

"I heard her on the phone. She called you Helen."

My brain scrambled around, looking for a good answer. "It's my great-grandmother's name." This answer had the benefit of being true, but the downside of being totally unrelated to what he'd asked me.

"Does your grandma confuse you with your great-grandmother a lot?

I laughed loudly like this was the best joke ever told. My mouth clicked shut when I saw his expression.

"It's my middle name too and she really likes it." I chewed on my lip. "You know, grandparents, they're weird . . . " My voice trailed off.

"Well, I better get you back to your car, Helen."

"Don't call me that," I said sharply. My eyes shot over to the corner to make sure Lauren hadn't heard him. "I mean, it drives me crazy when my grandma does it."

"Well, I wouldn't want to drive you crazy," he said, standing up. He walked toward the door and I followed him. Things had been going so well and I blew it by acting like a spaz. We drove back to my car in silence. When we got to the movie theater parking lot I waited a beat in case he wanted to do the arm-stroking thing again, but he kept his hands on the wheel.

"I had a nice time tonight," I said finally.

"Me too."

I waited to see if he would say anything else, like that we should do it again, but he just sat there.

"So, thanks for tea and telling me about the movie."

"They do the classics every Tuesday."

"Cool."

"Really? I thought you didn't like old movies." Christopher rubbed his chin. "What was it you said? You could take them or leave them?"

"I'm a girl. I'm supposed to change my mind." I flipped my hair. "Besides, didn't you tell me that you liked that I didn't fit into any one category?"

He didn't say anything. If I could stop acting like Claire and instead act like Helen, I somehow felt sure things would go better. I could admit I loved old movies too, and I wouldn't always have to be trying to cover things up. Of course, giving up Claire to go back to Helen would mean giving up getting revenge on Lauren. "I should go," I said finally.

"See you around."

I slipped out of his car and into my own. He waited for me to start my engine and then waved before driving off. I sat in the car thinking over the night. It was most likely for the best that he didn't try to kiss me. After all, I was out for revenge, not a relationship. The universe was going to get confused if I kept changing the goal. The important thing with Christopher was to keep him from Lauren, not to fall for him myself. The point of this year wasn't to have a relationship with anybody. Although I hadn't yet achieved the complete and total revenge that I had been hoping for, clearly things were starting to move in the right direction.

In theory I should be thrilled, so it wasn't clear why I felt like crying.

chapter twenty-nine

Bailey and Kyla had potential careers as interrogators for the CIA. Bright lights and a cattle prod were the only things missing from their technique. The questions about my date with Christopher started in French class and continued straight through until lunch. By the time we sat down in the cafeteria every minute of the date had been broken down and we were now moving on to establish motivation.

"So when you held hands, did you take his or did he take yours?" Bailey leaned over the cafeteria table as if we were discussing espionage secrets. "I mean, who started things?"

"Who cares," Lauren asked, trying to change the subject. She had a smear of lipstick on her teeth. I noticed none of us had mentioned it to her. She wasn't eating at all, just drinking herbal tea.

"Are you kidding?" Bailey said. "Who took whose hand first is superimportant. It lets you know if he's taking control of the relationship or not. You can tell a lot from hand holding."

I popped a cherry tomato from my salad into my mouth. "It was somewhat of a meet in the middle. I had my hand out there, but he took it."

Bailey squealed. "I knew it! He likes you. He doesn't strike me as the kind of guy to hold hands with someone by accident."

I wondered if holding hands with someone by accident was something that came up a lot in Bailey's world.

"Pretty impressive, Dantes," Kyla said. "I can tell you, a lot of girls have had their eye on him. You move here and sweep him off his feet in record time. He must have been waiting for the right woman."

"Maybe. He didn't call last night and he hasn't said anything to me today," I pointed out.

Kyla waved away my concern. "Men. He has to prove he's independent. It's something to do with the testosterone they have. Let him come to you. Don't come across as easy. Play hard to get."

"Don't come across as easy? Interesting advice coming from you." Lauren smirked.

"What the hell is that supposed to mean?" Kyla asked, dropping her fork.

Lauren leaned back. She wasn't used to her lackeys speaking back to her. "Chill out. It was just a joke."

"Not funny. Maybe you're the one who shouldn't be giving out relationship advice," Kyla snapped.

All of us turned to look a few tables over, where Justin was sitting with Tiffany. She was an empty-headed sophomore girl who had more breasts than brains, but it was clear Justin had no trouble moving on post breakup.

"I said it was a joke." Lauren's face was flushed. "God, I was just sick of the conversation. They had one date and it wasn't even a real date—they bumped into each other at a movie. Excuse me if I don't want to spend my entire lunch hearing a blow-by-blow account."

"It's okay to be sad about your breakup." Bailey patted Lauren's arm. "But even if you're sad, you should still be happy for your friends."

Lauren wrenched her arm back. "Fine. I'm thrilled. The date sounds like it was freaking earth-shatteringly wonderful. I hope you have many more." She got up from the table and stormed out of the cafeteria.

"The prima-donna thing is getting old." Kyla stabbed a piece of lettuce. "She keeps that shit up and Justin isn't the only one who isn't going to want her around."

I waited a beat, but even Bailey didn't stick up for Lauren. Neither of them seemed remotely interested in following after her either.

I was still looking at the door where Lauren left when I saw Brenda standing with her tray a few rows over looking for a place. She smiled when she saw me. I spun back around. It wasn't that I didn't want to eat with her, but there was no way she could join this table. Not now. Not when things were going so well. My control on things was too fragile. The quickest way to stop being the center of this new orbit was to admit someone to the system who clearly didn't belong.

"So tell me again about what you guys talked about at the coffee shop," Bailey prompted.

Maybe it was because I had told the story at least six times already, but it felt like all the fun was washed out of it. I pushed my lunch away. I was getting sick of salad.

chapter thirty

Guilt is a funny thing. You end up undertaking all kinds of things you didn't picture yourself doing.

Brenda saw a posting about helping in the elementary school and got all excited. Something community service–related she could put on her applications. When she found out her assignment was helping second graders with an art unit, she convinced me to do the project with her. She didn't mention how I blew her off at lunch, but it was still there between us. Agreeing to do the project with her seemed easier than saying I was sorry. Certainly less complicated.

Brenda, being Brenda, did piles of research on art history and artistic techniques such as perspective and horizon lines. She hadn't counted on the fact that second graders are more interested in eating crayons than in learning how objects appear smaller when they are far away. There is a reason they make those things nontoxic. A group of second graders sat at our feet. A boy waved his arm madly. Brenda gave a sigh. He had already asked a few questions, and I could tell they weren't the kind of questions she had been hoping for.

"So the guy, van Gooey, who chopped off his ear, did he eat it?"

"His name was van Gogh. Wouldn't you rather hear about his paintings?"

"Did he chop off any other parts of himself?" He made some swipes in the air with his imaginary sword.

"Lots," I said, drawing out the word. "By the end of his career all that was left was one eye and a thumb."

"Cool," he whispered. Brenda shot me a look. The teacher wasn't paying any attention at all. She was sitting in the back of the room reading *People*. We could have taught a class on sex education and she wouldn't even have noticed. We could have had a room full of second graders strapping condoms on some bananas and she wouldn't even have looked up from an article on George Clooney.

"Claire is joking around with you. He didn't chop off anything else. Maybe somebody else has a question about art?" Brenda looked around the room with a hint of desperation in her eyes.

"If you eat green crayons, will you poop green?" the same boy asked. The class burst into giggles.

Brenda gave up and slumped down on the stool the teacher had provided.

"No. Trust me on this, because I've tried. It also doesn't work if you eat poster paints," I said.

"Gross," a little girl who had at least a dozen barrettes in her hair said.

"Very gross," I agreed.

"Way back then it was a time of artistic turmoil with competing views of what made something art," Brenda said, still trying to educate tomorrow's leaders on more than ear chopping and colored poop. The kids all turned to look at her and then back at me for clarity.

"'Turmoil' means really screwed up. No one could agree. It's like how some people think SpongeBob is funny and other people think he's disgusting."

"You know what, let's skip the rest of the art history lesson and go right into doing our own art!" Brenda said, changing gears. She pointed toward their desks, which had been pushed together in little islands around the room. The teacher had covered the desks with large pieces of paper and there were jars of bright poster paints sprinkled around. "We're going to break into groups and paint pictures. We talked about all kinds of art today—landscapes, still life, portrait, and abstract. You can choose to paint whatever you want. This is what we call artistic freedom."

"Can I paint people chopping off each other's ears?" Guess Who yelled out. I was starting to think that kid was going to grow up to be a serial killer. If I lived in his neighborhood, I would keep a close eye out for pets going missing in the area.

Brenda looked at the teacher for some guidance. She had to clear her throat several times before the teacher looked up.

"No, Richard, you may not paint chopped-up people," the teacher said in a bored voice before she went back to paging through her magazine.

"But then I'm not free," Richard said, indicating that he grasped the concept of artistic freedom, which I would have guessed was way above the second-grade brain.

"That's right. You're not free. You're in second grade," the teacher said.

Richard kicked the carpet in frustration but went to sit at his desk. We stayed to help for a while. I would have stayed all afternoon. I like kids. It's way easier to navigate elementary school than high school. Here I could be totally me. I didn't have to worry about keeping up the Claire front. Being popular took so much energy. You had to smile at the right people, or risk being labeled a stuck-up bitch, and ignore the wrong people, or be labeled a loser lover. Besides, I like the way poster paints smell. When our time was up, the teacher gave us each a candy bar to thank us for coming down. Brenda tried to tell her that we didn't mind at all, but I just said thank you. "Never turn down free chocolate" is one of my mottos.

I unpeeled the Kit Kat as we walked down the hall. I broke off one of the bars and handed it over to Brenda.

"Thanks for inviting me. It was fun, and not just because I got out of math," I said.

"And you can put it on your college applications."

"Right."

"You know there's still time to apply places."

I nodded absently. I had a bunch of applications piled on my desk at home, but it seemed surreal that I was expected to just figure out where I wanted go, pick a major, and come up with some sort of plan for my life. How was I supposed to know what I wanted to do? How could the adults in my life, who didn't trust me to choose to do the right thing after midnight, think I was supposed to make this kind of decision?

"I may take a gap year."

"What would you *do*?" Brenda's nose wrinkled up in confusion.

"I don't know. That's sort of the point of a gap year, isn't it? To sort out what you want to do, have a gap."

"You should apply to Boston University. Then if I get into MIT we'll be in the same city."

"Yeah, maybe." I couldn't imagine anything after this year. Everything had been about Lauren for so long that it was like I couldn't imagine what would follow. Where my future should be, there was just a blank screen.

"We could get an apartment or something together after a year or two. My folks really want me to live in the dorms for a while though."

"I don't think you should count on me to be there for you," I said.

Brenda looked over at me. "I'm getting that sense."

"Look, it isn't that I don't want to hang out with you more. It's just that I can't. There's all this stuff going on. Stuff I have to sort out."

"So who hurt you?"

"No one hurt me."

Brenda gave a disbelieving snort. "You don't have to tell me if you don't want to, but I can still tell. You don't let anyone get close to you. The thing is, no one can hurt you unless you let them."

"If you think that, then no one has ever really burned you," I pointed out.

"I don't mean to make it sound simple. It's just that if you hold on to a hurt then you never get over it. It's like picking at a scab."

"Let's stop talking about my scabs, okay?"

"But if you want to move on then you have to let go of what is holding you back."

"Look, Oprah, I asked you to drop it," I snapped.

"Friends look out for each other," Brenda countered.

"I didn't ask you to look out for me. In fact, I specifically told you there was stuff I didn't want to talk about, but all you do is push. Stop trying to make me into your friend." Brenda stopped walking and looked at me, her eyes wide. "What? I thought things only hurt if you let them," I said.

Brenda's head snapped back like I had slapped her. I wished I could rewind time and take back that last sentence. If I was Helen I would, but I still had to be Claire. At least a bit longer.

Lauren was so close to cracking. Brenda didn't say anything else, just marched back toward the high school. Her shoulders drew up under ears and she started to do that weird Frankenstein lurch that she had just about given up. I watched her walk away, then kicked the wall.

chapter thirty-one

Christopher was leaning against my car after school. He had this way of standing like his limbs were just barely connected, sort of loose.

"Do you like parties?" Christopher asked as I walked up.

The real answer to the question was that I didn't know. It was one of those things where I hadn't been invited to many in the past couple of years. However, Claire would have been to a zillion. I put a hand on my hip. "It depends on who's at the party."

"Do you want to come to one with me tonight?" Christopher asked.

"Like a date?" I hated how my voice came out all high and screechy.

"That's what I'd been thinking. I thought maybe we'd give the whole being together outside the movie theater thing a try."

"I do better in the dark." As soon as the words came out of my mouth I knew it didn't come across like I meant.

"Well, that sounds promising."

"I meant, I had a good time at the movie. You know, dark theater." I decided I better change topics. "Who else is going to the party?"

"So are you saying you don't want to go with me to the party unless your friends are there?"

"No, that's not what I meant." I didn't add that while I wanted to go to the party with him, I especially wanted to go if Lauren could see us together. "I'll go."

"Well then, it's a date," Christopher said with a smile. He took a step forward and then paused. He was going to kiss me. My heart started to beat super fast like I was running a sprint. His hand reached over and cupped the end of my elbow, pulling me just a touch closer. I swallowed. *God, I hope I don't have Kit Kat caught in my teeth*. That's all I needed, for him to kiss me and end up finding a snack in there. No one likes secondhand chocolate. If I'd known he was going to kiss me, I would have gone to the bathroom and swished out my mouth first. I closed my eyes and I could feel his breath as he leaned in. His breath smelled like mints.

HONK!

We both jumped back. A car driving by gave another loud honk and someone leaned out the window, yelling at a kid on the school steps.

"Joe! Suck this!" The kid in the passenger seat turned around and pressed his butt cheeks against the window. The pasty butt, quite hairy I might add, had a way of taking all the romance out of the moment. Christopher apparently felt the same way as he was rubbing his palms on the front of his jeans nervously and showing no signs of coming back in for a kiss.

"Yeah, so . . ." I wasn't really sure what to say, so the sentence sort of trailed off.

"Yeah." Christopher looked at me and then away. "How about I pick you up at your house around six? Julie Baker's parents are out of town and she's doing a sort of barbecue thing."

"Sounds good."

Christopher gave me a nod and walked off. It was framing up to be a very interesting evening.

Popularity Question: How do you know if a high school party is successful?

1. There is at least one person throwing up outside in the flower beds.
2. So many people have come that someone thought it would be a good idea to start parking on the lawn.
3. A minimum of three couples are having sex somewhere in the house—at least one of them in the parents' bed.
4. Doritos, chips, and other salty snacks have been crumbled into a fine powder and ground into the living room rug.

5. At least one priceless breakable has been broken. Someone will make an attempt to fix it with superglue or toothpaste. It will not work.

6. The kitchen floor will be sticky from spilled liquids, making it possible for a small freshman to become completely stuck to the floor like to a giant piece of flypaper.

7. Music is playing at a level loud enough to cause ears to bleed. Occasionally someone will yell to turn it down before the neighbors call the cops. This person will then be called a pussy by the others and the music will go a notch louder.

8. A group of jocks will be around the dining room table, playing a complicated drinking game to which no one completely understands the rules. It is possible that the rules are completely irrelevant anyway.

In the case of Julie's party, it was all of the above. Julie didn't seem to mind. She was wandering through the house wearing her mom's silk kimono-style bathrobe and drinking a wine cooler. It was possible that she had decided she was going to get the death penalty for the party when her parents got home so she might as well enjoy her final night on earth.

Lauren was already at the party. When Christopher and I arrived it was clear she'd had quite a few drinks. It looked to me like she'd left drunk behind a few beers ago and had moved into that stage where your brain starts to float free in all the alcohol.

Lauren lunged at Kyla declaring her to be her "very best friend in the world!" Kyla met my eyes across the room and shook her head in disgust. It didn't look like Bailey was there. I wondered who Lauren was counting on to hold her hair out of the toilet when she started puking, because it was clear to me that Kyla was not going to volunteer.

Christopher and I wove our way through the crowd of people until we found the cooler in the kitchen. He grabbed a beer for himself and then looked over at me.

"Is there any Diet Coke left?" I asked.

Christopher fished through the melting ice water and pulled out a can, taking the time to pop the top for me. And people say there are no gentlemen left.

We clinked our drinks together and wandered out onto the back porch where at least it was quiet enough to hear yourself think. The porch was screened in so it wasn't quite as cold as being outside, but it was still way colder than the house. You could see your breath in the air.

"You cold?"

I started to shake my head no and then realized there was no point in being polite; my shivering was most likely giving things away. Christopher pulled off his military jacket and wrapped it around me. It was a deep olive green wool and still warm from his body.

"Better?" he asked.

"Much."

We sat on the bench, watching people come and go through the kitchen. I knew I should talk about something, but I was at a complete loss to come up with a topic. The longer I didn't talk, the louder the silence was between the two of us. What if we had nothing to talk about but movies? Did that mean our relationship was doomed? Would it be easier to talk to him if I was being myself, or was he only interested in me because I was Claire? Maybe it didn't matter who I was because I was doomed in any relationship due to my lack of communication skills. There was a constant loop in my head, *say something, say something, say something, say something*.

"So did you know Katharine Hepburn did all her own stunts? She thought the stunt women didn't stand up straight enough," I blurted out. I then wished for a meteor to suddenly fall from the sky and take me out for saying something so completely random. That's the problem with space debris. It never causes a cataclysmic event when you want it to.

"I can honestly say that no, I didn't know that," Christopher said, no doubt taking pity on my poor social skills. "I would have thought it was part of the job requirement for stunt people to have good posture."

"Yeah. It could have just been her take on stuff. She was sort of a control freak about things. I mean, the guy I used to date who was into movies told me she was," I tried to explain while still waiting for the earth to swallow me whole.

"I always had the impression she wasn't the kind of person to be wishy-washy on issues." Christopher took a drink of his beer.

"What's wrong with knowing exactly where you stand on things?"

"Life isn't a vintage film," Christopher said. When he saw my confused face he explained, "Things aren't black-and-white."

"Some things are."

Christopher gave a vague one shoulder shrug. "Don't get me wrong. I like Katharine Hepburn. She was honest. You knew where she stood."

I swallowed. I wondered what he would think of my less-than-honest take on key issues like my real identity.

"I have no idea why I brought up Katharine Hepburn," I admitted.

"Don't worry. Random isn't a bad thing."

"The thing is, I'm not really good at this kind of thing."

"Just so we're on the same page, what kind of thing are we talking about?" Christopher asked, taking a long drink of his beer.

"Being with people."

"I thought it came second nature to the elite crowd," Christopher said.

"Sometimes it only looks like it comes easy. It can be a lot of work."

For some reason I had the urge to tell him about Lauren. About what she did and how it made me afraid to get too close to anybody. I don't know why, but I was sure he would know what to say, that he would have some kind of advice. I wanted to explain that I had been sure things were black-and-white, but lately there was all this gray everywhere. I opened my mouth to tell him when the door to the patio flew open and Julie spilled out. She spotted us and swayed back and forth while her mouth waited to catch up to whatever her brain was thinking.

"You guys have to come inside, we're playing a game," Julie said, though it came out more like, *"You'll gooz, come inziiid, waa plainning a guum."*

It was possible that an out of control party was not the place to spill your guts. Unless you counted Lauren, who dashed past all of us to spill her guts in the bushes in a nonmetaphorical sense.

Christopher stood up and took a step toward Lauren and then stopped. There wasn't anything he or anyone else could do to help.

"Splashdown!" one of the jocks yelled out the living room windows. I glanced over my shoulder. It looked like everyone was getting a good view of Lauren.

"Those are my mom's azaleas," Julie slurred.

"Not her finest hour," I said.

"What's your problem with Lauren?" Christopher asked.

"I don't have a problem."

"You spend a lot of time worrying about something that isn't a problem."

"I have no idea what you're talking about." I didn't meet his eyes. "Do you want to go inside and play a game?" I tried to make my voice sound flirty.

"You know, unlike most people, I'm not real big on playing games." He turned around and walked away.

chapter thirty-two

Christopher and I didn't stay at the party late. Things had started to go downhill rapidly once Lauren started throwing up. It's been my limited party experience that once people start spewing bile in public the fun is over.

Christopher pulled into my grandma's driveway but didn't turn off the car. It looked like our second date was over.

"I had a good time," I said.

"Really?" Christopher stared out the window.

"You don't believe me?"

"Honestly? No." He looked over at me. His face was tinted blue in the dashboard lights. "I don't know what to believe. Sometimes I get you and other times it seems complicated."

"Complicated can be interesting."

"It can also be a lot of work."

I wasn't sure what to say. Claire would have a flip comment about how some things are worth a bit of work, but I wasn't sure the line would work on Christopher. My grandma flicked on the driveway light indicating that she thought enough time had passed out there.

"I guess I should go."

"Have a good night."

I paused, wanting to say something else, but the lights flicked on and off again. "You have a good night too."

I replayed the night as I lay in bed. Public vomiting was a new low for Lauren. It was one thing for a popular girl to get a little wild and wacky at a party. It was a whole other dimension when you started spewing for the world to see. There was no official way to tell, of course—popularity doesn't have an official ranking list that can be checked—but I was almost certain Lauren's reign was at an end. She wasn't unpopular. It would take a lot more hurling for that to happen, but she was definitely less popular. I was one step closer to total victory, but it didn't feel nearly as good as I had hoped. Instead of the image of Lauren hurling in the bushes for all to see, the picture in my mind was Christopher looking disappointed.

I rolled over and looked at the digital clock—3 a.m. I clicked on the bedside lamp and pulled my revenge binder out from under the bed. I ran my finger down the list. Lauren had lost her boyfriend, the lead in the play, and her friends. Christopher hadn't been hers, and he wasn't exactly mine now either, but no way could he find her attractive after what she pulled tonight. The only thing left was cheerleading, and I even had finally come up with a plan for that. I should feel like celebrating. Something was missing. I ran through the list over and over trying to determine if I had left anything out, some angle on the plan that would click everything into place.

Then I saw it. I looked down at the binder. It was all about Lauren, what she had, what was important to her. Pages and pages all devoted to the great Lauren Wood. Maybe I needed a list about me for a change.

I pulled out a clean sheet of paper and wrote across the top: LIFE AFTER LAUREN.

I stared at the paper. There she was, right at the top of my list. I crossed off her name with a thick line. Nope. I scribbled over it. That wasn't right either. No way was I letting her ruin my list. I crumpled up the paper and tossed it toward my trash can. I grabbed a fresh sheet of paper and started again. LIFE LIST.

Now all I had to do was make a list of things I wanted to accomplish. Things I wanted for myself. I tapped my pen on the edge of the binder, waiting for inspiration. After a few minutes I wrote down a couple of items:

1. Friend.

It went without adding that I meant a real friend. Someone I could count on, someone like Brenda.

2. Christopher.

I was willing to admit it. I liked him. I wanted him to like me. The real me.

I stared at the list. Two items? That's it? How could I have only two things that I wanted out of my life? It has been easier coming up with things to take away from Lauren than it was to come up with what I wanted for myself. The only other item I could think of for the list was too vague. I wanted to be happy.

I added another item to my list:

3. Get a Life.

chapter thirty-three

I tried to call Brenda on Sunday night, but her cell wasn't on. I called her home number but her mom said she was studying and couldn't be disturbed. The thing with Brenda is she's the type who really could be into studying, all caught up with protoplasm or black holes, and not want to be disturbed, but I had a hunch that wasn't the issue.

I'd made a decision. I didn't want to hear a blow-by-blow replay of the party from Lauren's perspective. I didn't care what Kyla thought of what everyone was wearing. I had zero interest in spending another lunch pretending to find what they said even remotely interesting. Getting revenge on Lauren didn't have to mean giving up everything that I wanted for myself. At lunch on Monday, I gave the three of them a nod and then walked right past their table.

I stood at the front of the tables and searched up and down looking for Brenda. I wanted to talk to her about Christopher, and I also owed her an apology for always blowing her off in public. I looked right past her at least three or four times, not recognizing her. She was sitting at a table with a bunch of other girls from the play. She was wearing one of her new outfits and laughing at what one of the other girls said.

"Hey, there you are," I said as I walked up to her. Brenda looked up as if she didn't know who I was.

"Oh, hi."

I stood there with my tray wondering if she was going to ask me to sit down.

"I tried to give you a call last night."

"I was studying." Brenda's eyes didn't meet mine.

"Oh." The whole table sat there watching me. "Mind if I join you?" I asked.

"We're just finishing up actually," Brenda said.

I looked down at their trays. Unless they were on the anorexic diet, Brenda was dissing me. They hadn't even made a dent in their lunches. My jaw tightened. So that was how it was going to be.

"Fine. Now that I think about it, I've lost my appetite anyway." I walked to the end of the row and dumped everything, including the tray into the garbage and walked out. I slammed open the bathroom door, and once I was sure I was alone, I kicked the stall door. It swung open, whacking into the toilet paper dispenser, and then bounced shut again. It was not nearly as satisfying as I had hoped and it made my foot hurt. I gave it another kick anyway.

I heard the door open and before I even turned around I knew it was Brenda.

"I thought you weren't done with lunch," I said, hating how my voice sounded snotty.

"You can't do this, you know."

"Do what?"

"Act like you're my friend one minute and then not the next moment. Tell me you know exactly what I need to do and then the second I have any advice for you, tell me that I have no business giving it." Brenda tossed her hands in the air.

"I know," I said.

"I'm not interested in being friends with you if you're going to be all CIA. *I'd tell you, but then I'd have to kill you.* I don't even know if you *want* to be my friend."

My throat felt like it was getting more and more narrow. It felt like she was asking me to step out onto the window ledge of a tall building.

Brenda rested her hand on my arm. "I don't want to do all this back and forth. Friends one minute and then not the next. If you want me to understand that there are things you can't do, you should be willing to understand there are things I can't do."

"So where does that leave us?" I asked.

"What do you know about space walks?" Brenda said.

"Space walks? Is this your subtle way of changing the subject?"

"Stick with me and it'll make sense. What do you know about space walks?"

"My knowledge here is pretty slim."

"Here's the thing, space isn't built for humans. It's freezing cold;

there's no air. So the astronaut gets all dressed up," Brenda said.

"I'm not a complete idiot. I know people don't just go walking around in outer space."

Brenda ignored me. "So the astronaut goes into an air lock. It's sort of a waiting room. They suck the oxygen out, and then when the pressure is equaled they can go outside the spaceship, and then they do the same thing in reverse when they want to come back in. It isn't instantaneous. The transition takes some time. Go too fast and someone could get hurt; go too slow and you could run out of time."

"What does this have to do with us?" I asked.

"You asked where we are—we're in the air lock."

"Waiting for the pressure to equalize," I said.

"Exactly, and hopefully before we run out of air." Brenda turned around, and suddenly my chest felt tight like it was going to burst, and I had to do something to release the pressure. Before I knew it the words flew out of my mouth.

"My name isn't Claire."

Brenda turned around and looked at me with one eyebrow up.

"My name is Helen." My voice shook as I said my real name.

The first bell rang. Lunch was over.

"I'm guessing this isn't the kind of story that can be wrapped up in the next three minutes, huh?" Brenda said with a sigh.

chapter thirty-four

One of the benefits of being generally good is that the teachers trust you. Brenda marched down to biology and told Mr. Wong that we needed some time to work on our bacteria project. He gave her the keys to the lab and wrote us a pass in case anyone wondered why we weren't in class.

The biology lab was dark. The blinds were drawn so everything had that sort of hazy shadow lighting. Brenda and I sat on opposite sides of one of the lab tables facing each other. I held on to one of the microscope cords, winding it up one finger and then letting it go so it hung like a giant spiral curl, and then I would do it again. If you were going to film a horror movie, the empty lab would be a great place for it: posters of eviscerated frogs on the wall, strange chemical smells, trays of dissection tools off to the side, and microscopes casting giant shadows on the far wall like a line of marching Tyrannosaurus rexes. Then again maybe the room wasn't scary and it was just the fact that I was scared out of my mind.

"So . . ." Brenda's voice trailed off.

"I don't know where to start."

"Why don't you start with why you're calling yourself Claire if your name is Helen."

"Would you believe me if I told you I busted up a mafia drug ring and that I'm in the witness protection agency?"

"No," Brenda said, sitting perfectly still.

"Okay, I'll tell you, but you have to promise that you will never tell another soul."

"You want me to swear on a Bible or something?"

I grabbed a copy of our biology textbook off the table and passed it over to her. "I want you to swear on science, on Mr. Darwin here. It's that important to me."

Brenda placed one hand on the science textbook and raised her other hand. "I swear on this science textbook that I will keep whatever secret you tell me."

I took a deep breath and tried to sort out the story in my mind. "It started from the moment I was born."

It took me nearly forty minutes to tell her everything, how Lauren and I had been friends, what she did to me, and my master plan to get revenge.

"*You're* the Snitch Bitch?" Brenda asked sounding almost impressed. "I remember hearing about that freshman year.

Everyone was talking about how you had screwed over the seniors."

"I'm not the Snitch Bitch, Lauren is. So do you see now why I had to do this?"

"So you broke up her relationship with Justin?"

"Sort of. I mean, I put the pieces into place."

"And you poisoned her mascara?"

"Poison is a bit harsh. That stuff is just an irritant," I pointed out.

"But you also ripped her jeans." I nodded. "Took her shoes." I nodded again. It was only one shoe, but whatever. "You're sabotaging her friendships and trying to make sure her crush ignores her." Brenda looked vaguely in shock. I wasn't sure what she thought my secret was going to be, but I was pretty certain this wasn't it. "So everything you're doing this year is designed to get revenge on her."

"Yeah."

"What about me? Where do I fit in?" Brenda asked.

"What do you mean?"

"I mean how do I fit into your revenge plan?"

"You're not part of the plan. We met and I liked you," I said.

"So you didn't give me a makeover and get me to try out for the play with the goal of keeping Lauren from getting the part?"

"Uh," my voice stuck in my throat. "That wasn't just about revenge. I mean, I did think you would be really good, and you are. Really good."

"How lucky for you that you could help me out and screw over Lauren at the same time. Very efficient."

"Don't be mad. I should have told you, but I swear I thought it was a killer idea for you to do the play. I still do."

"Because it helps you out?" she asked.

"No. Honest now, are you liking it?" Brenda gave a deep sigh and I pressed on. "See, you do like it, don't you? It's fun," I said. "Not to mention it's going to look great on your applications."

"Yes, it's fun, and yes, I'm glad I did it, but you should have told me there was more to it."

I stood up and paced up and down the aisle. "You wanted to know, you made me tell you, and now you're mad."

"I think I'm entitled to be a little annoyed to find out you've used me."

"I am not using you," I said, my voice rising.

"I want you to leave me out of this plan from now on."

"Deal."

"I am sorry about what happened, the whole Snitch Bitch thing. What she did was lousy. You didn't deserve that," Brenda said.

I felt my eyes fill up. One nice word from her and I was ready to burst into tears. I shrugged instead of saying anything because I was pretty sure I would start crying if I opened my mouth.

"So when will you be done with this plan?" Brenda asked.

"When I've got revenge."

"How much is enough?"

"I don't know. It seems like I'm close. She's starting to fall apart. If I can push her just a little bit further then I think she'll crash and burn." I crumpled up a bunch of extra handouts that were on the table and chucked them into the trashcan.

"You want her to suffer."

"Exactly!" I pounded my palm down on the lab table. At last someone understood.

"What if she doesn't? What if you do your best to make her life miserable and it doesn't work?"

"Thanks for the vote of confidence."

"I'm being serious. How do you even know if you've won? What does revenge mean? It's just a vague concept. It doesn't mean anything," Brenda said.

"It means a lot to me."

"Okay, say you win, whatever that means. What in your life is going to be different after you get your revenge?"

I looked at her and opened my mouth, but I didn't know what to say so I went back to pacing back and forth for a minute while Brenda watched me. I looked over at the periodic table poster on the wall just in case there was an answer in there for me.

"What I'm trying to point out is that I totally understand why you would want revenge on Lauren, but it doesn't gain you anything," Brenda said.

"Satisfaction. A sense of justice," I offered, but in the back of my mind when she had asked what I wanted to gain, an image of Christopher floated in my mind.

"And then? I mean, unless you're willing to kill her, then whatever you do, she'll just get over it eventually. She'll move on." Brenda paused, giving me a careful look. "You aren't planning to kill her, are you?"

"No, I'm not going to kill her. Maim her maybe, a nice amputation or something." Brenda's eyes grew wide and I had to fight the urge to roll my eyes. "I'm not going to maim her either. I want to do something that will hurt her like she hurt me." I didn't mention that I already had put something into place that might just do the trick. Something that would get Lauren kicked off the cheerleading team and humiliate her all at the same time. I had the sense Brenda wouldn't want to know the details. Besides, I'd already planted the evidence in Lauren's purse.

Brenda sat at the lab table without moving. She had her hands folded on the table, and she was looking at them like they were a crystal ball with all the answers.

"I'm glad you told me."

"I'm glad too." I was about to say something else, but Brenda waved me off. She had more to say.

"I understand why you want to do this, but I have to tell you, I think it's a bad idea. If you want real revenge then live a great life, prove that what she did didn't matter that much. The fact that it still bothers you just makes her win last longer," Brenda said.

"You sound just like my grandmother. I can't explain it. This is just something I have to do," I said. Brenda was chewing on her lower lip. "I'm not going to be able to move on until I finish this. You're going to keep this secret, right?"

"I really don't think this is a good idea."

"You've made that pretty clear, but you promised. You promised on Darwin." I held up the book as a reminder.

"What if she gets hurt?"

"As much as it would give me great joy, I am not going to slip arsenic into her salad."

"What about what you did with her mascara? What if she had permanent eye damage?"

"Makeup companies have to make their products idiot-proof just in case someone sticks lip gloss in their eye by accident. Having chili pepper extract in your eye might hurt, but it isn't going to damage anything. That's why they test all that stuff. Better living through science and all that."

"I don't know."

"I'm not asking for you to help me with it, just to not say anything. I'm almost done. There is just one more thing I have to check off. We don't ever have to talk about it again. I'll move on. You can help me apply for colleges and all that stuff."

Brenda gave this big sigh. "I won't say anything." She looked over, meeting my eyes. "I promise."

I felt a huge weight lift off my shoulders. She was right, it did feel good to have told someone. It made me feel less alone even if she did think the whole plan was insane.

"You have to promise me something too," Brenda said. "Think about the law of diminishing returns."

"Huh?"

"Is all the effort you're putting into your plan worth it? In science sometimes researchers have to realize they've gone down the wrong path and turn around before they get further from what they really want. And one more thing," Brenda said.

"What?"

"I don't feel good about lying to Mr. Wong. We need to put in at least an extra hour on our biology project after school to make up for this hour."

"I will gladly spend an hour with you and your bacteria."

"Our bacteria."

I broke into a smile. "Of course, our bacteria." I reached over and we shook on the deal.

chapter thirty-five

I took everything off the kitchen shelves. The one downside of my grandmother's cooking habit is that she never throws anything away. She wants to be sure she has everything she might need to make any meal should all grocery stores across the county suddenly go out of business. She had drawers full of spices (cilantro, basil, fennel seed, coriander), different types of flour (cake, unbleached, whole wheat, enriched, multigrain), sugar (brown, white, castor, powdered, colored), and countless varieties of vinegar and oil. When I had gotten home from school I'd wandered around the house, practically bouncing up and down with nervous energy. The conversation with Brenda kept playing over and over in my mind. That's when tackling the kitchen occurred to me.

Once I had everything off a shelf, I wiped it down first with warm water to get all the sticky and spilled bits up and then with a quick spray of the kitchen cleanser. I had been at it so long a cloud of bleach hung over the room. While I cleaned I wondered what

Christopher was up to. I couldn't quite figure out what we were doing. Sometimes it seemed like he liked me. He'd held my hand at the theater and I would have sworn we were close to kissing at least twice. Then there were other times when I wasn't sure if he liked me at all. He was like this ghost; he drifted in and out of my life. Sure, I could call him, but it seemed like it should be his move next.

It was possible that he was busy with his film and that's why he didn't call. Instead of being annoyed, I should have admired him for having so much creative drive. I knew he had interviewed the whole cast because Brenda told me. He hadn't asked me for an interview, but it's possible that director flunky wasn't an important enough role to merit film time.

"What'd you do?" My grandma asked, surprising me. I was standing on the kitchen counter and turned so quickly I almost fell over.

"I thought you were going to the hospital to visit Kay," I said.

"I've been around a long time, kiddo. Don't think I didn't notice that you didn't answer the question."

"My parents like it when I help out without being asked."

"Uh-huh. You're their only kid, so they don't know any better. I had three, plus six grandkids. You don't get to be my age without knowing teenagers don't voluntarily clean out the kitchen cupboards."

"Well I do."

My grandma fixed me with a look and then shook her head.

She sat at the counter and started sorting through the mail. My parents had sent a postcard. She flipped it over to read the short note and then stuck it on the fridge.

"You see this from your folks? Sounds like things are going well."

I gave a nod and focused on the shelf. Some Karo syrup had spilled and created some type of chemical bond with the wood.

"Sometimes I clean because it feels like the only way I can make order out of something," she said. "When my life gets confusing, sometimes cleaning gives me the illusion that I'm at least making forward progress in one part of my life."

"Nothing that complicated with me. I went to get something and noticed the shelf was sticky. Once I did one shelf it just made sense to do the others. Everything's fine." I gave the syrup spill another swipe with the cleaner.

"Well then, I'll leave you to it." Grandma pushed herself up from the counter and headed off into the living room.

I waited until she was gone and then I sat down on the kitchen counter. I grabbed the postcard off the fridge and flipped it over. My dad had written a quote on the back: *There is no way to peace. Peace is the way." A. J. Muste.*

Suddenly I felt tired. Finishing the shelves seemed like entirely too much work. In fact, putting everything back seemed impossible. I fanned myself with the postcard. Maybe Brenda was right—the revenge plan might be the wrong path. Maybe my parents were right with their whole "give peace a chance" thing. Maybe there was such a thing as good enough. Maybe it was time to give it up, to stop worrying about Lauren. I thought every time I pulled something over on her it would feel like a victory, but so far it mostly felt frustrating. And lately it was an annoyance to worry about her at all. Instead of plotting my next scheme for her I could plot to see Christopher again. That had the potential for a pretty good payoff. Perhaps if my life wasn't so complicated, he wouldn't find me to be too much work. I picked up a soup can and rolled it back and forth between my hands. Andy Warhol did a great soup can painting. Brenda would most likely help me pull together an art portfolio if I wanted to try art or design school. I couldn't see myself doing advertising, but maybe something like fabric design. There were a bunch of art schools in Boston, or New York if I felt like going there. I wondered where Christopher was thinking of going for film school. Not that I was planning on stalking him or anything.

I popped off the counter and went back to my room. I would finish in the kitchen later; right now there was something else I needed to clean up. I shut the door to my room and fished my revenge binder back out from under my bed. I flipped through it. I had spent a lot of time on it, but looking at it now it felt like someone else had written it. I held it for a second. I almost felt like crying, but I couldn't have told you why. Then before I could think about it anymore I yanked my life list out and let the rest of it drop into the trash can.

Done. The fate of Lauren was officially in the hands of karma. From now on, I'd just worry about my own.

chapter thirty-six

The next day I couldn't talk to Brenda until rehearsal. She hadn't been in school all afternoon because of a dentist appointment. When I found her she was fiddling with one of the prop doors that kept sticking.

"Hey," I said.

"Do you know what we can do with this? I'm worried I'm going to end up stuck on the wrong side and miss a cue."

"I'll add it to the list for Ms. H." I looked around to see if we were alone. "I wanted to talk to you about something."

"Sure," Brenda said, opening and closing the door, trying to wear it down. "About the door?"

"No, ignore the door for a minute. You were right about the revenge thing. It's time to let it go."

Brenda looked at me for a second and then threw her arms around me as if I had announced that I had discovered a cure for Ebola during the only biology class she missed all year. "That's fantastic. What changed your mind?"

"All right, people, let's take our marks. We've got a lot to get through this afternoon. Let's start at the top of act two," Ms. Herbaut called out, interrupting our discussion. "Brenda? We need you."

Brenda looked at me and then over at the stage.

"Don't worry, I'll tell you all about it later."

Brenda skipped onto the stage and gave me a big smile.

"What is she, your girlfriend?"

I turned around to see Lauren standing there with her trademark smirk.

"She's my friend."

"Brenda Bauer? Brenda the space cadet?" She laughed. "Nice choice."

"Thanks. I thought so," I said. Lauren's face looked pinched like she had been chewing on a movie-size container of Sour Patch Kids. I looked at her and realized I felt nothing. "Excuse me," I said as I stepped past her.

I jumped off the stage on my way to my seat and saw Christopher standing at the back, setting up a video camera. I didn't know if I should say anything to him or act like I didn't see him, but before I could decide he raised a hand in greeting. I walked over.

"I'm doing some shots today of the rehearsal, but I wanted to know when I could meet with you. I haven't interviewed you for my film yet."

"Me?"

"You're part of the show, aren't you?"

"You know what? I am."

"All right. Can I call you later?"

"You bet," I stood there looking at him. I found it impossible not to smile. I was sure it would work out between us now that I had gotten rid of Lauren in the middle. Finally I shook my clipboard. "Time to get down to work," I said as if he were trying to keep me from it.

I sat down and chewed on the end of my pen. In theory I was supposed to be making a list of to-do items for Ms. H., but instead I tried to figure out if I could calculate how close Christopher was behind me without looking around. I was pretty sure Brenda would help me figure out a way to explain to him the whole alternate persona thing, one of the many benefits of having a smart friend. It was time to go back to being Helen. I looked at the script. The scene called for Eliza to pass through the flower market. I wrote down plastic flowers on the top of my list.

"Claire?"

I spun around and realized that Ms. Herbaut must have called my name more than once. She sounded annoyed and everyone was looking at me.

"Claire, can you come down here? I need your help."

I hustled down the aisle to join everyone on the stage. Lauren smirked at me.

"Forget your name?" she asked, and a few people laughed.

"Sorry, I was thinking of something else." I waited for the flush of anger I usually felt when Lauren pulled her condescending act, but I didn't care.

"Can you tape out where everyone is standing at the beginning of the scene?" Ms. Herbaut asked.

"Can you start with me, please?" Lauren asked. "I can't stand here all day, I'm supposed to run through one of the songs again with Rubin." Lauren motioned to the orchestra pit where Rubin was filling in as pianist for practices. He jumped when he heard his name, and I could see his giant Adam's apple bopping up and down.

"I can wait, Lauren," he said, his voice slightly cracking.

"Well, I don't want to wait," she snapped.

I bent down and taped an X on the floor where it met the tip of Lauren's shoe.

"There you go. You're free," I said. Our eyes met and she looked at me slightly confused.

"Actually, Miss Wood, I need to see you briefly," a voice said from the rear of the auditorium. It was Principal LaPoint.

"Me?" Lauren asked, pointing to herself. Everyone in the auditorium looked back and forth between Lauren and Mr. LaPoint. Lauren was not the typical student called into his office.

"Yes. Please bring your bag and come with me."

"I can't go now; we're in the middle of practice."

The vein in Mr. LaPoint's forehead began to pulse. People didn't tell him no very often.

"I've already called your mother. I think it would be better if we had this discussion in my office."

Lauren stomped her foot down. "Can't this wait? I've got to leave here and go straight to cheerleading. What's the big deal?"

"Miss Wood, I think we should discuss this in my office."

"Discuss what?"

"You've been accused of possessing drugs, Miss Wood," Mr. LaPoint spat out. My stomach fell into my shoes. Oh shit. This wasn't supposed to happen. If Mr. LaPoint had been expecting Lauren to cower in fright, he was wrong. She looked at him and laughed. Of course she had no idea what was coming. I didn't feel like laughing at all.

"You're joking," she said.

"I'm not joking. Now, if you will come with me."

"I don't do drugs," Lauren said with a toss of her hair.

"Then you don't mind if I search your bag?"

"No."

"Lauren, maybe you should wait until your mom gets here," Ms. Herbaut said.

"It's no big deal. This is obviously a mistake."

Lauren jumped off the stage and walked to the side of the auditorium where everyone had dumped their bags and coats on the floor. She pulled out her giant black leather tote. I wanted to stop what I knew was going to happen, but short of pulling a fire alarm I couldn't think of anything to do.

"If you look through my bag, then I'm free to go, right?" She handed Mr. LaPoint her tote and tossed her hair. "I'm assuming a strip search won't be required."

Someone in the front rows snickered and Mr. LaPoint looked over, his gaze freezing everyone into silence. He walked over to the table at the front and placed the bag down as if he were about to start a tricky medical procedure. He unzipped various pockets and stacked Lauren's things on the table: pens, three different shades of lipstick, a small notebook, her iPod, a roll of winter-green Life Savers, some nail polish, a stack of Kleenex folded into fours.

Lauren stood watching him, her hip cocked out to the side looking bored. The rest of the cast and crew didn't even pre-tend to ignore what was going on. They jockeyed for position to see what would happen. I could see Brenda standing near the back, and she looked as nervous as if she were the one in trouble instead of Lauren.

"Satisfied?" Lauren asked in a voice that implied she would have her daddy's lawyer down to the school first thing in the morning to bring charges against Mr. LaPoint.

For a second I thought it might work out okay, that he wouldn't see it. That however this had gotten screwed up would work itself back out. Then he found it, buried deep in the front pocket: a tin of Altoids. He popped the tin open and then smiled. Lauren's brow furrowed. He turned the tin and there, nestled in the paper were two joints.

The cast and crew let out an appreciative *ooh* for a trick well done. The blood dropped out of Lauren's face. I felt like I wanted to throw up.

"That isn't mine," she said.

"That's what I tell my folks too when they catch me!" yelled out one of the guys in the chorus, and everyone started laughing.

"Miss Wood, if you'll come with me." Mr. LaPoint reached for her elbow and she yanked it away. Lauren's lower lip started to shake. Any drug offenses were an automatic dismissal from the cheerleading squad. Not to mention what her mom and dad were going to say. I froze when I saw Brenda. She was looking at me in shock.

"They're not mine," Lauren said again, even louder.

Mr. LaPoint reached for her again, this time taking her by the forearm. Once he had a hold on her she crumpled. It was like every bone in her body turned to water and she collapsed to the floor.

"NO!" She yelled out. Ms. Herbaut stood up and moved forward, but it was clear she didn't know what to do.

"Please come with me, Miss Wood," Mr. LaPoint repeated.

Lauren didn't say anything. She just began to cry. Mr. LaPoint took her elbow and lifted her to her feet. He half carried and half led her out of the auditorium, her handbag stuffed under his arm. He gave Ms. Herbaut a stiff nod as he walked out the door. The room erupted with everyone talking to everyone else.

I turned around and realized that Christopher had caught the whole thing on film.

"Okay, everyone quiet down," Ms. Herbaut said, raising her

voice over the din. "Everyone give it a rest. We're going to move on with practice." She flipped through the script at random. "Casey, let's run through your scene."

Casey, a shy-looking sophomore, went on stage while everyone else dropped their voices back down to a murmur.

"I can honestly say I didn't see that coming," Ms. Herbaut whispered to me.

Brenda was standing at the edge of the stage looking at me. She shook her head before turning around and walking away.

"Me neither," I mumbled. This was only half true. I can't say it was totally unexpected. I knew how the joints got in her purse; I'd put them there a few days ago during lunch. The question was, who called Mr. LaPoint and turned her in?

chapter thirty-seven

I grabbed my jacket out of my locker. My mind kept replaying the situation over and over. No one could focus after the drug drama, so we ended rehearsal early, and the halls were already empty. Most of the students and teachers had gone home. I could hear people in the student newspaper office. I wondered if they would consider this a breaking story. The janitor was waxing up the floors, and the hum of the machine bounced off the tile floors and cement walls.

I shut the locker door and Brenda was standing there. I stepped back.

"Whoa, way to sneak up on people," I said.

Brenda didn't even crack a smile. "What are you going to do?"

"About what?"

"About what happened." Brenda looked to see if anyone was around and lowered her voice. "You were the one who put those in her bag, weren't you?"

"Yes."

"Where did you get the pot?" Brenda's head kept whipping back and forth as if the vice squad might swoop down on us at any moment.

"I asked Tyler from my gym class."

"And he just gave it to you?" Brenda looked appalled.

"Well, he made me pay for it. It wasn't like a charity thing or anything."

"What happened to giving up the revenge plan? You couldn't resist one last chance to get her back?"

"I did give up the plan. I stuck the stuff in her purse a while ago, but I swear I didn't call LaPoint. I'd been planning to make an anonymous tip to the cheerleading coach, but that was before we talked and I decided to dump the whole revenge plan. I never told anyone."

"The cheerleading coach? Why?"

"So Lauren would be kicked off the squad. They have a zero tolerance policy. Cheerleading was the only item that I hadn't checked off."

"Well, you wouldn't want to leave anything unchecked."

"I keep telling you, I'm done with all that," I said, throwing my arms up in the air. "Someone else called LaPoint." I was practically yelling at this point and I noticed that the janitor had turned off the floor buffer and was watching us like our little drama was better than cable TV. I gave him a smile and pulled Brenda down the hall. We went outside and stood by the door.

"I didn't plan for this to happen," I said. Brenda gave a snort. "Okay, I planned it, but I gave up the plan. I don't know who did this today. Maybe someone else saw a chance to get her back. Who knows, maybe karma finally caught up to her."

I shuffled in place. I'd waited a long time for Lauren's downfall. I'd dreamed about it for years. Now that it finally happened it didn't feel nearly as good as I'd anticipated. Especially with the way Brenda was looking at me.

Brenda's mom pulled into the parking lot and flashed her lights.

Brenda shook her head at me, then jogged over to the car and got in. I waved as they drove away, hoping it would infuse Brenda with confidence that somehow things would work out for the best.

So much for victory being sweet.

chapter thirty-eight

The door to the school slammed open, and I jumped back out of the way. Mrs. Wood stormed down the stairs, dragging Lauren behind her. Neither of them saw me. I was afraid to move and draw attention to myself.

"Never in my life have I been so humiliated," Mrs. Wood said. It was clear to see where Lauren's nostril-flaring talent came from: Her mom's nostrils were wide enough to comfortably hold a tennis ball in each.

"It wasn't mine. I'm telling you, someone planted it there," Lauren said. Her face was red and blotchy.

Mrs. Wood spun around and Lauren pulled back as if she thought her mom would hit her. Mrs. Wood yanked Lauren closer by her wrist so that she could yell directly in her face.

"I don't care if it's yours. What I care about is that you are dragging the name of this family through the muck. You better believe that there are plenty of people in this town who would love the chance to tear down your father and me, and you just gave them a way to do it."

"But it isn't true."

"I don't care about the truth, Lauren. I care about how it looks. I care about what people think is the truth. You know, I don't ask that much of you, just that you stay at the top of your game, that you represent this family to the best of your ability, and you can't even do that."

Mrs. Wood shook her head in disgust and stomped toward the street.

"Mom, I'm scared," Lauren said in a wobbling voice. She was still frozen on the stairs.

Mrs. Wood spun back around. "Well, Lauren, frankly I don't care what you feel. What we need to focus on is how we're going to fix this. Your father is going to get a lawyer and you're going to do whatever we need you to do to make this situation go away. You can save your tears for some other time and place." Lauren's mom yanked open the door to her Lexus SUV, her diamond bracelets winking in the sunlight. "Move it," she said, getting in and slamming the door behind her.

Lauren's shoulders slumped over and she walked slowly to the car. Her mom sat in the driver's seat staring straight ahead. When Lauren got to the car she looked up and saw me standing by the side of the school door. I saw her chest hitch and she started crying harder. She opened the door and crawled into the SUV and her mom tore off before she had finished closing the door.

"I'm sorry," I said, but no one was there to hear it.

chapter thirty-nine

There is no doubt in my mind that I have the strangest
parents in the world. They wear only all-natural fibers and
actually like the taste of tofu tacos. They've dragged me to all
kinds of weird self-exploration workshops where I learned to
meditate, chant, rub crystals, and burn sage stalks to smudge
the evil spirits from my life. I'm pretty sure both of them think
they have been through previous lives. They're weird, but they
love me. They love who I am, not what or who they wanted me
to be or thought I could be. They want me to be happy. I knew
without a doubt that if the situation had been reversed, if I were
in Lauren's shoes, they would want to know the truth and they
would stay with me until we figured it out together.

It was possible that the worst thing in the world wasn't being
betrayed by your so-called best friend; maybe the worst thing
was being betrayed by your family.

Lauren wasn't in school the next day and there wasn't a soul in all of Lincoln High who didn't know why. A couple of geeky juniors who had been on the receiving end of some of Lauren's cruel comments over the years spit on her locker as they walked past, and someone else had written BITCH on it in marker. It was clear that while Lauren might have been popular, that wasn't the same thing as being well liked.

Bailey, Kyla, and the rest of the cheerleading squad were warming up for a lunchtime practice. Apparently there was some big cheerleading derby or something coming up that called for extra practices. Bailey had asked me to come for moral support, so I sat on the slick gym floor watching and picking at my sandwich.

"Hey, can you give a message to Lauren for me?" One of the guys from the football team said as he jogged past.

Kyla gave a curt nod.

"Tell her if she's looking for blow, she don't need to do drugs. She can have this." He grabbed his crotch and gave it a shake. The rest of the guys burst out laughing.

"That was disgusting," Bailey said, looking away and pulling her leg effortlessly up above her head in a stretch. "I still can't believe the whole thing."

"It's not like it's the first time she did something without thinking," Kyla pointed out.

"True, but I don't think she did it," I said. "I think someone stuck that stuff in her bag for LaPoint to find."

"That's terrible. Who would do that to Lauren?" Bailey asked.

"That's what we need to figure out," I said.

"Now we're going to be Nancy Drew?" Kyla asked with a laugh. I had a sudden flash of Lauren cutting her palm so we would be in trouble together after our Nancy Drew adventure had gone bad.

"Yeah, now we play Nancy Drew. We figure out a way to clear Lauren's name."

"I feel terrible about what happened, but I don't want to get messed up in the situation." Kyla bent over, bouncing as she touched her toes. She looked back at me. "What? I've got my cheerleading slot to think about. Anyone mixed up in drugs is an auto off the squad. Who knows what happened? Maybe she was holding them for someone. Maybe they *are* hers. At the party last week she took a toke off someone's joint. She's no angel."

"Smoking that stuff is wrong." Bailey's mouth pressed into a thin line. Clearly Mary Poppins did not approve of recreational weed. "You start with marijuana and then it leads to heavier stuff. She could have ruined her life."

Kyla rolled her eyes. "Don't freak out, Miss Just Say No. She got caught with two joints. It isn't like she was shooting heroin. The whole thing is no big deal. Her cheerleading days are over, but Daddy's lawyer will keep her out of any real trouble."

I looked over at Bailey and she looked away, pulling at her pleated skirt.

"It isn't that I don't want to help Lauren. It's just, my parents told me I'm not allowed to hang out with her anymore. They're like superstrict and stuff," Bailey said.

The cheerleading coach blew her whistle and motioned that she wanted everyone to join her in the center of the gym floor. I stood up and chucked the rest of my sandwich into the trash.

"I don't know why you want to help Lauren so bad. You know she totally talks shit about you," Kyla said. "You might think she's your friend, but she's not. Lauren hates competition, and as far as she's concerned, you never knew your place."

"She never said anything that bad," Bailey said, clearly feeling awkward. "Lauren just gets sort of short sometimes. She hates change."

"Whatever," Kyla muttered, doing a few last twists at the waist. "I wouldn't worry about her. Things have a way of working out for Lauren." Kyla ran off with her skirt flipping up.

"It'll be okay. I think it's super nice you want to help her out, but maybe she needed to get caught to keep herself from getting into even deeper trouble. It might have been the best thing that could have happened to her." Bailey gave my arm a soft rub.

Oh no. She didn't.

"Bailey, did you turn in Lauren?"

She pulled back. I could read her like an open book. She was thinking of lying, but she didn't have the slightest idea how to do it. Dishonesty wasn't something that came easy to her.

"It isn't that I wanted her to get in trouble." Her eyes filled with tears. "Real friends do what's right, even when it feels wrong."

I sank down to the floor. Lauren was taken down by Mary Poppins. Bailey kneeled in front of me on the floor. "What happened?" I asked.

"I went in her purse to get a mint and I found the drugs." Bailey twisted her hands together. "Lauren was never into that stuff before, but she's been all weird and tense lately. I've been worried about her. I think she's getting on the wrong track."

"So you turned her in to LaPoint?" I glanced around to see if anyone else was paying attention to our discussion.

"I prayed about it first. I wanted to do the right thing. Now she can get the help she needs." Bailey's lower lip was shaking. "Are you going to tell her it was me?"

My mind was whizzing around like a salad spinner. "No. I won't tell her."

"I really did do it because I care about her."

"I know you did." The coach blew her whistle again. "You better go." Bailey squeezed my hand and then ran over to join the rest of the squad. I clamored up to my feet, brushing off my jeans.

I wasn't sure how she did it, but Lauren had found herself a true friend. I wanted another option, but I couldn't think of one. It wasn't about doing it to help Lauren; it was about doing it because the person I wanted to be would do the right thing. If I was going to get a life, it should be one worth having.

chapter forty

I sat outside LaPoint's office, my knees bouncing up and down.
I had to think that waiting to tell was going to be worse than
the actual telling, but the way the secretary kept shooting looks
over at me like my days were numbered made me wonder. I had
the sense no one who met with LaPoint got out alive. I had never
been in trouble like this before. I wasn't sure what the process
would be. Would LaPoint call my grandma? Would they kick
me out of school?

Suspension might not be a bad thing. There was no telling how it would go once the rest of the school found out
what I did. They might love me for taking down Lauren, but
more likely they'd think I was a freaky stalker psycho who
lied about everything. Maybe Grandma would be willing to
homeschool me for the rest of the year so I could graduate.
Then again, once my grandma found out I had lied to her
about the revenge plan there was the very serious possibility

that she wouldn't feel like doing me any favors.

The door to LaPoint's office swung open and he stood there like a leering Count Dracula. The secretary didn't say a word; she just pointed at me. I felt like doom-and-gloom music should start playing, but the only sound was my pounding heart. I stood up and tried to ignore the fact that every square inch of my body was sweating like I had run a marathon. I walked past Mr. LaPoint and sat in the chair across from his desk.

Mr. LaPoint's office was done in an early prison warden–style, stark and cold. He wasn't the kind of guy to have a lot of knickknacks and mementos hanging around. There was one framed picture on his desk, but it looked like the fake-family shot that came with the frame. I didn't notice any torture devices, like thumbscrews, but I supposed those weren't the kind of thing you'd leave laying around. I nibbled on the skin next to my thumbnail, but when I saw him looking at me I pulled it out of my mouth and sat on both of my hands. I waited for him to say anything, but he just sat there at his desk, his hands folded in front of him on the desk blotter.

"So . . . ," I said, my voice trailing off, but he still sat there silently. I wanted to look at my watch. It felt like I had been sitting there for an hour at least even though I knew it had been a couple minutes at best. Apparently Mr. LaPoint didn't subscribe to the "how to make things easier on you" school of discipline.

"I came to confess something," I said finally.

"Go on."

"I put the joints in Lauren Wood's bag."

"I see."

When I'd thought of how this situation might go, Mr. LaPoint simply saying "I see" hadn't been one of the possible outcomes I had imagined.

"So, I guess you'll clear Lauren's name. I don't know if you need to call my grandma to pick me up or not."

"I don't think that will be necessary."

"Okay." I waited for something to happen. I'd pictured Mr. LaPoint to be more of a yeller. I thought he was going to try to get out of me where I'd gotten the drugs or pull my fingernails out until I confessed my secret identity. Nothing. He sat there with his hands folded on the desk, looking at me. "Where do we go from here?" I asked.

"You go back to class, Miss Dantes." He pushed back from the desk and stood.

"Class?" Was that a joke? Would I go to open the door and find myself taken down by a taser?

"While I appreciate the sentiment, lying isn't tolerated here."

"What?"

Mr. LaPoint gave a chuckle. "You're friends with Miss Wood, aren't you? You hang with her little crowd."

Little crowd? How patronizing could this guy be? "Lauren and I aren't friends."

"Ah, perhaps you're hoping if you take the heat for this situation she'll be endlessly grateful. I know how young girls can be;

I've been doing this job for a long time. Cliques can be difficult to manage, especially for someone new. I don't know if she put you up to it or if you took it upon yourself, but either way, it doesn't matter."

"I put the drugs in there," I insisted again, as if repeating the information would somehow help. How could he not believe me?

"I know you're involved in the theater program, Miss Dantes, but allow me to remind you that drama should stay on the stage. I will refrain from granting you a detention this time, but I trust that your"—he made finger quotations in the air—"'confession' will be your last such attention-getting scheme." Mr. LaPoint strode to the door and opened it. "I have confidence this is the last time we'll have this discussion."

I trudged past him and he shut the door behind me. I held my hands out and they were shaking. If I pushed Lauren to the very edge of a cliff, did it really matter that she took the last step herself? I would feel just as guilty as I would if I had shoved her. If you try to do the right thing and no one believes you, does it still count?

chapter forty-one

I told the secretary I was sick. She took one look at me and decided I wasn't lying. I wasn't. It wasn't the flu, but I had a serious case of guilt-induced stomach upset that made the whole strawberry to the handbag incident look minor. The idea of sitting in class and acting like everything was fine seemed impossible.

Grandma wasn't home when I got there. I walked around the house. I didn't want to lie down and couldn't think of anything that I wanted to do. I clicked on the TV and flipped through the afternoon court TV shows. I tried to get interested in who got justice, but it seemed too complicated to follow. When Judge Judy starts being too complex you have to know you aren't at your best. The Turner movie channel was showing *What Ever Happened to Baby Jane?* Even a creepy Bette Davis movie wasn't going to do the trick.

I picked up the phone and put it down. Then I saw the number stuck to the fridge with a magnet. I pulled it off and dialed it without thinking about it any more. The receptionist at the meditation camp went to get my mom.

"Hey, Poppet, is everything okay?" As soon as I heard my mom's voice, I felt better. I clutched the phone close to my face as if that would bring us closer together.

"I hope I didn't interrupt you from reaching enlightenment or anything."

"You're never an interruption."

"Mom, how to do you fix karma?"

"Karma isn't a broken thing."

"What if someone did something, say, a bad something, but when they did it they knew it was wrong, but thought they were doing it for the right reason, but then they realized it wasn't the right reason, but the situation was already out of control and then everything was all screwed up?" The words flew out of me in a giant run-on sentence.

"Well, assuming I followed that last bit, I guess I would tell this mysterious someone that everything we do and say has an impact on the world around us. If this person has put something out in the world that was wrong, then she needs to double her efforts to put in something good."

"Sort of balance things out," I said, with a sniff.

"Exactly."

"What if she tried to make things right, but it didn't work?"

"What do you do when you draw something and it doesn't come out right?"

"I erase it and do it over."

"There you are. We need to redraw the world when we don't like what's in front of us."

I could hear the chime of a bell in the background. "I suppose I should let you go," I said.

"I can stay and talk longer if you want."

"No. I'm okay. Will you tell Dad I said hi?"

"Of course. One more thing: Karma is a heavy weight. Hard to move, hard to change."

"Yeah, I'm getting that idea."

"That's why it's always best to get a helping hand. You can leverage so much more when you don't do it alone."

I hung up the phone and then picked it up again before I could talk myself out it. Brenda picked up on the second ring.

"I need your help," I blurted. "All those times I was giving you advice? You were right, I should have been taking it from you instead. You're clearly the smart one in this relationship. I'll say I'm sorry a million times in a row, but you have to help me."

"Anyone ever tell you that you're sort of intense?"

"So if I say I'm sorry, say, a hundred times in a row that would cover it?"

"Maybe." I could hear a thaw in Brenda's voice.

"The thing is, the person who turned in Lauren actually did it for the right reason. I don't want to get that person in trouble, but I need to make things right somehow."

"And you think I'll know how to sort this out?"

"I'm pretty much counting on it."

Brenda sighed. "Okay, this is a bit outside my usual area of expertise, but in science if you screw up, the honorable thing to do is make it public. You write a paper about where you went off track and publish it where all your colleagues will see it. You have to own the error."

"You think I should take out an ad in the school paper saying I planted the drugs?"

"I'm not saying it's the best plan, but it is an option. Do you have any other ideas?"

"Not really. Science isn't my thing."

"What's your thing?"

"Movies."

"What do they do in the movies?"

"In the movies when a character wants to redeem himself, he has to make a noble sacrifice. Like when Rhett Butler leaves Scarlett O'Hara in the middle of the invasion of Atlanta to join the army, even though he knows they'll lose."

"I think joining the army and heading off to war to your certain doom is going a bit far."

"Yeah, I look lousy in a uniform. I can sacrifice something though." I picked up a pen sitting by the phone and tapped it on the counter. "I'm going to have to kill off Claire."

"At least she'll die with a purpose." Leave it to Brenda to find a silver lining.

"Before I put her obituary in the paper there's someone I need to talk to." My voice shook slightly.

"What do you think he'll say?"

"I don't know. I might end up sacrificing a chance with him too."

"Or it might make a chance possible."

chapter forty-two

I got to the theater early, but Christopher was already there. He was sitting near the back with his eyes closed while he waited for the show to start. They were showing *Flying Leathernecks*. I took a deep breath and moved down the aisle. He opened his eyes when I sat down. I motioned to the pile of junk food in his lap—a bucket of buttered popcorn, a giant box of Junior Mints, and a bag of those SweeTart knockoffs that taste like sour sugar cubes.

"Hungry?" I asked.

"Dinner of champions." He shook the popcorn in my direction and I took a handful. "I take it you've decided you like old movies?"

"I think I always did." I took a deep breath. "I need to talk to you."

"Now?" He looked confused. Talking and movies don't usually go together. The lights went down and the Dolby sound kicked into overdrive. It was so loud, the sound waves pushed me back into the chair. The previews were apparently being screened for those with hearing impairments.

"No, it can wait." I wasn't sure what he was going to do when I told him the truth. He might be Lincoln High's bad boy, but he had his own clearly defined sense of right and wrong.

"I'm glad you came," he said, before scrunching down in his seat.

"Me too," I whispered, but I wasn't sure he heard me.

"How can you not like John Wayne?" Christopher asked as we walked out to our cars after the movie. "It's like saying you don't like baseball or apple pie. It's un-American."

"It's not exactly the same as flag burning or marching for anarchy."

"It might be worse. What about his film *Fort Apache*?"

"Nope."

"Okay, *Rio Grande*?"

"Meh." I waved my hand back and forth.

"*Hellfighters*?"

I gave a shrug. "*The Quiet Man* was okay."

"Oscar-winning film and she says it was okay."

"You know what happened to Lauren? Those drugs weren't hers." I said it in a rush, before I lost my nerve.

"Holy changing topics, Batman," he said.

"No, I'm being serious. I know they weren't hers."

"Why do you always bring her up?"

"I don't always bring her up," I protested.

Christopher gave a laugh, which ticked me off for some reason.

"I don't bring her up that often," I said, trying to calm my voice.

"Hey, don't get mad. You can talk about whoever you want. Everyone else is talking about her these days."

"That's what I'm trying to talk to you about."

"Now listen here, pilgrim, you don't want to get involved with the law, " he said with a really bad imitation of John Wayne. I crossed my arms across my chest. "Oops, that's right. I forgot you hated him. Look, you're right. The stuff wasn't Lauren's."

I suddenly felt light-headed. "How do you know?"

"That girl is wound way too tight to be smoking weed on a regular basis. I mean ask yourself, does she strike you as someone that people would call mellow?" he asked.

My mouth clicked shut. The logic there was hard to ignore.

"I put the stuff in her purse."

"Why would you do that?" He took a step back. I had to fight the urge to step closer.

"This is a long story. Is there some place we could talk?"

chapter forty-three

Christopher had a tree house. It was built high in a giant
oak tree in the woods that ran behind his neighborhood.
He jumped up to pull down a rope ladder and motioned that I
should climb up first. I hadn't been in a tree house since I was ten,
but this was about a thousand times better than any tree house
I had ever seen. The floor was straight and felt solid. The roof
was large, shingled with a generous overhang. The walls went up
only half way so you could look out between the branches. It felt
more like an outpost than a tree house.

Christopher climbed up behind me. There was a giant
Rubbermaid container in the corner, and he popped it open
to pull out some blankets. He spread one on the floor and
then passed me a worn blue fleece blanket.

"It's getting cold," he said. He pulled another blanket out for
himself and then a lantern, which he fired up. It gave the space
a sort of yellow glow. If we'd had some marshmallows and a fire

it would feel like camp. Of course I suspected Smokey the bear frowns on campfires being set in trees, given that they are flammable and all.

"Nice place," I said, breaking the silence.

"It's a little elementary school, which is fair since it's been mine since elementary school, but you wanted a place we could be alone. This would be it."

"You make it yourself?"

"Me? No. My dad and I built it when I was a kid. He knew how to make stuff last, but he wasn't as good with keeping relationships going. This tree house will be around for years, which is more than I could say for him."

"I'm sorry."

"Don't be. I got over feeling bad about that a few years ago. All my family trauma will give me something to talk about when I'm interviewed as a famous director. Gotta have something to fill up those behind-the-scenes DVD sections. And if nothing else, this gives me a place to go when my mom and I aren't getting along. I like to think of it as my dad's lovely parting gift."

I pulled the blanket around me so I was wrapped up like a fleece burrito. I took a deep breath and began at the beginning. "When you said things with me were complicated you were right. You know how my grandma calls me Helen? Well . . ."

Christopher didn't interrupt while I told the whole story. I wasn't sure what he thought, but I was considering it a positive that he didn't get up and leave.

"That's it," I said, in case he hadn't guessed from the silence that the story was over.

"Can't say I expected that."

"The thing is, I didn't call LaPoint." I felt it was important that he knew that I hadn't done this final piece of damage.

"But you would have. I mean, maybe not LaPoint, but you would have gotten her in trouble at some point. Your point was to destroy her, wasn't it?"

I pulled at the thread on the edge of the blanket. "Yes." A tear ran down my face, it felt hot on my cheek. That was the first time I realized how cold the night had gotten. "I'm sorry that I did it. I'm sorry that it ended up hurting Lauren, and I'm sorry that I lied to you and Brenda. I always thought that Lauren ruined everything for me, but the truth is, the reason I never made any other real friends is because I'm lousy at it."

"I'm pretty lousy at the people thing too."

"You're better than me."

"Take this in the nicest way, but you haven't exactly set the bar real high."

It was hard to argue with that. I pulled the blanket closer. "The whole thing will come out tomorrow after school."

"Should make for an interesting day."

"Can you forgive me?" I held my breath waiting for him to answer.

"How can I forgive you? I don't really know who you are."

Do not cry. Do not cry. I reminded myself that you didn't see

Rhett Butler crying. You can't be noble and a crybaby at the same time. Tomorrow was another day and all that. "Fair enough."

I stood up and folded the blanket. I passed it back to Christopher without saying anything else and crawled down the rope ladder. I jumped down the last few feet.

"Hey, Helen." Christopher poked his head out of the tree house. I could hardly make out his features in the dark. "I don't know who you are, but it might be interesting to find out," he said.

My face burst into a huge smile. "I can promise you, with me it will almost certainly be interesting."

chapter forty-four

I left school early. I didn't want to be around when they distributed the paper with my CLAIRE DANTES=HELEN WORTHINGTON ad in it at the end of the day. Besides, there was one other person I had to talk to. Lauren's mom answered the door. She was wearing slacks that looked freshly ironed and a scarf tied at her waist like a belt, an expensive, all-silk belt. I wondered if she stood up all day to avoid being wrinkled. The dark circles under her eyes were the only things out of place. Otherwise she looked perfect. She didn't say anything; she simply raised one eyebrow as a question. I guessed my paint-stained yoga pants weren't kicking her hospitality gene into action.

"Is Lauren home?" I held up the tote bag full of books I had brought. "I go to school with her. I have all her homework and stuff."

"I'll see that she gets it." Mrs. Wood held out one perfectly manicured hand.

"I sort of need to see her. Some of it has to be explained."

Mrs. Wood didn't say anything else but led the way. I followed after her, past the designer kitchen that looked as if it had never been used, through the living room with its uncomfortably stiff furniture, and up the stairs. She tapped on the door to Lauren's bedroom with her fingernail and walked away.

"Come in," Lauren said.

I pushed open the door. Lauren was propped up in bed; she had the TV on showing a rerun of *Gossip Girl.* When she saw me she clicked it off. She sat up straighter and ran her fingers through her hair, which looked a bit grimy. I had felt panicky on the way over, but for some reason, now that I was in the middle of everything, I felt strangely calm.

"I brought you a bunch of stuff from school."

If I had been waiting for her to say thanks, then it looked like it was going to be a long wait.

"Are you feeling okay?" I asked.

"I'm fine."

The conversation seemed to have run out of steam again.

"Did you want anything else?" Lauren asked.

"I came to say I'm sorry."

"For what?"

"Remember when you said you started having all kinds of bad luck when I showed up? That wasn't all by accident."

"Did you do this too? Did you stick that stuff in my purse?"

"Yes." From the look in Lauren's eye I could tell she was already planning to sic her daddy's lawyer on me like a pit bull. "I suppose you want to know why I did this?" I said.

"No, *Helen*, I know exactly why you did it."

I backed up until I hit the wall. "How long have you known?"

"I suspected for a while. I didn't know for sure until now. Did you really think you could keep it a secret forever? I *know* you. I know you better than anyone. I would have guessed even sooner except I didn't think anyone could be that twisted." Lauren got off the bed and walked across the room. She crossed her arms and looked at me. "I bet you're really proud of yourself, huh?"

"Not really."

"I doubt that."

"I came to say I'm sorry."

"You should be." Lauren stepped closer so that our faces were inches apart. "Is this where you expect me to say I'm sorry too? To throw myself to the floor and beg you to forgive me? Maybe we could sit down and talk it all over and end up swearing to be best friends forever? Maybe your mom and dad could make a peace circle out in the woods and we could dance by the moonlight in some weird pagan ritual."

"I don't expect us to be friends, but you know we used to be. There was a time when I would have done anything for you."

"That was your problem, not mine."

"You're right. It just took me a longer time to catch on than it should have. Friendship is supposed to go both ways."

"Wow, that's deep. You should make up T-shirts or something."

"I came to tell you I'm sorry. What you did to me was wrong; what I did was wrong too. It's even now. We're done."

"What if I say it's not done? What if I have my dad get his lawyer and sue your family for every stupid trinket they own? You do own some things, don't you? What do you think the kids at school are going to say when this comes out? You think they're going to like you, knowing that you basically came here to stalk me? Why don't you just admit you want to be me? This was all about trying to steal my life because you're jealous."

"I've been confused about a lot of stuff, but the one thing I'm certain of is I never want to be you." But I realized as I said it that she was almost right. In getting the revenge, I almost turned into her, and that would have been the worst outcome I could imagine.

"Whatever. We'll see what everyone has to say."

"The people who matter to me already know who I am. As for telling everyone else, you don't need to worry. I'm guessing it's public knowledge by now." I put the bag of books down on the floor and turned to leave. That's when I saw them. How could I have missed that when I had been in her room last time? I walked across the room and ran my fingers across one of her bookshelves, along her collection of hardcover Nancy Drew mysteries.

I picked one up and flipped through the pages. Stuffed in the back were our detective agency business cards and some pictures of the two of us together. I smiled when I saw one of the photos. It was a sleepover. I don't remember the occasion, but my folks had allowed us to pretend we were pioneers. They'd turned the heat down in the house and we had slept in front of the fireplace. In the morning my mom had made pancakes, and we had drowned them in a lake of maple syrup. The photo was of the two of us sitting in front of the fireplace with our plates balanced in our laps. I could remember everything about that moment. The way the smoke of the fire mixed with the smell of pancakes and how I ended up with sticky syrup in my hair. We had laughed so much that night I couldn't even remember if we ever went to sleep. I flipped the photo over so she could see it.

Lauren's lower lip was shaking.

"We had some good times," I said softly. Lauren shrugged. She wouldn't look me directly in the eye. "You take care of yourself, Lauren Wood."

chapter forty-five

I slipped out of Lauren's room and down the stairs. I let myself out the door without saying good-bye to Mrs. Wood. I didn't owe her anything.

I heard a honk and looked up. Christopher's car was parked across the street. He and Brenda got out. I felt a smile break out across my face.

"How did it go?" Brenda asked.

"I don't think she and I are going to be best friends, if that's what you're asking."

"Of course not, I'm your best friend. The position is already taken," Brenda said.

"What are you guys doing here?"

"If you can believe it, she just admitted she's never seen an Audrey Hepburn movie," Christopher said, motioning to Brenda.

"What? I told you to watch those weeks ago," I said.

"Things got a bit busy."

"We've rented the whole series: *Sabrina*, *Breakfast at Tiffany's*, and of course, *My Fair Lady*." Christopher counted them off on his fingers. "We're going over to her place to order pizza."

"And you came to get me?"

"How can I get to know you unless we spend time together?" Christopher leaned over and kissed the corner of my mouth. "Besides, Brenda tells me you've got only one night before you're doomed to be grounded. I thought I better see you while I still had the chance."

"Good point. Lockdown begins tomorrow. If Lauren gets my parents involved there may even be forced community service hours."

"Don't worry. In addition to heist movies, I've seen a lot of prison break movies. There's hope for you yet."

I was almost afraid to ask, but I had to know.

"So what was the response to my ad?"

"I think you should look at transferring schools," Brenda said. My mouth fell open and she burst out laughing. "I'm joking."

"Most people I heard talking about it thought the whole thing was sort of cool," Christopher said. "Who knows, maybe it will make you even more popular."

"I don't care about being popular anymore. Well, except with the present company."

We piled into Christopher's car. While Brenda and Christopher debated the merits of different pizza toppings, I flipped through the DVD movie cases they had picked up.

Old movies are black-and-white; they've got good guys and bad guys. The thing was, I didn't want to live in the past anymore. It was time for my life to go full color.

acknowledgments

When I buy a book I always read the acknowledgments section. I think I'm hoping to see my name in it. In that spirit, my first thanks go to you for picking this book to read. Feel free to pencil your name in here. You deserve it.

Big thanks to my friends and family who put up with me. At times this is harder than you might think. You can't choose your family, but if I could, I would choose the one I have. As for my friends, I couldn't imagine better, and that is saying something because I make stuff up for a living.

One of the best parts of writing has been the support and friendship of other writers. For all the help with brainstorming, talking me off the ledge, and inspiring me with your writing, thanks go to Joelle Anthony, Allison Pritchard, Robyn Harding, Shanna Mahin, Carol Mason, Nancy Warren, Eileen Rendahl, Serena Robar, Carolyn Rapanos, Meg Cabot, everyone connected to the Debutante Ball, Joanne Levy, Brooke Chapman, Lani Diane Rich, Jen Lancaster, Allison Winn Scotch, Alison Pace, and Barrie Summy. A special nod to Dumas, who wrote *The Count of Monte Cristo*, the inspiration for this book.

My agent, Rachel Vater, continues to be both a great business partner and friend. Thanks for all your guidance, support, and late night discussions on skeptical topics. Huge thanks to my editor, Anica Mrose Rissi, who shares my love of good books, good food, and dogs, even when they're being bad. Your feedback is wonderful and makes each book better. I'd write books with you anytime. The entire team at Simon Pulse is fantastic. Special thanks go to Cara Petrus, who designs covers that are so wonderful I want to lick them.

Special thanks to my husband, Bob, who always believed this was possible. You are my happy ending. My two dogs deserve thanks for providing me with disgusting half-chewed toys as a distraction. It's like having a live action Cute Overload in the house.

Lastly a huge thanks to my readers. There are so many good books to choose from, I appreciate people giving mine a chance. Please be sure to drop by my website and let me know what you think of the book. I'd love to hear from you! www.eileencook.com

about the author

EILEEN COOK spent most of her teen years wishing she were someone else or somewhere else, which is great training for a writer. When she was unable to find any job postings for world-famous author, she went to Michigan State University and became a counselor so she could at least afford her book-buying habit. But real people have real problems, so she returned to writing because she liked having the ability to control the ending. Which is much harder with humans.

You can read more about Eileen, her books, and the things that strike her as funny at eileencook.com. Eileen lives in Vancouver with her husband and dogs and no longer wishes to be anyone or anywhere else.

Want more funny?

Here's a peek at

EILEEN COOK'S
What Would Emma Do?

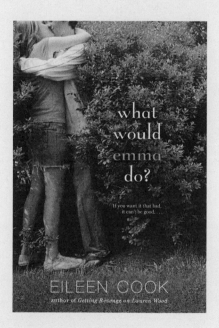

From *What Would Emma Do?*
by EILEEN COOK

chapter one

God, I've been thinking about our relationship. The way I see it, most people look at you as either (a) a Santa Claus figure they pray to only when they want something, their wishes granted depending on if they are on the naughty or nice list, or (b) a bearded vengeance seeker who gets his immortal jollies from smiting those who annoy him. It occurs to me I've been talking to you my whole life and I don't really know who you are. In fairness, I've always relied on formal prayers, which really haven't given you a chance to get to know me, either. I'm thinking we need a bit more honesty in our relationship—you strike me as the kind to support honesty—so from here on I'm just going to tell you what's on my mind.

We spend a lot of time at Trinity Evangelical Secondary discussing "What would Jesus do?" You have to wonder how the Son of God finds himself in so many ethically questionable situations. I'm guessing he hangs out with a bad crowd.

We've covered how Jesus feels about:

- low-rise jeans (negative)
- underage drinking (although this is the same man who brought us wine transformed from water, we've decided he would just say no)
- gossip (to be avoided—which goes to show he would never make it in Wheaton, where gossip has been perfected to near Olympic levels)

All in all, the Son of God is coming across as a very no-fun kind of guy. I prefer to see him as not so uptight. This puts me in the minority here, where the motto for our church could be "Trinity Evangelical: Sitting in judgment on others since 1849."

At the moment we were supposed to be discussing in great detail, as if this is an issue the president of the United States might need to consult us on, what Jesus would do if he accidentally came across the answers to the math test before the exam. Everyone stared off into space, pondering how our savior might handle this tricky situation.

I left the issue of exam ethics to my capable classmates and went back to trying to get my best friend Joann's attention. I risked a look over my shoulder at her. Mr. Reilly, our religion teacher, has been known to hurl erasers at the heads of students he feels aren't paying attention, so being subtle was key. Joann was either ignoring me or in a catatonic state. I gave a fake cough to draw her attention. Nothing. I coughed again, this time drawing it out as if I might be in the final stages of TB, but not even a glance.

Darci Evers raised one perfectly manicured hand in the air. Darci looks like she jumped out of a spread in *Seventeen* and the teachers always talk about how she makes a great role model, but don't be fooled. She's the kind of person who laughs if you trip in the cafeteria. If your mom forces you to wear the sweater your nearly blind grandmother knit for you, she gives a brittle, thin smile and says, "Nice sweater." Then her posse of friends giggle. In elementary school she dotted the *i* in her name with bubbles and hearts.

"If Jesus saw the test before the exam, he would tell the teacher and ask for a new test, one where he didn't know the answers," Darci said. She paused, her head cocked to the side as if she was getting direct communication from heaven. "Our Lord doesn't like cheaters."

I fought the urge to roll my eyes. The rest of the class all nodded, seemingly relieved to have this conundrum solved and Christ no longer at risk for blowing the hell out of the bell curve. Mr. Reilly smiled. He adores Darci Evers.

"Excellent answer."

I raised my hand. Mr. Reilly's smile withered.

"God is all-knowing, right?" I asked.

"Yes, Emma. He knows everything, what you've done and even what you will do." Mr. Reilly took this moment to look out over the classroom in case anyone had evil or impure thoughts in their hearts.

I looked to see if Joann was following my line of intellectual debate. Joann has never been a huge Darci fan, and I figured it wouldn't hurt to remind her that we had this in common.

"So if God knows everything, won't he know what questions the teacher is going have on the new test too?"

Mr. Reilly's head started to turn red, and I could see the vein in his forehead bulge. For a guy so close to Jesus, he has a lot of repressed rage issues.

"Are you trying to be smart?" Mr. Reilly said.

I hate questions like this. There is no right answer. If you say you are trying to be smart, you get in trouble for being a wiseass, and if you say you're not, you're admitting to being stupid. It's what they call a lose-lose situation. What would Jesus do if faced with this question? I'm guessing he would go for honesty, but Jesus didn't have to worry about getting lower than a C in class and losing his track eligibility as a result.

"No, sir," I answered.

Mr. Reilly gave a snort and turned back to the board. Darci shot me a look of annoyance and raised her hand again. Joann still wasn't paying any attention to me.

"Mr. Reilly, do you mind if I make an announcement? It's related to student council business," Darci said.

Darci never misses an opportunity to make an announcement. She finds excuses in nearly every class to take center stage.

I suspect that if it were up to her as senior class president, she would get to wear a small crown or sash to denote her over-all superiority. I'm shocked she doesn't demand that the rest of us scatter palm fronds on the floor in front of her as she walks through the halls.

"As everyone knows, the big spring dance is coming up in just a few weeks, and we still need volunteers to help with the decorations. This year we've selected the theme 'Undersea Adventure.' Please show your school spirit by helping to make this a great event. Even if you haven't been asked to the dance, you could still decorate. We'll be accepting nominations for king and queen for the next two weeks, and the three couples that get the most votes will be announced as the court. The queen and king will be announced at the dance."

"I nominate you," Kimberly said so quickly she must have bumped her nose on the way to kissing Darci's ass.

Darci placed a hand on her heart as if she were overcome by the honor.

"Why, Kimberly, thank you so much! I feel a bit funny about putting myself down on the list, but if you insist." She pulled out her pink gel pen to inscribe her name before she forgot it.

"Why do we even have a king and queen?" I asked.

"We've always had a king and queen of the spring dance. It's tradition," Darci shot back.

"Maybe it's time for a new tradition." As the challenge shot out of my mouth, I couldn't tell who was more surprised, Darci or me. It felt like the air was sucked out of the room for a second as people held their breath, waiting for Darci to whack me back down to size. At least I had Joann's attention now.

"You can't have a new tradition. Then it's not tradition, it's the opposite; it's new," Darci said, giving me a look, as if shocked that someone of my low intelligence was even allowed in school.

I slunk down in my seat.

"What would Jesus do?" asked Todd.

The entire class turned around to face him. Todd Seaver is the guy in our class who never says anything. There have been rumors that he's an elective mute. Todd has the dubious honor of being from "away," a non-Wheaton native.

"What are you talking about?" Darci asked.

"Would Jesus approve of people setting themselves above others? Sounds like false gods."

"It's not like that at all. Besides, you're Jewish, how would you even know what Jesus would do?"

There was a gasp. It's an unwritten rule that we don't bring up Todd's Jewishness. In a town that is all born-again, his religion is like a deformity, one of those things everyone is painfully aware of and tries to act like they don't notice.

"He was one of the tribe when he started out, you know," Todd said. "I'm thinking he would see the whole king and queen thing as a bunch of false idols, golden calves." He gave Darci a lazy half smile and then looked over at me.

I slunk farther down in my seat, not meeting his eyes. If I

went any lower I would slide completely out of the chair and onto the floor. Part of me was glad someone else was standing up to Darci. I just wished the person I was aligned with wasn't the class pariah.

"Interesting point," Mr. Reilly said, tapping his thin fingers on his Bible. He adored Darci, but stamping out fun was his favorite thing in the world.

"It's tradition," said Darci, her voice cracking.

"I think we need to discuss the dance at the next advisory board meeting," Mr. Reilly said as the bell rang.

Darci's mouth opened and shut silently like a fish flopping on a dock. A fish with pink-bubble-gum-scented lip gloss. Everyone got up and moved toward the door. I stood up and grabbed my bag.

Darci bumped into my back. "Way to go, Emma," she hissed, shoving past me.

"Yeah, way to go," Kimberly parroted, following two steps behind her.

Joann walked up next to me, and I gave her a smile.

"My mom already bought me a dress for the dance," she said, crossing her arms. "Why can't you leave some things alone?" She walked away without another word.

Recent events, combined with years of religious study, have clarified for me that at the ripe age of seventeen, I am pretty much already damned to hell. Let's recap:

- Gluttony: I have, on more than one occasion, eaten the entire gut-buster ice-cream sundae at the Dairy Hut that you get for free if you can finish it. What can I say? I run a lot; I get hungry.
- Greed: I have a passion for my running shoe collection that others might reserve for the members of a boy band. It's not just fashion; it's also about function.
- Sloth: Every time my mom sees the state of my room, she is compelled to say, "If you're waiting for the maid to come along, you've got a long wait ahead of you." Then she sighs deeply, like being my mother is her burden in life.
- Wrath: I detest Darci Evers, and if I had the opportunity it is quite likely I would replace her shampoo with Nair.
- Envy: I would give just about anything, including possibly my soul, to run like Sherone Simpson (ranked number one in the world for the hundred meters).
- Pride: I won the state championship last year for hurdles and plan to repeat this year. I've been accepted to Northwestern, and if I can nail down a track scholarship, I've even got a way to pay for it and a way out of town.
- Lust: I kissed my best friend's boyfriend over Christmas break.

Yep, it's pretty much the last one that's going to do me in.

chapter two

God, I know you're busy, and to be honest, what with famine, pestilence, and war I feel a bit bad about bugging you in the past over silly things like getting breasts (although—hey, it's never too late), but the situation with Joann is really bugging me. Is there any way you could remind her that we're best friends? A small vision, perhaps? I really am sorry for what happened with Colin. Think of the benefits: If we were close again, I wouldn't need to come to you with the small things, I could sort them out with her. Consider it less like granting a prayer and more like a time-saving device for yourself.

There is no greater sin than kissing your best friend's boyfriend. It's such an obvious screwup it didn't even make the Ten Commandments. God figured he shouldn't even have to make a note of that one.

I've known Colin since I was two, which is long before he started dating Joann. Not that I'm trying to offer that up as an excuse, more of an explanation. After my parents divorced, my mom (for reasons that have never been clear to me) moved us from Chicago (a perfectly good city without a single silo, which is more than I can say for Wheaton) to live near her parents, my grandparents. Colin's family farm is right next to my grandparents. We grew up together with everyone making smoochy kissy noises around us with elaborate winks and nudges. His dad and my grandpa would always joke about how the fence between their two farms could come down with no trouble at all. Then there's the humiliating childhood photo that gets pulled out every so often, of the two of us around age five sharing a bath. It was expected that we would become a couple, which pretty much guaranteed it was the last thing that either of us would ever want. In a small town like Wheaton, it is an accepted fact that getting married is the high point of your life. Big church wedding with big hair and a big bouquet and then a bad buffet at the Veterans' Hall. Shoot me.

Even though I never planned to date Colin, I always liked him. I don't mean *like him* like him. Just regular like. He's a good guy. He doesn't mind renting chick flicks, and he introduced me to the Matrix movies (which despite having Keanu Reeves are pretty good). He's into football, but if I ask, he'll watch me run on the track, and he'll scream out my times as I fly by. Since I've known him forever, I can tell him stuff without feeling like I'm talking to a guy. He'll tell you the truth about how you look in stuff (like if your jeans make your ass a mile wide). Colin even asked me what

I thought about him asking Joann out this past summer before he did it. I did the emotional reconnaissance for him, so he knew she would say yes. I was glad they hit it off. Honest.

It was my idea to drive into Fort Wayne and go to the mall at Christmas. Wheaton is so lame we don't have a mall. There is one clothing store in town, the Hitching Post. All their clothing smells like old people and has an elastic waist. Wheaton is not exactly fashion central. Colin was trying to figure out what to get Joann for Christmas. They had been dating since July, and this was their first major "couple" holiday, which put on the pressure for gift giving. The Hitching Post was not going to cut it. A trip to a real shopping destination was required, and who better to help him with the gift selection than his girlfriend's best friend?

The mall was insanely busy. They had decorated with huge garlands covered with ornaments the size of border collies strung between the stores, and there was a giant winter wonderland in the center. A single loop of Christmas songs kept repeating over and over. Every time you walked into a store, one of the clerks would yell, "Season's greetings!" in this frantic voice like they'd had one too many rounds of eggnog. Colin was starting to drag, and I could see he was ready to buy something and leave. I gestured to the Gap up ahead and started to lead Colin into the store.

"Let's go sit on Santa's lap instead," Colin said, pulling me down the slick white floor.

"Santa? Don't you think we're a bit old?"

"You're never too old for Santa."

Colin was practically racing down the hall. We stood in line for Santa with all the little kids. The kid in front of us had his finger jammed up his nose and watched us warily while doing his nasal drilling. I tried to ignore him.

"What are you leaning toward getting Joann?"

"I can't decide. What do you think of the sweater?"

"She'd like it."

Colin sighed.

"What? She would. She looks nice in green," I offered.

"There must be something that she'd really like. A sweater seems boring. I mean, I got my mom a sweater."

"Well, don't get Joann the same one. That's creepy."

"Thanks, Freud," Colin grumped, and then pushed me forward. Santa could see me now.

I sat down slowly on Santa's lap. The last thing I needed to do was hurt the old guy. Up close he didn't look that old. Nor were his eyes very twinkly. However, he was built for the part: His belly had definite jellylike status. I think sitting on Santa's lap used to be better when I was a kid, or else I was too young to notice the ick factor back then.

"What do you want for Christmas?" Santa asked with what looked an awful lot like a leer to me.

"Santa?" Colin asked, his voice low and serious. Santa and I both turned to face Colin, who was standing next to the elf photographer. "Santa, why have you taken Christ out of Christmas?"

I burst out laughing just as the camera flashed. I thanked Santa for his time and chased after Colin, who was dancing near the printer, waiting for the photo. When it came out, it was worse than I expected. My mouth was wide-open, mid-laugh, and my eyes were squeezed shut. Santa looked confused and annoyed. I gave Colin a shove. The elf assistant gave us a look, and I noticed that Santa was getting up to take a break. I'm guessing minimum wage was not cutting it to put up with people like Colin and me.

"Must you torture Santa?" I asked. Colin grabbed the photo and paid for it.

"Christmas is more than shiny paper and Rudolph. I would hope as a student—no, an ambassador—of TES, you would know that. Have you forgotten the real reason for the season? Has Satan won you with nothing more than a shiny jingle bell and some cookies?" Colin asked in a solemn voice before his face cracked into a smile.

"Lemme see the picture again." I took it out of his hands. "I look like someone who wanders around with tinfoil on her head."

"No, you don't. You look good." He took the picture back.

"Good? My mouth is hanging open, and see that shiny bit there? I think that's drool. I drooled on Santa."

"You never like your pictures. It's nice."

"You're a freak. Tear it up."

"I'm not tearing it up, I paid for it."

"Just because you were dumb enough to pay for it doesn't mean I want a picture of me like that hanging around." I reached for the photo, and Colin held it above his head. He's annoyingly tall, so I was reduced to jumping up and down trying to snatch it from him.

We were laughing, and Colin kept yanking the picture just out of my grasp. I leaned in to try and take it. Suddenly our faces were inches apart, and then he kissed me.

Or I kissed him.

It's possible we met in the middle. The picture fell out of his hand and drifted down to the floor like an autumn leaf. We just stood there, looking at each other.

I think if things had been different, we might have walked away and acted like it never happened. The whole thing was weird, some kind of space-time vortex, like on sci-fi shows when the screens gets all wavy and wiggly to indicate reality isn't what it used to be. I really think we would have just left, gone to get the sweater for Joann, and maybe stopped at the food court for a burger. However, that isn't what happened, because right behind us, with a front-row seat for the kiss, was Joann's mom.

Don't miss the novel Lisa McMann calls
"Thrilling and creepy, super sexy,
and so very hilarious."

EILEEN COOK'S
Unraveling Isobel

Turn the page for a peek!

From *Unraveling Isobel*
by EILEEN COOK

Chapter 1

When the minister asked if anyone knew any reason why these two shouldn't be married, I should have said something. I could think of at least five reasons off the top of my head why my mom shouldn't have married Richard Wickham.

1. His name is Richard, which is really just a fancy version of Dick. I don't think anyone should be in a relationship with a Dick.
2. My mom met Richard (Dick) three months ago on the internet. If I wanted to go to a movie with a guy I met on the computer, I would get a lecture about creeps who lurk online. Not to mention, when you can measure your dating history in weeks (twelve!), then you have no business getting married.

3. Dick has a son my age, Nathaniel, who happens to be unbelievably good-looking and is now officially off-limits because we're related.
4. Just because my mom wanted to be married, I have to go along for the ride. I'm being forced to move my senior year from Seattle to an island where there are more endangered birds than there are people.
5. Dick's first wife and daughter died seven months ago, and it seems to me he could have given it at least a year before bringing us in as the replacements. I may not be the queen of etiquette, but even I know some things are in bad taste.

As the ferry chugged closer to Nairne Island, suddenly I noticed reason number six looming over me.

"Well, there she is," Dick said in a booming voice. He sounded like an actor on a stage waiting for those around him to burst into spontaneous applause at his mere presence. "What do you think of your new home, Isobel?" He gave my back a hearty slap that nearly knocked me to the deck.

I looked at my mom for confirmation. I hoped it was a joke, but instead of laughing, she was looking at Dick like a slice of chocolate cheesecake after an extended sugar-free diet. She'd said the house was big and that it had been in Dick's family since the late 1800s when his family established a town on the island. However, she'd neglected to mention that it wasn't big; it was *huge*. Most hotels are smaller than this house. It sat on the top of the tip of the island like a fat brick lady squatting down to get a good look at what was coming in and out of the harbor. The center of the house had a row of large arched windows with a stone terrace in front. The wings on both sides were covered in ivy. Not in a nice Big Ten–campus sort of way, but more like a wild-jungle-vine-gone-rabid kind of way.

"What's that style called? Early Ostentatious?"

"Isobel!" my mom said, shooting me the look that meant *Boy, are you in for it when we're alone.*

Dick gave one of his hearty "yo-ho-ho, I'm Lord of the Manor" laughs. "Now, don't be mad at her. Seeing Morrigan for the first time can be a bit overwhelming."

My eyebrows went up. "Morrigan? You gave your house a name?" I bet Richard was the kind of guy who names everything, including his car, his favorite golf club, his dick. Dick's dick. I shuddered. That was the kind of image that could leave some serious emotional scars.

"Most estates have names," Dick said, subtly pointing out that while normal people live in houses, this was an *estate*. Like I needed a reminder. Our old two-bedroom bungalow would most likely fit in the foyer of this place.

"I'm sure Morrigan will feel like home for us in no time," my mom said.

Nathaniel snorted, and the three of us looked at him. My new stepbrother was good-looking, but his mood was a downer. The phrase "turn that frown upside down" didn't seem to be his personal motto. It wasn't clear to me if this was part of his personality, or if he was just unhappy with my mom and me as the recent additions to the family. He stood apart from us with his hands jammed into his pockets, and his expression looked like he smelled something nasty. It wasn't me. I'd had a long shower that morning, and knowing this day wasn't going to be an easy one, I'd applied enough deodorant to keep an Olympic swimmer dry. There was no reason for him to always try to stand a few steps away from me. At least no reason I could figure out.

"What did you mean by that?" his dad asked. Nathaniel shrugged. Dick opened his mouth to say something else, but Nathaniel was already turning away and heading back inside the ferry's main cabin. My mom put a hand on Dick's arm and they shared a look, which I could tell meant *Kids . . . what are you going to do? No one will adopt them at this age.* I would have snorted too and followed Nathaniel inside except for the fact that apparently he couldn't stand me.

"I should get our things together. We'll be docking in a few minutes," Dick said, patting my mom's ass. I turned around and looked back at the island so I could miss their parting kiss. I knew they would kiss as if he were heading off to war instead of leaving for ten minutes to go get the car.

My mom stood next to me after Dick left. Her hands gripped

the metal railing as if she planned to vault up and over. Of course, with her wedding ring on she would sink to the bottom of the ocean in record time. The ring Dick gave her is so large it practically requires its own zip code.

"You could make this easier," she said.

"So could you."

"We're not talking about this again. You can't live with Anita." My mom had dismissed the perfectly rational idea of me living with my best friend as if I had instead suggested that I live on the streets in an old washing-machine box.

"Why not?" I couldn't help pleading again. "Her mom's fine with it." I twisted the ring on my finger and added in a softer voice, "It's my senior year."

"All the more reason I want you to be with me. You'll be leaving for college after this." She tucked a strand of hair behind my ear. "Honestly, Isobel, you don't have to act like it's a prison term. As you keep pointing out, it's just one year."

I knew it was a lost cause, but I couldn't help expressing my misery anyway. "If it's just one year, then maybe you could have waited to marry Sir Dick."

"His name is Richard, and drop the 'sir' stuff."

"Are you telling me you don't notice that he does it? The whole fake British accent thing?" There was no way she could be that oblivious.

"Isobel, don't push it. I know you're not happy about this, but someday you'll understand."

"I don't want to understand later. I want to understand now." I knew I was pushing it, but I couldn't stop myself. "Why couldn't we all live in Seattle for the year?"

"Because Richard's life is here."

I felt my throat tighten. "What about *our* life?"

"In case you didn't notice, we didn't have much of a life." My mom spun and stalked off.

I sighed, and it was lost in the wind. The ferry whistle blew as we pulled into the dock. The boat bounced off the giant wooden pylons as it came to rest, and I grabbed the railing to keep my balance. The tide was out in the harbor; the water had peeled back, leaving a graveyard of crushed oyster shells and slick seaweed. Two seagulls were fighting over a piece of some nasty dead bit they had pulled from an oyster shell. The sour smell of dead fish and rotting seaweed washed over me.

Home sweet home.

Chapter 2

We were setting new records for family dysfunction. It was only a few hours after the wedding and already Mom and Dick weren't talking. When he drove off the ferry, Dick asked my mom if there was enough room on her side of the car for him to clear the metal gate. I could have told him this was a bad plan, as my mom has zero skills in the spatial-relations area. Of course she said yes, and the next thing you know Dick had a four-inch scrape on the side of his Mercedes. He was pissed. My mom was pissed that he was pissed, because she felt like his car's paint finish shouldn't be more important than her feelings, blah blah blah. The honeymoon was over. I bet they were wishing they had done some time in Cancún instead of rushing back here so Nathaniel and I could start school.

Nathaniel and I didn't fight. That would have required us

to have an actual conversation. Since we met for the first time over an awkward dinner a month ago when our parents had announced their engagement, we had exchanged about ten words in total. I felt like pointing out to him that none of this was my idea either. While he might not have been that crazy about us moving in, at least *he* didn't have to leave all his friends and his life behind right before his senior year. While both of us felt screwed over by our respective parent, in my opinion, he was still less screwed than me. However, he didn't seem like a glass half full kind of guy, so I didn't bother to point this out.

Nathaniel sat as far away from me in the backseat as possible and stared out the window without saying anything. I sat as close as I could to my own window. The only sound in the car was Dick grinding a few layers of enamel off his teeth. One big, happy, blended family.

We turned off the main road and slipped through Morrigan's tall, black wrought-iron gates. The driveway was gravel and in real risk of disappearing under the encroaching trees and bushes. The tips of a few of the branches slid along the sides of the car as we drove past. This place was in desperate need of a serious weed whacking. The driveway went on forever. I hoped I wasn't going to be expected to walk down to the end of it every day and pick up the mail. I'd have to bring a compass to make sure I made it back.

"This used to be an orchard when my grandparents owned the estate," Dick said, waving out the window at a section that looked like an evil forest of twisted trees. I wouldn't have been shocked to see a troll lurking under a bush. "It's gone wild in the past few decades. I plan to bring it back to its former glory one of these days."

It looked to me like the only plan that made any sense was to burn the whole thing down and start over. I kept that thought to myself. The sickly sweet stink of fruit rotting on the ground made my stomach turn.

"I see some apples," my mom said, spinning around to look closer at the trees. "I'll have to come down here and pick them. We could make a pie."

Dick patted my mom's knee. One mention of pie and their fight seemed to be over. I didn't break it to him that my mom couldn't bake anything that didn't come out of a box. Ever since she met Dick she had started to remake herself into the ultimate happy homemaker. She talked about taking up knitting and making her own jam. I could tell she was fantasizing about wandering down to the orchard with a floppy straw gardening hat and a basket over one arm. My mom is like a kid who never outgrew her imaginary world. Only instead of imaginary friends, my mom has an imaginary life.

As long as I can remember, my mom has talked about how things would have turned out if my dad hadn't ruined everything. She married my dad with the idea that they were going to be a part of Seattle's top society. They'd had a deal: she would be the pretty one, throw all the right kinds of parties, and keep the ultimate house, and my dad would earn buckets of money in advertising.

Things were all going according to plan until my dad went crazy. Not just "oh, he's a crazy guy" kind of crazy. My dad went full-on hearing-voices, lock-him-up, heavy-meds-and-a-padded-room kind of crazy. "Psychotic break" is the term. I don't remember any of it. I was only four when it happened. Eventually my dad's mental state was stabilized with medication, but by then he was off the fast track and even farther off the family track. He decided he wanted to make real art instead of creating dancing toilet-paper characters to push tissue. He left us and moved to Portland. Now he lives in someone's converted garage, where he paints all day. My mom was left with a toddler, a pile of debt, a dead-end job as a secretary for a law firm, and a serious case of bitterness. We weren't poor, but we were a lot closer to food stamps than to trust funds. Dick was her second chance at her dream life. She wasn't letting go, even if it meant ruining my life—or if not my whole life, at the very least my senior year.

The car snaked around the final curve, and there was the house. We piled out and stared up at it. Dick stood there with his hands on his hips, looking as proud as if he had built the whole thing himself. I had to admit, the place was impressive. If the entire cast of a Jane Austen movie suddenly burst out the front door, it wouldn't have surprised me. The house looked like it had been transported directly out of the English countryside and plunked down on the island.

"Isn't it stunning?" my mom gushed, turning to me.

"I should warn you, this house is my mistress. She takes up a lot of time," Richard said, pulling Mom close.

Nathaniel and I rolled our eyes in tandem. When we caught each other doing the same thing, we both looked away quickly.

"As long as this house is your *only* mistress, we'll be just fine." Mom linked arms with Dick. I fought down my gag reflex.

"The west wing of the house is closed up." Dick pointed to one side of the house. His eyebrows drew together in concern. "It needs a few repairs."

I looked closer at the one side of the house. There were shingles missing on the roof and a few of the upstairs windows looked as if they had been boarded up from the inside. Here and there an occasional brick had broken free of the facade like a missing tooth. A few repairs? No wonder Dick and my mom got along: they both lived in fantasyland.

"The roof has a tiny leak, and the wiring is a bit old," Dick explained. "Of course, most rooms on that side aren't needed for daily use—the ballroom, the library, the gallery . . . that type of thing. It's been closed up for years, but not any longer. In the spring we'll open it up and get started on some repairs. You girls deserve the best." Mom beamed and nodded along as if the idea of renovations excited her. "There are plenty of bedrooms in the east wing. Isobel can have her choice."

Dick looked at me like he expected me to fall to my knees and thank him for not requiring me to sleep on a dingy mat in the kitchen. If I could really have any bedroom of my choice, I would choose my old room back in Seattle. He wasn't doing me any favors. I hadn't even been allowed to bring any of my own furniture, because Dick's place was full of family heirlooms that his great-great-grandfather had chiseled down from trees planted by some other long-dead relative. My mom sold most of our stuff at a garage sale. The U-Haul trailer we'd brought contained nothing more than our clothes, my art supplies, and a few knickknacks my mom wanted to keep that used to belong to my grandparents. I'd seen people go on vacation with more stuff than we had with us.

"Honey, how about that? A library in the house!" Mom turned to Dick. "She's such a bookworm. I don't know who she gets that from, because it certainly isn't me."

He gave her nose an affectionate tap with his finger. "It would be a tragedy for you to hide your pretty face in a book."

My mom laughed and squeezed Dick's arm. I noticed no one mentioned that it would be a tragedy if I kept *my* face in a book.

Dick bent over and swept my mom off her feet, and she let out a high-pitched giggle. "Nathaniel, bring in the luggage. I'm going to carry this fine woman over the threshold and make this marriage official."

Nathaniel and I stood in the driveway and watched our parents acting like idiots. There is something especially gross about knowing your parents have sex. Especially if you have no sex life of your own. I peeked over at Nathaniel. His face was made up of strong lines, like someone drew him with a ruler. He wore his hair just a bit too long, and he was always pushing it out of his face. I couldn't help but notice he had these amazing lashes models could only achieve with multiple applications of plumping mascara. I stuffed my hands in my pockets and tried to think of something to say that didn't involve either of our parents, the weather, or weddings. Nothing came to mind.

Without a word, Nathaniel started to unpack the U-Haul trailer. Before now I hadn't noticed how cheap and shabby our luggage was. The large roller bag had a piece of duct tape holding the side together, and there was a huge ink stain on my duffel bag where a pen had exploded in a pocket years ago. I felt myself flush and made a grab for my bag as soon as he unloaded it.

"I'll get it," Nathaniel said.

"I can carry my own stuff," I insisted. "Seriously, I'm not handicapped." As soon as the words flew out of my mouth, I winced. Nathaniel's younger sister had been mentally disabled. *Super,* I chided myself. *Insult his dead handicapped sister. Great way to win him over.*

"Fine." His mouth set into a firm line.

"Sorry. That didn't come out the way I wanted."

"Whatever." Nathaniel tossed a few more of our bags out of the U-Haul and onto the driveway. He paused, looking over at me. "How do you see with all that black crap all over your eyes?"

I raised my hand and touched the corner of my eye. Who did he think he was? The makeup police?

"How do you see with your head shoved so far up your ass?" I fired back and twirled around before he could say anything else. I stomped toward the house. It would have been a really dramatic exit except for the fact that the driveway was covered in at least six inches of gravel and my right foot slid out from under me. I went down hard on one knee. I heard Nathaniel start to laugh before he managed to choke it back down. I pulled myself up. My knee was bleeding.

"You okay?" Nathaniel asked.

"No. Actually, I'm not okay, and if possible, could we skip the whole part where you act like you care?" I dusted myself off and glared back at him.

Nathaniel stood with his mouth slightly open. "Whatever you want."

"If I got what I wanted, I wouldn't be here." I shouldered my bag and climbed up the front stairs.

Home sweet home. Yeah, right.

Chapter 3

The entrance hall was designed to impress. The floor was a buttery cream-colored marble and the walls were paneled in dark wood. I'm not a lumberjack, so I had no idea what kind of wood it was, but it looked expensive and it had been carved into elaborate scrolls and designs. A huge staircase dominated the room. It looked like it had been stolen from the movie set for *Gone with the Wind* or *Titanic*. At the bottom of the stairs, at either side of the railings, were two carved women holding aloft what I think were supposed to be the lamps of knowledge. The house smelled like lemon furniture polish and old books. All that was missing was an English butler named Jeeves to take my coat and bag. Impressive, but no one was going to call this place cozy.

I dragged my duffel up the main staircase. I really hoped Dick didn't think part of our "one big, happy family" plan included me cleaning this place. The main banister had been polished, but I could see some cobwebs near the ceiling. Dusting would be a full-time job in this place.

I dropped my bag at the top of the stairs and started peeking in the various rooms, looking for one I could tolerate. The bedrooms on the second floor were decorated in a style I would call uptight fussy meets grandma's house. The curtains had giant flouncy ruffles. Each of the beds came with a herd of small pillows in flowered fabrics. They looked hard and uncomfortable. A lot of the furniture seemed to be perched on tiny fragile wooden legs designed to break. A few of the rooms had wallpaper that could be used as a torture device. I was fairly certain constant exposure to those patterns could lead to blindness or insanity.

As soon as I opened the next door, I knew I'd found Nathaniel's room. The lack of floral wallpaper was a giveaway, along with a giant bag of sports gear that was spilling out onto the floor. Instead of shutting the door, I took a few steps inside after shooting a look over my shoulder to make sure he wasn't coming up the stairs. He wasn't a slob, other than the duffel bag on the floor. There weren't piles of laundry in the corners. Unlike Anita's brother's room, which always smelled like old socks, his smelled a bit like campfire smoke mixed with vanilla. There were no posters of bands or half-naked women draped over cars on his walls, instead he had a bunch of framed black-

and-white photographs. I wandered around the room touching the odd thing here and there. I wasn't sure what I was looking for—maybe something that would help me understand him. I ran my fingers over the stacks of things on his desk: a pile of loose change, a pen with a chewed cap, his music player, a stack of books for school.

There was a small frame on top of his dresser. I picked it up. A woman stood on the beach looking at the camera, shielding her eyes from the sun with one hand. Her other arm was draped around a little girl. There was an elaborate sandcastle in front of them, the sides decorated with shells and rocks. It had to be a photo of his mom and sister. It struck me that when this picture was taken, they had no idea they were going to die. I put the frame down. I didn't want to see their smiling faces. They probably thought their biggest problem was that the tide would come in and destroy the castle they spent hours making. I heard a noise in the hall and my heart sped up. I could only imagine what Nathaniel would say if he found me in his room. I backed out quickly and shut the door.

There was another room stuffed with antiques, and the next had to be the master bedroom. The room was large, but all the dark colors and heavy fabrics made the room feel claustrophobic to me. Above the dresser was a giant painting of a woman I was pretty sure was Dick's mom. The idea that he wanted a life-size portrait of his mom in his room was creepy. The windows were covered in thick red velvet draperies, and in the center of the room was a giant four-poster bed. The idea of my mom and Dick rolling around on that football-field-size mattress while his mom watched made my stomach clench. The idea of Dick in general made me nauseated.

I stood back out in the hallway. I was out of bedrooms. I wondered if it would be rude to ask Dick if he was open to some major remodeling. I'm not a giant pink cabbage-rose-bedroom kind of person. I was trying to picture Dick's face if I used pushpins on his walls to hang up my poster of Klimt's painting *The Kiss*. Then I noticed the door. It was covered in the same paneling as the wall, and the handle was a small brass knob designed to blend in to the wood detailing. I must have walked right past it. I'd barely touched the handle when the door clicked open to reveal a narrow staircase leading up. I was surprised. From the outside, it hadn't looked like the house had a third floor.

At the top of the stairs there were two more doors. I opened one and found the attic. It ran the length of the wing. The ceiling was sloped, giving the room the appearance of a huge wooden tent. The room was dusty, with piles of old leather trunks that looked like they were last used in the 1800s when the Wickham family moved in. I wandered in farther. I pulled a sheet off one of the giant lumps to expose a rack of dresses. They were ball gowns. My hands ran down the sides of an emerald-green silk dress. The bodice was covered in blue, green, and gray beads. There was a handwritten dry cleaning tag on the hanger. Elizabeth Wickham.

That was Dick's mom. Apparently, she didn't just keep her house like a royal estate, she liked to dress as if she were a queen too. The dress was stunning in a cool vintage over-the-top way, but since I was hardly ever (as in never) invited to royal balls, I hadn't a clue where I would wear it. Across the aisle I spotted a row of boxes marked TOYS. A lonely stuffed zebra sat on top of one box. One of his eyes was gone, and someone had sewn a black button on in its place.

"Tragic war injury?" I asked, picking him up. I expected the zebra to smell musty, but he smelled clean and almost minty, like toothpaste, maybe. I touched his button eye. "Don't you worry about it," I told him. "Real women dig men with scars. Gives them character." I tucked the floppy zebra under my arm and went back into the hall.

As soon as I opened the only other door, I knew I had found my bedroom. It was larger than the other bedrooms downstairs, but much of the space was lost, due to the ceilings that sloped down to the floor like a Parisian garret. Two big windows opened to the back of the house, each with a deep inset window seat. I kneeled in the first and peered out. The view was amazing. You could see the stone patio I had noticed from the ferry, and beyond that, the cliff edge jutting out, and then the ocean. The waves marched along in perfect formation, and I could hear the sound of them breaking against the rocks, even through the thick glass.

The floor was wide-planked hardwood that had been stained

so dark it looked nearly black. The walls were a soft gray instead of the insipid pinks of downstairs. There wasn't a single inch of ugly wallpaper or giant floral fabric anywhere. There was another door, which led to a small bathroom. My own bathroom! I gave the zebra a hug in glee. The bed wasn't made up, but a soft white blanket had been pulled over the mattress. The only other furniture in the room was a desk tucked into one of the corners and a low bookshelf that was completely empty.

I put my duffel bag down and looked around the room. It was perfect.

"What the hell are you doing?"

I jumped when I heard the voice. Nathaniel was standing in the doorway looking at me, his eyes the same cold gray color as the ocean outside.

"Your dad told me to pick out a bedroom." I hated how my voice sounded so defensive.

"Well, you can't have this one."

"Look, if you wanted it, you should have called dibs before now. I saw yours downstairs."

"You went through my room?" He yanked up his sleeves as if he was getting ready to start a fistfight with me.

My face flushed red-hot. "I didn't 'go through' your room. I opened the door and figured it was yours since it was one of the few places that wasn't pink," I said, hoping he wouldn't call me on my lie.

"You're a girl. You're supposed to like pink."

"Tell me you did *not* just say that."

"What? Pink doesn't go with your goth image?"

"My image isn't goth," I said through clenched teeth.

"What is it then?"

"Nothing. I'm capable of coming up with my own look instead of dressing like a clone."

"Dressing all in black is being a rebel clone. Low rent."

"Fuck you."

"Isobel!" My mom and Dick appeared in the doorway. My mom's face was flushed. I had the sense she wasn't impressed with my language choice.

"Did you hear what he said to me?" I asked her.

"No, and we don't want to know." Dick crossed his arms and gave both Nathaniel and me a stern look. "We're not going to get in the middle of you two. Do you think we can't see what you're doing? We're a family now. You can't ask your mom to take your side any more than Nathaniel can expect me to take his. The two of you are going to have to work things out on your own, and I would hope that you could learn to do it without resorting to foul language."

"But she—" Nathaniel started to say.

"Nathaniel, remember your breeding," Dick barked. Nathaniel swallowed whatever he was about to say and stood up straight as if he were in a military prep school. "Honestly, you two are acting like children."

"She wants this as her bedroom," Nathaniel said, biting off

each word. "I was trying to explain to her that wasn't possible."

I wasn't backing down. "You said I could pick out whatever bedroom I wanted. No one is using this room, so what's the big deal?" This was the room I wanted. Not only was it the only room I could possibly imagine myself living in for the next year, it was also separate from the rest of the house. I needed some distance if I was going to survive.

"How did you even get up here?" Nathaniel asked. "The door to this floor is kept locked."

"It wasn't locked," I said.

"It's always locked."

"Okay, you busted me. I jimmied the lock, just a little trick I learned on the wrong side of the tracks with my low-rent buddies."

"Isobel, honestly. What has gotten into you?" My mom shook her head as if she didn't know me.

"The door wasn't locked," I repeated.

"This was my sister's room," Nathaniel said.

The air was suddenly sucked out of the space. My mom looked at me as if she blamed me for bringing up this awkward issue. How was I supposed to know this was Evelyn's room? It wasn't as if there was a nameplate on the door, and there wasn't a thing left on the walls or shelf that would indicate it belonged to anyone. Besides, why would her bedroom have been so far away from the others? I suddenly remembered the stuffed zebra. Shit. I bet that belonged to Evelyn too. The zebra was propped up next to the duffel bag at my feet. It didn't look like anyone had seen him yet. With a silent apology, I nudged him under the bed with my foot so he was out of sight. I didn't need to be accused of poaching the dead girl's toys in addition to her room.

"If Isobel wants this room, it should be hers," Dick said. I couldn't tell who was most surprised by his announcement.

"Dad!" Nathaniel looked shocked. I could tell he had expected his dad to back him up on this one.

"She can pick something else," my mom rushed in to say. "She doesn't need to be a bother."

"We can't keep this room a shrine to the past." Dick gave a weak smile. "I should have realized a girl would want her own bathroom and some space to herself. You go ahead and move your things up here."

"Seriously?" I asked.

"This was Evie's room," Nathaniel said again. His jaw was tight and it looked to me like his eyes were starting to tear up.

"The house is centuries old. If we saved rooms for all the people who were gone, we would have run out of rooms by now. We'd be forced to sleep in the garage." Dick chuckled, but I could tell Nathaniel didn't find the situation even remotely funny. I couldn't really blame him. His mom and sister hadn't even been gone a year and Dick was acting like it was no big deal. "Nathaniel can show you where the linens are kept, Isobel, so you can make up your bed. Now, you get settled, and your mom and I will rustle up some sandwiches for dinner. It's been a long day. Later we can play a round of Scrabble together." Dick clapped his hands like he was a kindergarten teacher and it was activity time. My mom was giving him a tearful smile like she couldn't believe how brave and caring he was being by letting me have the bedroom.

Nathaniel and I stared at each other. I wasn't sure where things had gotten so off track between us. Actually, we'd never really been *on* track. When I met him, I thought he looked rich, like when he was a baby his diapers had been cashmere. He came across as the kind of person who would never hang out with someone like me, and so far, that had proven to be the case.

"Look," I began, but before I could say another word, Nathaniel turned around and left, slamming the door behind him.

"I'll talk to him." Dick followed him out, treating the door more gently.

Now that we were alone, my mom shot me a look.

"I didn't do anything. Dick told me to pick out a bedroom."

"Would you *please* call him Richard?" My mom paced the room and then stopped to gaze out the window. "I know you're not happy, but is it asking too much that you try to make this work?"

"Mom, this is my senior year—" I began.

"This is the beginning of the rest of my life," she cut in. "Do you know how many things I put on hold for you? How much I sacrificed over the years? Now I have a chance to start over. *We* have a chance to start over. Having Richard as a stepfather is going to open doors for you, too. Can't you give me one year of your life when I've given you seventeen?"

I loved how she had this way of making my entire existence a burden to her when I hadn't asked to be born in the first place. "You don't believe me, but I'm doing the best I can. I'm here. I'm trying, but it's hard. I don't know anyone."

"You know Nathaniel."

"Nathaniel hates me," I pointed out.

"He doesn't hate you. He's just having a hard time with all of this."

"Welcome to the party."

"Nathaniel is sensitive because of what happened to his mom and sister."

"What *did* happen? Was it a car accident?" My mom had always been vague about how Dick's first wife and Evelyn had died. It didn't seem like the kind of thing I could ask a lot of questions about without coming across like an insensitive jerk. For some reason, with all the wedding planning there had never been a good time to bring up the dead first wife.

"No, it was a boating accident."

My knowledge of sailboats and yachts was pretty sketchy. All I could picture was some kind of *Titanic*-type incident, but there weren't even any icebergs out here. What else could happen to a boat? Did it run into another boat? Isn't the ocean big enough that they shouldn't run into anything else?

"Wow." I was at a loss for anything else to say. How did Nathaniel stand this house, with the sound of the ocean in the background like a constant reminder? No wonder the guy was edgy.

"Richard says Nathaniel hasn't been the same since the accident. He withdrew from his friends, quit the soccer team, and won't talk about it with Richard no matter how hard he tries. He won't even step foot on the boat."

"Dick kept the boat?" My voice came out a little screechy, and my mom raised an eyebrow. "I mean, Richard still has the boat? Isn't that weird?" By weird I meant disturbing as hell, and morbid, but I was trying to be more balanced in my communication style.

"If it were just any boat, that would be one thing, but it's a handmade wooden sailboat from the 1950s. It's been in his family a long time. Richard's dad was the one who restored it."

"Huh." Maybe Dick's dad had restored it, but his wife and daughter had *died* on it. I'm all for family memories, but this felt wrong on so many levels.

"It was an accident, after all. It wasn't like it was the boat's fault." Mom's face flushed, which told me that she thought it was creepy too, but she wasn't going to admit it. "He understands how upsetting it is, especially for Nathaniel, so he keeps it locked in the boathouse for now."

My mom started picking at her thumbnail the way she always does when she's stressed. During most of my childhood, she had raw, bloody cuticles from where she would tear the skin off. She'd stopped in the past few months. For the wedding, she'd even gotten a manicure. "I'll try harder," I said, giving in.

My mom gave me a huge smile. I could see her take a deep breath. She crossed the room with a quick stride and hugged me.

"That's all I can ask, just give it a try. Richard likes you. He's trying really hard to make you feel at home here."

I didn't bother telling her that the harder Dick tried, the more it made me want to run away. My mom brushed the hair out of my eyes and slipped out of the room. I could hear the waves outside. I sat down on the bed and pulled the zebra out from underneath.

"Looks like it's just you and me, buddy."

When you're seventeen and the only friend you have in town is a stuffed animal that doesn't even belong to you, I think it's safe to say your life is officially in the shitter.

Chapter 4

"You did *not* move into the dead girl's room!" Anita's voice screeched through my cell phone. My best friend has two volume settings—mute and screaming. She's never going to make it as a librarian, that's for sure. She has never understood the concept of using your inside voice. Then again, "moderation" isn't a term I would ever use when describing Anita.

"It's the nicest bedroom in the place." I looked around the room from my vantage point of the center of the bed. After a dinner where Dick and my mom pretended everything was fine and Nathaniel ignored me completely, I decided against an evening of board games, no matter how fun Dick tried to make it sound. Apparently his mom was some big Scrabble nut, so he wanted to carry on another fine family tradition. Most likely there was an heirloom Wickham Scrabble set with tiles some distant relative whittled out of trees that used to grow on the estate property.

Instead I went up to my room to get organized. I made the bed and hung my poster on the far wall. I stuck Mr. Stripes back under the bed so I wouldn't be accused of stuffie stealing. I unpacked a bunch of postcards of paintings that I had bought from the art museum in Seattle or had picked up at the various galleries, and made them into a collage on the wall above my bed. I piled my books onto the shelves and stuck the few other things I had brought around the room so it felt more like my own space. I stared out the window. I'd never had a room with a view before, unless you count looking directly into our neighbor's house. Mr. Turken tended to dance around in his boxers a lot. I usually kept my curtains shut. The wind was picking up now and it looked like it was going to turn into a big storm.

"I can hardly hear you," Anita yelled in my ear.

"I know, the reception here sucks. I didn't want to call you on the landline in case Dick has a rule about long-distance charges."

"Dick's a dick. Let's talk about someone more interesting. How's lover boy?"

"He's my stepbrother now, remember? Most states have laws against sleeping with a sibling."

"He's not your real brother, which means he's fair game. Totally legit. Besides, could he be better looking? It's always open season on someone that hot. If you don't want him, I'll swim over there and take him off your hands."

"He's not on my hands. He can't stand me."

"Not stand you? With all your wit and charm? He must be playing hard to get."

"More like impossible to get. Besides, he's my stepbrother. I'm hoping that somewhere on this island there will be someone who is reasonably attractive, not a weirdo, *and* not related to me."

"Negative energy! Blow it out. You want to attract positive energy. Think white-light stuff. Happy thoughts."

I suddenly missed her like crazy. "I wish I was there. This sucks."

"Just remember, by this time next year we'll be roommates." We had already vowed to apply to the University of Washington and get an apartment together near campus. "Visualize the end goal so the universe knows what you want. Besides, you're living on an island in the middle of nowhere. Think of it like an artist's retreat. People pay big money to go to those things, and you're there for free. You can get a bunch of stuff done for your portfolio without being distracted by civilization and stuff."

"My mom is still dead set against me getting a degree in art."

"You don't have to do what your mom says at that point. You'll be eighteen."

"Eighteen with about a hundred and fifty bucks to my name. I'm pretty sure college tuition is going to cost me more than that."

"That's why they have student aid, to aid students. Have faith that the universe will provide, but you have to be willing to do your part. You can't expect fate to carry the whole load.

Take steps toward your goal to show your commitment. The universe needs to know you're not screwing around. A portfolio demonstrates to the universe that you're serious. Draw some pictures, suck in all that island air and inspiration."

"That assumes living in an old, broken-down house will inspire me."

As if in protest to my statement, a burst of static blared, and I yanked the phone away from my ear. I could hear Anita call out my name, but her voice was distant. It sounded like we were talking on one of those tin can string phones.

"Anita? Can you hear me?"

The phone gave a blare of static in return. I called her name again, but the call went dead with a click and then silence. The lights flickered, and then they went out completely. A second later they were back on, but it was long enough without power to make my clock radio blink 12:00 at me.

I knew the storm outside, combined with the poor cell service, was to blame, but for an instant it felt like the house was mad I'd insulted it.

I shivered and then shook off the feeling. I checked my phone, but there was zero reception. Annoyed, I tossed the phone into my bag. Well, if I couldn't finish my conversation with Anita, at least I could take her advice. I pulled my sketchbook off the shelf and flipped through it until I found a clean page. Anita was flakey, but she was also right a lot of the time. I had my heart set on being accepted into the art program at U-Dub, which meant

I had to have a portfolio ready to show by the time I sent in my application, especially if I wanted any kind of scholarship. I was going to need some money to pay the bills, because when my mom found out I wanted to major in art, she was going to freak out. "Freak out" being an understatement.

My mom blamed my dad's passion for art for everything. She often pointed out that van Gogh cut off his own ear and you never heard of accountants doing something like that. She wasn't sure which came first, the crazy or the art, but she wasn't taking any chances with me. As far as my mom was concerned, I should go to school and study nursing or accounting. I think she thought she was being supermom for giving me a choice at all. The fact that I got a D in tenth-grade biology and couldn't stand math didn't faze her. Art was the one thing that I was really good at. Sometimes drawing felt like the only thing keeping me sane. It was like my pencil could figure things out before the rest of me.

There was no point worrying about it right now, though. I got myself settled on my bed and started sketching the room, trying to catch the angle of the walls and the deep-set windows. I smudged a pencil line with my little finger to give the corner the feeling of piled shadows. I felt my focus narrow down to the point where my pencil met the paper. The wind outside picked up speed. I got lost in the picture, trying to make it work.

Somewhere along the way, I must have fallen asleep.

That's when I saw her.

How many lies does it take
to break a heart?

Find out in

EILEEN COOK'S
The Almost Truth

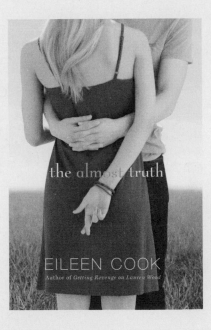

the almost truth

EILEEN COOK
Author of *Getting Revenge on Lauren Wood*

From *The Almost Truth*
by EILEEN COOK

chapter one

You know it isn't going to be a good day when you have to choose between food and proper hygiene.

"Can you take the milk off the bill?" I asked the cashier. My cell phone began to ring. I dug around in my bag for it.

"You don't want it anymore?" The cashier tapped her impossibly long fingernails on the register with one eyebrow raised.

"That's right. I don't want the milk," I repeated. This wasn't true. I wanted the milk. Eating dry cereal for a week was going to suck. Not to mention having so little dairy in my diet that I would likely end up with a raging case of osteoarthritis when I was old. But until my mom got paid on Friday, there were limited funds in the house, and there's no way I was going without deodorant. I finally found my phone buried at the very bottom of my bag and yanked it out.

"Sadie, it's Brendan." I didn't need him to tell me his name. Brendan has this habit of yelling into his cell as if it were a tin can on a string.

"Hey," I said. I looked at the new total on the register. *Shit.* "Can you take the toothpaste off too?" We'd have to squeeze a few more days out of the old tube. Now in addition to having brittle bones, I could be toothless. My future was looking brighter and brighter all the time.

The woman in line behind me gave an exasperated sigh. Screw her. She was probably one of those people who always makes you wait while they count out the exact change from their Coach wallet. I turned around. Great, it was Rebecca Samson and her mom. Their cart was piled high with groceries, including that expensive cheese made by yaks that costs something like twenty dollars for an ounce.

"Gosh, Sadie, do you need to borrow a couple dollars?" Rebecca asked, fighting to keep a smirk off her face. Her mom might have also been trying to smirk, but her face was so Botoxed she was incapable of expression.

"Hey! Is that Blow Job Becky I hear? What are you doing hanging with the cheerleader from hell?" Brendan bellowed. His voice carried out of my phone like he was on speaker. Rebecca's face froze as hard as her mother's.

"The total's twenty-two fifteen. How does that work for you?" The cashier tapped her fingernails again.

"Hang on, I'm at the store," I said to Brendan. I plunked my phone down on the conveyor belt and pulled some cash out of my bag. I made sure to spread the two twenty-dollar bills out in a fan shape so they could be clearly seen by the cashier and Blow Job Becky, too.

The cashier snapped her gum when she saw the money. No doubt she wondered why I had nickeled and dimed my bill when I had forty bucks. She handed over my change. I palmed the ten-dollar bill she gave me and, with my thumbnail, pulled a folded five-dollar bill from under my watchband. I made a show of counting the bills. "I'm sorry. I think you didn't give me enough change." I held out the two fives, a couple ones, and eighty-five cents.

The cashier screwed up her face. "I swore I gave you a ten. Sorry." She pulled another five out of the drawer and handed it to me.

"No problem." I tucked the money into my bag and took the groceries from her. An extra five bucks was going to come in handy. I could use it to buy milk, but I had more immediate needs than staving off osteoarthritis. I smiled at Rebecca and her Botoxed mom and stepped outside. As soon as the automatic doors closed behind me, it felt like I was slapped in the face with the hot, wet air. It might sound good in theory, but summer sort of sucks unless you can spend it sitting by the ocean with a fruity drink. Spending it in a parking lot with your T-shirt damp and sticking to you isn't that much fun.

"Sorry about that, you caught me in the middle of something,"

I said into the phone. I leaned against the warm cinder-block wall. A small kid was standing near me, staring at the pony ride next to the row of gum-ball machines. I tried to ignore him, but he looked like someone had shot his puppy. I sighed and handed him a quarter. He broke into a smile and climbed up on the mechanical horse, leaned forward, and fed the machine the coin. Ah, when joy could be purchased for less than a buck.

"Are you still running that wrong change con for five bucks?" Brendan said. "I keep telling you to up the ante. If you cashed in a hundred-dollar bill, you could easily clear twenty bucks."

"Twenty bucks is more likely to get noticed," I pointed out. "Not to mention if I start flashing hundred-dollar bills around town, that's going to seem weird."

"So you're doing the small con just to be careful? Are you trying to tell me it has nothing to do with the fact that if the short is less than five dollars then the cashier doesn't have to pay it out of their own pocket?"

I dragged my sneaker on the cement. "Being a cashier at the Save-on-Food Mart is punishment enough. She doesn't need to cover me."

Brendan laughed. "Your ethics are getting in the way of the big score, but hey, it's your choice. What are you up to tonight? I was thinking we could go over to Seattle and grab dinner."

I snorted, knowing full well Brendan's idea of grabbing dinner. "You buying or is the restaurant?" I asked.

"Now why in the world would I pay?" Brendan wasn't teasing.

He actually was incapable of understanding why he should have to pay for anything when he was clever enough to steal it without getting caught.

"While stealing a meal with you sounds like an attractive option, I'm going to have to say no."

"For a con artist you have a highly overinflated sense of morals," Brendan said. "Especially when dinner is on the line. We could go for Japanese if you want."

"Don't call me that. Besides, you hate Japanese."

"Yet another good reason I shouldn't have to pay for it."

I rolled my eyes. If you wanted to get technical about it, I *was* a con artist. I'd learned the tricks of the trade from my dad. Then I taught what I knew to Brendan, who happened to have some sort of freakish natural ability in the area. He was like a con genius savant. However, unlike Brendan, who just loved getting away with something, I preferred to see it as a means to an end, an end that was finally coming to a close. "I can't go to dinner, I've got stuff to do tonight."

"Like what?"

Most people would take a polite brush off and move on. Brendan was not most people. "I have stuff to get ready for school."

"You're not going away to college for months. C'mon, a night in the city would be fun."

I knew down to the exact day (sixty-four, counting today) how soon I would be leaving Bowton Island for college. If I were better at math, I would be counting down the hours in my head. "I want to do some packing," I said. The truth was, it wouldn't take me that long to pack. My bedroom was the size of a closet. Even if I took the time to fold each item of my clothing into a tiny origami crane, there'd be no need to start now. The problem was spending time with Brendan felt weird lately. We'd known each other since we were kids, and on an island where 90 percent of the residents measured their wealth in terms of millions, and those of us in the remaining 10 percent measured it by having enough to buy groceries, we were automatic allies. Brendan had been my best friend as long as I could remember.

Brendan was the one who'd realized that the pranks I'd taught him could be used to pull cons to raise cash. He helped me figure out what I needed to do to escape my life. I would always owe him for that. The problem was, he didn't want me to leave. Or at least he didn't want me to leave without him, but where I was going there would be no room for him. I was planning to make over my entire life, and that meant leaving the old me behind.

Then there was the uncomfortable realization that Brendan maybe wasn't thinking of me as just his best friend anymore. There'd been a few awkward moments where I'd caught him staring at me, and at graduation I'd thought he might try to kiss me. And not in a "wow, we're great friends and we survived high school" kind of way.

"Maybe we could do it another time?" I asked.

"Fine, but you can't blow me off forever," Brendan grumped.

"I'm not blowing you off. I'm tired, that's all."

"Then get some sleep and we'll do tomorrow night. No excuses." Brendan clicked off before I could say anything else.

I tossed my cell back into my bag. I pulled out the ten-dollar bill I'd dropped in there after palming it and stuck it in my wallet. Taking a five at a time wasn't adding up fast, but combined with the money from my part-time job at the hotel, it did add up. Brendan could tease me if he wanted, but I knew that while larger cons might pay off better, they also came with much bigger risks. My dad was a living, breathing example of that. For as long as I could remember, he had been in jail more often than he'd been out. I suspected the correctional officers knew him better than I did. One year when he was on probation, they sent him a birthday card.

For Brendan, the point was the con, not the cash. As soon as the money came in, it went right back out. I'd been stockpiling mine. In three and a half weeks I would put most of it down to hold my place at Berkeley. I was going to college, and I planned to leave all of this behind me.

The doors to the grocery swooshed open and Rebecca and her mom came out. Her mom pushed their cart past me as if I didn't even exist. I suspected she saw me like the help, best ignored unless she needed something. Rebecca glanced over at my Old Navy T-shirt and my cutoff shorts. Somehow she managed to look cool and unphased by the heat. It was like being really rich also made her immune to humidity and the need to sweat.

"Nice outfit," she said, her smirk in full force.

"Aw, that would hurt my feelings if I cared about your opinion," I said. This was a concept Rebecca had never fully grasped. She felt everyone should want her love and approval. She was also open to ass kissing. It really chafed her fanny that I didn't care what she thought of me. It must have made her job as the popular mean girl so much less enjoyable when what she said didn't bother me. She was also apparently unaware of the fact that high school was now over, making her the queen bee of nothing. I noticed a glint of silver on her perfectly pressed polo shirt. "Is that your cheerleading pin?" I asked.

Rebecca fingered the silver megaphone. "It's my captain's pin."

I couldn't decide if it was merely sad or full-on pathetic that she was still wearing it postgraduation. Rebecca was going to grow up to be one of those overly skinny women who hang out at the country club bitching about how their husbands are never around, how their maids don't scrub the toilets to their satisfaction, and how high school was the best time of their lives. Personally, I was planning on my life getting better from this point forward.

I picked up my bag of groceries. "You have a good rest of the summer," I called over my shoulder at her as I walked away. Being nice to Rebecca would screw with her head more than any sarcastic comeback. I tucked my bag into the basket attached to the back of my scooter. Rebecca might mock my secondhand clothes and Brendan might make fun of my five-dollar cons, but in sixty-four days none of it would matter.

Unlike Rebecca, I didn't plan to look back on high school with fondness. I didn't plan to look back on it at all.

Love. Heartbreak.
Friendship. Trust.

Fall head over heels for
Terra Elan McVoy.

THERE'S A FINE LINE
BETWEEN *bitter* AND *sweet.*

bittersweet

SARAH OCKLER

AUTHOR OF *TWENTY BOY SUMMER*

EBOOK EDITION ALSO AVAILABLE

From Simon Pulse
TEEN.SimonandSchuster.com
SarahOckler.com

Sweet and Sassy Reads

One book. More than one story.

LOOKING FOR THE PERFECT BEACH READ?

SimonTEEN

Simon & Schuster's **Simon Teen**
e-newsletter delivers current updates on
the hottest titles, exciting sweepstakes, and
exclusive content from your favorite authors.

Visit **TEEN.SimonandSchuster.com** to
sign up, post your thoughts, and find out what
every avid reader is talking about!

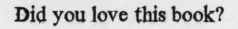
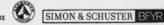